PROOF OF LIES

PROOF OF LIES

an Anastasia Phoenix novel

by diana rodriguez wallach

Entangled Publishing, LLC
2614 South Timberline Road
Suite 109
Fort Collins, CO 80525

Entangled Teen is an imprint of Entangled Publishing, LLC.

Visit our website at www.entangledpublishing.com.

Edited by Alycia Tornetta
Cover design by Clarissa Yeo
Interior design by Toni Kerr

ISBN: 9781633756083
Ebook ISBN: 9781633756076

Manufactured in the United States of America

First Edition March 2017

10 9 8 7 6 5 4 3 2 1

For Jordan, who always believed

For Juliet and Lincoln, may we teach you to believe in yourselves just as much

"There is nothing more deceptive than an obvious fact."
Sherlock Holmes
-The Bascombe Valley Mystery

PROLOGUE

Only my parents could make a trip to Europe seem dull. But they were always heading to some far-off country, to the point that, if they stayed home for more than five days in a row, *that* was unusual. Tonight, my dad was flying to a chemical conference in London. Last week, my mom spent three days in Tokyo meeting with government officials about a prospective deal. Before that, they both spent an entire week in Egypt ironing out problems with a potential investor.

For a teenager, I was home alone a lot—and not in the let's-throw-a-keg-party kind of way. Literally, home alone. Especially now that my sister was in the seven-year medical program at Boston University and living in the dorms, but at least she was just down the street.

"Hon, have you seen the garment bag?" my father yelled from the master bedroom as we listened to him rifle through the closet.

"It should be hanging on the back of the door!" Mom hollered back.

"Don't you think I looked there?"

"Maybe it's still in the car?"

"Can you check the trunk for me?"

"I will, after I eat. You should sit. We got Chinese."

"Come on, Dad, we're all eating together, and it's not even my birthday!" I teased.

Takeout was a primary food group in my family. Neither of my parents cooked—and they had no desire to learn. In the few months since we'd moved to Brookline, we'd acquired an impressive amount of menus. We could get Ethiopian delivered.

But of all the places we'd lived, this was one of my favorites. For the first time in years, I had my own bedroom. Whenever we moved to Europe, the flats were so tiny, Keira and I always landed in side-by-side twins. And I don't even want to begin to describe the bathroom situation in our home in Morocco.

But the biggest perk of moving to Beantown was the obvious—I knew the language, even if everyone here was *pahking the cah in Hahvahd yahd*. It was nice not to have to conjugate verbs in my head.

"Can you pass the soy sauce?" Keira asked. I slid the bottle across our rustic table, an antique my parents had flown in from Tuscany. Another perk of their travels—lots of souvenirs.

"How's your biochem class coming along?" asked Mom.

"It's coming." Keira singsonged, clearly not wanting to talk about it.

"Have you gotten into genetics yet?" Dad asked, suddenly appearing in the kitchen. He leaned against the counter, digging a plastic fork into a carton of lo mein. "If I could go back, I would study human genomes, DNA. It's the future, absolutely fascinating. You should look into it."

"Well, I'm thinking pediatrics," Keira mumbled, staring at her food.

"Really?" said Mom. "Not research? Because cancer research—"

"No," Dad interrupted. "I'm telling you, the advances in human genomic DNA will lead to personalized medicine. You'll want to be in front of that. Look at our DNA, for example—"

"Or we could talk about something else," Keira interrupted.

"You're right. Advanced scientific research is not nearly as interesting as a career changing diapers," Dad mocked.

"I wouldn't be changing diapers. I'd be treating sick children," Keira defended.

"Hey, at least, she's not thinking dermatology," said Mom.

"Or podiatry!" Dad headed back to the master bedroom as if he were done listening to whatever defense my sister had for her seemingly subpar career path.

"I know, I'm such a disappointment," Keira griped, aggressively stabbing her food. Despite our parents' frequent absences, they had an unusually strong desire to control our futures. It was why I took martial arts and not soccer, and Keira transferred to BU from the University of Miami. They were hard people to stand against. "Seriously, I'm becoming a doctor, just like you wanted. Do you really want to choose my specialty? Pick my classes? Arrange my marriage?"

"Don't tempt us." Mom raised a teasing eyebrow. My sister did not look amused. "We're not trying to control you," Mom continued, "we're trying to give you the benefit of our experience. We're taking an interest, leading you down the right path."

"Sure you are. Look, just because you and Dad are engineering gods who flit around the world solving every biochem problem known to man, doesn't mean that some weird advanced organic chem gene was passed down to me. I have to work just as hard as everyone else."

My sister complained often about her classmates' snarky opinions regarding our parents being the heads of the Dresden Chemical Corporation. They assumed she didn't have to study, or even try, because there was a research job waiting for her the moment she snatched her diploma. In all fairness, there probably was. Dresden was big on hiring families. But that wasn't the future Keira had planned. Or me, for that matter. Still, it was like studying computer science when your dad was Bill Gates.

"I never said you didn't have to work hard. Don't you think we work hard?" Mom said, unfazed by Keira's attitude. Nothing rattled our parents. Ever. We could scream obscenities until our cheeks burned (like when they told us we were moving to Morocco), and they still would barely blink in response.

"Why are we talking about *me* anyway?" Keira turned my way. "Aren't we here to talk about something else?"

The sounds of my father packing ceased, as if he could hear our conversation from the bedroom, down the hall, with the door closed. My mother leaned back in her chair, her eyes suddenly serious. Then, on cue, my father appeared in the kitchen entry, his hazel eyes possessing a familiar look, a scary look, a look I knew too well.

I dropped my spoon. "No. No way. I refuse."

"We don't have a choice," Mom said.

"Of course you have a choice! There's always a choice. Don't. Move," I snapped. We'd been living in Boston for only three months. Three months! If we moved again, it would make this our shortest stay ever. And they swore this was our home, this was where I would graduate. Keira enrolled in BU. We relocated to Dresden's corporate offices; my parents took desk jobs in their headquarters downtown. I was actually making friends. I joined a local karate studio. I was invited to a party, for the first time in my life. I was not moving again.

"It's not that simple. When projects come up..." My father's tone sounded like he was talking to a toddler on the verge of a tantrum.

"Send someone else!" I screeched. "Come on, you guys run the company. Send a different employee. Let someone else pay his dues. What about Randolph Urban? He's been living in Boston for years now. Why can't *he* go for once?" I rose from my chair, too livid to sit.

Urban was my parents' best friend. They'd started the company together, after having met at Princeton University, back when he and my mom used to date. Now he sat comfortably behind a desk barking orders as the CEO. He hadn't been in the field in years.

"Randolph's not an option. That's not how we run things. And this is a government project in Montreal. We can't trust it to just anyone," my dad reasoned.

"Think of it this way, at least they speak English in Canada," Keira chimed in. "You'll be fine."

That was when it hit me—she wasn't coming with us.

"You're staying in Boston."

"I have to. I'm in college. If I want to be a doctor, I can't keep transferring. I'm lucky BU accepted my credits from Miami."

That was the last place we'd lived, for a whopping six months. I was actually excited to move there until I realized exactly what Miami humidity felt like. The entire city needed to be tarped and air-conditioned. And the people were way too tan. My milky skin blinked tourist almost as drastically as it had in Africa. But at least for those moves, I had my sister. We didn't fit in together. Now, I'd be moving to Canada alone.

"I'm not going," I insisted, shaking my head. "I'll stay here with Keira."

My parents exchanged a look. "You'd rather be with your sister than us?"

"I've been with Keira more than you my entire life! How would this be different?"

"For starters, she lives in a dorm," Mom replied.

"She can move here. What's wrong with the brownstone?" I cut my sister a look. "You promised you'd never leave me, that you'd never be like *them*."

If my parents were insulted by the comment, they didn't show it. They never would. "I'm in med school," Keira said, her eyes sympathetic but her tone definitive. She didn't want me.

"Anastasia, *we're* your parents," my dad stated.

"Then *be* my parents! Don't make me move again. Put *me* first!" I yelled, fingers clenching. "I don't get it! You're engineers. Why do we have to move so much? You promised this was it. You said this was home. Were you lying to me this whole time?" I backed away from the table, away from all of them.

"We weren't lying," my mom defended, her voice annoyingly calm. "We believed it when we said it. We never thought things would progress so fast."

"But you knew it was a possibility?" I picked apart her words. "I can't believe you're doing this to me. I hate you! And I swear I won't go anywhere with you."

I stormed off to my bedroom, bare feet stomping on the hundred-year-old floorboards. I'd never said "I hate you" to my parents before, but I wanted to hurt them. They were hurting *me*.

I slammed my bedroom door and locked it tight, guilt rushing through me. I wasn't going to apologize. Maybe I'd said something wrong, but what they were doing was wrong. I couldn't spend my entire life as the new kid. I couldn't keep pretending it didn't bother me. Of course I wanted friends, a social life, and a bedroom where the boxes were actually unpacked. My parents were the ones who needed to say they were sorry, for *all* of that. Then maybe I would take back those three mean words.

I stayed in my room. Hours later, they knocked on the door to tell me they were leaving for the airport; I didn't say good-bye. Instead, I listened silently as they told me that they loved me and that they wished things could be different. Still, I didn't apologize. I didn't say a word.

I didn't realize that would be our last conversation.

I didn't realize they'd never come back.

CHAPTER ONE

Three Years Later...

When you meet a girl who's lost both of her parents, your gut reaction is pity. I get that, and I'd probably feel the same way if I weren't *the girl*. But it had been three years since my parents died, and I'd learned to stop feeling sorry for myself. Somewhat. I've tried to move on, but unfortunately my classmates haven't.

I pushed my orange tray along the cafeteria line with my only two friends at Brookline Academy—Tyson Westbrook and Regina Villanueva. They got to know me before the accident, so maybe that was why they were able to see me as a person rather than the tear-jerking star of a Disney movie. (I often thought of my life as the first five minutes of *Finding Nemo,* only both my parents got eaten.) Not that I blamed my classmates. They couldn't relate, and not just to the joint parental tombstones, but to the fact that my legal guardian was my twenty-four-year-old sister who often spent more time partying than signing permission slips. Tonight, there was a rager planned for our living room. Great.

"Come on, guys! It'll be fun, I swear. You have to come,"

I begged, pushing my scratched orange tray down the metal rails past the cups of zero-calorie Jell-O with crusty sugar-free topping. I brushed my dark bangs from my face. "What teenager doesn't want to go to a party?"

"For starters, you don't," Regina stated plainly as she plucked a tiny bag of baby carrots from our "healthy alternatives" snack bar. "And you know how my parents feel about parties, or teenage fun in general."

Regina came from a loving two-parent household that happened to be a part of some fanatical Filipino sect of Catholicism that Regina dubbed "the cult." Only, unlike her enormous family, Regina was a vocal atheist, which made me like her even more. Not that I was anti-God or anything, but it took guts to stand up to the pack, and I was nothing if not respectful of the lone wolf.

"My sister will be there, so it's technically chaperoned," I defended, snatching a milk carton from a cooler of ice. Our school offered only milk, water, and organic orange juice as part of a healthy lifestyle campaign. Most kids chose the two-dollar bottled water.

"Your sister and the nursing population of Boston General will be drunk before five p.m.," Regina said pointedly.

"Maybe, but your parents won't know that."

She shot me a look. The Villanuevas didn't see Keira as a responsible guardian, and often neither did I. My sister had a history of hitting happy hours at the bar across from the hospital and bringing home random meatheads who bought her drinks, but she also paid the bills on time. And it wasn't like I had any alternatives aside from foster care.

"Tyson, how about you? Talk your girlfriend into this," I pleaded. "You know Keira's gonna wear something crazy. Don't you wanna see an armful of jelly bracelets? Purple hair extensions?"

My sister had a weird fascination with eighties fashion. Sometimes she'd put a lavender streak in her hair and crimp it with an iron that belonged to my mother thirty years ago. Amazingly, it still worked, though the lights dimmed when she used it.

"Sorry, but the plans are set. Regina just can't get enough of *this*." Tyson patted his broad chest, trying to look seductive.

"Ew, I have a lunch to eat." I pretended to gag, though Tyson's chest was muscular, thanks to his double black belt in karate. It was how we met. I knocked him on his butt during our first sparring session. At six-foot-one, he was more than embarrassed until he learned I received my double black belt from a master in Singapore—one of the perks of having an international childhood and of having two parents who met at a boxing match and thought organized fighting was a more valuable sport than T-ball.

"Tyson's mom is actually *working* tonight. On a Friday. We have to take advantage," Regina pointed out, rolling a tiny red apple onto her tray.

Tyson was one of the few people at Brookline Academy who unfortunately knew what it was like to lose a parent. One night, his dad walked by the wrong bar in East Boston and accidentally took a bullet meant for someone else. It had been six years since the police arrived at his door hat in hand, and still, his mother needed a fistful of pills to get out of bed in the morning. But Tyson went to school every day. He made the honor roll. He worked part-time at a convenience store. He helped keep the lights on as his mother bounced from job to job. And he was the sole reason we selected the two-percent milk, fruits, and vegetables from the snack bar—we knew he didn't get many fresh groceries at home.

"Can't you do date night *at* the party?" I suggested,

desperately not wanting to be the only sober person in a room full of stumbling nurses vogueing to Madonna.

"It's just a party. You can handle it." Regina shrugged.

"Besides, I'll see you tomorrow at karate." Tyson yanked a mess of crumpled bills from his pocket.

"If you don't come, I swear I'll knock you on your butt," I threatened.

"Like you could."

"Says Mr. Second Place."

"I just don't want to hit girls…"

"No, you try to hit her. You just can't." Regina pushed his shaved head in that playful-girlfriend way. Tyson was one of those guys who could pull off a dark shiny Bic'd scalp, like a young Michael Jordan, only without the endorsements.

"Wow, that's coming from your girlfriend. Ouch!" I mocked.

"Girl power!" She slapped me a high five.

"I feel so loved," Tyson grumbled. "You know I have first place trophies…"

"Of course you do, honey." Regina's tone was mocking.

Tyson's full pink lips pursed to the side, his eyes looking insulted. "Okay, well, maybe I should go to the party—"

"That sounds like an amazing idea!" I prodded, hoping to urge the fight along.

"I'm just messing with you. I know you've got mad skills. So proud…" Regina hugged him, burying her face in his chest and making kissy sounds. He touched her butt, and she giggled. I averted my eyes. I couldn't compete with that, which meant I'd be attending a party in my own home. Alone.

I knew after two drinks, Keira would pretend I wasn't there, which was probably how she'd prefer to live the rest of her life. My sister gave up everything to care for me, from her freedom to med school. She was currently a nurse at Boston General, scrubbing in with doctors who used to be her classmates, a fact she mentioned often. And while she'd never openly admit she resented me for her plummeting career trajectory, it was so obvious, I couldn't help but resent her right back—especially when she bossed me around or acted like she deserved a trophy for not dropping me off at a firehouse.

Keira was not my mother (a fact I pointed out regularly), so that only made the Mother's Day Eve celebration she was throwing in our home tonight more infuriating. She had eleven months until I turned eighteen and she got to relinquish her guardian title, and she was practically marking the days on a calendar with giant red Xs.

My friends and I headed down a row of rectangular tables set in prison-straight lines. We sat near the windows on the outskirts, one of the few parts of the cafeteria untainted by the stench of meatless veggie burgers and drugstore body sprays.

I bumped the backs of carrot-colored chairs as we neared our seats. I could see a pack of baseball players headed from the opposite direction, which was unusual given that the popular table sat in the cafeteria's center. It was like seeing Mickey Mouse in the parking lot of the Magic Kingdom.

"Hey, look who it is!" said Wyatt Burns in a voice so loud he was obviously working to draw an audience. He hovered over a male student seated alone with his tray, two empty plastic chairs beside him. "Where's your Harley now, *empanada*?" Wyatt backhanded the guy's head, not hard enough to be an actual hit, but too hard to be considered friendly.

What was strange was that I didn't recognize the target. He was well-built, with black spiky hair, dark eyes, black T-shirt, and a tattoo of a bull with curved horns showing on his neck. Not exactly someone you could easily overlook.

I stopped en route to our table, twisting my head toward Regina. "Who are they messing with?"

"He just started here. Some exchange student or something. I think he's Mexican. Could you imagine moving to a new school in May? The year's almost over." She mindlessly flicked the part in her shiny black hair, which fell toward her waist like a silk curtain. I'd kill for hair like that. Instead, my hair reminded me of my mother's every time I looked in the mirror—long, thick, and espresso brown.

"Sometimes you don't have a choice," I grumbled, as we continued to our table. I put down my tray, but I didn't sit; I was too busy watching the scene.

"Oh, sorry. I forgot about your nomad days." Regina made a whoops-my-bad face, though it actually was nice not to be considered the new girl anymore. At seventeen, I'd lived in nine cities, in five countries, on four continents, and spoke four languages—including upper-class Moroccan French. "I heard his parents work at Boston General, doing research or something. Hey, maybe your sister knows them?"

"Maybe he'll be invited to your party?" Tyson added.

"Yeah, I'm sure Keira invited the entire hospital staff and their families," I deadpanned, still gawking. Wyatt wasn't letting up. I didn't know what this kid had done to draw the ire of three hulking baseball players, but the entire lunchroom was now involved. Conversations lulled.

"You know, I think they serve tacos up there," Wyatt pointed to the cafeteria line. "Did you grab a couple *burritos, ese*?"

The guy said nothing, and even in his silence, I could see

he wasn't Mexican. I'd traveled enough to recognize the basic physical differences between cultures. His features looked European—maybe Spanish, assuming all the politically incorrect digs were based on something other than idiocy.

"Maybe next time you cut me off on that stupid bike of yours, I won't slam on the brakes." Wyatt jerked like he was going to punch him, but the guy didn't flinch (good for him). Wyatt quickly covered by reaching for the boy's untouched veggie burger. He plucked it from his tray, took a huge bite, and threw it on the dirty tile floor.

"*Bon appétit!*" he shouted, probably not realizing that was French, not Spanish, though I doubted he cared. He was laughing like he'd just told the best joke in the world, bits of food flying from his mouth as his buddies cackled beside him. Then they marched away, straight toward us, patting one another's backs.

I'd watched a lot of TV in my seventeen years, and I'd heard theories about "crimes of passion," people who claimed to pull the triggers of guns yet had no recollection. They swore there was no conscious decision made, it just sort of happened. That was me in that moment.

I stood watching the cocky smile on Wyatt's face, his cheesy high fives to his buddies, his undeserved swagger, and I simply stuck out my foot. I wasn't even sure my brain registered the action, but when Wyatt charged past my right side, my leather sandal wrapped around his ankle, just above his Nike, with perfect timing, and Wyatt tripped.

Wow, did he trip.

He stumbled forward in three awkward lunges, arms flailing for balance, until he fell splat on the gritty linoleum floor. Face first.

The roar of laughter that followed could rival any Comedy Central performer. I pressed my palm to my mouth, trying to hold in the giggles, but I'd just tripped the most popular guy at Brookline Academy.

Wyatt pushed to his feet and spun toward me, blue flames in his eyes.

"Sorry," I sputtered, fingers covering the laughter spurting from my lips. "I didn't see you."

Regina and Tyson doubled over, crying with giggles, as Wyatt's scruffy hands twitched into fists at his sides. His eyes darted around viciously, but after a few heated moments, he did nothing. He didn't say a word. He just stomped off in the opposite direction, preserving what little dignity a teen who trips in the cafeteria can muster.

"I think I love you," Regina choked. "Like, really love you."

"Oh my God. That was awesome!" Tyson added, patting my back with his big sweaty hand. "You're my hero."

Everyone in the cafeteria was staring—the teachers, the lunch aides, probably the roaches in the walls, and especially the new kid.

Our gazes met for a second. His eyes were as dark as his hair, but when he smiled, they lit with the glint of a rock star on stage. "*Gracias*," he said. With that one word, I could tell I'd been right. He was from Madrid. I'd spent only a summer there, but it was good to realize I hadn't lost all of my nomad skills.

"*De nada*," I replied, noticing the dimples in his cheeks. What was it about a guy with dimples that sucked you in, like you couldn't look away, even if you wanted to.

And I didn't want to.

CHAPTER TWO

Apparently, being the hero of the cafeteria did nothing to inspire a change in plans from Tyson and Regina. Not only was I still attending my sister's party alone, but I was now watching Keira and Charlotte, our roommate and our mutual best friend, decorate the offensive fiesta.

Only my sister could turn Mother's Day into a drinking holiday.

"Don't you find this a little tacky?" I asked as I watched Keira wind pink and black streamers around an empty curtain rod. Charlotte held the other end of the crepe paper roll.

"Not at all." Keira smacked her lips. "I deserve some recognition for not screwing you up these past three years."

"Who says you haven't?"

Keira shot me a look. "I wouldn't mess with the one thing standing between you and a group home in Jamaica Plain." She cocked her head, her ironed platinum blond hair falling over her shoulder.

After decades of looking like our dad's Mini-Me—with hazel eyes, a pointy nose, pale skin, and light brown hair— Keira decided to dye her hair Madonna-platinum and coat herself in tangerine tanning solution. It was a reaction to the funeral, and I didn't have room to criticize. I hardly waited a week before cutting my espresso-colored locks to my shoulders to avoid seeing my mother's reflection in the mirror. But eventually, I let my hair grow out, confident that my eyes set me apart. They were a smoky gray-blue color that was unique amongst my family, which, depending on who you asked, either made me look perpetually gloomy or a tad mysterious. My sister voted for gloomy.

"Even if you wanted to celebrate Mother's Day, which I still think is weird, shouldn't we be doing brunch and mimosas, not kegs and Cheetos?" I commented as I watched Charlotte shove rosy carnations into an empty vodka bottle.

"Who said anything about kegs? We're talking *martinis*." Keira fluttered her fingers near her unseasonably tan face as if she were suggesting a cotillion. "We're classing it up." Though as she said this, she stepped onto the sofa, lifted a giant metallic "My Mom Rocks" sign, and adhered it to the wall with Scotch tape.

"What if there is a Happy Legal Guardians' Day? Did you even look into it? Maybe we should be throwing this party in October or something? I mean, if Hallmark can peddle Grandparents' Day, Secretaries' Day, and Valentine's Day, I'm sure they thought of this, too." I plopped onto our leather recliner, which expelled a stale puff of air as if it were as exhausted as I was.

"First off, it's Administrative Professionals' Day. Let's keep it PC," Charlotte corrected, blowing a stray dirty-blond curl from her eyes. "And second, the first known association of Valentine's Day with sappy love is in Chaucer's 'Parlement of Foules.' So you can blame him. Hallmark just added the singing cards." She cascaded fuchsia "I Heart Mommy" napkins on the glass coffee table, looking as if this obscure knowledge simply rested at the tip of her brain.

"Why do you know that?"

"Because I read."

And she did. Charlotte had a bedroom library that consisted of everything from *Pride and Prejudice* to *JavaScript for Dummies*. She actually read law reviews for enjoyment. It was amazing she still was fun to hang out with, but she really was, even if she spent so much time plugged into her computer that she made Mark Zuckerberg seem low tech.

"So exactly how many people are going to be invading our house tonight?" I asked, hiking up my unwashed jeans. There seemed no reason to wear fancy going-out clothes for a bunch of guests who would probably arrive in hospital scrubs.

"Like, thirty, depending on who shows." Keira stacked hot-pink paper plates next to the cheese and pepperoni tray, then twirled a lock of blond hair around her index finger in that way she did when she was nervous. "Hey, did anyone call for me today?"

"You mean, like, on the landline?" My forehead creased. "Why would a guy call you here?"

"I never said it was a guy," she hissed defensively.

"You didn't have to." I rolled my eyes and propped my bare feet up on the table next to the crackers, crossing my ankles. "Unless it's a telemarketer, that phone doesn't ring. So let me guess, he lost your number?"

Keira had a history of spending the night with guys who suffered from crippling cases of selective phone-number amnesia. And I had a feeling she might be seeing someone new, because she'd been "working late" and "pulling double shifts" a lot recently. The last time she used those excuses, she was dating a married man who she worked with. It didn't end well, and it looked like her new romance might be headed down the same path.

"It's not like that. I was just expecting something…"

"As long as it's not his wife," I mocked. "That scene on our front steps wasn't too fun the last time."

"Don't be a bitch," she snapped. "And get your feet off the table!" She chucked a package of uninflated pink balloons at me, a little too hard.

"All right, ladies, let's not fight," Charlotte interrupted in a calming tone. "It's Mother's Day Eve, a time to bring us together. So let's rock in this holiday like it's never been rocked before!"

"That's because it never *has* been rocked before," I noted.

"Cue the playlist," Keira ordered.

Immediately, Ozzy Osbourne's voice boomed through the living room speakers, wailing "Momma, I'm Coming Home," and I watched as their hair flew, headbanging, shouting lyrics. If this was what they looked like sober, I could only imagine where the evening was headed after a few martinis.

People tended to think that hospital employees were the epitome of stoic professionalism. *"Get me ten cc's of epinephrine, stat!"* That might be true, but I was watching those same employees missing their mouths as they tried to swill back cups of vodka-something while attempting the MC Hammer and yelling catchphrases from at least two decades ago ("Loser!" with an *L* hand gesture propped on their foreheads).

I pulled myself up from the sofa and shoved another handful of Dorito crumbs into my mouth as I started toward my bedroom. It had better be unoccupied. I turned in the hallway, my bare feet collecting cracker bits from our creaky pine floors. The brownstone was one of the few things inherited from our parents—a four bedroom, 1,500 square foot, walk-up in Brookline. After lifetimes of relocating, our family had become experts on housing markets from here to Morocco.

Good thing, too, because apparently our parents weren't big on saving. We inherited little cash, and it wasn't until months after the funeral that their best friend and colleague, Randolph Urban, stepped in, claiming Mom and Dad had a life insurance policy through Dresden. He said he was terribly sorry he hadn't informed us of it sooner and handed us a check. We didn't ask any questions (mostly because we were sick of eating ramen noodles), but we were never quite sure if such a policy existed or if he'd simply wanted to help.

"What up, Phoenix sistahs?" cried Charlotte as she flung open her bedroom door. She stepped into the hallway in ripped jeans and a thrift store T-shirt, looking about as dressed up as me. "How hot am I?"

"The hottest computer science geek the corporate world has ever seen," I joked.

"Don't you know it!" She waved her hands in the air, staggering slightly, her messy curls flopping in her face.

Charlotte was a major reason why Keira and I still functioned in society. After the funeral, our grief got stuck at the anger stage. We screamed over everything—my grades (which tanked from B's to D's in a single quarter), my suspension rate (which accelerated alarmingly due to skipped classes), and even whose turn it was to unload the dishwasher ("I may be your guardian, but I am *not* your maid!"). We resented our parents. We resented each other. And we resented the Red Sox for winning the World Series and making everyone in the city so damn happy.

Charlotte helped. She was a friend of Keira's from BU

who had a high-paying full-time job and was in need of a place to live. Plus, she came equipped with every season of *Buffy* on DVD, an insane knowledge of everything in the known universe, and unquestionably sound judgment. ("Keira did the dishes yesterday. It's *your* turn.") She was our judge and jury.

"Hey, where's Keira? 'Cause I need to fill 'er up!" Charlotte slurred as she waved her empty plastic cup.

"In the kitchen, but—"

"Anastasia!" Keira shouted as if sensing her name in the wind. "Where's the sugar?" She stumbled out of the kitchen in a new pair of too-tight skinny jeans, gripping a pink-and-white striped plastic pitcher in one hand and a yellow cocktail in the other. Her eyelids hung heavily, and her right shoulder was exposed, her wide-necked black shirt sliding down her arm like a modern version of *Flashdance.*

"It's next to the coffeemaker," I griped, taking in her drunken spectacle.

I didn't drink. Not because I was a goody-goody, but because there were a lot of things social services was willing to overlook, but an orphaned teen being supplied illegal substances by her twenty-something guardian wasn't one of them. It was a one-way ticket into foster care, and as much as I questioned my sister's right to boss me around like a lowly subject, I knew I had it pretty good. There was no lock on my fridge and no bruises under my clothes. Keira and I were the only family we had left, and even if we'd never admit it to each other, that meant something.

"No, that's sweetener. I need sugar. The real stuff," Keira spat, her head flopping like a bobblehead.

"You threw out all the sugar when you went on Weight Watchers."

"No, I didn't! And I'm not on points. *Mom* was on points, or so she said. Not that she needed it. Not that she needed anything…or anyone, apparently," Keira rambled as she took another gulp. "I'm on South Beach, by the way."

"Whatever." My sister had a habit of bringing up our parents when drunk. The anniversary of their deaths was two months ago, and she had spent the entire day polishing off a bottle of tequila and slurring about the old days until she vomited. Repeatedly. "Just use Splenda. Or better yet, stop drinking." I rolled my eyes.

"Hey, I saw that look! And I'm allowed to have fun. I'm twenty-four! I'm, like, the *oldest* twenty-four-year-old on the face of the planet!"

"We're not old!" interjected her friend Rebecca, as she attempted the electric slide to a Snoop Dogg song.

"No, you're right. I just need to switch to dermatology, get some free Botox, and be discovered as the next Boston weather girl." Keira's expression turned dreamy.

"You know weather girls have degrees now, right?" I cocked my head.

"And they're called meteorologists," Charlotte corrected as she grabbed the pitcher from Keira.

"So?" Keira shook her head, her whole body so off-balance that vodka splashed wildly from her widemouthed martini glass. She rubbed her dripping hand on her shirt, cleaning under the vintage eighties *K* ring on her forefinger. I'd bought it for her for her twenty-first birthday, and she hadn't taken it off since, mostly because it was too small to remove. But still, I loved that she loved it.

The apartment door swung open, and we turned to see three guys standing in the doorway, looking like they'd arrived straight from a Nirvana tribute show, only their faux vintage T-shirts and wrinkled button-downs seemed a bit too clean, and their jeans were ironed. Two sported those messy haircuts that required a flatiron to sculpt, and the other had wavy dark blond hair that fell to his chin in layers that were obviously professionally cut and styled. They were trying way too hard to look as though they weren't trying. I glanced at my sister, and I could instantly see that this was who she was asking about earlier, the guy she'd been sneaking around with, desperately hoping would somehow call our landline. Thankfully, there was no wedding ring on his finger.

"Hey," said Mr. Wavy Locks. "I hope you don't mind, I brought my buddies." His voice was deep, not just deep but scratchy. It made my shoulders tense.

He pulled his lips in a cheesy duck-face, accentuating a thick scar on his upper lip that stretched past his nostrils. It looked as though his lip had been split, and the sight of it sent an uneasy ripple through my belly. It was like walking down a deserted street and seeing a stranger coming my way; sometimes, for no reason, I crossed to the other side. This guy had that vibe. "Nice place."

He narrowed his green eyes and scanned the room. Only it didn't appear as though he was admiring the décor, more like he was sizing up the guests, his gaze lingering on the faces of the men in the apartment more than the women. Maybe he was surveying his competition.

He stepped under the entryway light, his head nearly hitting the swinging pendant—he had to be at least six-foot-two. "I'm Craig," he said to me, his eyes landing on my chest. He licked his lips seductively. Ew.

"Glad you came," Keira cooed, mistakenly thinking the gesture was for her.

Score one for alcohol.

Two of Keira's nursing friends rushed to her side.

"This is Jocelyn and Rebecca." She nodded to her pals who were swaying drunkenly and looking just as smitten. The guys in the doorway scanned them from head to toe, and I could almost hear them mentally calling "dibs."

"You wanna drink?" Keira swiftly grabbed a pack of clear plastic cups on the table nearby and flashed a flirtatious grin. Craig grabbed a cup, his hand brushing her wrist, lingering a moment, while his other hand reached for the crotch of his pants, adjusting himself. My sister pretended not to notice, still batting her lashes like an adoring fan. It was as if I was the only one who could see how pathetic these guys were.

I grabbed my sister's elbow, yanking her toward me. "Are you serious?"

"What?" She shrugged, faking an innocent look.

"You know what." I nodded to the losers, but she shook me off, stepping closer to Craig.

It was like my sister was born without a douchebag detector. She had to know she was better than this. The guy was still holding his crotch while ogling my boobs.

Then he blew me a kiss behind her back, flashing his tongue.

"Keira, come on. Let's get some coffee," I reasoned.

"Coffee? Ugh," she groaned. "I'm fine, sis. You can go to your room now."

Did she just send me to time-out? I set my jaw, glaring at her, only she turned her gaze to him, her fingers flipping her hair as she giggled.

Fine. Be that way. She and these losers could have one another. I turned my back.

"Happy Mother's Day," I grumbled before stomping away.

CHAPTER THREE

I awoke the next day to a blissfully silent apartment, which was a welcome relief considering I had spent the wee hours of the morning covering my ears with two thick down pillows. Even through the feathers, I could hear Keira's bed squeak, which was beyond gross. First, she's my sister. I shouldn't be exposed to such acts—it could damage my fragile teenage psyche. Second, if she was going to subject me to such repulsive torture, she could at least pick someone who wasn't jerky enough to hit on her sister while she wasn't looking.

But that was Keira. She coped with our parents' deaths by "filling her soul" with "meaningless sex"—or, at least, that was what the shrinks said. I, however, was diagnosed with the opposite. Psychiatrists claimed I had trouble "forming attachments," which was a fancy way of pointing out that I had only two friends my own age and I had difficulty confiding in them with anything more significant than a grade on a pop quiz. But after years of moving around the globe, I'd learned to depend solely on my family. Then my parents died.

"Three Die in Fiery Wreckage." That was the headline on the front page of the *Boston Globe* three years ago on March eighth.

A man named Derek Wolf was driving down Storrow Drive, a picturesque expressway bordering Boston's Charles River. He had recently left a fortieth birthday dinner for his newlywed bride, Shawna Belkin, where the couple had consumed two pitchers of sangria, two margaritas, and several shots of tequila. He was traveling at a speed of seventy-two mph in a forty-mph zone—in the wrong direction—when he collided with my parents' car.

An explosion followed. Their bodies were charred beyond recognition and had to be identified by dental records. They were fifty-five years old. Derek Wolf died as well. According to the police report, his blood alcohol level was 0.33 percent. More than four times the legal limit. He probably didn't feel a thing. I doubt my parents were so lucky.

Now we were two orphaned sisters—one with hardly any friends at all, and the other with an overabundance of friends with benefits. How cliché.

I glanced at the clock—eight in the morning, like always. When I was little, my mom called me her walking alarm. Every morning I'd get up exactly at eight and crawl into their bed—even if they weren't home. Once, when we moved to Singapore and were still staying at a hotel waiting for the lease to close on our apartment, I tried to crawl into their room. Only I opened the door to the wrong hotel suite—thanks to a careless maid—and sank into an empty king-size bed. I slept there for over three hours. All the while, my family frantically searched the premises for their missing child. The police were called. There was a news alert for a missing American six-year-old. Eventually,

I awoke and returned to my room to discover the hubbub. They didn't let Keira and I share our own hotel room for a long time after that.

I crawled out from under my soft cotton sheet and headed toward the hall bath. Charlotte and I shared it, while Keira took the master bathroom. Considering people had spent hours partying and puking in our place the night before, I wasn't excited to see what awaited. I grabbed my toothbrush from the safety of the medicine cabinet, and caught a whiff of urine mixed with stale beer mixed with a juniper breeze candle. My stomach sloshed. I brushed my teeth while holding my breath, then washed my face with cold water and darted out, still dabbing my skin with a towel.

Keira and Charlotte had better clean up—their party, their mess.

I closed my bedroom door and slid into jeans and a black long-sleeved T-shirt. I was still running a brush through the knots in my hair when I slipped into my gray Converse sneakers and tiptoed toward Keira's room.

I knocked lightly, my attempt to be respectful.

No one answered.

I waited a few moments and knocked again, harder this time.

"Keira?"

I heard the rustle of movement. Then a raspy male voice whispered, and my sister moaned—like, *moaned*.

That did not just happen.

I stared at the cracked white paint and tentatively rapped again.

She moaned louder.

No freakin' way. I stood glaring, my fist balling so tight my nails dug into my flesh. *She knows I'm standing right here! I have ears.*

"Keira!" I snapped. "You probably don't care, but I'm heading out!"

She moaned in response. Seriously. It took everything I had not to open the door and chuck something at them.

I stomped down the hall. What was wrong with her? It wasn't like I was against her dating, I was against her dating dickwads, which was her entire romantic history for the past three years. Exhibit A) Matt, an unemployed thirty-year-old who ate our entire box of Cocoa Puffs and never called again. Exhibit B) Jeremy, who had the nerve to ask for money for the T every time he came over (it was a two-dollar fare). Exhibit C) Ted, who wore only black T-shirts so small they wouldn't fit me, just in case you missed the fact that he lived at the gym. Exhibit D) Gideon, who actually used the phrase "pretty dope, bro" in conversation. And Exhibit E) Jordan, who stole our entire mega pack of toilet paper before skulking out at sunrise (we still weren't sure if it was a prank or if he couldn't afford his own). Now I was going to have to watch my sister stare at her phone praying that some Kurt Cobain wannabe sent her a text.

I grabbed my wallet from my room and charged out the front door. She deserved better than this, better than *him*. All of them. How could she not see that? I bounded down the steps, flinging open the exterior door at the bottom.

The street was still. Actually, our tree-lined street in Brookline was usually hush-hush for a city block, but today it almost felt eerily so. There was no wind.

I closed my eyes and breathed the warm air. How long did I need to stay gone if I didn't want to see Señor Sketchy in my kitchen? Probably longer than it took to buy bagels, but it would have to do.

I walked to Comm. Ave. and a T-train rumbled past,

breaking the silence. It was almost empty due to the hour. College kids weren't big on the "early to rise" thing, not even when their mothers were in town waiting to sip mimosas. I crossed the intersection and swung open the glass doors to Shaw's Supermarket. Bouquets of fragrant flowers decorated the entryway with plastic "Happy Mother's Day" signs inserted between the pink buds. Celine Dion's "Because You Loved Me" played on the sound system, and before I could even grab a wire basket, an employee interrupted to announce a special on "Mother's Day Chocolates."

Times like these, it was quite easy to imagine what it was like to be Jewish on Christmas. Not that my family normally celebrated this holiday even when my mother was alive—well, this or Father's Day, or our birthdays, or Thanksgiving, or Easter. My parents were always working or traveling, which was curious given that over the years we'd met plenty of teens whose parents were engineers, and they worked Monday to Friday, nine to five.

It was just the Dresden Kids who sat around while their parents jetted off to India for three days and occasionally came back with mysterious bruises that they claimed were from "accidents at the plant" or a "slip in the lab." To be fair, my parents also boxed as a form of exercise. But this, combined with their immense computer skills and fluency in countless languages (including Arabic and Farsi), led to a running family joke that they were plotting to take over the world. Either that or they were secret spies, drug dealers, or mafia enforcers. (We did spend a year living in Milan.)

I wandered down a nearby aisle, past the pink greeting cards and pastry displays, winding toward the clinking registers as a steady stream of Jewel, Norah Jones, and Celine filled the air.

That was when I saw him.

He was standing in line at the overpriced grocery café, dressed in a black leather jacket, which was pushing it for May, even in Boston. From this distance, and safely hidden behind a rack of "Greetings from Beantown" postcards, I could get a better look at his tattoo—a black bull with angry crimson eyes. Not very subtle. I'd imagine anyone getting a tattoo would have to think hard about irrevocably marking himself, but to put that tattoo so close to your face—and not on, say, your butt—must mean you feel unusually attached to the image. It had me wondering what the black and red bull meant. Hopefully, it wasn't a nod to his affinity for highly caffeinated beverages.

A perky barista with a bouncy blond ponytail worthy of a cheerleading uniform grabbed a paper cup for his order and, even from a few yards away, I could see her smiling over the espresso machine in that way that Keira does, all giddy and twinkly. She was probably putting a little heart in his foam. He turned to shove his wallet into the back pocket of his weathered black jeans, a shiny metal chain hanging down—a bit too hipster for my taste— and that was when he saw me. Straight on. There was no denying it. I was hiding behind a rack of four-for-a-dollar postcards watching him order coffee like he was a piece of performance art.

Damn.

"*Hola.*" He nodded at me, flicking his hand.

Double damn.

I smiled sheepishly, my cheeks flaming. "*Hola*," I muttered. Now I had to walk over or it would look even weirder. I took an embarrassed breath and trudged toward him, staring at my sneakers the whole way.

"I never got to thank you for yesterday. *Muchísimas gracias, te lo agradezco de todo corazón*," he said, and I had to admit it, his accent was amazing. I knew a lot of Americans were suckers for British accents, but for me, there was nothing like a Spanish accent. It made you sweat. And he knew it. Otherwise, why would he choose to speak to me in Spanish before knowing if I spoke the language? He was trying to have an effect on me and, embarrassingly, it was working. My cheeks burned hotter.

"*De nada. Debe dar gracias a mi pie,*" I replied, showing that his language skills weren't that impressive, while also showing off my own. I switched back to English. "Seriously, I don't know why I did it. My foot has a mind of its own."

"Then your foot is lethal. You brought down a guy twice your size."

"It's a gift." I shrugged. I'd learned over the years that most guys preferred ballerinas to black belts, which was fine. I didn't need a boyfriend. And if my sister was any indication, most guys wouldn't even try to relate to our depressing family situation. If that wasn't what they wanted from her, why would I be any different?

"Your classmates seemed to enjoy it."

"Let's just say he had it comin'." I grinned, remembering Wyatt as he hit the dirty linoleum.

"I don't even know your name." He stepped toward me, staring intently in this unflinching, un-American way, like he didn't care about personal space or boundaries.

"Anastasia," I replied, pretending his proximity didn't bother me, but he was standing so close I could smell the citrus soap on his skin.

"*Ahnahstassia,*" he said, heavily accented with European flare. "Russian?"

I tried not to roll my eyes.

Most people linked my name to the Russian princess who possibly disappeared a hundred years ago after her family was murdered. There was a whole cartoon movie about it. I wasn't a fan. And I wasn't Russian. Though if the rumors were true and the infamous Anastasia *did* outlive her parents, then the two of us, unfortunately, had a whole lot in common.

"No, I'm an American mutt. Irish, Italian, Polish, yadda yadda." I shrugged my shoulders. "And you're from Madrid?"

"*Sí.*" He nodded.

"Marcus!" yelled the barista, gesturing to him with the white paper cup in her hand, a tan cardboard collar wrapped around it. "Double espresso."

"That's me. Marcus Rey." He continued looking at me as he said it, not glancing at the twinkle-eyed blonde, and I had to admit, that made me a little happy.

"Nice to meet you, Marcus," I replied, not breaking eye contact.

Just then, an intercom announced a two-for-one special on Mother's Day greeting cards, and I remembered Keira back in our apartment with a stranger. "I should probably get going. See you in school on Monday?"

Marcus nodded and grabbed his coffee from the bar. "*Buenos tardes, Ahnahstassia.*"

"*Adios,*" I replied, still loving his Spanish accent.

I rushed home, one of those dazed walks where you don't even know how you got there; you're just suddenly standing in front of your door. I couldn't stop picturing Marcus's dimpled grin or the way he looked at me while we spoke. I knew if I told Keira about him, she'd clap and cheer like our five-minute conversation was the most important moment of my life. Really, I had no idea if I'd ever speak to him again. But I wanted to. And I wanted to tell my sister about him.

I bounded up the creaky wooden steps of my brownstone and reached for the brass handle to the apartment, but the door fell open as if it had been left ajar. I was positive I'd slammed it before I left, so that could mean only one thing—lover boy had left the building. *Thank heavens for small favors*. Maybe Keira cleaned the bathroom while I was gone, too. (And then we won the lottery, and I was named prom queen.)

I threw my keys on the mail table, which was still decorated with a half-empty lemon martini with a floating cigarette butt. Water was running in the master bathroom. It sounded like the tub, but I couldn't remember Keira taking a bath. Ever.

I headed down the hallway.

"Keira? Is that you?" I hollered.

I was still debating what to tell her about Marcus. I hadn't mentioned the cafeteria incident yesterday, so I'd have to start at the beginning. She was going to love that he was European. Actually, she was going to love me talking to a guy, period. Not that we were really talking; I'd only just learned his name.

"Keira, I've got something to tell you…" I sang cheerily as I knocked on the door to the master bedroom, our parents' old room. I hated going in there, which was why I let Keira have their bathroom. The room still smelled of them—lilac perfume mixed with dust mixed with old leather.

No one answered, so I reluctantly walked in, newspaper pages rustling on my father's antique desk as the wind from the door breezed through. We never touched a thing. It wasn't like we were creating a shrine, more like we were too overwhelmed—with grief, with memories, with the sheer magnitude of our parents' belongings. So we left everything where they'd put it, saying we'd deal with it later. But we always seemed to have enough to deal with.

A white light shone from the crack below the closed bathroom door, water roaring behind it.

"Wow, are you really taking a bath? How gross was that guy?" I knocked on the door. "Seriously, I don't think there's enough cucumber melon in the world to save you now…"

She didn't respond, so I knocked again. "Keira? You there?"

Still nothing.

Suddenly, ice ran through my bones. I shivered.

"Come on, it can't be that bad…" Only something told me it was. Visions flashed in my brain: Keira being hurt, him hurting her, him touching her, him *forcing* her.

I grabbed the handle to the door, my hand trembling.

"Keira, I'm coming in. Okay?" I struggled to keep my voice calm.

The door swung open.

All I saw was blood.

CHAPTER FOUR

I rocked silently on a kitchen chair. The patchwork quilt my parents brought back from Indonesia was loosely wrapped around my shoulders. It was black and blue, torn, and smelled faintly like a thrift store from the years spent resting at the top of a hall closet. I didn't know who draped it over me—probably Charlotte—but I didn't need it. I wasn't cold. Still, I hugged it tighter.

Bam! Bam! Bam! Police charged through my apartment. There were dirty footprints covering every inch of our wood floors, plastic yellow teepees were scattered about marking evidence, and caution tape hung in the doorways.

My ears throbbed from the squealing police radios, the squawking voices.

"We're so sorry about your sister…"

"Can we get you some water?"

"Is there someone you can stay with?"

I swayed, fists pressed to my ears, trying to drown them out. *This isn't real, this isn't happening…*

But it was.

"Miss! Excuse me. *Miss!*" someone shouted.

A clenched hand shook my leg, blue veins bulging around the pale white knuckles. I followed the arm up, dazed, and saw Charlotte gesturing to a detective with her chin. A forty-something African-American woman in a dark navy suit stared down at me, fidgeting slightly as if my pain made her uncomfortable. Believe me, I wanted to stop crying, but the tears were leaking from a broken faucet.

"Miss, I'm Detective Dawkins," she introduced. "I'm sorry for what you're going through, but I have some additional questions." She averted her eyes. "I know this is difficult, but did your sister have a history of mental illness?"

"What are you talking about? Why would you ask that?" My forehead wrinkled.

"Maybe a history of depression? From your parents' accident?" she continued, clutching at a tiny spiral notepad.

"Why would that matter?" She wasn't making sense.

"It's just, we need to understand her state of mind." Her expression was serious. "We need to know what she might be capable of…"

What *she* might be capable of? My jagged fingernails dug into my palms. I glared at the detective. "Are you serious? Do you think my sister drowned herself in a pool of blood? And then what? She got up and walked away? Without leaving a trail? Someone cleaned up this place!" My vision blurred into a crimson film. "My sister is hurt, seriously hurt. Someone attacked her, took her, and they're out there. You have to find him! Find *her*!"

My mind flipped back to that bathroom.

When I opened the door, blood flowed everywhere, gallons and gallons of vibrant red liquid spilled from the claw-foot tub and pooled so deep on the ceramic floor you couldn't make out the white of the tiles.

There was no body. There was no Kiera.

Steam weighed heavily in the air, making me dizzy as it mixed with the scent of her vanilla bean lotion, her floral hairspray, her bodily fluid. It was like I could taste her. She had been here. This was her blood.

In an instant, my body flipped into primal mode. I howled, twisting off the spigot as it spread bits of Keira far and wide. I sank my bare arms into the boiling water, searching the blood as if I expected to find her, find something. Anything. That was when Charlotte appeared. Her zombie-like reaction left her frozen in the doorway, palm covering her mouth. I shrieked for her to call 911, my knees slipping on watery blood as I continued searching, calling Keira's name in an endless loop.

When the paramedics arrived, I was covered in so much gore that they searched me for wounds. Charlotte had to strip my clothes.

"Okay, if your sister didn't hurt herself, then who did?" Detective Dawkins asked, her plastic pen poised above her notepad as if not wanting to miss a word. "You need to tell us everything you know about the man she was with last night. What do you remember?"

"He was a douchebag."

"Yes, I know. You said that." She sighed. "But what was his name?"

"Craig," I recalled.

"Craig, what?"

"I have no idea. I already told this to a different cop." I hated that they kept making me repeat myself. It was painful enough the first time. Didn't these people talk to one another? "The man was tall, white, twenties, long dark blond hair. He had a scar on his lip."

"I know, but how did she meet him?" the detective

continued, sounding irritated with *me,* like the least I could do was make her job easier.

"I don't know. But I had a feeling she was waiting for him to call earlier. Maybe his number's in her phone."

"We'll check." The detective made a notation. "Do you remember his friends' names?"

"No, but they might have hooked up with two of the nurses who were here, Keira's friends."

"Okay, good. We'll need their names." She nodded like I was finally being useful. "You said Craig was sketchy? In what way?"

"In every way," I responded. "He grabbed his crotch when he saw me and blew me a kiss when Keira wasn't looking. His outfit seemed fake, like he'd bought it at a nineties costume store. Everything was ironed and too clean. And his eyes kept darting around, but not at the girls. It was like he was sizing up the men. He just gave me the creeps, like I knew he was going to do something bad when he walked in the door."

Why didn't I stop him? I knew she was drunk. And I let Keira spend the night with him. What if all those squeaks from her bed weren't consensual? What if I spent the night listening to him attack her? Please, God, tell me that wasn't what happened. Please tell me my sister wasn't pleading for help, and I left her.

Keira was alive in our apartment when I woke up. She was there and breathing when I knocked on her door, when I went to the grocery store, and when I flirted with Marcus. *If I had just opened the door, if I had come back sooner, if I hadn't been so damn judgmental, so pissed off, I could have stopped this. Please, God, let me go back and stop this. I'll do anything. Absolutely anything.*

Air drained from my lungs. The room grew hot. Too

hot. I couldn't breathe. I pulled at my heather gray T-shirt, the crew neck tightening like fingers around my throat. Someone pushed my head between my knees, then a cold cloth was pressed to my neck.

"Breathe, breathe," Charlotte whispered in my ear. I could hear the tears in her voice. "You're okay…"

"Miss, I'm sorry if I upset you. I know how difficult this must be," the detective continued. "But we need to know—"

"Stop calling me *miss*," I hissed when air returned to my lungs.

"Sorry, Anastasia. Right now, we're working on the assumption that the blood is your sister's, but—"

"The *assumption*!" My head snapped up, my dark sweaty hair sticking to my face. I smeared it to the side. "What do you think this is, a practical joke? You think some rival high school came and dumped pig's blood in our bathtub? Who else's blood could it be?"

"For starters, the man she was with. We haven't done any lab work yet," said the officer beside her, piping up for the first time.

"This is my partner, Detective McCoy." She nervously gestured to the man beside her like she already knew how I'd react to his comment.

"Well, Detective *McCoy*." I snarled, jumping to my feet, my heavy quilt sinking to the kitchen floor. "Unless you're suggesting that my sister, the woman who put herself through college, who gave up everything to take care of me, who works as a nurse treating people in an emergency room, suddenly woke up this morning, became a serial killer, and left me to be raised by wolves, then I think we can all assume that *she* is the victim! Why don't you stop standing around here, and go out and *find my sister*!" I shouted so loud the Hazmat team carrying jars of watery blood stopped mid-step. Everyone quieted, making a siren in the distance—someone else's emergency—seem impossibly loud.

"They will. Calm down." Charlotte grabbed my arm, pulling me back. I hadn't realized it, but I was within inches of Detective McCoy's face. I'd spat on his cheek.

"Okay, everyone, take a breath," said Detective Dawkins, shooting her partner a look. He coughed awkwardly into his chubby fist. He was fat, sweaty, bald, and smelled of onions. He didn't look healthy enough to run around the block, let alone chase a criminal. "Anastasia," she continued. "You mentioned your sister caring for you. I know your parents passed away. Again, I'm sorry. But we need to consider motive here. You said you think this man came here with the intention of causing harm. Why? Were he and your sister fighting?"

"I don't even know if they were *dating*. I just know she was waiting for a call earlier in the day, and whenever Keira is waiting by the phone, it's usually because of a guy. But she never mentioned him to me before. How about you?" I looked at Charlotte, who shook her head no. "This guy is a psycho. Plain and simple. That's your motive."

"What about your parents? They died in a car crash, correct? Three years ago?"

My jaw tightened. Why did she keep bringing this up? I had enough to upset me, without adding those memories. "You know what happened to my parents; it was in the newspaper."

"Did they have any enemies?"

"No." I folded my arms tightly across my chest. "And if you want me to keep answering these pointless questions, you better assure me that the rest of the Boston Police Department is out looking for my sister. Right this second. Tell me you have choppers, dogs, amber alerts…"

Detective Dawkins shot her partner a look, then they both stared at the ground.

"What?" I asked. Charlotte reached for my hand, like she needed support.

Detective Dawkins sighed warily. "We spoke to the medical examiner." She looked up at me with softer eyes; it was a practiced look. It was her "I need to deliver bad news" face, big eyes full of sympathy. "It's still preliminary, but the amount of blood at the scene...it's significant."

"I know. That's what I'm saying. That's why you need to be out there." My stomach started twisting. I didn't like where this was headed.

Charlotte tightened her grip.

"Look, it's still preliminary, but it's the opinion of the medical examiner that no one, especially not someone the size and weight of your sister, could survive that much blood loss." The detective's voice was steady, resolved. She stared me straight in the eye. "It's very likely that the department is going to rule this case a homicide. So if it is determined that this *is* your sister's blood, you should prepare yourself for the worst."

Keira is dead.

That was what she was saying. *She thinks my sister is dead.* Little streaks of light danced before my eyes as a seething rage bubbled within me. Sweat covered my forehead, my body. I couldn't see clearly, but I could feel the heated words blistering in my throat.

"*What?* What are you talking about? You're wrong! Some dirtbag was in her room this morning! I was gone for less than an hour, and my sister went missing. Did you hear me? *Missing.* She can't be far. She's *not* dead. Why would he take her body? It makes no sense. Keira is out there! I *know* she's out there!" I thrust my face within inches of the detectives. "You have to find her! *You have to save her!*"

"Anastasia, they're doing their jobs." Charlotte grabbed me, holding me back. Her frizzy hair was gathered into a high ponytail that looked ridiculously pep-rally-ish given the situation. But her gaze was lifeless.

There was a buzzing in my ears. "No, they're not! Some guy could be torturing my sister, some pervert could be doing God knows what, he could be—" I doubled over, my stomach wrenching. I heaved at the ground, only nothing came out. Charlotte rubbed my back.

"We will find out what happened to your sister," said Detective Dawkins.

"No. You will *find my sister*," I choked out.

"Yes. Of course. That is our objective."

"You're the one insisting the blood is hers," interrupted McCoy, his liver-spotted nose wrinkled, his eyes almost annoyed. "We don't want to give you false hope."

Fire shot through me, a burning, licking fire, and the buzzing in my ears hit a piercing level. "My sister is *alive*. And if you don't believe that, then *get out*. All of you, get out of my house! Stop touching her stuff! Stop wasting my time! Either save my sister or *get out!*"

Charlotte gripped me by the shoulders and shoved me, dragging me from the kitchen. I couldn't fight back. I could barely see. Black spots swirled before me. She yanked me down the hall and pulled me into my bedroom, quickly closing the door. The sudden silence engulfed me, and I collapsed on the floor, wailing. She tightly wrapped her arms around me, but she couldn't stop the shaking.

My eyes clenched shut, sobs ripping through my chest. *This can't be happening again.*

I stayed on the floor, an old memory hammering in my head.

I was lying on my bed, no pillow beneath my head. It was black. Night. My comforter was in a heap by my feet. Goose bumps covered my skin, my shirt was pushed up to my chest, my belly exposed. I shivered, but it wasn't from the cold. My latest argument with my parents still churned in my brain. They told me that we were moving to Canada. I told them that I hated them.

I didn't, of course. It was one of those things kids say when they're too upset to think of other words. But it wasn't fair to move me again, not after all the promises. So I let them leave for the airport without saying good-bye.

Now it was 12:32 in the morning, and my guilt had awoken me.

I reached for the heavy comforter balled at the foot of my bed. Its pale beige cotton glowed from the light of the streetlamps slicing through my mini blinds. It felt unseasonably cold for March. Maybe the heat was off. I pulled the covers tight against my chin, tucking my pillow back under my head.

I felt myself get heavy, drifting away, until the noise of the front door jolted me alert.

I held still, listening for the sounds of my mother returning. A key slid from the lock, and the hinges whined. I waited for the familiar tread of her footsteps.

Only that wasn't what I heard.

These steps weren't my mother's.

My chest tightened. I sat up, waiting for the sounds to move closer, the old wood beams moaning with each movement.

I knew those steps.

What was *she* doing here?

"A?" Keira called. She sniffled, her breath staggered. "*Ah-Anastasia?*"

Something was wrong.

I knew my sister's voice, and that wasn't it. This voice was warped, tortured. I'd never heard her sound like this before.

The sniffles repeated. She was standing in the hallway. She'd stopped walking. Even with the door closed, even without seeing her face, I could tell she didn't want to come any closer to my room. She was waiting for me to come to her. Only I couldn't move.

There are moments in your life when you know that everything is about to change. Time isn't whizzing by, your mind isn't in a blur, you're in it, living it, and you know, consciously, that your world will never be the same again. *You* will never be the same again. And I knew, somewhere in the hollow of my being, that this was one of those moments. I could feel it in every hair follicle, every skin cell. I had never been more awake or alert in my life. And I didn't want to open that door.

I stared at the six rectangular panels carved in the white-painted wood, the only things protecting me.

"Anastasia?" she cried again, her voice quivering. "A? Are you up?"

She hadn't called me "A" since I was in kindergarten and called her "KayKay."

I heard her footsteps walking closer, her sneakers squeaking. I could almost picture the pink and white Nikes on her feet. I was there when she bought them, and for some reason, in that moment, I couldn't help but be annoyed that she didn't buy the yellow and gray ones. I thought they were better, less girly.

"A," she said again. There was a long pause. I could almost feel the heat of her breath on my face. "Something's... *happened*."

That was when the fragile bubble burst in my brain.

She'd said it. Out loud. Something's happened. I couldn't ignore her anymore.

Robotically, I rose from my bed. My trembling hand reached for the brass knob, and I stepped into the hall. The golden light of the entry cast a haunting glow around her, creating a dark silhouette of my sister's frame. She was shaking, her head hung.

"What happened?" I asked, tears already leaking down my cheeks.

Somewhere inside, I already knew. I'd known the second I awoke with the chills.

Keira looked up, biting her lip, her hands clenched below her chin.

"Say it," I insisted, stiffly wiping my tears.

Keira breathed a long inhale, then pressed her hands into a prayer position at her lips. Pain hung in the air between us. This was the last moment of my normal life, of *our* normal lives. I knew it, as surely as I knew it was Friday, March eighth.

"They're…they're dead," Keira said.

And that was it.

The next evening, Keira moved out of the dorms and back into our brownstone. She planned their funeral. She bought our groceries. She fought with social services. And she cried herself to sleep.

Now it was my turn.

Now *she* needed *me*.

Keira was missing, and I had to find her.

CHAPTER FIVE

Time passed.

I yelled, I bargained, I pleaded—but no body was found. No attacker brought to justice. No one would listen.

Keira was gone. Simply gone.

DNA confirmed that the blood was hers and, given its significant volume, the case was ruled a "probable homicide," as Dawkins predicted. *The Globe* carried the story for a couple of weeks, so did the local TV stations, but then the case got cold and a little girl was kidnapped in Southie, consuming the headlines. We were old news.

Even Charlotte stopped looking, and I thought her faith in her hacker powers was unrelenting. At twenty-four, she was a software engineer at one of the largest firms in Boston, who transformed into "ChartreuseWeb" every night. She was famous in underground cyber circles. Only, after weeks locked in her room, sifting through emails, bank records, phone calls, and hacked security footage, all she turned up was a low-res video from a local juice bar showing a white SUV leaving our street around the time Keira probably was taken. She didn't even get the license plate.

That was when she gave up and planned a memorial.

It was held at BU's Marsh Chapel. A poster-size photo of Keira's face was mounted to cardboard and placed on an easel at the altar.

I wore a black dress. Charlotte never left my side. Neither did Randolph Urban, my parents' former colleague and best friend. In fact, half of Dresden attended in a show of solidarity, including Marcus and his parents. Turned out his parents didn't work for Boston General, but instead were high-ranking researchers for the Dresden Corporation who were simply utilizing the hospital's facilities. They'd been with the company for a decade, meaning our parents probably knew one another, though I didn't have the energy to ask, not even when I saw them at the post-memorial brunch that Urban hosted. It had been only three years since he'd hosted the same brunch for my dead mom and dad.

Only Keira wasn't dead. I couldn't shake the image of my sister out there, breathing, scared, captive, and *alive*. But even Charlotte dismissed my claims. She thought Keira was murdered, and, sure, she wanted to find her killer, but that wouldn't bring Keira back. I was alone in hoping for that possibility. Actually, I was alone, period.

So I returned from the memorial and crawled into bed wearing my itchy bereavement outfit, picturing my sister's photoshopped face on that poster. I shoved my guilt into my belly and tried to shut out how much I'd failed her.

I'd let this happen. I walked away from her door.

I walked away from her.

I pulled the covers over my head and breathed in the silence, the darkness.

I shut my eyes. I rejected the world, and I fell into the funk.

CHAPTER SIX

One month later...

JUNE

The trays of food came three times a day. My bedroom door opened and in came Charlotte with a well-balanced meal. Oatmeal. Turkey sandwich. Pizza. Oranges. Sometimes I ate it. Mostly I didn't.

Instead, the trays served as a way to acknowledge the passing of time. It was hard to tell day from night anymore. My blinds were always shut. I stayed in bed.

The door opened again.

Spaghetti.

Keira and I ate spaghetti almost every night after our parents died. It was cheap, easy to make.

Keira…Keira…

I scrunched my eyes. I went back to sleep.

JULY

"Mom, I know you guys are her guardians, but I don't know if moving her is a good idea. She won't even leave the bed,"

I heard Charlotte say through my closed bedroom door. She was standing in the hallway. They were talking about me. Again.

"That's exactly why she needs to leave. You don't know how to help her," said Mrs. Conner. It sounded like she was dragging something.

"And you do? You don't even know her."

"That's my point, and we're legally responsible for her. What if she…hurts herself? That will be on us."

I'd thought about a fistful of pills. Really, who would miss me?

Keira, I thought, every time. *Keira would miss me. Maybe she is out there, maybe she needs me…* My head hurt. I rolled over, pulling my covers over my eyes.

"Charlotte, I know you're doing your best. But this is over your head." It was her father's voice, deep and authoritative. "The psychologists think she needs a stable influence. She needs to return to her routine."

"And what routine is that? Her entire family's dead!" Charlotte snapped.

"Don't you think we know that? But we finally got the school to pass her from eleventh grade. She won't even have to take her finals. Come September, she can start her senior year, and everything will be better."

"Do you honestly think that's possible?"

"Yes. And you're moving in with us, too. You both need to get out of here. The memories…they're horrible."

More silence. Then my bedroom door creaked opened. I tugged down my bedsheet and saw Charlotte standing backlit in the doorway alongside her parents. They had stuffed suitcases, a steamer trunk. I could see my puffy silver down coat bundled under her father's arm. They'd been touching my things.

"Anastasia, it's time to get out of bed," her father said sternly.

I didn't move.

"We're here to take you home," her mother added, her bright red hair in a messy bun. She was holding a Sam Adams box full of my shoes. She'd taken them from the hall closet. I squinted my eyes. On top of the pile of sandals and boots sat Keira's gray and pink work sneakers. They had no right to touch them. They belonged to her, in this house.

"Look, my parents think we should come home with them for a while." Charlotte pleaded their case. "They're your guardians now, and we don't want the social workers to threaten foster care again."

I continued staring at Keira's sneakers. The hot pink laces were still double-knotted in bows. She never untied them, just wiggled her feet in.

"It's time to get up," Mr. Conner insisted, the wrinkles on his face setting deeper. "Let's go."

He flicked on the overhead light; the dusty bulbs stung my eyes as he reached for a black wool sweater on the back of my desk chair and tossed it into a liquor store box. Then he moved to my bookshelf, grabbing paperbacks at random and flinging them into the pile. He grabbed a white fuzzy teddy bear holding a heart-shaped pink pillow claiming, "I love you beary much." He chucked it into the box. For an entire year, Keira and I gave each other only drugstore presents—partly because of financial necessity, and partly to be ironic. That was my Valentine's Day gift from her. She'd placed it on my pillow along with a bag of conversation hearts, which she knew I hated but she loved. Now the bear sat on my shelf, smiling. It was mine.

I started screaming.

Like, *screaming*.

I'd never heard that sound come out of me before. It originated somewhere in the back of my throat, somewhere that burned.

Everyone froze, and I kept yelling. Then cursing. Then flailing.

I couldn't leave my sister. Or my parents. Or this apartment. It was all I had left.

What if she comes back? What if she comes back? What if she comes back?

They left my room.

August

"Anastasia, talk to me!" Charlotte shouted, shifting the bed with her weight. "You can't keep going like this!"

I swung my head toward her. I had been taking a nap. Her disturbance annoyed me.

"My parents are talking about group homes, hospitalization," she squeaked. "You've got to snap out of this."

The threat registered in my brain. I had been told I didn't look healthy. I wasn't sure how I was supposed to look, and I was too tired to care.

"Anastasia, there's something I need to tell you."

I closed my eyes. I wanted to sleep, and the light in the room was too bright. Charlotte had lifted the blinds.

"Look at me. Open your eyes."

I struggled to push up my heavy eyelids, my vision blurred.

"I don't know how you're going to react. I could be making things worse. The shrinks told me that you can't take much more. They're worried you'll shut down further." Charlotte was rambling. It was hard to concentrate on the words. There were too many. "But I don't see how you could get any worse. It's been *months*, and you're still a zombie."

She shook my leg. I let her.

"Look at me."

I tried to focus my eyes on hers.

"The cops found surveillance footage of Keira and the guy who took her, Craig. He was at the hospital."

I blinked.

"Did you hear me? Someone called in an anonymous tip. They're still trying to track down who, but it means somebody out there knows what happened to her."

It was as if her voice suddenly pierced my brain, a pang of clarity.

"The cops never would have found the footage otherwise. Keira wasn't even working at the time, and she was nowhere near her floor. She's outside in the back near the ambulance dock, and I swear she's with *Craig*."

My eyes blinked rapidly as if a blindfold had been removed. I sat up, my muscles stiff.

Everything around me suddenly seemed shinier, louder.

"Anastasia, did you hear me?" Charlotte's freckled face sparked to life.

I coughed, my throat raw from disuse. My covers were damp with sweat; I peeled them off, stretching my legs.

I got out of bed.

I ran a comb through my dark, wet hair, split ends brushing my back. My shampoo smelled pungent, citrusy. It hurt my nostrils.

"Can I come in?" Three taps sounded on my bedroom door. Charlotte opened it before I could answer.

"You look *so* much better." The relief in her voice was as if she'd just finished a marathon; there was a distinct air of "thank God that's over." Only it wasn't over. Part of me still wanted to curl up and go back to sleep, but I couldn't do that anymore. So I tried to smile, hoping to ease her mind, but it actually hurt. Who knew cheek muscles could atrophy? I rubbed my jaw.

"I think we need to burn these sheets." She looked at my bed, rumpled with unwashed, previously white linens, and pretended to gag. "Seriously. It's *ripe* in here."

She was right. When I returned from the shower, I detected a very strong odor coming from my room that I hadn't been aware of before: BO, dirty laundry, and humidity. Her parents had begged me several times to let them clean the room, but I refused. It would have meant leaving the bed.

I turned to my closet and reached for a pair of jeans. I hadn't worn much more than PJs lately, and I was surprised to see I owned ten pairs of jeans. I had no idea. I'd never seen them all clean and stacked up before. I yanked some skinny denim over my hips. They were much looser than I remembered. I must have lost weight.

"I'm ready." I nodded, eying her nervous expression as she leaned against the doorjamb. She'd promised to take me to the police station, but she seemed to be already regretting the offer, like any contact with my sister's case might send me spiraling back to my rumpled bed.

"You sure? Because we don't have to go right away," Charlotte insisted, tugging anxiously at her frizzy curls. "I plan on hacking into the police system and downloading the footage tonight anyway. So if you want to wait till tomorrow, we could just watch it here."

"No. I gotta do this," I said, marching past her at the door. "I need to see my sister, the sooner the better."

CHAPTER SEVEN

Charlotte and I sat in a windowless room at the police station waiting for Detective Dawkins. My knee couldn't stop bopping. I glanced at the giant mirror on the wall so reminiscent of TV crime dramas, I had to wonder if a team of detectives was sitting behind it, watching us as they drank stale coffee in environmentally unfriendly Styrofoam cups.

I needed to see my sister alive. It was the only thing squashing my grief.

I fidgeted in my metal chair, yanking at my T-shirt. I felt exposed being out of my bedroom, like I'd walked through the squad room naked with tragedy.

"You okay?" Charlotte asked again.

"I'm fine," I muttered, already knowing how often I'd be repeating this sentiment. "You don't have to keep asking."

"Yeah, well, maybe someday I'll describe exactly how bad you've looked these past two months. 'Cause you weren't the only one grieving, you know," she grumbled, aggravated, and I felt a pang of guilt. Charlotte was abandoned by both the Phoenix sisters, and forced to be the de facto head of a family that wasn't even her family. I didn't think "sorry" would suffice.

The door to the interrogation room swung open, and Detective Dawkins walked in carrying a large black laptop. She rested it on the metal table and pulled out the chair across from me, its legs squeaking on the linoleum like cardboard edges rubbing together. A shiver crept up my spine. She plopped down with a sigh, looking like she'd aged a lot in the weeks since I'd seen her last. There were squishy bags under her coffee-colored eyes, and her full lips looked dry, almost cracked.

"Anastasia," she greeted. "I'm glad you're feeling better."

I fought the urge to roll my eyes. Obviously, I didn't feel better. Did she really think there was an alternate reality where a person could return home to a bloody tub from a slasher film and then "feel better" in a few weeks. But I nodded in response.

"Charlotte, you were right. You got through to her."

Charlotte stared at her hands, at least having the good sense to realize it was bad form to discuss me right in front of me.

I pointed to the laptop, ready to move on. "You want me to watch the footage? You think I can help?"

"Well, *help* might be too strong a word. We just want you to tell us if you see anything odd. You knew her best, you might notice something we don't." Dawkins flipped open the laptop's oversized screen and moved her finger across the black mouse pad, cueing some software.

Charlotte looked like a Saint Bernard eyeing a steak. "That's an impressive system."

"Well, after the marathon bombings, our analysts got an upgrade to the forensic video equipment." Her tone was matter-of-fact, but I could tell by the light in her eyes that she was thrilled with her toy.

To me, it looked like we were watching the video on split screen, only we weren't using the second screen. I was guessing it was for enlarging images or doing some sort of manipulation, but I didn't ask. Bordering the window that held the black and white footage were multiple boxes showing squiggly lines, folders, and scales with adjusting levels. It reminded me of the software music producers use, only as soon as she pressed play, I realized I was wrong.

There was no audio.

"Just tell me if you see anything," she instructed again.

Keira walked out, and breath instantly expelled from my lungs. Tears flooded my eyes. It was an involuntary response. There was my sister. Alive. Healthy. No blood.

She turned toward the camera, whipping her long platinum hair behind her bony shoulder. It was tied in a loose ponytail at the base of her neck, strands falling into her face. She was wearing light-colored scrubs, probably peach, and those familiar pink sneakers Charlotte's parents tried to confiscate. There were small silver hoops in her ears, and her forehead was shiny. A few moments later, a man stepped out behind her. He wasn't facing the camera, but it didn't matter. I would have recognized him in a pitch-black pit—long, greasy blond hair, tall posture, and a too-wide wrinkled T-shirt covering the thick muscles that moved beneath it.

My face burned as I sat back in my chair, my still-damp hair clinging to my cheeks. I held my breath. It was him. Craig.

I scrunched my eyes tight as I pictured him dead and beaten. I pictured his body in a tub full of blood. I pictured my knuckles raw from hitting him again and again. My fingers formed fists in my lap.

"It's okay," Charlotte whispered.

But we both knew it wasn't.

I looked back at the footage, and Craig reached for my sister. He held her hand. And for a few moments, they just stared at each other, arms dangling, fingers entwined, looking comfortable, familiar.

They really had been dating.

I'd always suspected that he was the guy she had been asking about earlier and the reason for her "double shifts." But even so, she didn't introduce him to me at the party, and especially not as her boyfriend, not as anything more serious than a hookup. Why would he visit her at work?

I watched as Keira let go of his palm and started talking rapidly, her eyes wide and her lips flying. We couldn't hear what she was saying, but she looked upset. No, she looked *worried*. Like she did before we got our parents' "life insurance," when she wasn't sure her paycheck would keep the lights on.

Craig's large hand reached out once more, rubbing her shoulder, stroking her face. He looked almost tender, and she leaned in to his embrace.

White fire zipped through me. I wanted to strangle him. Then her.

My teeth ground together, and for the first time I realized how angry I was at my sister for letting him into our lives, our home. Because as much as I hated myself for not opening the bedroom door that morning, part of me also hated her for letting him behind that door in the first place. She let him do this to us, and now, who knew what he was doing to *her*. All because her grief had morphed into an unfathomable case of poor taste in men.

I watched as my sister wiped at her eyes, hiding her face with her hand. She hated raw displays of emotion. She didn't even cry at our parents' funeral. It was as if she shed all her tears the night she showed up at our home to tell me about the crash, and then decided that was enough. She never shed a tear in front of me again. (Instead I heard her sobbing in the shower, in her bedroom, behind closed doors. Always alone.) But there she was, crying in front of him. I felt betrayed. Craig held out a tissue, and she took it, muttering something more as she swiftly dabbed at her cheeks. Then they strolled back into the hospital together.

Craig concealed his face the whole way, like he knew exactly where the camera was located.

"Okay, did you notice anything?" Dawkins asked, her dark eyes skipping between Charlotte and me.

I peered at my roommate, swallowing hard, and she nodded slightly as if she already knew what I was thinking.

"They were more serious than we thought," I admitted reluctantly. My sister was seeing a guy she felt comfortable crying in front of, a guy who would show up at work and hold her hand.

"Yes, there seems to be a familiarity in their interaction," Dawkins replied, nodding like we were getting somewhere. "So was this normal for Keira? Did she like to keep her relationships secret from you?"

At this point, I had no idea. "No. I mean, I don't know. The last time she hid a relationship, the guy was married."

"Okay." Dawkins nodded, jotting in her notepad. "That could be a possibility."

"I've checked her phone, emails, texts, contacts, former patients, everything. There's no mention of a Craig," Charlotte pointed out. "If they were talking, I have no idea how they communicated."

"Well, this video was shot five days before the party, and she seems upset." Dawkins noted. "Maybe they broke up? Tell me, how did they seem at the party? Were either of them angry?"

"No." I shook my head. I would have told them that already. "Like I said before, I think she was expecting him. She had asked earlier if anyone had called for her. But when he showed up, there was no boyfriend-girlfriend interaction. They didn't hug or kiss hello, nothing like that."

Dawkins nodded, her eyes distant as she contemplated something.

A few moments passed, and Charlotte sat up straighter. "You think this was a crime of passion," she deduced, watching the detective. "What, that they broke up in this video and he came to the party anyway, and this is all about some relationship gone bad?"

Dawkins held up her wrinkled palms to stop her, leaning cautiously back in her chair. "We don't want to get ahead of ourselves. It's a possibility. The video is being analyzed as we speak. I just wanted to take this time to see if the video sparked any new memories for you; we'll also canvas her colleagues at the hospital again."

It was the first motive anyone had presented since the cops showed up in my apartment that morning. This wasn't some random psycho who showed up to attack the first girl he saw. They knew each other. And by the look of this video, they were having a serious discussion. *They* were serious. If we could find out what they were talking about, that would change everything.

"When do you think you'll know what they're saying on the video?" I asked.

"Hopefully, by the end of the week." She snapped the laptop closed.

"So, Friday? We can come back then."

She tucked the large black laptop under her arm and eyed me quizzically. "I'm glad that you came by and that you're doing better. But this is an ongoing police investigation;

we can't share these sorts of details, not even with you."

"But you wanted us to come in so we could help you," I pointed out, feeling like I needed to show my name to a bouncer with a clipboard.

"Yes, and if we need your help again, we'll ask. Trust me, it's better for *you*." Her tone was flat.

"How is it better? This is my life, Keira's life. Are you seriously not going to tell me what they're saying?" I rose quickly from my metal chair, almost knocking it to the floor.

"I understand you're frustrated, and I know what you must be going through—"

"You have no idea what I'm going through," I snapped through gritted teeth.

"You're right, sorry, but I do know that we will do our best to find out what happened to your sister. Informing you of every line of inquiry could not only compromise the case, but give you false hope. You've got to let us handle this."

"What about the anonymous tip? Any lead on who called in the footage?" Charlotte asked, standing solidly by my side.

Dawkins sucked in her lips for a moment, deliberating. "Whoever called used a burner phone, impossible to trace. We can't even triangulate a location."

"So they knew what they were doing," Charlotte translated.

"Why would someone trying to help go through all that effort?" My eyes narrowed.

"That's what we need to find out." Dawkins moved toward the door. "We'll be in touch."

I watched her exit into the bustling station, as if this were over, as if she'd pacified us. But I knew, without even looking at Charlotte, that by sundown she'd have the video analyzed by a suite of illegal software on an NSA-worthy computer.

We'd get our answers ourselves if we had to.

CHAPTER EIGHT

I'd underestimated my hacker friend. Charlotte broke into the Boston Police Department's security system and had the footage on her laptop less than an hour after we returned home from the station. Though after watching it for three days in endless rotation, we still weren't able to decipher any clues. At best, I thought I caught Keira say my name, which was both eerie and heartwarming, but still didn't tell us much.

Currently, Charlotte was tinkering with the video in recently "acquired" forensic software that claimed to have an algorithm for lip-reading speech recognition, but so far it had produced only gibberish. Regardless, it was better than the video montage I was presently watching. Charlotte had made it to commemorate her friendship with Keira. It was twenty-seven minutes long. "That's What Friends Are For" was the opening number.

"This is really sad, and I mean pathetic-sad, not sad-sad," I mocked as *Toy Story*'s "You've Got a Friend in Me" trailed off to a selfie of their close-up faces.

"Hey, you were semi-unconscious when I made that. I

had to do something." Her fingers flew over the keyboard. She could continuously type for three minutes while looking at me and holding a conversation. I timed her once. Her green eyes flicked my way, still rapidly typing. "I'm glad you finally exited the depression stage of your grief."

"Don't speak too soon. I haven't *accepted* anything," I quoted the five-stages-of-grief book that her parents were mandating I read if I was to continue under their care, though most of the stuff I'd learned from psychologists while grieving for my parents. Turned out not much had changed in grief philosophy since then. "The only thing keeping me going is the fact that there isn't anything to grieve about. We have a lead. Keira is out there."

Charlotte's eyes turned worried. Yes, she wanted Keira's body found, and her killer brought to justice, but I knew she had no hope of finding my sister with life in her veins. I had enough hope for both of us, though.

"Eat something," she insisted.

I dug my fork into a plate of mac and cheese with hot dog slices. Charlotte made it every week. On Wednesdays, Keira used to make Hamburger Helper. On Thursdays, we ate pasta, and on Fridays, pizza. The other days were up for grabs—canned soup, sandwiches, cereal. It was our routine. Our *old* routine. And Charlotte seemed determined to recreate it, or more accurately "assimilate back to our normal lives and focus more on our personal relationships." It was the shrink's suggestion.

"How did you have time to make a sappy montage, hack computers, *and* go to work?" I garbled as I chewed on a gooey bite.

"It's called insomnia. Turns out a tub full of blood has the opposite effect on me as it does you," she quipped.

A bite lodged in my throat as I realized the magnitude

of my overdue apology. I never thought about Charlotte's pain during my funk. I hadn't thought about anyone else actually; it was one of the beautiful side effects of going numb. "I'm so sorry I disappeared on you." I forced down the noodles. "What your family's done for me— I could be in foster care right now."

"It's okay. You've been through enough," Charlotte shivered, running her fingers through her frizzy curls, already greasy at the scalp from mindlessly repeating the gesture. "This software is getting us nowhere!" she groaned, thudding her hands on the keyboard. "I've got to start looking at more hospital footage. I'd focused only on the days and times Keira was scheduled to work. But whoever called in the tip knew she'd be on camera at a time she wasn't scheduled to be on duty. I mean, why was she even there?" Boston General was not only one of the leading hospitals in the U.S., but in the world. It was affiliated with Harvard. Searching every camera, at every minute of every day, would be nearly impossible, especially for one person.

"Maybe she was working overtime?" I suggested.

"I already checked that."

"Covering someone's shift?"

"It would be on her timecard."

I stabbed another hunk of noodles.

"At this point, I'm going back as far as the hospital system will allow," Charlotte continued. "I'm gonna focus on the outdoor cameras, see if I can find her with Craig elsewhere."

"Okay. I'll help you."

Charlotte shook her head. "No way. Absolutely not. You gotta get out of here."

"What?"

"We've been at this for days. You've recently returned from the *Walking Dead*, and you've spent all of your time either hounding the police or staring at a computer screen."

"So have you."

"Yes, but I have a clean bill of mental health," she said pointedly, grabbing her fork and stabbing a hot dog. "You don't. Not yet. The doctors, the social workers, my parents, all say you need to 'see friends and loved ones who can offer support.'"

I rolled my eyes. "I'm seeing you, aren't I?"

"That's not enough. You need to 'set personal goals, learn a new skill'…"

"Now you're just quoting Web Doctor."

"Well, it's better than watching you slip away." She tugged at her hair aggressively. "Tyson and Regina have been calling nonstop. They're about ready to send up smoke signals to find you. Why aren't you calling them back?"

She knew why.

Tyson and Regina had tried to be supportive. They attended the memorial. They cried, dropped off lasagna, made donations. ("In lieu of flowers, gifts can be made to Boston General's Children's Hospital.") But I could see it in their eyes—if I was hard to relate to before, I was an eight-legged Martian now.

To Regina's credit, she was incapable of understanding. She hadn't lost anyone, ever. Her childhood dog was still alive. And she saw the whole ordeal as some atheistic circle of life. "It's up to you to keep on living. We never know how much time we'll have." Then she patted my head like a puppy. Tyson took the opposite approach. He didn't get within ten feet of me at Keira's service, afraid touching me might spread the death disease. He was only one step away from my situation. If his mother cracked, took one too many pills, it would be him, the sole surviving member of his family.

Then I slipped away, and so did they. They stopped calling, stopped trying to visit—not that I really wanted people to join in my funk. But it was a little obvious that my phone was suddenly blowing up now. Charlotte had clearly tipped them off about my return to functioning society, only I wasn't sure any of us were really ready to communicate.

"You're shutting out people because you *think* they won't understand. You have to give them a chance," Charlotte said, as if reading my mind.

"What do you want me to do?"

"Go. Out." She rose from the kitchen table and grabbed my empty dish encrusted with cheese the color of traffic cones. "It's not like you're going to miss anything. I'll continue the search. My nightly activity of scanning surveillance footage will not cease just because you leave the house. So make plans. Do something. It would do a lot to get my parents off my back. They're already talking about us moving in with them again. You know how well that discussion went last time. Please, let me tell them how much better you're doing."

I may have been semi-catatonic, but I remembered that argument well enough to be embarrassed by it now. I had turned into a primal-screaming cave girl. And from making dinner to watching *Wheel of Fortune* to buying trashy magazines, Charlotte had been working overtime to make my days so normal I'd never want to sink away again. If she was getting a hard time from her parents, or worse, from social services, I owed her this favor. Actually, I owed her a lot more.

"I'll call him back," I said, like I was agreeing to take out the garbage.

"Good." She smiled, relief on her face.

I reached for my cell phone. Tyson answered on the first ring.

CHAPTER NINE

Turned out the student body of Brookline Academy had very sophisticated plans for the evening. While I would have preferred my first night reentering teenage civilization to have been more of a reality-show-fest on Regina's couch, I was instead seated at Boston Harbor. My classmates had gathered to watch a movie on the outdoor screen set up alongside a gazebo on the edge of the wharf. We weren't the only ones there, of course. Café tables were packed with yuppie couples sipping Sam Adams and gray-haired retirees slurping buttery lobster as water lapped against the massive yachts docked nearby.

It was a starless, humid night, and we were watching *The Princess Bride*. Most of my classmates were present, because a cousin of Wyatt Burns had been an extra in the film. (You can see her briefly during the wedding scene right after the priest says, *"Mawidge is what bwings us together today…"*) Tyson and Regina were attending as part of a "grown-up date night," and I was the grieving third wheel who had to smile awkwardly as they ordered ice cream in decorative glass cups and took little bites from each other's spoons. At one point, Tyson put a dollop of cookie dough on Regina's nose then licked it off. It was making me more depressed.

"We're so glad you came out," said Regina as she wiped her mouth with one of those unusually thick paper napkins, courtesy of the five-star hotel attached to the café. "You look so much better than when we saw you last."

"You mean at my sister's memorial?" If that was the standard to which I was being compared, I'd imagine I must look like a runway model now.

"Yeah, that." She stared down at her melting fudge ripple, sweat on her brow, which I hoped was due to the heat and not the uncomfortable conversation.

"How's Charlotte?" Tyson asked, his gleaming head also beading with perspiration.

"She's good. Worried about me."

They nodded, eyes locked on their melting ice cream as they visibly strained to come up with a gentle topic of conversation. Finally, Regina sat up, her smile perky.

"You get the summer reading list for English?" Her voice was high and squeaky like this was the greatest subject matter ever. "I can't believe we have to read Sophocles."

"The plays are pretty short, actually. I already finished them," said Tyson.

"Really? Give me your notes."

"No way. Read them yourself. The Oedipus one is famous."

"Some guy killed his mother, blah, blah, blah…"

"There's more to it than that."

"Like I care."

I looked away, staring at the boats swaying in the harbor. When we were younger, Keira and I used to complain endlessly about having to switch schools and read the same books over and over because the curriculum never aligned from one district to the next (or one country to the next).

Every time we whined, my mother would roll her eyes and say, "Pray this is the biggest problem you ever face in your life." Now, I understood what she meant. I wished I could worry about summer reading.

"It's, like, the basis for an entire psychological condition," Tyson continued.

"What, are you auditioning for *Criminal Minds*?"

"No, but I'm planning on passing English."

"Good, then you can write my essay for me."

"That would be cheating!"

"So?"

I popped to my feet, certain that if I had to pretend to be normal for one more second, I'd start howling like a lunatic. "Do you guys know where the bathroom is?"

They both pointed toward the café, hardly looking my way as they continued debating the validity of classic texts being mandated as required reading during vacation hours. I pulled at my knotted shoulder, my body aching from disuse. I needed to go to karate; *that* could be my "normalcy"—wailing on something repeatedly.

I cut through the rows of round tables, squeezing past the backs of wrought iron chairs as I wove toward the café's interior, the flickering blue lights of the movie lighting my way. I slapped a mosquito on my arm as the crowd started laughing.

"*As…you…wish,*" the hero called from the screen, followed by the sound of actors toppling down a grassy hill. Keira and I had watched this movie so many times that I didn't need to look at the film to know what was happening.

I spotted the electric sign for the restrooms and veered toward the red neon letters.

That was when it hit me.

Right between the eyes.

A chicken wing.

I never saw it coming.

Even with the blackness of night surrounding me, and the movie blasting from the speakers above me, I could still hear him laughing and spy his hulking silhouette.

Wyatt Burns.

He'd pitched a barbecued chicken wing at my head and was now barking out a hard hollow laugh that rivaled the sound system. He wasn't alone. An entire table of baseball players and their girlfriends flanked him, all laughing hysterically, hands clapped to their mouths.

"That's what you get for tripping me!" he shouted, leaning back in his chair and stretching out his long arms, black armpit hair peeking through his T-shirt.

I wiped the sticky burgundy sauce from my forehead with the back of my hand, too shocked to do anything else. He looked so smug, as if my tripping him months ago was still a hardship he considered worthy of revenge. I was almost jealous of the simplicity of his life as I stared at the goo coating my fingers.

"Dude, didn't her mom just die or something?" someone whispered.

"No, her sister died. I think her parents are already dead."

"All of them?"

"Pretty sure. Yeah."

"Omigod."

"Seriously?"

"Dude, that's messed up. You should apologize."

"Whatever." Wyatt shrugged, pulling his hairy arms down and adjusting his intentionally dirty Red Sox cap. "I didn't do anything to them. Maybe they all just wanted to get away from *her*."

I closed my eyes, unable to move, to speak. Logically,

in my brain, I knew that words coming from someone like Wyatt shouldn't bother me. He was almost too dumb to be allowed in society without supervision. But still, it hurt. After everything that had happened to my sister, my parents, I couldn't take much more. Not from him.

I could feel the tears building behind my eyelids, my heart thumping too fast. Only I couldn't make my feet move. I opened my eyes, and a pathetic tear fell, making me hate myself even more.

"Puta madre! Que te folle un pez!" cursed a voice in Spanish, rising up from behind me. "What is wrong with you people? Do you not hear what you're saying? You are disgusting." He grabbed my hand, hot breath brushing my skin.

I turned, slightly dazed, but immediately recognizing the familiar accent. Marcus.

"Vamonos." He tugged my arm, dislodging my feet, and I followed him, not knowing where we were going, but letting him lead me away.

CHAPTER TEN

I was seated on the back of an extremely loud, puttering Harley Davidson, my thick hair squished inside a black helmet, my arms wrapped around Marcus's waist, the smell of his leather jacket engulfing me as I crushed myself against his back. We were speeding through Boston's Italian North End. Over cobblestones.

A white SUV cut us off as it turned right, and we swerved, flying down the narrow bumpy road lined with Italian restaurants and old-fashioned storefronts sitting below weathered brick buildings with old metal fire escapes.

I'd been down this street a million times before, usually traveling at a much slower pace in Charlotte's lime green VW Beetle as we stopped to pick up penne a la vodka and cannoli for dinner. This felt a little different as wind whipped my cheeks, lights zoomed by, and every cell in my body clenched to keep me from toppling over. Images flashed in my brain—twisting metal, burning steel, my parents' crash, Keira's memorial poster.

A death wish—that had to be it. I had a death wish. Otherwise, why would I get onto the back of a bike with this guy? Given all of Keira's shifts in the ER, she once said she'd rather see me base jump from a skyscraper than get on the back of a bike.

And here I was.

I could picture the news coverage: *Two teens died today in a motorcycle accident in Boston. Reports say the female passenger boarded the bike with a Spanish teen she hardly knew after having been struck in the head with a chicken wing. No word yet as to what she was thinking...*

Only I *wasn't* thinking.

I simply followed as Marcus clutched my hand and guided me from Wyatt and his lapdogs. Then I took the napkin he handed me, wiped away the barbeque sauce, and blindly trailed him to a massive heap of metal, leather, and tires. He tossed me a helmet, saying, "I'll drive you home," and hopped onto the bike. It almost felt rude *not* to throw my leg over the side and accept his offer. So I got on.

Besides, I could handle myself. I'd fought guys twice my size in karate tournaments. I found my way back to my hotel in Lower Manhattan when I was eight years old and my parents lost me in a crowd in Times Square. I even bought my own metro card and read a subway map. And when we lived in Morocco, I once chased down a pickpocket and got my sister's wallet back. I was thirteen at the time.

Only...I couldn't drive, nor did I enjoy spending much time in motorized vehicles.

It wasn't that I was scared (exactly), it was more that I'd been of legal driving age for a year, and that year was spent in a major metropolitan city with an excellent public transportation system. I didn't need to drive. I had the T. Plus, my parents died in a fiery auto explosion that landed on the front page of the *Boston Globe*. That sort of thing sticks with a girl, and it made me a bit cautious when it comes to vehicular transportation. (Charlotte calls me "chicken.")

The lights of Faneuil Hall and Quincy Market came into view as I felt the bike begin to slow. My pulse gratefully calmed with it until, finally, we pulled alongside the curb. I exhaled, not letting go of Marcus, my cheek still pressed to his leather-covered shoulder.

"You okay?" he asked when I didn't release him.

"Oh, fine." I unlocked my grip from his waist, peeling my face from his leather jacket. "I thought you were taking me home." I yanked off my helmet and swung my leg off the bike. I stumbled slightly, the ground feeling oddly off-kilter, like when you take off your ski boots after a day on the slopes. I ran my fingers through my matted hair, not because I cared how I looked, but more because I was hoping to appear casual and not completely nauseated as I regained my balance. My fingers jolted on a knot, and I silently wished I had Regina's stick-straight locks.

Wait, Regina. Damn. I left her and Tyson at the movie. They were probably wondering where I was. I pulled out my phone and pounded a quick text with my thumbs. **With Marcus. Fine. TTYL.** Let them try to figure *that* out over shared spoonfuls of fudge ripple.

"I can still take you home. I just thought maybe we could get some coffee?"

Coffee... That was what Marcus was doing that day at the supermarket—ordering coffee from a perky barista. The air reeked of espresso. I stayed too long, talking to him, trying to flirt, making a fool of myself while my sister was alone in our home with a deadly psycho. The sight of the bloody bathroom flickered in my brain as if it had been resting behind my eyelids ready to be drawn upon at any moment. It all bubbled up. Blood, blood, blood...

cops, tears, Marcus, blood…

"You okay? Was it the ride? I was going too fast, yes?"

He grabbed my arm like he thought I might faint. I guess the color had drained from my cheeks. Dizzy spots swirled before my eyes as familiar rolls of nausea ripped through my belly.

"Do you need to sit?"

I shook off his arm. "I'm fine. Sorry." I stared at the pavement until my vision cleared, wiping the sweat from my lip as my eyes focused on one black, flattened dollop of littered chewing gum.

Slowly, I felt steadier.

It wasn't his fault that I'd left that morning to buy bagels, that I didn't open the bedroom door, that I didn't get home in time. If anything, he'd done enough already. Apparently, I'd needed an alibi for my sister's disappearance, and Marcus was it. He was questioned by police. *"Yes, officer, Anastasia Phoenix was flirting with me when her sister was brutally attacked…"*

"Do you want to stay? Eat something?" Marcus asked, gesturing to the pillared façade of Quincy Market. The building was old, like part of the Freedom Trail old, constructed of brick with a massive domed ceiling, and full of food vendors and souvenir shops.

"Sure, I guess. Unless, do you have someone waiting for you back at the movie?" I asked.

Marcus glanced away, a flush on his face. "Oh, well, you know what it's like. New kid. I don't have too many friends here yet, and I saw online that everyone was going to the movie, so I thought I'd show up and see…" His voice trailed off, then he shrugged like his solo status was no big deal, though clearly it was. Being the new kid sucked. "Anyway, I can't believe those guys. *Idiotas*. I don't understand—"

"It's fine," I cut him off.

"*Lo siento*."

"I know."

"I can take you wherever you want," he mumbled, shifting awkwardly. "If you want to get coffee, that's okay. If you want to go home, that's okay, too."

I looked up as he fiddled with the shiny metal chain that connected to the wallet in the back pocket of his black jeans, which matched his black leather jacket, black T-shirt, black hair. He ran his hand through his messy locks, flattened from the motorcycle helmet, fidgeting nervously in an all-too-familiar way. I remembered what it was like to try to win over the Dresden Kids who'd lived in town longer. For most of my life, they were my only friends in the world. Every time we relocated, our parents would introduce us to the other Dresden families with an expectation of insta-friendships. We had a shared uncommon childhood, like military brats only without the military.

But I'd been out of pajamas for barely a week. I had to be the worst friend Marcus could find, and there was a part of my brain that couldn't unknot him from my sister's tragedy, from that bathtub. Still, if I went home now, I'd have to tell Charlotte about Wyatt and the chicken wing, which would only make her worry more. I didn't think bullying counted as a sign of "emotional support" from my peers.

"How about some soup?" I asked.

Marcus smiled. "Soup it is."

My family had a tradition. In every new city where we relocated, we spent our first meal at a restaurant eating the local cuisine. I don't just mean eating Italian at the best-rated place on Yelp! I mean, we ate whatever made the city famous. When we lived in New Orleans, we ate crawfish and beignets. When we moved to Morocco, we had some ground beef and powdered sugar served alongside a belly dancer. When we were in Madrid, it was tortilla Española with a side of ham.

And when we visited Paris after Keira's high school graduation, we ate bouillabaisse and snails. They call it escargot there, which sounds slightly more appetizing, but it's still snails. Those slimy little things that cross your driveway coiled up in hard round shells. They even serve the shells with them in case there's any doubt as to what you're eating.

I remember Keira and I staring at our plate, eight tiny snails displayed in a circular dish with cups like an egg carton. They douse them with a gallon of butter and herbs—again trying to drown the "you're eating snails!" aspect of the meal—and I remember debating whether it was time to draw the line. After all, we weren't moving to Paris, we were just visiting, so acquiring an appreciation for the local cuisine really wasn't a necessity. That was when Keira spoke up. She said that if we ate this, then at least we knew from here on out, it would be the most disgusting thing we ever tasted. All food would go up from here. And I had to agree.

So we ate them.

They tasted like buttery pencil erasers.

Then we moved to Boston, and the tradition carried on. Our first night in town, we went to Quincy Market. We each ate a cup of Boston clam chowder with a two-pound steamed lobster served in a cheap plastic tub.

Now I was sitting with Marcus, two wooden tables away from where I'd sat that evening, eating Boston clam chowder in a bread bowl, and none of my family was with me. Like, none of them were with me *in this world*. There was a toddler sitting at our old table, babbling in her high chair as her mom fed her peas.

I felt my throat closing around a chunk of warm, creamy potato. I was having trouble swallowing.

"I've never had clam chowder before," said Marcus as he gulped another plastic spoonful, white goopy soup dripping on his chin. He didn't seem to notice the reaction I was having.

"It's called 'chowda' here," I corrected, forcing down the bite. I could not go through life tearfully skipping down memory lane every time I saw a place my family had visited. We traveled *a lot*. To find a location completely void of memories, I'd have to move to a farm in Idaho or something. I wasn't farm material.

"I stand corrected." Marcus smiled, dimples flashing on both sides. For someone who tried very hard to produce a bad-boy vibe (neck tattoo, black leather, and motorcycle), his dimples crushed it. It was hard not to look adorable with a grin like that. I bit my lip, immediately feeling guilty for thinking that, for even noticing his smile, for sitting across from him at this table. My sister was missing.

I peered down at my soup, my emotions conflicted.

"So how are you doing? With everything?" he asked.

"I'm fine," I muttered, wishing I had a button I could press that would repeat this phrase at will.

"Do you want to talk about it?"

Did I? I honestly wasn't sure. My brief outing with Tyson and Regina proved I wasn't ready to discuss normal topics like schoolwork. Marcus's glowing smile showed I wasn't ready to feel even a flicker of happier thoughts. My sister was my singular focus lately, and I'd shared my dark reflections with only Charlotte, because her mind was as traumatized as my own. Still, the shrinks and social workers insisted that if I wanted to stay off the meds, I needed to expand my "circle of support." The question was—did Marcus really understand what he was asking, and did he want to hear the truth?

"You can trust me," he offered as if sensing my worries. "If it helps to talk about it, I'm here. But if it makes things worse, I understand."

Okay, here goes nothing...

"I can't stop thinking about it—Keira and the tub," I admitted.

"I can't imagine."

"You really can't. It's like a horror movie that never ends." The tub flickered in my mind once more. Always there. "I wish I could think of something else, anything else, be normal, but it's like there's no room in my head for other thoughts."

"I hear the Red Sox won last night."

"What?" I asked, perplexed.

"Against the Yankees. Two home runs in the bottom of the ninth. Almost went to extra innings."

"I didn't know Spaniards followed baseball."

"When in Boston..."

"I think a visit to Fenway is a requirement for residency these days."

Marcus smiled once more. "See, you thought of something else. Even if for just a second."

"I guess a second counts." I ripped a thick piece of sourdough from my makeshift bowl and dipped it into my soup. A shopper pushed against the back of my plastic chair, hoisting her tray over my head, her paper shopping bag tapping my shoulder. "The problem is, when I do let my mind drift, which is rare, I feel so guilty. Like I'm betraying her or something."

Marcus nodded, his eyes turning sad. "We didn't get to talk at the memorial, but I was with you that morning, when everything happened…" His voice trailed off.

"I know."

"After I heard—my parents told me—I wanted to reach out, come by, talk to you, but I wasn't sure what you'd want."

"That's because we hardly know each other," I pointed out.

Marcus sat back as if I'd thrown an insult, but I was simply stating the truth. I didn't know him.

I spent the last three years judging my sister for every brain-dead loser she flung herself at in an attempt to cope with her grief, all the while ignoring the sacrifices she made for me in the process. I never really thought about what it would be like to be a junior in college and suddenly put in charge of a pissed-off teenage sibling.

Keira had to pay the bills and be a grown-up when everyone else she knew was doing keg stands and studying in Paris. And how did I treat her? Like she had no right to tell me what to do, like she was overstepping every time she asked me to so much as take out the trash, like she was pathetic because she cared so much whether some random loser called. And what was I doing when she needed me most? Flirting with a boy I hardly knew.

I was an ungrateful hypocrite who devastatingly failed her.

My throat started to close, a familiar side effect of my funk—the feeling of my muscles constricting, my grief rejecting my food, a mushy potato lodging en route. I squirmed in my seat, coughing slightly, trying to push the dark thoughts far enough away that I could swallow.

"I don't know many people in Boston, *anyone really*," Marcus said. "But I have a brother, Antonio. And I know what it's like to have parents move you around the world. My brother, my parents, they're all I've got. Now Antonio works for Dresden and travels all the time. This is the first time I've moved someplace without him, and if anything happened to him…"

My eyes snapped toward Marcus with a sudden feeling of kinship as I thought of my last conversation with my parents, about moving to Canada, how I would have been moving without Keira and how much worse that made the relocation. I swallowed my uncomfortable bite of food, feeling relief as my muscles relaxed. "That must suck."

"It does. And starting school in May—" He stopped mid-sentence, abruptly adjusting his posture, his expression severe. "I can't believe I'm talking about myself after what's happened to you."

"No, it's fine," I said. "It's refreshing, actually."

"No, it's not. *Lo siento.*" He held up a hand with an apology I didn't need. "So how did your friends get you to come out tonight?"

"It's part of my depression-release program. I need to prove to my new guardians that I'm not a danger to myself and/or others."

"Should I be worried?" His tone was teasing, very unlike the *Pleasantville* normalcy Charlotte had been creating recently. I missed my sister making fun of me.

"We'll see. I've been out of the house for, like, only two hours." I raised a menacing eyebrow. "But I wouldn't get too comfortable if I were you."

"Understood." He smirked flirtatiously. "Are you coming back to school in the fall?"

"I don't have much of a choice, not that I care very

much about calculus these days."

"Does anybody?"

My phone buzzed, and I noticed a text from Regina. **Marcus who?** she asked in response to my earlier message. I didn't reply. She could stew a few minutes longer, likely with Tyson's tongue down her throat.

"So your brother's working at Dresden?" I switched topics, remembering Keira's med school days and the job she could've had after graduation.

"Yeah, he's in sales. Hardly returns phone calls anymore. I can't picture him in a suit." Then he looked down at his tray, fidgeting with his plastic spoon. "My parents said they knew your parents. They used to work together."

"I figured. My parents helped found the company; they knew everyone."

"I'm sorry about what happened to them."

"Everyone's sorry." I sighed. I lived in a never-ending stream of empathetic apologies. "Good news is the cops have a lead."

"On your sister?"

"Yeah, they found footage of her at work talking to the guy from our party."

"They'll be able to find him now, yes?" He sounded so optimistic, I almost smiled at his reaction.

"I want them to find *her,* but yeah, someone called in an anonymous tip."

"This is good." He reached for my hand, his fingers covering mine, a simple gesture of comfort. I thought of Keira on the video—Craig's fingers entwined with hers, and I instantly pulled back.

"Yeah, it is." I rested my hands in my lap. "I just wish we could hear what they're saying on the video. There's no audio, and Charlotte's been downloading every form of software she can find to try to figure it out, but so far nothing's worked."

"Can't the police tell you what they're saying? They must have people who can analyze such things."

"They do, but they're not sharing information with us. They keep saying it could *hinder the investigation.*"

"You have a copy of the video, *verdad*?"

I nodded, wondering where he was going with this.

"And you can see your sister's lips, her mouth moving?"

"Yeah, why?" My eyebrows drew together.

Marcus sat up straighter, his dark eyes bright. "Because I know somebody."

"What do mean?"

"There's a woman in my building, Madeline. She's thirty, kind of lonely, sits on the stoop a lot in the afternoons. And when I come home, sometimes I sit with her. Like I said, I don't know many people in Boston." He brushed off his loneliness, but I unfortunately knew that feeling all too well. It comes with being a kid without a hometown. "Anyway, Madeline's deaf and can read lips. So sometimes we spend afternoons peering into apartment windows while she translates conversations of the people inside. It's surprisingly entertaining."

A surge of emotion ran through me, releasing a sensation I hadn't felt in a long time—hope. "Are you saying you think she can read what Keira's saying on the tape?"

"I know she can." He grinned.

CHAPTER ELEVEN

Two days later I was sitting in my living room with Marcus, Charlotte, and our new best friend, Madeline.

"I can't thank you enough," I repeated again as I shifted on our couch, the leather creaking below me with a musty puff of air. Charlotte was cueing the footage.

"I'm happy I can help." Madeline tossed her dark ashy brown hair behind her shoulder; it fell nearly to her waist, which was an accomplishment given that she was at least six feet tall. Judging by her shoulders, she must have played sports when she was younger, maybe a swimmer. "Marcus is one of the few cool people in our building. At least, he thinks he is." She nudged his shoulder teasingly.

Her voice had the cadence of someone who couldn't hear herself speak, but having now spent nearly twenty minutes with the woman, I could attest that she understood everything we said. And she was funny. I could see why Marcus hung out with her.

He shifted a little closer to my side, leaning in to me, a tingle flooding my skin. "I'm so happy I can help. I know this will work."

"Me, too. It means a lot," I replied, glancing at my goose bumps.

He nodded supportively, his eyes on mine in a way that made my stomach flutter.

I inched closer to Charlotte, pushing the feeling away. "You ready?"

"Yup." She tapped her finger on the tiny white triangle on the screen, and the clip began to play. Just like before, Keira walked out to the ambulance bay and Craig followed suit. Only this time, as soon as Keira started talking, Madeline began to translate.

"She's saying, '*You knew I was going to do this. You knew that was my plan all along. And you told me you thought I had every right*,'" Madeline said, pulling words from the air like a magician in a Vegas showroom. "*I thought you agreed with me, I thought you were on my side.*"

Charlotte and I exchanged a look, like even we couldn't believe we actually had context to what was transpiring between Keira and the bastard who kidnapped her. I smiled for what may have been the first time in months.

Madeline's thin lips drew silent as it appeared Craig was talking, though we couldn't see his face. Still, we could see Keira's reaction, and she was looking increasingly worried, wrinkles creasing her shiny forehead.

"She's asking, '*What do you think I'm going to find out?*'" Madeline continued, her tone robotic. Craig must have answered her question next, though we couldn't be sure. I would have paid a kidney to know his end of the conversation.

"She's saying, *I don't know*," Madeline resumed as Keira spoke. "*I just feel like something was going on, something we don't know about. The more I think back, the more things don't add up.*" Madeline quickly translated as Keira's speech accelerated. "*All the moving, all the trips, all the late-night phone calls, the languages, the bruises. There is something about my parents that's never made sense.*"

My jaw dropped, eyelids frozen in shock. What? Was Madeline still translating *Keira*? This couldn't be right.

"*I know we joked about it, but I don't think it's a joke anymore. I think it stopped being a joke three years ago. I think my parents were involved in something other than engineering,*" Madeline continued, monotone and unreactive, as if she were translating a conversation about traffic on the Mass Pike, not my parents' unorthodox careers and untimely deaths. (To be fair, she really had no way of knowing the gravity of the conversation.)

I looked at Charlotte, who seemed equally stunned, her forehead creased and her eyes unblinking.

"What the hell?" she mouthed to me. I said nothing back. I had no words.

"She's saying, *It's a start. I owe it to myself to find out the truth about them. I owe it to Anastasia.*" Madeline flicked a glance at me, as if just now the conversation was getting uncomfortable.

"Now she's walking away, upset," Madeline noted, translating her body language. Though to be accurate, Keira wasn't just upset, she was crying. "I can't make out what he's saying, but he hands her a napkin."

We all watched as Keira wiped her teary eyes, my heart pounding with a mix of anxiety and confusion, like those nightmares where you show up to a final exam after not having attended a single class. Nothing made sense.

"Now, she's saying, *You're right. I don't owe her anything, but our parents sure as hell do. They owe us both.*"

That was it. We watched them walk back into the hospital, and Madeline sat back against the couch. Her work was complete. Only no one spoke or moved, and Madeline nervously began scanning our faces to see if she'd done a good job.

Finally, Charlotte and I popped up like the couch had suddenly tossed us off.

"What the hell was that?" Charlotte squawked.

"She was talking about our parents? To some random loser? To a psychopath?" I yelled.

"Where did that come from?"

"I don't know. I mean, she got really wasted on the anniversary of the crash, remember? She almost needed her stomach pumped." I shivered at the memory. Keira kept slurring, *"Why did they do it? Why did they leave us?"* over and over until she vomited all over the bathroom, and we had to put her in a cold shower—the same claw-foot tub where she eventually disappeared.

"Yeah, but that was in March," Charlotte pointed out. "This conversation was in May."

"We always joked about Mom and Dad not really being engineers, but she couldn't actually believe that, could she?" I shook my head, bewildered. How delusional had my sister become? Did she really think our parents were mob enforcers? Super spies?

"If she was looking into your parents' jobs or lives, there's no record on her computer, her phone, anything."

"Well, one thing's for sure, she and Craig aren't breaking up on this tape."

"There goes our crime of passion theory," Charlotte muttered.

Marcus and Madeline sat silently on the sofa staring at us like kids uncomfortably watching their friend's parents fight. My head pounded as I glanced heatedly around the apartment. This was where it happened; this was where we hosted the party. I sat on that couch, listening to Keira's music, watching her friends dance, then the next morning she was gone from a bloody pool. *What the hell was she up to those last few days?*

Madeline raised her index finger. "There's something else." We looked at her. "The napkin that he hands her on the video—"

"You mean the tissue?" Charlotte corrected.

"No, it's a napkin. From a bar, McFadden's Pub. I recognize the logo. It's not far from our place." She glanced at Marcus who quickly nodded in agreement.

"She's right," Marcus added. "That bar is right across from the hospital. Our building's down the street. My parents like the proximity to work."

I looked at Charlotte who immediately plopped down in front of her laptop and cued up the scene where Craig wipes Keira's tears. Sure enough, barely visible, was a tiny, dark logo on what we thought was a tissue. "I can't believe I missed it." Charlotte sounded deflated.

"Don't feel bad. The deaf are more observant. Occupational hazard," Madeline quipped.

The police should seriously put this woman on their payroll. Actually, the police should have told us this first. I angrily reached for my phone and punched in the detective's digits. Voicemail. She was probably screening my call.

"I need some air," I hissed, aggressively shoving my phone in my pocket as I stomped toward the door.

Marcus followed me outside.

We sat on my front stoop, scratchy concrete digging into the backs of my thighs, my gray khaki shorts hiked up. I picked at a dandelion peeking out of a crack in the step, flicking the petals again and again.

"I'd ask if you're okay, but I think I know the answer," Marcus said as he tapped his black motorcycle boots on the pavement. It seemed it didn't matter how hot the temperature was, Marcus always wore jeans and boots. And he always looked good.

"I feel like an idiot," I grumbled, annoyed at myself.

"*Que?*"

"First, I didn't know that Keira and Craig were a thing. Now, I didn't know that she was investigating our parents. And *he* was helping her. Not me. She asked *him*," I spat.

"You don't know what any of this means," he pointed out, trying to be positive. No, we didn't know exactly what the conversation on that video meant, but we knew it wasn't good, and we knew it wasn't a lovers' quarrel.

"It means she didn't trust me enough to tell me what she was up to." I yanked the dandelion from the ground and began twisting its spaghetti-like stem around my finger.

"Did you use to tell her everything?" Marcus asked, raising a doubtful eyebrow.

"No, but this was big. This was our parents."

"*Sí.* And I don't know what you and your sister went through, *after everything…*" His eyes flicked away as his voice trailed off.

I'd found over the years that people often didn't like referencing death directly, as if it might somehow invite it into their lives. They found other ways to simply *imply* my parents were six feet under.

"But my brother's not much older than Keira, and I can't imagine how he'd react if he suddenly had to take care of me. This is a guy who taught me how to ride a motorcycle and talked me into this tattoo." He pointed to the giant black bull with angry eyes permanently inked on his neck. "He'd be a horrible parent. At least Keira was trying."

"I wasn't going to ask, but that is quite a tattoo." I stared at his neck.

"*Sí*, and it was Antonio's idea. Our *abuelo* was a matador. He died when we were young. I'm named after him, and he had this same tattoo on his calf." He pointed to his left leg. "My brother has a lot of tattoos. Everywhere." He ran his hands up and down his arms to suggest full sleeves of ink. "I have a hard time saying no to him, and he has a hard time accepting it." He chuckled to himself, as if remembering something. "Anyway, my family lived near Plaza de Toros in Madrid, so we went to a lot of *corridas*. It seemed like a good idea, and now it's pretty badass, no?" He smirked at me.

Keira and I saw a bullfight when we lived in Madrid. Bull after bull was slaughtered until one finally bested the matador and walked out of the arena alive. My sister and I were so excited we actually hugged; that was until spectators informed us that the beast would be killed backstage. I was eleven at the time. We had gone by ourselves, because our parents were busy with work. *Here, kids, go enjoy a death match!*

"Would it offend you if I told you I find bullfights disgusting?"

"It depends. Have you actually seen one?"

"Unfortunately. My family spent the summer in Madrid six years ago."

"Huh." He nodded, his gaze far away. "I could've been there. We were in Madrid then."

"You did say our parents knew one another." I ripped a pinch of fuzzy yellow petals from the dandelion. "Though I'm surprised we weren't introduced, Dresden Kids and all."

"You're right." He cocked his head, seemingly puzzled.

"But we really weren't there that long, only a couple of

months. We didn't meet anyone."

"Still, it would have been nice to know you then."

"You mean before my life became a Shakespearean tragedy?" I raised a brow.

"No, I just don't always like the Dresden Kids I meet. But I like you." He smiled as he said that, leaning toward me with a glint in his eyes, like he was incapable of feeling self-conscious. I, unfortunately, did not share his confidence. And the buzz I felt every time he was close, too close, only made me fidget more.

I tore my dandelion stem in half. "Considering you just brought a woman to my place to translate a video of my missing sister and her potential kidnapper, I'd say you have odd taste in friends."

Before he could respond, my phone vibrated in my pocket. I slid it out and saw the name of the person I'd been waiting for—Detective Dawkins.

They acted like we were complete strangers to Keira. The Boston PD had finished analyzing the tape the day after we left, and Detective Dawkins swore she had every intention of updating us, but she "wanted more concrete information."

Honestly, I cared less about her by-the-book police procedures than I did the latest pro tournament golf standings. My sister was caught on-camera discussing my dead parents with her psychotic soon-to-be kidnapper only days before she disappeared—I had a right to know that. Not in at some point, not once they confirmed their leads, but now. Right now. This was my sister and my parents, but instead of coming to me with that information, they went to my parents' best friend. That was all Detective Dawkins wanted to talk about. Did I know Randolph Urban?

Gee, let me think... Randolph Urban: CEO of Dresden, the man who dated my mother when she was a sophomore at Princeton and he was a grad student ten years her senior; they broke up and remained friends. He became *best* friends with my father. They started Dresden together. He stood as best man at their wedding. He paid for their funeral, their brunch, Keira's brunch. He possibly cut us a personal check after they died claiming it was "life insurance," and he still invites us to the over-the-top Christmas parties at his mansion every year. He was the closest thing to family, aside from Charlotte, I had in the world.

Yeah, I knew him.

Dawkins seemed to think Keira's comments on the footage were referencing my parents' jobs at Dresden, and thus Urban. And while Keira was ranting about our parents' "work," what was missing were my sister's crazy theories that Mom and Dad weren't chemical engineers, but actually super-secret spies with exotic code-names and high-tech hydroplanes. Or maybe mob enforcers stroking Persian cats. Or possibly superheroes saving the world from nuclear annihilation. When we were younger, this was funny (so were farts). But after they died—after the tombstones, nightmares, and parent-size void in our home—I let it go. I thought Keira had, too.

But on that video, she said she wanted to prove something, to find out "the truth" about them, which had me worried that Keira thought one of our crazy theories was true and was actually looking into it before she disappeared. But how could you possibly prove your dad is Clark Kent or the Godfather? Sharing these theories with Dawkins would make Keira sound unstable at best and full-blown delusional at worst. So I left them out of my conversation, along with Madeline's tip about the napkin.

If the police analysts uncovered it, they didn't share it with me. So I didn't see why I needed to share it with them.

"Dawkins is gonna freak when she finds out we came here," Charlotte griped as we exited the humming T station, climbing the filthy concrete steps and dodging droplets of unexplainable black water that fell from the ceiling.

"Well, if she wanted us to share information, she should have told us what Keira said in that video instead of us having to hear it from Marcus's deaf neighbor."

I had asked Marcus if he wanted to come with us. After all, he lived down the street from the bar, and he was responsible for us finding this lead. But it turned out all the focus on my sister had him thinking of his own brother and how long it had been since they'd spoken. He seemed to be having an "appreciate every second you have with your loved ones" philosophical crisis, so he set up a time to Skype with Antonio. They should be talking right this second.

We crossed the traffic zipping past Boston General, all blue glass and towering buildings creating a complex of structures renowned for everything from newborn care to Alzheimer's and anything in between. In the shadows of the towering facade sat a tiny Irish pub with a wooden sign featuring gold letters in an antique-looking font.

"What if we're wrong in coming here? What if we screw something up?" Charlotte whined. "What if—"

I grabbed her wrist, jerking her to a halt on the wide sidewalk, my eyes pleading. "I'm sorry, but I can't sit around going nuts not hearing from the police. I don't know how you've remained sane for so long. At least I was semi-unconscious for most of this." I brushed off an image of myself marinating in a bed of filth. "We're just going to find out if there's info worth knowing. We're not *hindering* anything."

I caught a shift in her golden-green eyes. "If we find out something important, we're telling Dawkins, right?"

"I promise." I crossed my heart.

"Fine." She nodded. For a girl who'd been illegally hacking into electronic systems for most of this investigation, she was rather squeamish when it came to face-to-face confrontations.

We entered McFadden's Pub. As expected, it was packed with hospital employees in pastel scrubs throwing bent darts, eating drippy burgers, and sipping frothy beers. It had glossy amber wood paneling on the walls that released a stale scent of alcohol that probably never washed out. The ceiling was tin, painted a smoky gray, with brass lights barely illuminating the dim space.

Charlotte swiveled a green leather barstool my way, which had been ripped and sealed with packing tape, and I took a seat. I'd never been to a bar before, unless you count the cafés in Europe, but they're not really bars. Wine is served in McDonalds there. She signaled for the bartender, and he glanced at us briefly, continuing to dry the dripping pint glass he was holding, then cautiously looked back, eyes squinted.

"Okay, ladies, you're hot and all, but there's no way that girl's twenty-one." He pointed at me with the tattered white rag in his hand.

"She's not drinking," Charlotte countered. "We just want to ask you a few questions. About Keira Phoenix?"

His head jutted back, recognition clear in his eyes.

"You knew her, right?" I asked, already knowing the answer. "I'm her sister."

The look of pity I'd become so familiar with instantly washed over him. He nodded slowly, his brow furrowed as he sucked on his lips, looking sad and a bit uncomfortable. "I'm Seamus, the manager. Yeah, I knew Keira. She was a cool chick. I'm sorry about what happened."

"Uh-huh." I ignored his sympathy. "We're actually hoping you could help."

"Anything. How?" He walked over.

Charlotte pulled out her smartphone encased in a pink and turquoise cover. Earlier, she'd uploaded a still image from the surveillance footage. She showed it to Seamus. "This was taken at the hospital a few days before Keira was... attacked." I knew Charlotte wanted to say "murdered," since it was what she believed, but I was glad she refrained. "We think maybe this is a napkin from your place."

Seamus took the phone, pinching his giant fingers across the screen and enlarging the napkin blotted against Keira's eyes. For being so Irish that he had a name like Seamus, he looked about the size of an NBA all-star. "Yeah, that's from here. Doesn't surprise me that he'd have it. He came in with Keira a few times."

"You know him?" My pulse hit the accelerator. Seamus had seen them together, more than once.

"I don't know his name or anything."

"What do you know?"

"He's a douche."

"No shit," I grumbled. "Anything else?"

"They always sat in the back, near the jukebox." He pointed toward a dark booth in a secluded corner. It would be the perfect place to go if you wanted to be alone. "And there was this one time I took a picture of them, on Cinco de Mayo, and they totally freaked, which was weird. Keira was usually the life of the party. She follows us on Instagram. We get a lot of likes." He nodded like this was a notable achievement.

"So the picture's online?" Charlotte's eyes perked up.

"That's just it. There are lots of pictures of Keira on our

Instagram account, which she loved." He continued drying a pint glass with a rag that looked dirtier than the glass. "But this time, the dudes she was with went ballistic."

"*Dudes*?" I leaned forward, my palms sticking to the tacky surface of the bar. "You mean more than one?"

"Yeah. They were with some Italian guy."

"Italian, like from the North End?" Charlotte asked.

"No, Italian like fresh off the boat. Accent and all." He set down the pint glass and grabbed another. A wrinkle tensed above my nose. I couldn't think of anyone Keira knew who had an Italian accent—not a coworker, former classmate, doctor, no one. It was starting to feel like my sister had a secret life.

"But after I took the picture, the Italian guy grabbed my shirt, started cursing about what he'd do if I posted it. The guy couldn't have been much taller than you." Seamus gave Charlotte a look to emphasize the ridiculousness of the mismatch. Seamus was at least six-foot-four. "I didn't want any trouble, the customer is always right, you know the drill. So I told them I'd delete it. Instead, the bigger guy grabs my phone and starts deleting *all* the pictures from that night. Every one. I was pissed."

"So why'd you let him do it?" I asked, irritated.

"The place was filled with a bunch of drunks who'd been downing tequila since noon. It was Cinco de Mayo. I didn't want a brawl."

"Irish pubs celebrate Cinco de Mayo?" Charlotte asked.

"We celebrate Yom Kippur with a beer special. We're a bar." He stated the obvious.

I slumped, disappointed. "Did you ever see them again? The guys?"

"No." He shrugged, then suddenly stopped drying the glass in his hand. "Wait, are they the ones who attacked her?

Because that was like two weeks before everything happened, and the cops never came in, so I didn't say anything. Holy shit, I'm an asshole."

"You couldn't have known," Charlotte offered politely.

Though really, he could have. A regular at his bar got kidnapped (or murdered, if you believed the news), and he was involved in a near violent altercation with the two guys she was with only days before. He should have mentioned this sooner.

"I'm sorry, I just—"

I cut him off. "You're positive they deleted the photos? Can we check?"

"Yeah, but they're gone." He shook his head as he pulled his black smartphone from his pocket and handed it over.

Charlotte scanned the images, skipping back to last May and the weeks before it. I could see over her shoulder that she'd found nothing. "Can I take this?"

"What?" Seamus's head jerked as if she'd asked him to part with his leg, not his phone (though Charlotte would react the same).

"It's an Android. I have software that can retrieve deleted images. I might be able to recover it."

"Shouldn't the police do that?"

I cocked an eyebrow at Charlotte. She was the one who insisted we not "hinder" the investigation. Let's see what she thought now that the lead involved electronic communication.

She looked at me sideways. "The cops have been giving us the runaround. They're not telling us anything," she admitted. "I just want to give it a shot before we surrender the phone."

Exactly. I'd happily share whatever we uncovered with Detective Dawkins, *after* it was "concrete." It was her rule, after all.

"I hear ya." Seamus nodded, grabbing another glass. "Once, I had my car stolen. Cops totally gave me the brush-off. It was the same thing."

I stared blankly. This wasn't exactly the same thing, but I doubted there were enough words in the English language to explain that. Besides, Seamus had a potential picture of my sister's attacker, hopefully in the "cloud" or the moon or wherever regrettable photos go to not die. I wasn't about to pick a fight.

"Charlotte knows more about computers than anyone at the Boston PD, and no one wants to find my sister more than me. Please, will you let us try?" I gave him my most pathetic puppy-dog face.

"What am I supposed to do about a phone until then?"

"I'll get you a new one," Charlotte promised. "I'm supposed to order my assistant a new phone at work. I'll order two. They'll never notice. You'll have it in two days. I swear."

"And until then?"

"Like you seriously don't have an old phone lying around. Come on, this is life and death," I insisted.

He sighed heavily, glancing at the tin ceiling. "Fine. But I'll hold you to it. I expect a new phone by Monday. Newest model."

"Done." Charlotte tucked his phone into her pocket and turned to me, excitement fresh in her eyes. If anyone could find out who my sister was with in that photo, it was my hacker friend.

It was like I was starting to feel my sister getting closer.

CHAPTER TWELVE

All she needed was a few illegal software programs and one sleepless night, and Charlotte was able to do what the Boston Police Department didn't even know they were supposed to be doing—retrieve the photo of Keira's attacker (or attackers, plural. We really weren't sure anymore.).

"I deserve a medal," Charlotte boasted as she pulled the cord that connected Seamus's smartphone to her silver laptop. "Seriously, how awesome am I?"

"Pretty awesome." I yawned as I stretched my aching back. I didn't have much to contribute to her hacking endeavors, but I stayed up all night out of moral support. Plus, I wanted to be present the moment she found my sister's image.

"Just give me a second. I'll open all the pictures in Photoshop and blow them up." Her fingers clicked away as I waited beside her at the kitchen table, sipping my fifth cup of coffee.

"Okay, done." She punched a key. "Let's see what we've got."

She opened new windows for each image time stamped

with the date of May fifth. There were twenty-two. We began skipping through them, her cursor jumping from frame to frame—smiling drunks in sombreros, gigantic neon margarita glasses with sloshing green liquid, and cheap plastic leis rung on sweaty necks (though I didn't see how leis connected to a party commemorating a Mexican military victory being hosted by an Irish bar). My vision blurred as I forced myself to stay alert, focusing on the too-bright glow of her laptop.

Charlotte continued clicking until suddenly I froze mid-yawn, blinking once.

Charlotte was just as still.

There was Keira.

She was seated in a booth in McFadden's Pub, right next to the jukebox where Seamus said she'd be. Three half-drank pints of amber beer cluttered the table before her, along with a spread of crumpled and now very familiar napkins. To her right was the guy who haunted my nightmares every night: six-foot-two, dark blond greasy hair, greenish eyes, and a noticeable scar on his lip—Craig the Psycho. He even looked like he was wearing the same T-shirt he had on in the surveillance footage. Maybe he didn't own more than one.

Across from her was a man as Italian as a stereotype—olive skin, cropped dark shiny hair, near-black eyes, and the short stocky frame of a wrestler.

"That's Craig and Keira," Charlotte choked, almost in disbelief, touching the screen as if the image might disappear. "I can't believe it. Wow. So who's the other guy?"

"Luis Basso," I answered, my drained voice sounding as stunned as I felt. "I know him."

•••

An hour later, we sat at the kitchen table with another photo added to our collection—one from an album that belonged to my parents.

It wasn't easy to locate. Not because I didn't know where it was, but because to find it, I had to enter my parents' bedroom. I was never the type of grieving kid who took comfort in smelling her mother's perfume or in handling her father's cufflinks. It just hurt. All of it. Pain, pain, and more pain. And now the room had the added feature of an ominous bathroom that seemed to pulse with images of blood like the hallway from *The Shining*. I hadn't stepped foot inside since Keira went missing.

But I did it.

I got through it.

I crept to the closet, swung open the door, and yanked down all of the dust-covered albums (the ones with the plastic film and sticky paper that destroy pictures as much as they preserve them). My family had gone to Italy as part of Keira's high school graduation gift. All four of us traveling through Europe for three weeks: London, Paris, Munich, Prague, and Tuscany. Then we spent the rest of the summer living in Madrid. The trip was well documented, photos galore, including one very nice snapshot of a family from Tuscany.

I tapped it against the kitchen table. *Click, click, click*.

"You're sure she never mentioned that she ran into this guy?" Charlotte asked for the third time.

"I'm positive. Don't you think I would have mentioned it?" I stared at the matte image with thin white borders.

There were four sons featured alongside their father. The older gentleman was gray-haired, about sixty, distinguished, with kind eyes and a soft belly. His teenage sons stood beside him, their arms locked around one another's shoulders, no more than two inches separating their height. Each had dark hair, cropped and shiny. Their builds were athletic, and not one was taller than five-foot-nine. They almost looked like quadruplets.

The one standing closest to their father was also in the photo at McFadden's Pub with Keira—Luis Basso.

"Well, what do you think they were doing with him?" Charlotte glanced back and forth between the pictures. He looked exactly the same, almost ageless.

"I have no idea. It wasn't like that part of the trip was very memorable. I can't imagine Keira kept in touch with Luis. Maybe they just ran into each other randomly?"

Luis's father, Salvatore, was a friend of my parents. Well, friend might be too strong a word. He was an antique dealer, and my parents bought a rustic wooden writing desk from him during our trip. It still sat in my parents' bedroom. Apparently, they'd met during their travels years before and fell in love with his quaint little shop in Cortona, Italy, not far from Florence. They insisted we pit stop during our travels, only the visit dragged on longer than two kids in an antique store could tolerate.

The town is miniscule, with one row of souvenir shops and one coffee shop. That left Keira and I idly playing tic-tac-toe with the dust on the furniture for amusement until Luis, the oldest son, offered to take us for a ride outside the walls of Cortona. He sped up a narrow, windy, unpaved hill in his tiny, beat-up car, and parked at the peak. There we sat on the white car's dented hood, layered with grime from diesel fuel, and stared at the rolling hills of emerald and gold, dotted with skinny cypress trees and postcard-worthy cottages.

All the while, Luis meandered along the graveled edge plucking wild flowers. There was no guardrail. Every time a car turned the curve, it had to perilously swerve to avoid him. He never flinched, as if getting hit and tumbling down the mountain never occurred to him. He just continued picking straggly flowers for the family dining table with the confident swagger of someone who thought nothing could go wrong. Then he drove us back to the shop, and I hadn't thought about him since.

I didn't think Keira had, either.

Charlotte glanced at me nervously. "Keira was talking about your parents on the surveillance footage, and Luis knew them. He could have been helping her somehow; he could be involved in what happened to her."

I rubbed my temples with locked fingers, my head throbbing. So far, there was no motive for what happened to my sister. All we really knew was what *wasn't* true. It wasn't a lovers' quarrel, and it wasn't a random attack. My sister was secretive in the weeks before everything happened. I thought it was because she was dating someone we wouldn't like (and truthfully, I wouldn't like Craig the Psycho under any circumstances), but things no longer looked that simple. Keira and Craig weren't just dating; they were discussing my parents. She was *investigating* my parents. Then she disappeared.

Now it turned out that right before our tub filled with blood, she spent the evening with a guy from our parents' past who was capable of threatening a bartender over a simple photo.

"We have to show these pictures to the cops," said Charlotte.

"I know." I peered at her, my eyes weary. "But not tonight."

"Why?"

I sighed heavily. "Because I need a minute. They're going to ask me tons of questions about the Bassos, about

Luis, and I don't know what to say. It's like we're talking about someone other than Keira. How could all of this have been going on and we not know?"

"Because we weren't her keeper."

"Actually, she *was* my keeper. She was my guardian, *is* my guardian," I quickly corrected. Keira was out there, alive somewhere. I had to believe that. If I didn't, the funk would swallow me whole.

Charlotte's freckled face grew concerned, as it did every time I insisted my sister was alive. "False hope" was a term used often by the people around me, but what they didn't understand was that searching for Keira was the only thing keeping me from drowning in her absence.

My phone buzzed in the back pocket of my jeans, and I slid it out onto the kitchen table. It was a text from Marcus. Ever since he and Madeline left, he'd been texting for frequent updates, for more ways he could help, for us to get together. But we hadn't seen each other since. I told myself, and him, that it was because I was busy, but I didn't think either of us believed it. The truth was, a tiny part of me leaped every time I saw Marcus's name on my screen, then the rest of me took turns beating that tiny traitorous part to a pulp.

MARCUS: *Hola. How did things go with the photograph? Did Charlotte find it?*

ME: *She did. Long story tho.*

MARCUS: *Want 2 talk?*

I stared at the screen—*did I?* Conflicting emotions funneled like a tornado in my brain, images of Marcus mixed with Keira mixed with Luis Basso. My head pulsed from revelations, and my eyes ached from staring at photos. I typed the only response I could.

ME: *Not yet.*

It was the truth. And not just because I was tired, but because, regrettably, it was Marcus. No matter how unfair it was and how much I knew he sincerely wanted to offer support, I feared my guilt-ridden soul would forever be incapable of disassociating him from that morning. I was distracted by Marcus when my sister was attacked and taken. I couldn't afford to be distracted by him now.

I needed to think.

I needed to find her. I needed to find someone who knew something.

Finally, I thought of someone who did. Someone who knew many of the players involved in my sister's final weeks, especially the one willing to attack over a Cinco de Mayo photograph—Luis Basso's father.

CHAPTER THIRTEEN

I t seemed the economy had been kind to the antiquities business in the Tuscan town of Cortona. Salvatore Basso's shop still existed. It even had a poorly optimized website that took several search pages to find, but it was there — *Cortona Antiqueria.* On the home page was a photo of Salvatore, his hair a bit more silver and his cheeks a little rounder, but his eyes just the same.

On the bottom of the page was a phone number.

I had promised Charlotte that we would take our newly discovered photographs of Keira, Craig, and Luis to Detective Dawkins during Charlotte's lunch hour today. I fully intended to make good on that promise. What I left out was that I planned on calling Salvatore Basso the second she left for work. I knew she'd just try to talk me out of it, tell me that this was a job for the police and that we'd already overstepped enough. Of course, she had no problem *hindering the investigation* electronically, but when the leads to my sister required face-to-face communication (like with Seamus) or phone communication (like with the Bassos), she thought we were going too far.

I did not.

I held the phone in my hand as I prepared for an incredibly awkward conversation. *"Hi, I'm not sure if you remember me from that one time my parents bought a desk from you, but my presumed dead sister was seen with your son not long before she disappeared. Any chance he might have taken her?"*

That script might be a bit too literal to go with.

I punched the digits and listened to the low pulsing tones of a phone ringing overseas. He answered on the third ring.

"Sí?" said a deep voice.

"Ciao, posso parlare Salvatore Basso?" I asked in Italian. It'd been awhile since I'd spoken the language, but the words still sat ready at the edge of my brain. I may not be a competitive softball player, a concert pianist, or the next astrophysicist, but I excelled at languages.

"Sí, parlando."

My heart thumped, my knee bouncing as I sat in my desk chair, a tsunami of questions flooding my brain. If this man knew where his son was, I might finally get some answers; I might finally know what Keira was up to those last few weeks, where Craig was now, where Keira was now. I took a deep breath, sweat breaking under my arms.

"Signore Basso." I aimed to sound respectful as I continued in Italian. "I hope this is a good time. I wish to speak to you about your son Luis. He was recently in the United States, correct? In Boston?"

"Yes," he replied in English. I guess my American accent gave me away. "What is this about?"

"My sister, Keira Phoenix. I don't know if you remember, but my family visited you several years ago. My parents bought an antique desk, and—"

"Anastasia?" he asked.

My leg stopped bouncing. I stared at the splinters of raw wood on the unfinished pine desk Keira and I had planned to paint years ago. "Yes," I replied, my voice suddenly hoarse. "How do you know my name?"

"Your parents and I were good friends."

"You were?" My head tilted, perplexed, dark hair dripping over my shoulder. "I thought they were just customers."

"No, we knew one another quite well." He didn't elaborate, and a long silence hung. Already, this wasn't going as planned.

"Well, um, I'm calling because my sister was seen with Luis back in May, and not long after, she was attacked in our home and kidnapped. She and Luis were photographed with a guy named Craig, who we believe took her. I'm wondering if Luis knows something? Maybe he could help?"

I'd thought about it all night and determined this was the best way to approach Salvatore—suggest his son was a witness. Accusing Luis of potentially being involved might send his father into protective mode, but if I gave the impression that his son could help save my sister, then I might appeal to Salvatore's savior instincts.

"I knew they were reacquainted. Luis told me he ran into your sister at the hospital. She's a nurse, no?"

"Yes, she is." So that was how they met. That made sense. "Have you spoken to your son recently? Does he know anything about what happened to Keira?" My voice quivered from the mix of nerves, hope, and fear pumping through me.

"I am aware of what happened to your sister, but I don't think we should discuss it over the phone."

"Why not?" I leaned back, my wheeling desk chair swiveling to the side. When else would we talk about it?

"You may not realize it, but I was close with your parents.

So were my sons. I know Luis had nothing to do with what happened to your sister, if that's why you're calling. He's very concerned."

"Good, can I speak with him? Do you know where he is?" My voice clicked up an octave as my nerves heightened. I wasn't expecting him to already know about Keira's disappearance, but the fact that he did was a good thing. It meant he'd talked to his son recently; it meant he potentially knew where he was.

"I think there's a lot about this situation you don't know."

"I don't know *anything*." I sat still as a statue, fearful that moving might make him stop speaking. This man had answers, something he was nervous about discussing over the phone, and my body tensed with the desire to reach through the airwaves and yank the information from inside his brain. "Does Luis know where we can find Craig? Because Keira—"

"I'm not talking about Keira. I'm talking about your parents."

The breath caught in my throat as my hand started to shake, gripping the phone tighter. Why did my parents keep bubbling into this situation? I didn't want to think about them. I didn't want to think about their deaths, their lives, or their pasts. But their constant mention was making me feel sick, a physical reminder that the horror I was living with my sister could spread to everyone else I knew like a virus of torment.

"What do you know about my parents? Because Keira was looking into their pasts before everything happened. Was Luis helping her?"

"From what he told me about your sister, I believe there are larger forces at work here, and I'm not comfortable discussing this over the phone. Believe me, when you hear what I have to say, you'll understand."

"No, I won't. Please, tell me *now*. My sister was kidnapped—who knows what she's going through. If you know something—"

"I know my son had nothing to do with what happened, but he did see her before she went missing, and he told me a few things. I don't want to get him into trouble or drag him into this, and I definitely don't want to say anything over the phone that could be misconstrued."

"I don't care about things being *misconstrued*, I care about finding my sister," I snapped. "How are you going to help me from another continent if you won't talk to me?"

"Come here. To Cortona. Let's speak face-to-face."

"You expect me to hop on a plane?" I uttered in disbelief, though I already knew I would. I'd take a rowboat to South Africa, if I thought it would lead me to Keira.

"I'm too old to come to you, and…" He paused. I could hear him breathing. "Let's just say there are some things you need to see."

"Please, every second counts. If you could just—" I pleaded.

"I hope to see you soon." Then he hung up.

Charlotte thought I was crazy. I'd repeated the conversation multiple times to both her and Detective Dawkins, whom we visited during Charlotte's lunch hour as promised. Each time I relayed Salvatore's words, I looped back to the same conclusion—I was going to Italy.

No one agreed.

In fact, I worried that the Boston PD was going to charge me with being an accessory to some sort of fabricated crime after Dawkins learned we'd talked to Seamus, recovered a photo, and talked to Salvatore Basso, all before informing them of our leads. (Though they did offer to pay for Seamus's new phone as long as Charlotte surrendered his old one.) But when I said I wanted to go to Italy, I might as well have suggested hang gliding in the Swiss Alps without a helmet or a lesson. Both Charlotte and Dawkins hollered in unified protest, insisting I let the Boston PD work with Italian law enforcement via the proper channels.

Did they really think I would do that? My local precinct wasn't keeping me apprised of my sister's case, but now I was expected to trust a police department overseas. Not to mention, Salvatore said he was worried about getting his son into trouble, and to me, that meant he'd probably be less inclined to share information with the cops, whether they be from Boston or Cortona. He wanted to share it with me—specifically, and in person. How could I not go?

"Okay, I realize I started this," Charlotte said as we sat in my bedroom, continuing the argument that had been going on all day. She paced barefoot. One, two, three steps to my closet; one, two, three steps back to my desk. "I hacked into the surveillance footage, I recovered the photo, I let us talk to Seamus. But Italy? You've got to be kidding me. It's like you're Nancy Drew with a James Bond complex!"

"But Salvatore's not just talking about Keira, he's talking about our parents, my entire family. I have to hear this." Just the thought of my dead parents somehow being connected to my sister's disappearance had my hands shaking like I'd drank too much coffee. Because burrowed deep in my brain was a fear I didn't want to admit was relentlessly worming its way to the surface—I never listened to Keira's theories about our parents, because I didn't want to. I wanted to believe she was joking, and I didn't want to admit that I found their careers just as suspicious. If this was what Keira was investigating, if this was what got her taken, then she was doing it alone because she didn't think she could come to me, because she didn't think I wanted to go there—and I didn't.

If I had only been more receptive, more honest, more open to what she was going through...

"What if Luis is involved?" Charlotte snapped suddenly. "What if he and Craig were in it together, hurting Keira? What if his dad's just as crazy? They could be luring you to the Manson compound."

"I realize we've watched a lot of *20/20* lately, but that isn't the impression I got on the phone."

"You're not an expert! The cops are, and they're telling you not to go."

"If you're worried about me going alone, then come with me."

"How?" She tossed up her hands in aggravation, her nails chewed into tiny stubs. "You expect me to leave work and tell my parents I'm jetting off to do investigative work with their grieving teenage dependent?"

"We're just going to talk to an old man." I slumped onto the bed. Charlotte's parents had replaced my funky sheets with a crisp new set in icy blue, which according to online research, should have a calming, Zen-like effect on my mood. "This isn't a covert op."

"No, but it also isn't necessary. Look at how much we've uncovered in the last few weeks. The police are *on* this. And it's time for you to go back to school. Senior year starts in, like, two weeks." She stopped pacing, her toes wiggling in the fibers of my new pale blue rug.

I looked at her and sighed audibly. "Okay, let's be real—do you actually think I'm going back?" I knew we were all going through the motions, but my sister was taken from a pool of steaming blood— Did anyone really expect me to start AP bio in a few weeks and doodle sketches of prom dresses in my lab notes?

"Yes, you're going to school. My parents are your guardians. You're still a minor. You can't just leave the country without their consent." Her voice was firm as her fingers dug into her frizzy hair, pulling hard. "You have to graduate. What do you think Keira would want? She gave up *everything* for you, and now it's up to me to follow through. *For her!* Do you get that? Do you get the kind of pressure I'm under?"

I squeezed my eyes tight, shoving my new pillow against my ears.

I may not have appreciated it when it mattered, but I now realized how much Keira gave up to take care of me and how much grief I gave her in return. I was not going to make that mistake with Charlotte. No more lives were going to be detrimentally altered because I was an orphan. Yes, her family saved me from foster care, but that meant they were a form in my file, an emergency contact. They weren't my parents, not because I didn't appreciate what they'd done, but because I refused to burden them any more. My real guardian, my sister, was out there. I believed that, and I was going to find her. For all of us.

I looked at Charlotte, feeling completely resolute. "Nothing will matter to me, ever, for the rest of my life, if I don't find my sister," I stated plainly. "She's all I have left. You have to get that."

Charlotte's mouth snapped shut at the severity of my tone. Then she shook her head aggressively. "No, no, no. You can't go. It's too dangerous. Besides, where are you going to get the money? How are you going to fly off to Italy? I know I'm not paying for it!"

Actually, I was pretty sure I already knew somebody who would.

CHAPTER FOURTEEN

I crossed my chilled arms over my chest as I waited in Randolph Urban's reception area. The air conditioning was cranked to Arctic levels, which matched the harsh white lights and white marble corridors. I hadn't stepped inside the building in years, not since the funeral, but it hadn't changed. It was still lofted with a ring of executive suites on a metal catwalk overlooking a pit of employees— all rushing around shiny stainless steel desks or clicking computer keys as they blabbed on phones in their cherry red chairs. Modern art hung on the walls, and I couldn't be sure, but some looked like original works of Mondrian.

In the five minutes since I'd arrived, Urban's assistant, Donna, hadn't stopped typing, not even when she reminded me three times of how my meeting—without at least two weeks' notice—was "extremely rare." The fact that the exception was made for me, a teenager, made her left eye twitch.

My phone buzzed in my pocket, already set to vibrate per Donna's instructions. I pulled it out, expecting to see another shouty-capital text from Charlotte threatening to revoke her family's guardianship if I dared to even Google the word "Italy." Instead, I saw Regina's name.

Hey! Going 2 movie 2nite w Tyson. New Channing Tatum! Wanna come?

To say our lives were moving in different directions would be a radical understatement. How was I supposed to answer? "OMG! But I'm visiting with my dead parents' former BFF to secure funding for a solo trip to Italy to hunt down my presumed dead sister! Maybe next time!"

I didn't reply.

An intercom buzzed on Donna's desk. "Send her in," the voice barked.

"I rescheduled your four o'clock for four thirty, moved your five o'clock until tomorrow, and asked Hester to meet via teleconference," she said into the speakerphone as she glowered my way.

"Fine, fine. Just send her in." The voice was curt.

Donna frowned at the lack of recognition, then straightened a stack of papers on her desk and rigidly rose from her chair. "He'll see you now."

I followed her to a heavy steel door, more fitting for a bank vault in Zurich, and watched as she opened it wide, spreading her arms like Vanna White. If this were Take Your Daughter to Work Day, I didn't think I'd be very impressed by Donna's job. It required too much unappreciated stress and fake niceness for my taste.

"Thank you," I said, forcing a grin as I walked into the cavernous loft, its black marble floors shining below stark white walls decorated with colorful splatter art, that was probably very expensive, and a massive collection of hand-printed black and white photographs. Urban remained seated, his desk a mile away, and I stopped to admire his pictures. He was featured in every photo with just a sprinkling of Dresden employees mixed in—including my parents.

In the center, hung a large, eleven-by-fourteen, professionally matted image. My parents and Urban were standing alongside the president of France. I had seen it before. It was taken at a summit a year before their deaths. They'd just won a massive project. It was a huge accomplishment, even made the newspapers. Next to that, was a small five-by-seven photo in a simple black frame, taken in Venice. My parents were seated in an ornately carved gondola with Randolph Urban standing beside them, steering the boat with a long stick, one hand resting on my mother's shoulder. They were floating in the Grand Canal, and behind them was one of its many stately hotels. My parents couldn't have been more than twenty-five in the photo. They looked so happy.

I swallowed the rock swelling in my throat and turned my attention to the photos around it: Urban and some world leader dressed in African garb; Urban flying his own jet plane; Urban mountain climbing, scuba diving, wind surfing, sky diving. He was like an aging X-Gamer, and he featured his unusual accomplishments right beside his images of the prime minister of Japan and the president of Russia.

"I miss your parents every day," he said as he finally stepped behind me, eyeing the picture of Venice. The scent of his woodsy cologne coated the air, so familiar I was instantly reminded of company barbecues and holiday parties. "I don't know if I can say this enough, but I'm so sorry about your sister. The memorial... It was lovely," he continued. "She touched so many lives at the hospital. I could tell that people really loved her."

"They still do," I corrected.

"Yes, you're right. I'm sorry."

I turned to face him. He kept his beard longer now than when my parents were alive. I was used to a thin coat of stubble, but now it was full, white, and bushy, giving off a skinny Santa-Claus-on-crack vibe.

"I'm so happy you've come for a visit. I've been worried."

"I'm fine," I said, repeating my mantra.

"That's good to hear. Tell me, what can I do for you?" He wrapped his arm around my shoulders, leaning over as his athletic six-foot-three frame guided me to a scarlet leather chair nestled in front of a wall of windows. Not a decibel of street noise could be heard from below. He moved behind his glass desk and waited for me to sit before he lowered himself into his extra tall cherry red chair.

I'd practiced this conversation on the T-ride over, but now that I was facing him, my words seemed obnoxiously greedy. After our parents' funeral, Keira and I avoided Urban and everything Dresden that went along with him. We dodged his phone calls, his emails, his Christmas cards, but we accepted his "life insurance" check. Then Keira disappeared, and now I sat before him, nervously running my hands up and down my thighs, prepared to ask for money yet again. "I'm not sure how much the police have told you."

"They filled me in this morning."

I raised an eyebrow. The detectives weren't offering me those kinds of updates.

"Well, then you know my roommate and I uncovered a photo of Keira from a few days before she was attacked. She's with two men; one is definitely the guy from our party, Craig. The other is Luis Basso."

There wasn't a micro twitch of recognition on Urban's face.

"Do you know the Bassos?" I asked. "Apparently, they

were friends with my parents?"

Urban carefully folded his palms on his modern glass desk, which was impossibly void of a single smudge. "Yes, Luis's father, Salvatore, was a friend of your parents. I bought an antique dining set from him for my home in Martha's Vineyard, but that was the extent of our relationship. The police said you spoke to him?"

"I did. And he knew Luis was in contact with Keira." I tapped my thighs, struggling to keep my mind from dashing too far ahead of my words. "He claims Luis didn't have anything to do with what happened to her, but then he started talking about my parents and 'larger forces at work.' He sounded nervous and refused to talk more over the phone. He was acting like there was something he wanted me to *see*, in Italy. Do you have any idea what he's getting at?" If anyone could offer an educated opinion about this situation, it was Randolph Urban. He knew everyone involved, my parents especially.

He pressed his lips together tightly and stared down at his desk, breathing heavily through his nose. He exuded the uneasy vibe of someone about to tell you that the cancer had spread.

"I told the police this, but they already knew. You deserve to hear it from me." He peered at me warily.

"What?" I asked, a pit sinking in my belly.

"You know I've always thought of you as family, you and your sister. I loved your parents, and I thought it was my job to protect you, to make things better, not worse. That's why I didn't say anything to you sooner." This was bad. Randolph Urban was an accomplished businessman who dined with foreign dignitaries; he wasn't the type to start conversations with long, unnecessary, lead-ins.

He placed his palms flat on his desk, as if bracing himself.

"A few weeks after your parents' deaths, a group of men came to the office. FBI. They demanded all of your parents' employment records—their computers, their travel logs, their expense reports, their pay stubs, their project reports. Everything. They had a warrant."

I squeezed the metal arms of my chair, my sweaty palms leaving sticky prints on the chrome. "What did they find?"

He looked me square in the eye. "The agents claimed that your parents were spies, that they were enemies of the United States."

Everything slowed. I could see Urban's ivory nose hairs twitch with each inhalation, his tongue lick his whitened teeth in a tedious motion, and a single blade swirl around on the ceiling fan.

I blinked, mouth agape.

My parents were spies? He'd actually just said that. This was really happening.

"*What?*" I finally choked.

"The FBI claimed that every time your parents went on a business trip, in addition to doing their work for Dresden, they were also performing secret *missions*." He spat the word like it was ridiculous, which it was. "They wouldn't tell me what these missions were, but they implied that they were acts of treason, that they were working *against* the United States, that they were…traitors."

"That's insane. My parents are Americans. Why would they work against their own country?" I snapped, my eyelashes suddenly fluttering uncontrollably.

"They wouldn't tell me anything more, and nothing was ever made public, so I don't think their proof was concrete. Still, I pulled every string I could, because I agree with you. It makes no sense. I met your parents at Princeton. I started this corporation with them. I *knew* them."

"So did I. At least, I thought I did." I shook my head, the words clattering around like a mixed-up jumble with one accusation bolded and in CAPS lock: "**TRAITORS.**" How could anyone believe that? Even if my parents had a lot of bruises and spoke a lot of languages, even if we moved a lot, and even if you were willing to entertain the idea that they weren't simple engineers, how could anyone think they were evil? I thought of Benedict Arnold, and the Rosenbergs, and other notorious American traitors— did the U.S. government really think my parents' names deserved to be on that short list? For what?

"After the agents left, after I had time to think, I hired a private detective and a forensic accountant. I had them look into every trip your parents ever took for Dresden." He clasped his hands, the white hair on his knuckles standing on end as his fingers twined together. "There are large gaps of time in your parents' project reports. There is evidence of multiple cell phones, multiple credit cards. There's evidence that they'd often leave the city where they were working and go someplace else, unauthorized."

"That doesn't mean anything. That's doesn't mean they were *traitors*." I choked on the word.

"No. But it means your parents were involved in something outside the scope of this corporation, which amazes me, because they were two of the best engineers I've ever known. They did incredible work for Dresden. They shaped this company."

"Then it's not true," I said defensively.

"That was what I thought, too. But now, after what Salvatore said, I believe this is to what he's referring. He was friends with your parents, good friends. Maybe he knows something? It would explain why he'd be uncomfortable discussing it over the phone."

I sat back in my chair, my hands trembling in time with my voice. "On the surveillance footage from the hospital, Keira was talking about our parents. She said the more she thought back—about the languages, the trips, the bruises— the more things didn't make sense. She said she had a plan to find out the truth. Maybe she did? I mean, Keira always joked they were spies. We both did. At least, I thought we were kidding."

"I never even considered the possibility. I trusted them implicitly." There was an edge to his voice. Maybe betrayal? Because if this were true, then my parents deceived him, too—their best friend, their business partner.

"No." I shook my head, rejecting the theory. "Even if we are going to make some insane link between my parents and espionage, I am not willing to make the jump to them being traitors. Maybe they worked for the CIA? In black ops or something? That's a real thing, right? Maybe the FBI and the CIA just aren't sharing information?" My knee bopped, rattling the pens in the ceramic mug on his desk as my mind desperately searched for a more acceptable conclusion.

"I considered the same thing. I even put out feelers with a few contacts at the CIA, but they were never able to confirm anything."

"You really think this is what Salvatore wants to talk to me about? Because even if Keira did find out something about them, I can't imagine she uncovered information you weren't able to find, information so horrible it got her kidnapped."

"I don't know, but it would explain why Salvatore was so nervous. Maybe your parents had enemies? Or maybe Luis and Keira stumbled onto something together, and he's afraid to repeat it over the phone? At the very least, if I thought I were sitting on any information that might help you find your sister, I wouldn't be able to live with myself. That's why I'm telling you now." He rolled out his crimson leather chair and stood, walking around his glass desk until he was hovering right above me. "No matter what anyone says about them, *we* knew them." He gestured with his hand between the two of us. "What we think is what matters. And I owe it to them to help you now, to help your sister. So tell me, what can I do?"

My head dropped toward my now frantically bouncing knee, my long dark bangs brushing my lashes.

Blink. Blink. Blink.

This was why I'd come.

"I need to go to Italy," I declared, my voice suddenly clear, unwavering. "I know the cops say they'll work with local police, but Salvatore said he would talk only to *me*. In person. I can't ignore that. She's my sister."

"Done," he said simply.

My lips parted, my head jerking back in shock. I'd hoped he'd help me, but even I was surprised at the ease with which he agreed.

Then Urban turned to a picture of his granddaughter, his finger lightly touching the laser-cut crystal frame. Sophia was four years older than me, and we both briefly lived in Los Angeles at the same time, when I was in fifth grade. We weren't friends. She was closer to Keira's age than mine, but they weren't friends, either. Sophia was serious, very studious, rather rude, and tightly wound. I heard she'd graduated from the London School of Economics, which is like the MIT of England. That made sense.

Turned out Urban had a very brief marriage in his twenties, before he ever met my parents. That relationship ended in divorce (an ex-wife my parents never mentioned), but not before they produced a child, Sarah, who sadly died of an aneurysm not long after giving birth to Sophia.

So Urban was a grandfather by his mid-forties, raising his only heir. And even knowing her just loosely, I understood she was Urban's greatest source of pride. He paraded her around at company parties. He worked her name into many conversations. He gave her a job right out of college.

"If anything, *anything*, ever happened to Sophia, if she went missing, if she were hurt, I would spare nothing—no expense—to find her." He looked at me, his gaze intense. "You owe your sister the same, and I must think of your parents. I'll give you anything you need."

"Anything?" My eyes stretched.

"You want to go to Italy? I'll have Donna book the tickets."

I looked around his office—original works of art, marble floors, gold-plated light fixtures—this was the type of money that could accomplish things. That could find my sister.

"I...I don't know what to say. Thank you." I jumped from my chair and hugged him before I even knew what I was doing. He embraced me back, squeezing tightly. It had been a long time since I'd had a fatherly hug—my family wasn't big on touching.

He sighed, his snowy beard scraping my neck. "I was younger than you when I set off on my own. People these days act like seventeen-year-olds are children, but in my eyes, anyone who's survived what you have is already more of an adult than most of the people who work for me. This is your decision to make. I'm proud of you for standing by your family."

I gripped his neck tighter, inhaling his woodsy scent. Finally. Someone who understood.

Then an alarm buzzed on his desk.

"Mr. Urban," Donna's voice was annoyed. "*Another* teenager is here. He doesn't have an appointment…"

My brows tensed. For a man who was booked solid for the foreseeable millennia, he sure got a lot of unexpected teen visitors.

"Send him in," Urban urged, looking at me with a grin. "I'm expecting him."

I turned to the door as Donna heaved it open and watched as Marcus sauntered through, his jaw falling when he caught sight of me.

"What are you doing here?" we asked almost in unison.

"I'm here about Antonio. I sent you a text this morning." He gestured to me.

Oh crap, he did. I remembered seeing his name pop up on my screen, but I was sprinting to catch the T at the time, so I ignored it. I forgot to go back and read it, because I was too nervous imagining my conversation with Urban. "What's going on with your brother?"

He had told me Antonio wasn't calling him back, but I'd thought they'd Skyped last week. At least they were supposed to. *Did I ever ask if that conversation happened?* I was a terrible friend. I'd warned him of that.

His black motorcycle boots squeaked as he walked across the marble floor toward Urban and me. "I tried Skyping him, but he never picked up. My parents haven't heard from him, either, but they're acting like I'm being paranoid. I was hoping Mr. Urban could tell me where he is." He looked at him.

"Milan," Urban said definitively. "After I got your email, I had Donna look into it. He's trying to land a big client."

"But he's okay?" Marcus sounded relieved.

"As far as I know. Probably drinking too much wine." Urban joked easily as he turned to me. "Actually, Anastasia and I were just talking about Italy."

"I'm gonna try to track down Luis's dad, see what he has to say," I offered. I'd been keeping Marcus updated via text, but ignoring his requests to hang out, which made seeing him face-to-face now a little awkward. It wasn't that I didn't want to spend time with him, it was more that I *did*. Every time I was with him, I felt this pull, this buzz when he touched me, this flutter inside that brought with it a fresh wave of guilt for even thinking about smiling. I needed to focus on Keira, not a boy, and especially not after all the grief I gave Keira about her boyfriends over the years.

"I think you should go to Italy. You need to do this," Marcus agreed, a sharp contrast to the black hole of negativity that had been trapping me lately.

"Well, I must say I'm delighted the two of you know each other so well." Urban grinned. "I love seeing our Dresden Kids sticking together."

It had been a long time since I identified as a Dresden Kid, but I guessed it still applied. Keira and I were a part of the corporate history, so much so that the CEO was about to fund my trip to Europe.

"Marcus, I spoke with your parents," Urban continued. "I know you're worried, and maybe a little lonely, and I don't like that. Your parents and I think you should visit Antonio, maybe even go to Madrid, see some friends. And since you're both here, I think we should plan this trip together." He wrapped his arms around us like this was the greatest idea ever. "I'll expense both; that way your parents won't have to foot the bill, and *you* won't have to go alone."

My eyes bulged with a mix of shock and horror. I'd hoped to travel with Charlotte, somehow convince her this was a good idea, but even if she refused, I couldn't imagine strolling beside Marcus. I couldn't end up that girl flirting in the grocery store again when my sister desperately needed me. Keira had to be my priority this time.

Marcus peered at me uneasily. "I don't want to impose. I know how important this is."

"Well, I don't want to put you in danger," I retorted.

"Do you think you'll be in danger?" he asked.

"I don't know."

"I can't imagine," Urban interjected, stepping between us. "I've met Salvatore; he's not a dangerous man. He's old and sells armoires. I wouldn't agree to this trip if I thought I was putting you in harm's way. I just think you deserve to hear what he has to say, and if there's a way for you not to go alone, I know I'd feel better."

Talk about putting us on the spot.

"I really want to see my brother," Marcus said sincerely. "And go home for a bit. I don't mind going to Tuscany with you as long as you're okay with it…"

"There. It's settled!" Urban clapped before I could respond. "You'll both go talk to Salvatore, then head up to Milan and, if you have time, take in a bullfight in Madrid before school starts." He smiled like he'd just closed a deal.

"Um…uh." I looked warily at Marcus.

"If you insist," said Marcus, acknowledging how we seemed to have no choice. Then his eyes met mine. "I really do want to help."

I knew he meant it, and it wasn't *him* I didn't trust, it was me when I was around him. But I also didn't want to go alone, traipsing through family memories, searching for Keira, *by myself*. I hadn't been out of the funk long enough to handle that emotional load alone. I nodded in agreement.

"Wonderful. Donna will make all the arrangements."

Urban guided us toward the steel door, his long arm slung around my shoulder. "I would do anything for you, Anastasia. You're family to me, a part of Dresden. I really hope you find the answers you're looking for."

Then he practically pushed us through the exit.

I looked at Marcus, wondering if he knew what he was getting himself into.

If either of us did.

CHAPTER FIFTEEN

Having access to unlimited funds made it a whole lot easier to get a last-minute ticket to Europe. Within a week, Randolph Urban's assistant had arranged for Marcus and I to fly first class, with a make-your-own-sundae bar, restaurant-quality sea bass, individual entertainment system, entire cans of soda and, when we lied and said we were eighteen, we even got free champagne. It was my first alcoholic drink, ever, which Marcus swore would erase the image of Charlotte returning from work to find a three-line note on her canary yellow bedspread.

With Marcus as my mandatory traveling buddy, I'd decided not to ask Charlotte to come with me. I knew she'd say no; she might even warn Detective Dawkins or hack my name onto the no-fly list. So I opted for a Post-it. It read: *Headed to Italy. Call when I get there. Sorry.*

Tyson and Regina got a similar text, only I added that the Italian trip was a backpacking vacation because "I needed a break." They responded, "Have fun!" I doubted Charlotte would offer the same response. But honestly, I could have written a novel-length explanation and she'd still react like a mom with a toddler lost at the mall.

So I flew to Florence.

The plane touched down around seven in the morning, local time, and we hopped a cab to the train station.

Marcus sat beside me as we zipped through picturesque Florence, the ochre morning light gleaming behind the massive Duomo. It is one of the most beautiful and romantic cities in the world, and I was traveling with someone who made me choke on survivor's guilt. I leaned away from him, refusing to let our arms touch, our knees touch. It had been a constant battle during the flight, to ignore the feeling of static electricity rising between our bodies, but I was determined to ignore the diversion. Marcus was there to help and visit his brother. That was it.

I kept my eyes locked on the Duomo. It was an impressive cathedral, with an intricately carved marble exterior and a towering burnt orange dome at least thirty stories high. Personally, I wasn't a huge fan of cathedrals as tourist attractions—if you've seen one gilded Jesus, you've seen them all. But even I had to admit that Italians did churches right—all marble, frescos, and gold-plated reverence.

"*Que hermosa*," Marcus noted as he eyed the same view.

I nodded, noticing that outside our car, tourists were gazing at store windows full of leather gloves and colorful ceramics, and I couldn't help but think that a few years ago, that was my family, carrying overflowing bags of souvenirs before dining on plates of steak Florentine. Now, I was just hoping to find my sister alive and prove my parents weren't lunatics screaming, "Death to America!" Things had changed.

We stopped in front of the station and made our way to our high-speed train. We trudged our way through the narrow cabin aisles with our luggage, knocking passengers' elbows until we found our designated booth—there were two seats on either side and a gray plastic table set between them. I heaved my wheely carry-on onto the overhead metal rack and plopped down as the train lurched forward. I rested my laptop bag on the empty seat beside me, forcing Marcus to sit opposite the table. I yanked out my copy of *Ok!* magazine and blindly leafed through it, eyes buried. I'd bought it along with an international cell phone I'd use to call Charlotte once we arrived at our hotel.

I scanned the glossy pages as Marcus settled into his royal blue cushioned seat, the train roaring through a pitch-black tunnel. Amber overhead lights flickered, illuminating the cabin as I eyed an article on *The Bachelor*. Keira could practically teach a PhD course on the show, reciting the contestants' names and hometowns as if she shared their childhoods. I think she secretly wanted to audition, but didn't because her seventeen-year-old dependent didn't scream "free-spirited love interest!" Chalk it up as another way that I held her back.

The next page featured a "Stars Like Us" page with a picture of a British media heir, his bright blue-green eyes looking sad and horrified as he darted into a luxury car. Above his head, the editor had scrolled "Wanker" with a white magic marker along with streaks of snot coming from his nose. Halfway around the globe and stars still got the same classy treatment.

"I didn't know you were into celebrity gossip," Marcus noted, eying the magazine.

"I'm not. Keira is." I flipped a page, trying not to engage.

"You're hoping to catch your sister up once you see her?"

"Well, she might want to know Katy Perry's relationship status."

"It's good to be prepared."

I nodded, keeping my eyes buried in the photos.

"You were quiet on the flight." Marcus's voice was apprehensive. "You don't like that I'm here."

Damn. I didn't want to offend him, especially after all he'd done and all he was currently doing. But I didn't know how to explain my situation or how I was feeling. *Sorry, Marcus, but I just think this trip would be easier if you were unattractive.* That didn't sound right.

"It's not you, it's just…" I gazed at the dreamy farmland whipping outside our window, and again felt a misplaced sense of betrayal for even being in the presence of beauty, even natural beauty. "You don't know Keira."

"I know you, and you shouldn't have to do this alone." He placed his hand on the table, as if inviting me to take it. I didn't. "Dresden Kids stick together."

"This might be taking that slogan too far."

"I'm also here to see my brother, who would love that I'm doing this. Antonio lives for adventure, at least he used to. He was always running off, getting into fights, drinking too much. Sort of a rebel, before he became some serious business man." He uttered that last part like he still didn't believe the words. "Maybe you'll get to meet him."

"You know I might not be able to go to Milan, right?" It was probably rude of me to back out given that he currently was sitting on a train to Cortona holding up his end of the arrangement. But I couldn't commit to going anywhere that didn't lead me to Keira.

"I know. We'll see what happens." He glanced at the skinny cypress trees lining the farms as perfect as a painting.

"Do you think it's weird that Urban sent you here to see your brother? Why couldn't he just connect you over the phone?" The question had been gnawing at me ever since we left Dresden's offices. Not that I wanted to tell a CEO how to spend his cash, but it seemed like a Send-

Your-Kid-to-Europe program was an auditable misuse of corporate funds.

"My parents knew I was homesick. I think it was a good excuse to get me to stop moping and stop waiting for *you* to call." He gave me a teasing grin, and I felt instantly guilty for dodging his requests to hang out. I seriously was a terrible friend. "Besides, with everything that's happened to your family, I don't think anyone wanted to say no to you or send you here alone. I *want* to be here."

"To track down a guy whose son may or may not be involved in a violent kidnapping?" I pursed my lips. Most friends balk at helping you move.

"*Sí.* I'm with you." He looked at me so intently I felt my body involuntarily leaning toward him. I wanted to touch him. I wanted to reach across the table and grab his hand, touch his face.

Only I didn't.

I broke eye contact, clearing my throat as I stared down at my lap. *Stop it,* I reminded myself. "I don't think I've said it, but thank you for coming. It's nice of you." My voice was overly formal.

"*De nada*," he replied.

When I peered up through my lashes, I caught sight of his dimpled grin once more, and I couldn't help but think that Keira would really like him.

The conductor's voice bellowed through the croaking static of the train's audio system, announcing upcoming stops.

"Looks like we're next—Cortona," Marcus translated.

"*Sí. Parlo Italiano*," I replied, grabbing my bag from the overhead rack.

"Oh, I forgot, our Dresden education." He hoisted his duffle bag as the train pulled into our quaint Italian village.

Last time I'd been here, I sat in a rental car with my family: my dad driving, Keira humming the tune from *The Godfather,* and my mother spouting historical facts.

The scene looked a little different now. As did the company.

"So what's your total? How many cities?"

"Madrid, Berlin, London, D.C., back to Madrid, and Boston," he replied.

"You can't count the same city twice, you know that. Still, I gotcha beat. Seattle, Singapore, New Orleans, Morocco, Los Angeles, Madrid, Milan, Miami, and Boston," I recited.

"You got to live in Asia; that must've been cool."

"You couldn't chew gum."

Marcus chuckled, but it sounded forced, and I noticed a crease between his dark eyebrows. He looked worried. Maybe he was tired from travel, or maybe the fact that he was thrusting himself into the middle of my family's mess was finally hitting him. It should be.

"You sure you want to do this? You can just head up to Milan if you want." I placed a hand on his shoulder, offering him an out. It was the first time I'd touched him since we'd boarded our flight, and he seemed to notice. He looked down at my palm and smiled, that familiar tingle flushing my skin once more.

I returned my hand to my side.

Still, he moved toward me, his face so close I could feel the warmth of his breath. "I wouldn't think of leaving you. Lead the way, Miss Phoenix."

He followed me into Tuscany.

CHAPTER SIXTEEN

We rattled over cobblestones very reminiscent of our motorcycle tour of Boston as our taxi headed through the opening in the stone wall that encircled Cortona. The tiny village probably housed fewer people than could fit inside Fenway Park, but what it lacked in size, it made up for in charm.

We stopped in front of a swinging wooden sign and grabbed our bags from the trunk, trudging tiredly into the lobby of the same hotel that I'd stayed at with my parents. Only a few years ago, I watched as my father sat on the olive-green velvet sofa in the lobby reading the paper with his tiny espresso cup while my mother talked on her cell phone, her high heels resting on the intricately carved wooden coffee table. Nothing had changed in the hotel since, and it felt odd to see the décor continued to exist even though my parents didn't.

"You okay?" Marcus asked, noticing my dazed expression.

"I'm fine." I repeated my mantra as I shook off the memory and stepped toward the front desk. "*Buona sera.*"

The clerk confirmed our reservation, his eyes occasionally glancing toward us like our youth clashed with the ambiance. Donna had booked the last two available rooms—one on the same floor I'd stayed on with my family, and the other, the honeymoon suite. I chose the latter.

We rode up in the coffin-size elevator, stopping on the second floor (which was really the third floor, but they counted the ground level as '0,' as if it were nowhere). Marcus turned my way. "So we're meeting Salvatore tomorrow, *verdad*?"

"Yeah, the store opens at ten. I'll meet you in the lobby?" I had considered going straight from the airport to the antique shop, but given the amount of travel we'd just completed, and my lack of sleep, I thought it would be best to save extremely vital conversations until I wasn't slurring from jet lag.

Marcus nodded, and I exited the elevator into a lounge of empty couches. Dark wood beams lined the ceiling as I headed toward a narrow hall, dimly lit by wall sconces. I unlocked the honeymoon suite and placed my plastic key-card in the slot inside that powered the room's electricity. As expected, there was a massive, romantic canopy bed draped with sheer flowing white curtains nestled between a vase of wild flowers and a shutter-framed window that looked onto a beautiful stone courtyard.

There was even a congratulatory bottle of free champagne.

I dropped my bags with a thud and plodded into the bathroom, its bright white walls and fluorescent lights clashing with the rustic decor. I stopped at the mirror, glaring at my droopy eyes rimmed with dark purple circles, and splashed cool water onto my cheeks. The room was silent. Cortona was so small that it lacked street noise— like, *any* street noise. And being a girl who was used to T trains, car horns, and recycling trucks, the vapid sound of nothingness felt like a weight on my chest.

I moved to the bed, pushing aside the dreamy curtains, and dropped my head onto a fluffy down pillow. It smelled musty and foreign. I could hear myself breathing. I could feel my heart pulse. I suddenly felt alone, *completely* alone—in this bed, on this trip, in this world. My parents took me to this hotel. My sister gave me my first cup of cappuccino in the restaurant downstairs—doused with loads of sugar and a dash of cinnamon. I told her I liked it (I didn't), and she told me I'd learn to appreciate it (I did).

Now I was here with *Marcus*.

My mouth grew sour. It wasn't good to be so wrapped in my thoughts, to be so still. I could feel the funk lurking around me like a poisonous gas seeking a weakened, porous entry. The tears began to fall as I closed my eyes.

Welcome to Europe.

I woke hours later. The sun had set. My pillow was damp with tears.

Pull it together. I rubbed my eyes. *You are going to find your sister. That's why you're here.*

I looked at the clock, and panic gripped my chest. It had been almost twenty-four hours since I'd left Boston, and I'd forgotten to call Charlotte. I couldn't believe helicopters hadn't descended by now. I grabbed the cell phone I'd purchased at the airport and dialed the familiar digits.

"Hello?" asked a breathless, frantic voice.

I already felt guilty.

"Charlotte, I'm so sorry," I immediately apologized, sitting up in bed.

"I can't believe you did this! Are you okay? Do you have any idea what you've put me through?"

I winced at her tone. She wasn't worried or upset. She sounded pissed. "I had to…" My voice trailed off.

"No, you didn't! I told you not to do this! I told you the cops would handle it! And to leave the way you did, I can't believe—"

"Charlotte, I'm sorry," I apologized again. "But you wouldn't come with me, and I couldn't just let the police sit around and do nothing."

"They're not doing nothing! They spoke to Salvatore Basso, they contacted Italian law enforcement, they're working the case, all in ways that don't involve *you*. I tried to tell you this, but you wouldn't listen. Now you're off in Europe alone and—"

"*Well…* I'm not completely alone." I cringed, imagining her reaction on the other end looked something like the woman in the shower before the knife comes down. "Marcus came with me."

Static hung on the line for several moments, then she started screaming. "Are you *kidding* me? Why would you bring *him*? Is this, like, a vacation for you? Are you running away?"

"No! Omigod! No!" I spilled the whole story—about seeing him at Dresden, about his brother working in Milan, about Urban offering to pay, about us really having no say in becoming travel buddies, and about me being unwilling to turn down a free ticket that might possibly lead to my sister.

"So let me get this straight. Randolph Urban, the CEO of the Dresden Chemical Corporation, shipped two teenagers across the Atlantic and didn't think to mention it to their guardians?" Charlotte asked harshly.

"Actually, Marcus's parents know he's here." I fidgeted with my wrinkled bedsheet, twisting it around my wrist.

"Oh, well, I'm glad they got a phone call. Meanwhile, I've been trying to convince my parents that *I* gave you permission to go to Europe on some 'finding yourself' expedition, so they don't report you as a missing person."

"So I guess I'm in trouble?"

"With *me*? Hell yeah!" Charlotte snapped. I twisted the sheet tighter, my wrist turning a blotchy magenta. "My parents think I'm some irresponsible flake who superseded their judgment and let a teenager fly halfway around the world by herself to get raped and murdered."

I winced. "When you put it that way…"

"Do you have any idea what will happen if social services finds out you left the country alone, and my parents had no idea?"

"I know. I'm sorry," I apologized again. The guilt I felt lately was so heavy I was surprised I could move. From failing my sister, to flirting with Marcus, to running off on Charlotte, it felt like everything I'd done for the past several months was wrong. All of it. I was wrong. My family was wrong. Everything I knew was just wrong. That was why I had to find my sister. It was the only way to make anything right again. "I just…had to."

Charlotte sighed so heavily I could practically feel her breath through the phone.

"I can't believe you lied for me," I said, my tone thankful.

"I can't believe you lied *to* me."

"I left a note."

"Gee, thanks for that."

"And technically, I'm not alone."

"You know, as anti-feminist as it sounds, I'm actually

relieved you're with Marcus. Safety in numbers and all that. But if you're not on a plane back to the States by tomorrow, I'm coming to get you," she threatened, though I could hear the calm returning to her voice.

"It's weird," I admitted. "We're in the same hotel I stayed at with my parents and Keira. Only, they're not here anymore, none of them…" I swallowed hard, trying to force away the grief. I couldn't let myself feel that right now. I couldn't let the funk in, not when I was so close to learning something that might lead me to Keira. I had to focus on her.

"I'm sorry," she replied sincerely.

"You don't have to say that."

"You don't get to tell *me* what to do," she huffed. "So I take it you're meeting with Salvatore Basso? When?"

"Tomorrow morning, as soon as the store opens. I left a message telling him I was coming."

"Oh, so *he* got a phone call," she griped.

 I said nothing.

"Well, you better phone the second you leave that store." She groaned, clearly exasperated. "I swear, I'm turning prematurely gray."

"No, you're not. You're a lovely honey blonde, but I'm sorry I worried you."

"There's not much I can do about this now. Just be careful, or I *will* come get you."

"I know. Thanks."

 We both hung up, and I stared at my phone. There was one more person I needed to call.

 Straight to voicemail.

"Mr. Urban, it's Anastasia. I wanted to thank you, and Donna, for arranging this trip. Marcus and I are in Cortona and meeting with Salvatore tomorrow. Hopefully, he'll have some answers. This was really nice of you. I owe you."

I hung up and looked at my hotel room door, wondering what Marcus was doing in his room. Wondering if he was wondering about me. Then I instantly hated myself for thinking it. Still, I stared at the door handle, debating whether I should open it, whether I should go to him.

My fingers itched to turn the knob.

CHAPTER SEVENTEEN

I stayed in my room. I didn't visit Marcus; I didn't surrender to the distraction. Instead, I spent the night pacing my hotel room, mentally preparing my questions for Salvatore. Then I awoke the next morning with the determination of a Navy SEAL. I jumped into the hotel's tiny shower, dried my hair, put on a pair of slim gray jeans and my favorite blue-gray T-shirt, which almost matched my eyes, and headed down to the hotel lobby, my threadbare army green laptop bag slung across my shoulder and my mind on my mission.

Marcus was already waiting for me, lounging on the same velvet green couch where my father once sat, sipping a similar tiny cup of espresso and flipping through a newspaper.

"Want some coffee? Breakfast?" he asked, peering up from his cup when he saw me.

"No. I'm ready." I nodded to the door.

"*Bueno*. Let's go antiquing." He gulped down his espresso as we headed from the lobby.

The streets of Cortona are steep, like San Francisco steep, and my Converse skidded on the pavers as Marcus

puffed beside me. Every day since my sister had disappeared, I'd pictured myself being the one to find her: I'd
burst into a room and see Keira alive and grateful, then
I'd spin around and knock some guard unconscious with a
scissor kick before flinging a glass ashtray at the head of
another. I'd stare at the attackers on the floor, beaten, then
run to my sister, hug her, and whisper that we were safe,
we'd done it, and we were going home. But never in all
the times that I had this daydream did I picture myself
standing next to the guy I met in my high school cafeteria.

"It's just up ahead," Marcus said as he looked at the
colorful cartoon map distributed by the hotel. Cortona was
everything you pictured Tuscany to be—aging chipped
facades, burnt-orange shingled roofs, and battered wooden
doors. The entire scene breathed like a hometown, all quaint
and picturesque, full of locals sipping cappuccino and tourists
buying handmade goods. We turned onto *Via Nazionale*, and
I immediately saw the sign for the *Cortona Antiquaria*. It was
just as I'd remembered—its glass windowpane stuffed with
dusty terra-cotta pots, copper pans, and wood-framed chairs
with fuzzy embroidered cushions.

"We're here," Marcus said, watching as I moved robotically toward the entry.

I pushed open the glass door, bells tinkling overhead
as I stepped onto the creaky wooden planks, inhaling the
smell of dust that came with age. Salvatore stood behind
the cashier's counter, adjusting the brown plastic glasses
covering his heavy-hooded eyes, which sagged below wild
black eyebrows surrounded by decades of deep wrinkles.

We stared for what felt like forever.

"Anastasia," he finally greeted, his wiry gray mustache
twitching.

I could hardly move.

...

Marcus and I sat on decorative upholstered stools in a dank storage room in the back of the antique store. Salvatore Basso sat before us on an expensive-looking wingback chair illuminated by a bare light bulb on the exposed-beam ceiling.

He handed me a cup of straight espresso. I hated black coffee, so I doubted espresso would be any better, but I accepted the colorfully hand-painted ceramic cup. "*Gratzi*." I smiled, forcing down a tiny bitter sip.

Marcus sat beside me, easily drinking his.

"Thanks for meeting me," I said to Salvatore. "But I'm still not sure why I needed to come. Why couldn't we talk on the phone?"

"I know this must seem strange, but as I said, I was very close with your parents. May they rest in peace." He made the sign of the cross.

"That's just it. Why didn't I know that? When we came here, my parents acted like they were just fans of your store." I rested my cup on a gritty bookshelf.

"Well, your parents were very private people."

"You think?" I raised an eyebrow.

"They used to come through town on business."

"So there's a lot of chemical engineering being done in Cortona?" My sarcasm was thick.

Salvatore grinned in response. "No, it wasn't that type of business. And that's what I didn't want to share with law enforcement." He sipped his espresso. "Your Boston police called not long after you. They had questions about the photo of Luis and your sister's attacker. He was *not* friends with that man. He was introduced only once."

"But does he know where I can find Craig now?" I squeaked, hope dripping in my voice. "Can I talk to Luis?"

"I don't want to get my son involved further. He..."—Salvatore took a deep sigh—"has a record here. He got into trouble years ago, nothing serious. But I'm worried about how it might look."

"How it might look for *him*?" I snapped, my head vehemently shaking at the blatant selfishness in his words. "My sister left behind pints of blood in our tub, so I'm a little more worried about *her*. What does he know about Keira?"

"He doesn't know anything about the attack, *but* he does know that she was looking into your parents' pasts right before it happened. That's what she was talking to him about in Boston. She thought he might know something about their...*work*."

"Does he?" I asked. Was I the only one who didn't?

"Yes, and so do I." His voice was cagey, his drooping eyes tightening like a psychiatrist assessing a patient. I knew that look all too well. I had a history with shrinks, and this was the *Can she handle what I'm about to say?* look. "That's why I wanted you to come. There's something I need you to see."

He slowly rose from his chair, his knees creaking under his stocky heavyset frame. Marcus and I popped up beside him, following him to a hulking armoire on the far back wall. Salvatore yanked it open, revealing a secret door with a hidden staircase quite reminiscent of Anne Frank's attic. "Your parents used to stay here when they traveled through town," he divulged as he shuffled up the steps with the help of the arm rail. Marcus and I thudded behind him, my heart drumming a Metallica solo.

Then Salvatore unlocked a dead-bolted door. "This is a safe place. Or, a safe *house,* as you say in your country."

My stomach twined into a slipknot as we stepped into

the small windowless studio apartment, my eyes darting about. There were two thin sea-green floral-patterned mattresses resting on metal frames without sheets. A small kitchenette hummed with almond-colored appliances. In the living area rested a tattered brown and orange plaid sofa, a few rickety end tables, and a wooden bookcase full of thick tomes.

Salvatore waved me forward, and my eyes instantly caught on a silver picture frame nestled among the books. I stopped short. It was a photo of me. Or more specifically, of my family—my mom, my dad, Keira, and I were all standing in front of the Magic Kingdom. It was the Disney World vacation we took when I was six years old. It was one of the few times in my life I remembered my parents kissing and holding hands. We rode rides, watched princess shows, and even ate ice cream in the shape of mouse ears.

The next month, we moved to Singapore.

Salvatore held out the frame for me with a quivering hand.

"You okay?" Marcus asked as he slowly stepped to my side, afraid to make sudden movements.

The words slid down the back of my throat. It was an unanswerable question. I hadn't been okay in such a long time, but this pushed me to an incomprehensible level of confusion. I gazed at the image of my former life as I gripped the frame.

"There's more," Salvatore continued, and when I looked up, he was pointing to a handcrafted picture frame on a nearby end table. Constructed of salvaged barn wood, the frame held a yellowed newspaper clipping with a photo that, even from a few feet away, I could see featured my parents.

"That's how we met." Salvatore explained, plucking the thick frame from the table and handing it to me.

Displayed was a grainy black-and-white photograph

of a dead body contorted in the hatchback trunk of a car. Not exactly coffee table art. Around the vehicle were police officers and civilians. Among those present in the crowd were my parents—but not my parents as I knew them. This couple was young—maybe in their twenties—and fresh-faced.

The hairs rose on my arms.

"What is this?" I gasped.

"Your parents are heroes in my country," Salvatore stated proudly. "This is what I wanted you to see. It's an original copy. I couldn't part with it. I won't even travel with it. It means too much."

Has he never heard of a scanner?

I stared at their faces, round and full, their eyes stunned as if they had just stumbled upon the grisly scene. My mom's hair was feathered like a disco queen, and my dad had a long mustache. It must have been the seventies. Around them were policemen in uniforms that looked European; the car looked foreign as well, and the body in the trunk was completely unfamiliar.

"Who is that?" I asked. "*What* is this?"

Marcus pointed to the corpse. "That's Aldo Moro."

I could tell by the way he said it that the name was supposed to mean something to me. It didn't. I shrugged.

"Aldo Moro," Salvatore repeated slowly as if that would jog my memory. "He was the prime minister of Italy until he was assassinated in Rome in 1978." He again made the sign of the cross.

I shook my head, still oblivious.

"Aldo Moro is the Kennedy assassination of Italy," Marcus explained.

Now *that*, I understood. I nodded.

"He was kidnapped and held hostage for weeks," Salvatore continued. "This is a picture from when they discovered the body of the prime minister. Your parents saw the car pull up, and the information they provided tied the murder to the Red Brigades."

"Communist bad guys," Marcus clarified. "But a lot of people don't think that's who killed him. The assassination is one of the greatest conspiracy theories in European history."

"Nonsense," said Salvatore. "Your parents put themselves in great danger when they came forward, and they brought down a ring of political assassins. After this photo came out, they had to go into hiding. Their lives changed."

"Wait? Are we talking witness protection? Is my last name not Phoenix?" I squawked, horrified.

Salvatore shook his head. "I'm not sure."

"Well, what *do* you know? How did you get involved? And what does this have to do with what's going on now?" My heart was pounding so hard it felt like I might crack a rib. *Who were these people?*

"My brother, Angelo, was a member of the state police." Salvatore pointed to a man in the photo, then made the sign of the cross. I assumed from the gesture that his brother was also dead, which could explain why he kept a grisly photo displayed on an end table. "He worked the case, and he asked me to keep your parents safe until things calmed down."

"In this apartment." I looked around, understanding the situation. "So is this how my parents became spies? *Were* they spies? Was this the incident that started it all?" It almost made sense. They innocently stumbled upon a gruesome event, got entangled in a conspiracy involving an assassinated world leader, landed in danger, went into hiding, and after that, a career in espionage fell into their laps.

I took out my cell phone and snapped a picture of the image, then instantly sent it to Charlotte. With her computer skills, hopefully she'd uncover more information. Maybe the FBI had misunderstood my parents' pasts completely. Maybe someone out there could tell me who my parents really were.

As if hearing my mental confusion, Salvatore stepped toward me. "Your parents were complicated people. But after this day, our families were forever linked. They worked with my brother for years, in a nontraditional sense." He eyed me pointedly. "We became family." His jaw clenched when he said this, probably at the mention of his deceased sibling. I was familiar with the feeling.

"Well, what does that mean? What work did they do? And who were their enemies? Because somebody took my sister *recently*, and I think your son knows something. At the very least, he knows what she was up to before all of this happened."

"Luis is trying to track down some leads." He snatched the photo and returned it to the table.

"Where? How?

I was tired of people telling me things only when they felt like telling me. Urban knew the FBI was investigating my parents since their funeral (three years ago!), and he never told us. Maybe if he had, Keira wouldn't have felt the need to research our parents' pasts herself, maybe none of this would have happened. I wasn't going to let Salvatore get away with the same types of omissions. I wasn't going to play dumb anymore. "You brought me here for a reason. It wasn't just to show me a photo. What is going on? Because for all I know, your son's in on this. Maybe Luis helped Craig? Maybe *he's* the one who took her?"

Salvatore's jaw tightened. "Luis would never hurt your sister."

"And I'm supposed to believe you?"

"He loved your parents."

"Yeah, right. My parents never mentioned any of you! You keep talking about family, but honestly, you sound delusional."

"They were Luis's godparents."

My body froze, eyes blinking, and Salvatore watched the comprehension wash over my face. Then he walked over to the bookshelf, slid out a yellowed ivory photo album with dusty floral appliques, and opened the first page. He held it out for me to see.

"Now, do you understand why I am so certain Luis wants to help?"

I peered at a plastic-covered page with mustard-yellow water stains. An image of my twenty-something parents holding a newborn baby in a lacy antique christening gown was positioned dead center. Salvatore was standing beside them with an attractive woman I could only assume was his wife. It looked as though they were inside a Catholic church. "We might not have been family to you, but *you* were family to *us*," he stated. "That meant something."

I grabbed the book and flipped through the pages, searching every face.

"That's the only other image I have of them," he explained.

It was enough. I turned back to it and stared.

My parents had godchildren I never knew about? My parents were *religious*? We'd never gone to church. When Urban insisted on having my parents' funeral in the Catholic cathedral in Boston, Keira and I thought it was ridiculous. But he was footing the bill, so we went along. Maybe he was right? Maybe he knew what they wanted better than us? Maybe everyone knew our parents better than us.

I felt tears welling behind my eyelids. My parents had

close family connections we knew nothing about; they were witnesses in a political assassination; they were being investigated by the FBI, who thought they conducted secret "missions;" and they had enemies who were potentially willing to kidnap their children years after their deaths.

Suddenly, all that time I'd spent mourning them, crying for them, missing them, started to bubble into a new sensation in my chest—anger. Violent, pulsing anger. I had been betrayed, I had been lied to by the people who raised me, by the people who were supposed to love me the most.

I cleared my throat, trying to push away the bile that was rising. Marcus rested his palm on my shoulder; it felt like a brick.

"You obviously know more about my parents than I do," I said, my voice defeated as I handed back the album. "If Luis is innocent, I promise I won't implicate him in anything. I just need to hear what he knows about Keira."

"I'll talk to him. See if he'll meet with you."

"When? How?"

"You're staying at the hotel, no? I'll be in touch."

I hung my head. "How could my parents do this to us?" I muttered to myself.

Salvatore rubbed my biceps with a soft wrinkled palm, his other hand stroking the white tufts of hair standing upright on his head. "I'm sorry. Betrayal, it's the worst thing in the world, especially when it comes from someone you love, someone you trust. I wish I could tell you more. I truly do. But my only involvement in your parents' work was giving them a place to stay."

I scrunched my eyes, straining to hold back a waterfall of emotion, and Marcus stepped to my side. "We'll figure this out," he whispered in my ear. I was glad I wasn't alone, yet also embarrassed that he saw me so blindsided, that he learned the truth about my family right along with me.

"Go back to the hotel." Salvatore insisted. "I'll be in touch." Then he moved toward the door. "I hope you find your sister safe. No one should lose family so young." The sound of his heavy footsteps on the aged wooden steps trailed away, taking with them any bits I held true about my parents.

I probably would have stayed in that room for hours, dazed, haplessly searching for clues about the strangers who stayed here, only my phone rang in my pocket.

CHAPTER EIGHTEEN

We spoke for only a few minutes. Charlotte was on her way to work, the world continuing to spin in its usual nine-to-five loops. I filled her in on my conversation with Salvatore, and she said she was already researching the Aldo Moro photo I'd sent. Apparently, her hacker friends could analyze images with software that made Photoshop look like a Magna Doodle. I was really glad she was on my side.

"According to the map, the coffee shop's up here." Marcus gestured down the block.

I couldn't go back to the hotel. I wasn't built with the patience to wait; call me anti-Gandhi. And since I hadn't eaten all day, Marcus suggested we distract ourselves with food. He seemed to be picking up where Charlotte had left off—trying to create a sense of normalcy on a trip that only twenty-four hours in was already stupefying. But I appreciated his efforts. Every time he mentioned food, school, or the terrible font choice on the cartoon map he was holding, I felt a tiny moment of relief from the family revelations that were currently trying to eat my organs.

We entered the espresso-scented shop with an arching cathedral ceiling and crystal chandeliers swinging above tan leather benches and pastel walls with ornate silver stenciling. It was quite posh for a rural Tuscan town.

"*Perfecto*." Marcus nudged me toward the counter.

A barista stood behind the dark walnut counter, steam rising from the rumbling espresso machine. I ordered a cappuccino with cinnamon, a la Keira, and a ham and cheese croissant. Marcus ordered espresso and biscotti. Then we brought our dishes to a round pedestal table and plunked down on leather ottomans. "So, will you be annoyed if I ask how you're doing?" Marcus raised a teasing eyebrow.

"Oh, I'm just great," I said sarcastically, lifting my heavy ceramic cup from the table, rocking it slightly. "I'm thinking maybe I should call Urban. See what he knows about the Aldo Moro thing?"

"Wouldn't he have told you already? He told you about the FBI."

"Yeah, after he kept it secret for years. Who knows what else he's hiding?" I swallowed a too-hot gulp of foam, the burning sensation feeling good. I was surrounded by pathological liars: my parents regarding their pasts, Keira for looking into them, and now Urban for omitting the international incident that my parents had witnessed. I did the math—he knew my parents when they stumbled onto that crime scene.

Marcus cleared his throat like a kid about to tell his parents he crashed the car. "Okay, so, Salvatore said your parents were linked to the assassination of the dead Italian prime minster, and Urban said the FBI thought they were, um…"

"I know what the FBI thinks." I cut him off. "But my parents *weren't* traitors. They probably just misinterpreted their involvement in that crime scene. Everyone knows that the FBI and the CIA don't talk to each other. I'm starting to think that my parents witnessed a crime and maybe they got sucked into the espionage world, at least for a little while. Then maybe their work became classified or something?"

"*Es possible.*" Marcus nodded, but he sounded unconvinced. "How about Luis? Keira was looking into your parents' past, and she thought he could help her. Then the guy didn't want his picture taken. Now he's avoiding the cops. His dad is covering for something..." Marcus looked at me pointedly.

"You think Luis is a spy."

"*Sí.* Either that or a criminal working with Craig. Either way, I don't think he's someone we should be with alone."

"He's a link to Keira." I took a bite of my sandwich, aggressively chewing. "I need to know what he knows."

"Your sister wanted to know what he knew as well," Marcus pointed out. "Look what happened to her."

I gritted my teeth at his tone, like he thought Keira brought this on herself, like she asked to be violently kidnapped. I was pretty sure if it were his parents being accused of treachery and his brother who was missing, he wouldn't be so cavalier.

I took another scalding gulp of cappuccino, my throat tight. "Look, you don't have to come with me. I never asked you to be here."

"You want me to leave?" He sounded offended.

"That's up to you."

"I want to help you, it's just that when we came here, we thought we were talking to a little old man. Now, the stuff he said about your parents—"

"I know what he said." My hands shot up in frustration,

my shoulders pushed to my ears. "I know what everybody said." I abruptly stood. "I need to use the bathroom."

"I'm not trying to upset you..." Marcus started to explain, rising to meet me, his eyes apologetic, wounded, but I grabbed my messenger bag from the floor and marched away. I didn't come all the way to Italy to go home without answers. Salvatore said he would find Luis. Maybe I should just go back to the hotel and wait.

I spotted a sign reading *Il Bagno* in delicate cursive script. I veered toward it, entering a narrow hallway, lit by a glass door anchoring the far end. I didn't need to pee. I just needed a moment alone to think, free from opinions. Marcus didn't see our tub, he didn't dip his hands into that burning watery water, he didn't frantically search for his sibling's body. If he had, he wouldn't turn around and go home, because he'd understand that I didn't have a home without Keira.

I stepped toward a painting of a semi-naked Italian woman lounging in a bathtub, and as I was about to enter, I stopped short. Something caught my eye—a subtle movement, a change in light.

I pivoted toward the shop's rear exit and saw a figure passing by, a profile of a man—short, stocky, olive skin, with shoulders that spent hours lifting dumbbells and eyes that were all too familiar.

Luis Basso.

I darted toward the back door, swinging it wildly as it opened onto an alley and slammed against a stone wall. My head whipped around, split ends smacking my cheeks, my eyes searching for Luis. Not a shadow shifted. I sprinted in the direction I had seen the man walking, my laptop bag flapping against my rear. A rat scurried past a coffee-grind-infested dumpster and I jolted, then I carefully turned onto a narrow street. There wasn't a single pedestrian. I searched for flashing brake lights, listened for footsteps, stared at doorways. Nothing. It was like he'd disappeared—or I'd imagined him.

My shoulders sank. I trudged back into the alley, my feet heavy. Was I so desperate to find my sister that I was hallucinating in the middle of Tuscany? My Converse scuffed the pavement as I neared the rank dumpster, steering clear of the rat. What was I going to tell Marcus? That I ran off after a shadow?

That was when I heard the screeching tires.

I looked down the alley, the opposite way I'd run, and caught a small white sedan puttering in a burst of diesel fuel below the dense blanket of gray wooly clouds. It squeaked to a halt, and the passenger door swung open, a guy's head leaning across the seat from the driver's side.

"Get in," he ordered.

It was Luis.

CHAPTER NINETEEN

I did as I was told. Potential kidnapper or not, Luis was the entire reason I'd come to Italy. Now, he was driving a car right in front of me. I couldn't *not* get in. So I plopped my messenger bag on the passenger seat floor and willingly let him take me to a second location—Oprah would be so disappointed I didn't heed her warnings.

He spun through Cortona's maze of streets, under stone archways and past ancient facades. "How did you find me? Were you following me? What's going on?" I asked.

He didn't say a word as we sped out of the town limits and climbed the steep Cortona mountain. There was nothing but miles of deserted woods. Not another car passed. Still, I knew where we were going. I recognized the sharp cliff, the lack of a guardrail. It was the lookout spot where he'd brought Keira and me years ago, when my family had come to visit, when I still thought my parents were innocently buying furniture.

"Have you seen my sister? Craig? What do you know?"

His mouth stayed pressed in a hard line.

This was beyond reckless. He could have a gun. He

could have lots of guns. If he was a spy, or a criminal, he could have a weapon of mass destruction in the trunk.

I gripped the seat belt across my chest, my eyes flicking between him and the woods. *"I don't think he's someone we should be with alone."* Marcus's words echoed in my head. I should have called for help. I should have not gotten into the car until I told Marcus where I was going. Now the only person who could potentially save me was sitting in a café casually sipping espresso thinking I was having some serious intestinal issues in the bathroom.

Luis pulled onto the edge of the familiar lookout. An emerald valley spread wide with lush vineyard grapes twining in neat rows before small farms with burnt-orange shingled roofs and churches with green copper domes and pointed spires.

If it came to it, it would be a pretty place to die.

I flung open my car door and leaped onto the gravel path; only a few feet separated me from the edge of a cliff you could hang glide from. I maneuvered toward the dented trunk, leaving a solid barrier between us.

"Did you know I was at the coffee shop? Where is my sister? What happened? Say something!" I shouted, my eyes scanning the road, knowing the likelihood of another car passing was about equal to seeing a meteor propel toward the Earth.

"I'm not going to hurt you." He actually sounded annoyed by my questions as he leaned casually against the driver's side of his filthy white car. "I brought you here so we could talk."

"Why couldn't we talk at the coffee shop? I'm pretty sure that's why they were invented."

"Too many people listening."

"Marcus and I were the only ones there."

"That's one person too many."

"Did your father tell you I was here?"

"He told me you were coming to Cortona the moment you hung up the phone in Boston."

"So you were following me?"

"Does that surprise you?" He said it like I was stupid.

My jaw clenched as I glanced through the passenger window. My laptop bag was resting on the floor, my cell phone tucked inside. If Luis was as bad as we feared, if he whipped out a gun, I couldn't even call for help. Maybe I *was* stupid.

I tried to calm my voice, to sound tough. "I just want to ask you about my sister."

"Obviously." He glared back.

"I know you were with her at McFadden's Pub. I have a picture of you, her, and Craig."

He grunted in annoyance. "I figured someone would recover that eventually."

"So why were you with her?"

"I didn't take your sister, if that's what you think. I ran into her that *one* night at Boston General. I was in town on business."

"At the hospital?"

"I needed to get a few stitches taken care of."

"Stitches after a business meeting?" I cocked my head, suspicious.

"You'd be surprised." His dark eyes smirked in time with his lips, as if confirming he wasn't in a legitimate line of work. "It was back in May, that stupid Mexican holiday. Keira was drunk, and blabbing on and on about finding out who your parents *really* were, what they *really* did, slamming me with questions, talking about the CIA."

"Why was she telling any of this to *you*?" The betrayal sank in my gut like an anchor. She never said anything to me, and they were *our* parents.

"She thought I could help, and I needed a favor. I asked her to keep me out of the hospital's medical records." He flexed the hulking muscles of his right arm, almost reflexively, as if that was where he'd been injured. "She said she could get fired, and I told her I'd make it worth her while. I offered her money, but that's not what she wanted. She was looking for information."

"Why did she think you had it? Have you been keeping in touch with her all these years?"

"Of course not." He shook his head like it was a stupid question. "As soon as I recognized her, I tried to pay her cash to stitch my wound herself, but she said no. So I gave her a fake passport for the records, and after that, she was convinced I was some oracle who could tell her everything she ever wanted to know."

"Are you? Do you know something about my parents?" I asked.

"Let's just say your parents and I were in the same line of work."

"Which is what, exactly? Are you saying my parents were spies? Is Craig a spy? Are you? Is my mailman? Am I surrounded by 007s?" I knotted my fingers in my hair, tugging hard as I glanced at the darkening clouds overhead, wishing they would just let go and rain. I needed to wash this whole mess off me. I couldn't believe this was true. Is being a spy like being in *Fight Club*—the one rule is you never talk about being a spy? If so, they were all fantastic rule followers.

"Intelligence is a very lucrative business. It casts a wide net and employs more people than you think. As for Craig, I don't know him. I met him only that one time at the bar, and I figured he was some guy Keira was screwing. Obviously, I was wrong."

"No kidding," I snapped. I loved how he was so comfortable insulting my presumed-dead sister; it made me think of my own jabs, all the times I judged her. I hated her boyfriends. Did I sound just as bad? "You know what, forget my parents. Let's talk about Keira." I tried to refocus my brain on what was really important, right here, right now. My parents were another distraction. "What about the photo that Seamus took? If it was all innocent, why did you freak out?"

"Like I said, my line of work is complicated, and it's best to be camera shy. Besides, Keira was drunk and talking about your parents in front of anyone who would listen. She was acting like I was some James Bond character come to life, which is not only dangerous but honestly made me embarrassed to be seen with her. You really think I want photos on Instagram?" Luis scoffed as he walked toward me. He was only about an inch taller than me, but he had the body of a guy who grunts lifting weights at the gym.

"So you're saying it was just a one-time run-in? You saw Keira at the hospital and had drinks with her that one night? If so, and you had nothing to do with what happened to her, why not come forward with what you know about Craig?"

"I realize you can't possibly comprehend the scope of what I do for a living, what your parents did, but trust me when I say the cops and I don't share intel." The condescension in his voice was thicker than his Italian accent.

"Great. So Keira goes missing, and you have information, but you don't say anything because you don't like cops?" I was so frustrated I could hit him. I *wanted* to hit him.

He sighed in annoyance. "After your sister made the news, I learned that she wasn't just Googling your parents, she was trying to run a DNA test. She found some pathetic

CIA tech so desperate for a hookup, he told her that he'd run the labs, and that if Mommy and Daddy really were spies, then their DNA would be in the system. The kid was about as dumb as she was."

My jaw tightened at the way he constantly degraded my sister. Only I was afraid that if I defended her, he'd stop talking altogether. So far, he was the only person who knew anything about what Keira was up to before she disappeared. "What did the test reveal?" I asked, working hard to keep my voice level.

"Nothing." He shrugged as if it were obvious. "No one is going to let your parents' DNA turn up in a government database. You have to remember, decades ago when your parents were running around involved in these cases, DNA wasn't widely used. So as long as they were careful, there wasn't much that could link back to them or suggest any covert interference. But that doesn't mean evidence isn't sitting in labs somewhere. Cold cases have a way of coming back to life, new scientific tests are applied, and your parents' DNA would connect them to high-profile cases from around the world. There would be repercussions globally, historically. And believe me, there are a lot of people who had a reason to stop that from happening."

I sank against the grimy car. Keira's attempt to run an unauthorized DNA test caused this whole nightmare? Why didn't she tell me what she was doing? And why was this so important to her? It was just a lab test. *Wait. It was just a lab test!*

"Why couldn't you cancel the lab work?" I blurted as my mind flipped through scenarios. "You don't kill some-one, or kidnap someone, over lab results. You're spies—you could forge them or steal them. Why would someone hurt Keira over this?"

His gaze turned resolute, as if he were about to state a simple fact widely accepted. "Because your parents had a lot of enemies."

"What did they *do* exactly?"

"Are you sure you want to know?" His grin was cocky, like he enjoyed watching me squirm for each kernel of information he tossed my way. My chest filled with rage— at him, at Keira, and especially at my parents. This was *their* fault. Our parents did this to us. Every lie they told, every espionage act they committed, brought us here. So I was damn sure going to hear exactly what it was they did.

"Tell me."

"Well, I guess my dad already opened his mouth. So…" He shrugged, like just this once he'd let me into their secret club. "You saw the Aldo Moro photo, right?"

I nodded aggressively, growing impatient.

"That image was taken by a local photographer. It's incredibly famous. It ran in every paper, all over the world. Only the original that my dad showed you appeared in our local paper for a single day. After that, the photo was manipulated to remove your parents. *That's* what the rest of the world saw."

"So it was Photoshopped?"

"Well, Photoshop didn't exist then, but yes. Where your parents were standing was replaced with a wall of posters. Their involvement in the case was deleted." His voice was so flat, he might as well have been dissecting the Red Sox play-off chances. "This is in large part due to my Uncle Angelo. He hid your parents above our family store, he paid off the local photographer, he distributed the altered photo on their behalf. All to save your parents' lives."

"So they owed him."

"A lot." His words were clipped.

"And Keira's DNA test would somehow expose this?" I was trying to understand.

"You're not getting it." Luis ran his hand over his slick black hair. "The Aldo Moro case is just *one* example. Your parents were the first on the scene when that car pulled up with a dead prime minister. Their DNA is everywhere, yet their entire involvement as witnesses was covered up. Every copy of the Cortona newspaper that ran the original image was destroyed to protect them. If someone linked their DNA to Moro, it would raise questions about an assassination that's already riddled with conspiracy theories. And there are many more cases just like this."

"So you think Craig was working for some enemy of my parents? Someone who wanted to stop this test so much that they'd hurt Keira?"

Luis looked at me like I was finally catching on. "I've been digging into Craig. I think he might be tied to an underground criminal group based in Rome. That's why my father and I wanted you to come here."

"You think Craig's in Rome? Like, *Italy*? So Keira could be *here*?" My heart leaped to my throat. I pushed off the car and rushed toward him.

"No. I think whoever hired Craig to stop that DNA test is based out of Rome. Like I said, my uncle was a cop there, and his fellow officers still feed me information. They're very *loyal*." He emphasized the last word. "And *we* take our bonds seriously."

A raindrop plopped from the sky, and I gazed at the dense charcoal clouds about to burst. My brain felt just as full, overflowing. "Earlier, you said you didn't *take* Keira." I looked at him, wiping another drip from my nose. "Do you think my sister was kidnapped? That she's alive?" My optimism was as palpable as the humidity.

"In my business, people are always worth more alive than dead."

I exhaled a gush of air from my belly as the raindrops finally tumbled, relief washing over me. I knew it was far from a confirmation, and it was coming from a guy who lied professionally, but still, I could breathe. The cool rain splattered my face. After months of the police, my friends, the social workers, all swearing my sister was dead, I now stood in front of someone who agreed with *me,* someone with access to actual information, someone who worked in intelligence.

My gaze snapped toward him. "Hold on, you said that my parents were spies, that they conducted missions that could have global ramifications to this day if their DNA turned up. If so, where is the CIA now? Where are the helicopters full of men in black suits with laser-beam-shooting wristwatches ready to take down anyone who goes after one of their kids?"

"It's not like that."

"Why not?" I flung my hand, smacking the car. "Do your bosses know what's going on? Keira can't just be out there somewhere, being tortured because of work my parents did, and no one gives a shit? What's wrong with you people? What about the FBI? They think my parents were enemies of the state! If they weren't, then tell them the truth, have *them* look for her—"

"We don't deal with the FBI…"

"So make an exception!" I shouted, and the farmers working the vineyards below could probably hear me through the crackling thunder.

Luis pulled his keys from his pocket, looking officially annoyed. "I've said all I'm going to say." He strutted toward the driver's side.

"Are you nuts? You can't leave!" I reached for his arm, but he brushed me off like a mosquito. "You said you were looking into my sister's case, that whoever hired Craig is working in Rome. Do you have a name?"

"I don't have anything more to share right now."

"But your father practically insisted I come to Italy. *You* wanted me here, and I'm here. So help me find her."

"I am helping you. Go to Rome." He kept walking, and I stumbled behind, desperation tripping my every step.

"Who do I talk to in Rome? Where? Please! I'm sorry I didn't realize how close you were to my family. I get it now."

He never broke a stride, and I suddenly spied my laptop through the rain-splattered passenger window. "Wait! I have to get my bag!" I yelped, wiping my sopping bangs from my eyes. It was a lame stall tactic, but it was better than nothing.

He halted, pausing with his hand on the driver's side handle. He didn't look at me, but he didn't object, either, so I darted toward the passenger side and flung open the door. I had to keep him talking. I reached onto the crumb-riddled floor, my arm dripping as I scooped up my bag, its olive-green strap swinging loosely, the silver buckle clanging against another piece of metal. It caught my eye—a tiny piece of gold.

For some reason, I reached for it. I wasn't sure why; this wasn't my car. Whatever was lost on that dirty tan floor mat had nothing to do with me.

Only, it did.

I stretched my arm until my fingers touched the delicate piece of jewelry, and I slowly lifted a feminine yellow gold ring. It was vintage, 1980s. A *K* initial ring with a white topaz stone in the top cursive loop of the *K*.

It was purchased from eBay. It was Keira's birthstone. It was her twenty-first birthday present. From me.

CHAPTER TWENTY

I couldn't breathe. I pulled at the V neck of my stormy gray T-shirt like I'd opened the door to a sealed black car in Miami, and the heat was slapping my face. I gulped for oxygen.

Keira never took off this ring. It couldn't *come* off. It had gotten too small for her knuckle, so she'd left it on her middle finger for more than two years. She showered with it, slept with it, swam with it. I loved that she wore it.

Now, here it sat. In Luis's car. In Italy.

Only before I could shove the evidence into my pocket, Luis opened his door and glared across the seats at the jewelry in my hand like it might combust. "What do you have there?" His eyes were deadly.

"Nothing," I croaked, my fingers wrapping around the ring.

"Give it to me." He glowered at me through the car, both of us frozen like we were waiting for the other to make the next move. "Open. Your. Hand."

I squeezed my fist tighter. "Where did you get this?"

"It's mine."

"No. It's Keira's. Why do you have it?"

"I told you we hung out. The ring fell off, and I picked it up. I was keeping it for her in case we found her." He rose from the car and closed his door, then slowly inched his way toward me through a deluge of country rain.

I was standing on the edge of a cliff.

I rose gingerly and watched him pass the car's hood; he was only a few feet away. "It fell off her finger?" I confirmed.

"Yeah, I don't think she even realized she lost it." He shook his head, raindrops splattering.

I gripped the car door like a shield, my vision blurred by rain. "That's impossible. This ring couldn't come off. It's too small."

Luis sprang. His fingers reached through the stormy air for my wrist as I swung the car door into his gut. He wheezed, hunching over, and I moved toward the trunk, my sneakers perilously skidding on the edge. Finally, I reached the rear of the car, away from the cliff, and scanned my surroundings. There was nowhere to go. A life-threatening drop loomed on one side, wooded nothingness on the other, and a deserted road in between.

I looked at the gold ring in my palm, the letter *K* now indented into my wet pink skin. Luis's footsteps cut through the clattering drops as I maneuvered away from him, imagining all the sharp edges my body could crash against if I fell to the farmland below.

"That's how you're gonna play it? Ring around the rosie?" Luis mocked. "Just give me the ring."

"What did you do to my sister?" I wanted to sound strong, but my voice cracked with fear—for myself or my sister, I wasn't sure. "Was everything you said bullshit?"

"Actually, no. Everything I said was the truth—at least, it was from Keira's point of view. If you asked her, it was how everything in Boston happened, right up until we took her. She was just too gullible to see it coming."

He took her. He really took her.

I pictured Keira trapped in Luis's car, in the same passenger seat where I'd been sitting, a gun pointed at her head, maybe Craig in the back seat, tears streaking her face, wounds all over her body. "Where is she? Is she still alive? Tell me!"

Luis stopped, snorting as if exasperated by my endless questions. Then he sighed, shaking his soaked hair. "Well, I guess we're on to Plan B. So yes, your sister was alive and in Italy the last time I saw her."

"Are you serious?" My breathing accelerated, adrenaline coursing through me. *Keira was in Italy? Keira is* alive! I could have jumped off the cliff in a round of summersaults. I felt like Superwoman. "Where is she? Is she okay?"

"I have no idea. I just transported her here." We were now both standing near the rear of the car, only the trunk separating us.

"How?"

"Private plane, fake passport, lots of sedatives. It's one of my specialties." He puffed his damp chest, seemingly proud, and I wanted to punch him. Actually, I wanted to do a lot worse than that. "Once I threatened *your* life, she was pretty compliant. It's Craig you have to thank for the tub."

"But...I-I thought you were CIA," I sputtered, my mind spinning. "Why would the U.S. government want to kidnap my sister?"

"I never said I was CIA. I said I was in the same business as your parents." His voice took on the quality of a cartoon villain, and I half expected a flock of bats to fly out of a nearby cave.

"What does that mean? I thought you were spies," I asked in confusion, squinting through the unrelenting rain.

Then it hit me—I didn't care. Not really. Not about *them*. My parents were dead. Buried. Haunting us from the grave. They lied to us. They cost my sister everything from her medical career to her freedom. *She* was the one I needed to think about. *She* deserved my loyalty, my support, even if it took me too long to realize it. "You know what, forget my parents. Just tell me where my sister is."

"Oh, sure, no problem." He rolled his eyes, his right hand skimming the waist of his jeans, touching something hidden beneath the loose faded folds of his drenched button-down shirt. A gun. He probably had a gun.

Only I wasn't scared. The observation oddly seemed to make my mind still, as if I were taking a final exam I'd prepared for all my life. I'd watched my parents in times of stress, moments of anger, and they never lost their tempers, they never let their emotions win. At once, all the panic left my body, and I was strangely confident as I steadied my voice to face him. "Luis, I won't press charges. I promise. I won't tell anyone you're involved. People do crazy things all the time. Just tell me where she is, and this will all be over."

He squinted through the rain, looking almost insulted that I thought it would be that easy.

"Can you at least tell me why you took her? What do you want? Maybe *I* can help you. Is that why you wanted me in Italy?"

"Ah, the big 'why.' *Why* did I drag you into this? *Why* Keira? What's in it for *me*?" His dark eyes hardened, his deep whisper more frightening than a scream. "How about revenge for the uncle your parents had killed."

I jolted. "Your uncle?" My voice sounded as baffled as my face must've looked.

"Yes. My Uncle Angelo," he continued, "the dedicated police officer who worked with your parents for *decades*, who protected them, assisted them, and treated them like family. Only he obviously meant nothing to your parents. None of us did. The first time a mission went south, they bailed on him. They saved themselves and left my uncle to die alone in a gutter."

"Luis, I don't know anything about that." I shook my head, rain spraying from my bangs.

"Of course you don't! Because your parents treated you two like imbeciles. Doesn't that bother you? They lied to you. They have no loyalty, not for their friends and certainly not for their family. They'd betray anyone. You should hate them. I do." He started walking toward me once again, his boots kicking through puddles as I stood frozen, ignoring every neuron in my brain that told me to run. What good would it do? There was nowhere to go. If he had a gun, he clearly knew how to use it.

"We didn't do anything to you," I stated as I fingered the gold ring in my palm like a rosary, praying for divine intervention—this from a girl who'd been cursing God since the day her family died.

"Your parents did enough. And if I had my way, your sister would have died in that bathtub." Rage filled his eyes.

"So you were there all along? Not just that night at the bar? You were working with Craig from the beginning?" I squeezed the ring tighter, and he paused, his jaw twitching.

"No, what I said was true. I hung out with Keira only that one night. I was a bit busy with...*other matters.*" His smile was smug, like he enjoyed being obtuse. "Craig was running point on Keira, and I handled cleanup. Didn't you wonder why there wasn't a drop of blood in the entire rest of your flat?"

Actually, I did. I'd pointed it out to the police, and it led to the ruling of "foul play," though it never mattered. They still thought that she was dead and that the case was cold.

"That's just it. Keira lost so much blood, the medical examiner ruled it a homicide. Is she really okay?" I held my breath.

Luis shifted toward me, his eyes gleefully full of answers. "Your sister was a nurse. She donated blood. It wasn't too hard to covertly bank her donations for a private collection to be used later."

"But she didn't give blood *that* often. How long have you been planning this?"

"A lot longer than Cinco de Mayo." He cocked his brow. "You'd be amazed at how many contingency plans we have in place."

I wasn't sure I wanted to know what that meant, for either of us. So I focused on the positive—Keira was alive, the blood wasn't from a wound, and she was possibly in Italy. "What about the DNA test? The 'person' who hired Craig in Rome? Did you make up all of that?"

"No, like I said, the DNA test is real. Your sister tried to run it, and that's what drew our attention. *She* started this, in case you're wondering. We were sent to Boston to stop her stupid investigation, to try to convince her your parents were engineers and stop her from inadvertently exposing decades' worth of covert ops. But when that didn't work, I was sent to the lab to intercept the results, only things went sideways. We had to change plans."

"And those plans included kidnapping my sister?"

Luis inched closer, standing behind the latch of the trunk while I stood a few feet away beside the left rear tire, rain pounding off the metal. We both knew I couldn't out-sprint a bullet. There were no cars to help me. Given how he was freely spewing answers, I was betting he didn't expect me to be alive long enough to relay them. My only shot of getting out of here was somehow getting that gun.

"You should be grateful. The original plan wasn't a kidnapping. We were hired to leave her body, make it look like a drunken slip in the shower. Accidents in the bathroom happen all the time. *Your sister should be dead*."

Needles pierced the lining of my throat as I absorbed his words. They were familiar stabs, the same ones I felt when I spoke to police, went to that memorial, lay on my bed. Only this time I pictured Keira's casket, not empty, but housing her body. I clenched the ring like a talisman. "But why? Keira didn't learn anything. You said so yourself."

"Just be happy Craig changed things at the spur of the moment. Honestly, I wish I could say more, because I'd love to see your face when you realize the type of people your parents really were. But know that this thing is *huge*, and we're willing to take it pretty damn far, which does not bode well for either of you."

They could still kill her, kill both of us. Who knows what they'd done to her already. I looked at his hand, still clutching a hidden gun in his sopping wet jeans. "What do you want? Because I'll do it. We both will. Let me talk to your boss and work something out in exchange for Keira."

"Sure, let me give you his cell." He smirked sardonically.

"Look, I realize you think my parents did something horrible to your uncle, and maybe they did. Who the hell knows? But it has nothing to do with *us*. Luis, you have brothers. You know what I'm going through." I tried to appeal to his humanity, but his pupils were ominous pits. So I switched tactics, my mind growing sharper as I considered the facts. "Fine. You took Keira, this is all part of some big master plan. Well, I'm guessing it's not working, right? You've had her for *months*, and now you're dragging *me* into it. Your father practically dared me to come here, so I think somebody wants something from *me,* specifically. Let's get down to it. What do you want? Tell me what it's gonna take to get Keira back."

"Man, I *so* wish I could tell you!" He pumped his head, drops splashing as his eyes sparked to life, a toothy smile on his face like he was keeping the greatest secret in the world. It was the most excitement I'd seen from him all day, and I wanted to hurl his body off the cliff and watch it hit every rock. I'd never hated anyone more in my life—except maybe Craig the Psycho. I had a feeling the two of them would be tag-teaming my nightmares from now on.

Luis stepped toward me, his shoes splashing puddles on mine as he stood close enough to touch. "All I can say is you need to go to Rome. Your sister was getting help from someone. She's not smart enough to come across all the information she had on her own, and we think the person helping her is in Rome."

I gritted my teeth. Keira was *smart enough* to suspect my parents were spies while I lived obliviously. She was *smart enough* to leave her ring in a car for someone to find, for *me* to find. "If you think the guy's in Rome, then go confront him yourself."

"He won't talk to us, and believe me, I'd love nothing more than to drag you there by your hair. But the higher-ups are convinced he'll be more receptive to you. Alone."

"Why? Who is it?"

"You'll figure it out."

"I'm just supposed to guess who my sister was talking to?" As far as I knew, Keira wasn't friends with anyone in Italy. Though I was also unaware that she was dating a psycho and talking to Luis, so I probably wasn't the most informed on her actions. I was the worst sister in the world. "You know, this is the third time you've brought up Rome."

Luis's eye twitched, and he swiped at it through the rain. First he said he wanted me to go to Rome to see who Craig was working for; then he said my parents were responsible for his uncle's death, a Roman cop; now he was insisting there was someone there feeding my sister information.

"There's a trap, isn't there? You've got something planned? What's in Rome, Luis?"

"You'll have to find out. But can you think of another way to find Keira?"

They knew I wouldn't leave my sister in captivity while I sat around hoping for the best. This setup practically had GPS coordinates and a warning label, and they correctly knew I'd still walk into it. "I could call the cops," I blurted, my brain spinning through solutions. "Keira's alive. You just admitted it. I'll send a SWAT team to Rome to look for her."

He rolled his eyes. "Sure. Which law enforcement agency would you like to call? The Italian police who are still loyal to my uncle, the one your parents left for dead; the FBI who thinks your parents were terrorists; the Boston police who want you on the first flight home; or the CIA who is willfully ignoring this entire situation?" He tilted his head like he was speaking to a toddler. "Please, tell me, because we have agents working in every branch. I'll have someone give you a ring. It'll save you some trouble."

My body felt like a hot air balloon on descent, all the oxygen being let out as it plummeted to Earth, or in my case, reality. How could I fight an entire corrupt global system? I was a teenager. But how could I not try? Doing what they say might be the only chance my sister has.

"Is Keira even in Rome?" I asked, sounding hopeless.

"Maybe." He pumped his thick brows, amused by my reaction.

"Is she okay?"

"She was last I saw her." Then a new vicious glint entered his eyes. "But some of my colleagues are a little...*lonely*. And she's such a pretty girl—"

I swung. It was a reflex—one second I was feeling desperate, the next I was fighting a professional spy. I rushed at him, my right elbow connecting with his jaw and a splatter of rain. He took the hit with barely a jolt. I threw another quick punch with my fist, but he smiled like he expected my choreography, grabbing my arm and twisting it behind my back. He shoved my chest aggressively against the hood, rain cascading down my cheek as he bent me over, yanking my arm higher, pain ripping through my shoulder, the joint threatening to dislodge. White light filled my eyes as my free hand reached out, stretching for the windshield, slipping aimlessly as raindrops fell harder. I grabbed a wiper blade with my clamoring fingers, yanked it free and thrust it backward toward his head, stabbing him in the throat.

He let go.

I spun around. "What have you done to her?" I shouted, rolling my sore shoulder as his black eyes glared, seemingly entertained. He stepped toward me, and I jumped, the heel of my sneaker connecting with his chin in a massive uppercut. Then I watched as he spat blood, a tiny tooth fragment plinking into a puddle below.

"Not bad, little Phoenix," he growled, wiping his mouth and almost sounding impressed. "Your sister was too scared to break a nail."

Then he charged.

In all my years of martial arts training, I'd never been in a real fight—not outside of a mirrored room with an audience and a regimented scoring system. I doubted Luis

Basso was the first person I wanted to test my skills on. At best he was a spy, at worst he was an assassin. But I wasn't being given a choice in partners, and we weren't sparring.

He threw a punch at my head, and I blocked it, pivoting sideways and jamming an elbow into his kidney. Not a wince came from his lips. Then he turned with such force it was clear he hadn't been trying before, like I'd just now pissed him off and he was done playing *Karate Kid*.

His hand clenched my throat like a vise, squeezing all air as he slammed the back of my head into the hood of the car. My vision blurred, rain speckling my eyes as pain shot from my skull all the way to my toes. Then he hoisted my body into the air like a cheap plastic doll from a drugstore and slammed me onto the road by my throat, a deep puddle splashing, soaking my hair.

This was it. I'd lost. My life, my sister, everything.

I prepared to die. My head swelled with dizzying heat, ready to explode, as thunder roared overhead.

Then I heard the tires.

CHAPTER TWENTY-ONE

I might have passed out. I could remember floating, letting go, then suddenly I was jolted back to consciousness by the feel of a knife on my right biceps. The pain was sharp, but it returned the air to my lungs.

I breathed. Coughing, hacking, gulping at the rain-clogged air, my fingers clawing at my slick throat.

Then I heard the screaming male voices. *"Stop... Get away... I already called the police!"* The voices sounded far off in the distance, but when I fluttered my eyes, I saw Marcus looming down, directly above me. *"Are you all right?"* His words sounded warped. Was it the rain? My ears?

He lifted me to my feet. *"Can you stand?"*

My legs straightened underneath me. Apparently, I could.

Luis. Where was Luis? My head darted around, and a nausea-inspiring bout of wooziness took over. I clutched Marcus's shoulder to remain steady and saw the blood pouring down my upper arm. Then I spied Luis standing calmly by the passenger side of his car; a pocketknife dripping crimson hung by his leg. He'd cut me.

I glanced at my wound; it didn't look deep. Marcus had saved me. How?

"A little something to remember me by." Luis nodded to my bleeding gash, grinning like he'd had a blast on a roller coaster—despite a missing tooth. "See you in Rome."

Then he winked.

I blinked, trying to think of what to say, trying to process what had happened, but Marcus was already shoving me toward a motorbike idling a few feet away. "Can you hang on?" he asked as he threw me onto the padded leather seat, hopping in front and revving the engine. It didn't seem like he was waiting to find out.

I reached my hands around his sopping waist, noticing for the first time that my messenger bag was slung around his chest. He must have grabbed it from the ground. *Keira's ring.* My eyes futilely searched the ground for the tiny gold bit of my sister, but I'd lost it. I'd almost lost my life.

Marcus peeled off, the air reeking of rubber as tires kicked up a cloud of wet gravel. I looked back expecting to see Luis's car in pursuit, threatening to ram us off the cliff, only as I peered through a haze of grit and raindrops, warm blood streaking my arm, through my fingers, I caught Luis standing motionless beside his grimy car. A gun was pointed at our heads, a smile on his face, rain dripping from his features.

But he didn't fire. He let us get away.

We raced down the mountain through the pelting rain in a manner almost as frightening as my battle with an assassin. I kept looking back, searching for headlights, but we were alone on the road. Luis never followed.

We returned the bike to where Marcus had "found" it

(its rightful owner unaware), and ran back to the hotel. The bleeding on my arm had begun to slow as we threw our stuff into suitcases (most of which we hadn't unpacked). Then we changed into dry clothes, and Marcus washed my wound, applying Band-Aids as I told him what had happened. Apparently, he'd watched as Luis's white car darted past the café's plate-glass windows. Its speed drew his attention, and when I didn't return from the bathroom, he went searching. This led to him "borrowing" the motorbike and tracking our whereabouts up the mountain via two unsuspecting tourists who'd witnessed the speeding car. When he'd pulled up, Luis was strangling me with one hand and carving me with his other. Marcus had saved my life.

"Why did he let us get away? He had a gun. He could have killed us." My fingers lightly feathered my sore windpipe as Marcus hauled our bags into the first taxi we saw. We were getting out of town. Immediately.

"I have no idea. But he didn't challenge me at all. He backed off as soon as I showed up."

"It makes no sense."

"Let's not question miracles." Marcus squeezed beside me in the taxi's back seat. "What happened up there?" he asked softly, his eyes concerned as he rested a comforting hand on my leg.

I shifted away, abruptly yanking my phone from the messenger bag on the car's dirty floor. "Omigod, I have to call Charlotte." I punched in her digits as I gave Marcus a "she's not going to believe this" look.

"Keira's alive!" I shouted as soon as she answered, not waiting for hello. "*She's alive! Really, alive!*"

"What?" Charlotte gasped on the other end. Marcus looked at me, breaking into a dimpled smile as we both absorbed the joy pulsing through the phone line.

I blurted the story, from Luis's words, to the DNA test, to Keira's ring, to Rome. Only I left out the blood match. Charlotte couldn't do anything to change what happened on the top of that mountain, so why worry her from across an ocean?

"Holy shit!" Charlotte yelped when I finished the recap. "*She's alive…*" I could hear her soaking it in, basking in the glory of those two little words. "Anastasia, I'm so sorry. I should've believed you. I mean, I did believe you, deep down. I was just scared to admit it, you know? Scared to get my hopes up. I was trying to be realistic, listen to the cops… *I can't believe it!*"

"I know." I rested my head on the back of the taxi's leather seat and winced. I'd forgotten about getting my skull crushed against a car. From the purple handprint on my throat to the two-inch slice in my arm, my head injury seemed like a paper cut. Until I touched it.

"*You okay?*" Marcus mouthed, clearly worried as he saw my reaction.

I nodded, trying to shrug it off. Because I was okay. I was alive. And so was my sister. That made any battle wound not only worth it but insignificant.

We approached the rural train station with one lonely track and only a handful of people occupying the outdoor platform. The rain had stopped.

"Anastasia, you're not seriously thinking of going to Rome, are you?" Charlotte asked.

"What choice do I have? They said it was the only way to find Keira."

"Of course they said that. It's a setup. The guys practically bought you a ticket."

I thought of Luis's final words, "*See you in Rome,*"

followed by a not-so-subtle wink. "I know. But I can't exactly go back to Boston. Not now. Not when I *know* that they brought Keira to Italy." I stepped out of the taxi and walked toward the trunk where Marcus was already grabbing my bags, afraid I was too fragile to lift them. He was probably right. "They think that Keira was communicating with someone in Rome, and that this person would only be willing to talk to me. Though I have no idea who they mean."

"Well, I think *I* do," Charlotte said, sounding reluctant to add to the turmoil. "You're not the only one with news."

"What?" We walked into the station, and I stared at the departures board. Rome was the next train out.

"That photo you texted of Aldo Moro, Luis is right, it's all over the internet, and your parents aren't in it." I could hear her tapping on her laptop, fingers speeding. "But they're not the only ones who are missing. If you compare the pictures side by side, you'll notice there are two additional figures deleted from the crowd. So I sent it to a hacker friend in Norway. He has access to facial recognition software with an international database. It's sick…" She sounded jealous. "Anyway, he scanned the two faces. And you're not gonna believe this, but one of the men, standing not three feet from your parents, is the deputy director of the CIA. I mean, he wasn't the deputy director *then*. He's only, like, twenty in the photo, but still. He eventually grew up to run the CIA."

I stopped at a bench and shoved a balled wad of cash at Marcus. I was too tired to stand in line. He stepped to the ticket window as I sat. "Luis said he and my parents didn't work for the CIA. I have no idea who they actually worked for, but he claimed that if I called Langley, he'd have a double agent intercept it. Maybe it's this guy."

"I have no idea, but he's in the photo. That can't be a coincidence."

I sank against the back of the wooden bench. As much as I wanted to cling to the hope that my parents weren't evil country-betraying murderers, I was nearly strangled to death by their godson, an admitted spy. If their close family friends were psychopathic killers, it didn't bode well for them being on the side of the right and just. Who knew what type of espionage they were involved in or how high this madness went? Maybe the director of the CIA was in on it? Maybe the president? The pope?

My head hurt.

"That's not all," Charlotte continued. "The other man in the photo is all over the internet, too. He's a former *chemical engineer*," she emphasized the words. "Now he's a published author and a current professor at the *Sapienza Universita di Roma*."

"Rome," I repeated, the word sinking in.

"His name's Allen Cross. He's listed as faculty. I'm gonna try to see if Keira ever contacted him but, given everything we've learned, I'd bet my laptop this guy's a spy." I heard her crack a soda can and take a gulp. "This is who they want you to meet in Rome. I'm sure of it. They practically gift wrapped this picture for us. They knew we'd figure it out."

I stared at the cypress trees in the farmland across from the station, everything so serene it made the situation more surreal. "Allen Cross," I repeated. "The name doesn't sound familiar. Luis said the guy would be 'more receptive' to me, like I knew him."

"Study the picture. Maybe it'll jog your memory."

I rubbed the throbbing lump on my head. I doubted anything would make sense in my brain right now, but I couldn't say that to Charlotte without divulging the fight, which she really didn't need to know about. "Maybe when I see him, it'll click."

"When you *see* him!" Charlotte snapped. "You can't go there alone. Wait till I get there. I'm hopping a flight tomorrow."

"You don't have to do that. I have Marcus."

"Unless Marcus has SEAL Team Six training you forgot to mention, I don't see what protection he can offer."

"And you're so tough?"

"I'm legally responsible for your well-being. I have to be there."

"I'm not sure foster families are required to dive in front of bullets—"

"There were bullets?" she yelped, horrified.

"No! I'm kidding! Of course not," I lied, remembering how Marcus stopped a man with a knife and drove the getaway bike while a gun was pointed at our heads.

But he didn't shoot.

I was alone with Luis on top of an isolated mountain for a long time; he could have whipped out that gun at any time, but he didn't. If I'm to believe him, he didn't kill Keira, either. They changed their plans. Now they wanted me in Rome, and I had to assume they wanted me alive. Both of us alive. Otherwise, we'd both be dead already. Easily.

"Look, I'm calling Detective Dawkins. Screw Luis and his claims about crooked cops, we need help." Charlotte sounded determined.

"You're right," I admitted. For all I knew, Luis could have lied about having police connections to deter us from contacting them.

"And don't do anything until I get there. I'll text you my flight plan."

"I'll try," I said, though we both knew I wouldn't be able to sit in Rome waiting patiently for Charlotte's flight to land while Allen Cross was down the street. Every minute could cause Keira more pain. "She's alive." I sighed dreamily.

"She's alive." Charlotte reciprocated as if it were a standard good-bye.

Marcus plopped onto the bench beside me, two tickets in his hand. I could smell the stale sweat dried on his skin. He'd defended me against an armed attacker. He had no weapon, and he still got off that bike. He'd risked his life *for me*. "So, Rome?" He looked at me right then like he'd follow me anywhere, and for once, I believed him. A familiar flutter swept through my belly, and I shut my eyes, trying to force it away, but I was so tired.

Aches pulsed everywhere. Thankfully, the cut on my arm was shallow. It didn't need stitches. And my throat and head just needed time. Everything would heal eventually, but maybe next time I wouldn't be so lucky or, more accurately, *we* wouldn't be so lucky. Marcus risked a lot for me today. "Thank you," I said honestly. "For everything. You saved my life."

"You would have done the same. You *are* doing the same for your sister."

"Yeah, but she's my sister. I'm nothing to you."

He cupped my face and looked into my eyes. "You are *a lot* more than nothing." He emphasized the words.

I didn't pull away. I let his hands linger, feeling warm and comforted. It was a welcome sensation for once.

"You know, I've never been to Rome." His hands slid toward my shoulders then lightly drifted down my arms. "Maybe we can visit the Vatican or the Sistine Chapel while we're there." His tone turned teasing.

"Oh, sure. Then we can tour the Coliseum, see some Caravaggios…" I didn't take my eyes off his.

He reached for my hand, and I didn't pull away. I laced

my fingers with his.

"Or we can walk the Roman Forum." His dimples flashed.

I knew he was trying to distract me from the constant string of fears that plagued me since we'd left Luis. "*Your sister could be dead already. Luis is a professional liar. He wants you in Rome. They could have something horrible planned. These could be your last moments on Earth. You could be walking to your grave...*" But as I sat here with Marcus, our faces close, our fingers entwined, for a just a moment, the panicked voices lulled.

"It's gonna be okay." Marcus nudged closer.

"But what if it's not?" I stared into his eyes. "What do they want? Why do they want me chasing her?"

"Maybe we'll find out in Rome."

"You really want to go?" I asked, in awe of his commitment to two girls he barely knew.

"Yes. We're in this together."

I tried to read his face, studying him for some underlying motive, until suddenly, as if on autopilot, my hand reached up and touched his cheek, my finger lightly stroking the skin near his ear. He closed his eyes and leaned in to my palm. It was as if the adrenaline from earlier had heightened my senses; I could smell his skin, see his pores, feel his warmth. Slowly, my face inched closer, a heat growing between us. This pull I'd felt since the day we'd met, I was too tired to fight any more, too tired to overthink, too tired to push him away.

We could have died today.

These could be my last moments of life...

A train rumbled past in the opposite direction, and Marcus abruptly pressed his lips to mine, his hands cupping my cheeks. Pinpricks flooded my skin and washed away every ache and fear I had. I gave in. I knotted my fingers in his hair, kissing him back, forcing myself to focus only on his lips, our breath, his touch. He pulled me closer, and it was as if the buzz that was always between us had moved directly into my body. My breath stuttered at the sensation, and I suddenly realized how Keira could lose herself like this. I held him tighter, kissed him harder, until every painful throb in my body was forgotten. For once, I stopped fighting.

Until it was time to board our train.

Rome was waiting.

CHAPTER TWENTY-TWO

I spent the ride to Rome making travel arrangements with Urban's assistant. Currently, we had proof that three former "chemical engineers" were erased from a crime scene photo with a dead Italian prime minister: my two parents and some man named Allen Cross. I didn't know what that meant with regards to the Dresden Chemical Corporation, but the engineering connection seemed an uncanny coincidence. Still, I had to hope that Randolph Urban, my only pseudo family left on this planet, wasn't a pathological liar too, that he really did love me, that he wanted to help, and that he wasn't involved in my parents' alarming top-secret lives. I couldn't lose everyone.

And it wasn't like I could get far in Italy with fifty euros in my pocket.

So I accepted his offer to stay in a five-star hotel near the Spanish Steps. I even agreed to a "gelato date" with his granddaughter, Sophia. Apparently, she'd recently moved to the ancient city, and while I didn't have time for a social visit, she might be the only person alive who knew whether Grandpa Urban's generosity was based purely on compassion. The man raised her, after all; if she didn't have insight into him, who would?

We sped over cobblestones past rows of intricately carved sienna buildings with classical arched doorways and hunter green shutters. Dozens of Roman mopeds whizzed around our taxi like immersion therapy for a person with a fear of motorized vehicles. I scrunched my eyes in the back of the cab, my seat belt locked against me.

"You okay?" Marcus asked.

There was sweat on my brow. "Just tell me when we're at the hotel." A car honked as tires screeched beside us.

"You take on deadly spies, but you're afraid of traffic? *Interesante*."

The car slowed, and I gradually opened my eyes to see an ornate swirling fountain spraying water in front of a wide marble staircase, more than a hundred steps high, full of couples joined at the face and teens chugging wine. We sped alongside, then stopped in front of a massive, decoratively carved building that could double for a palace.

"Wow, Urban has good taste," I muttered as I tossed the driver our fare.

Marcus followed me into a gold-plated lobby befitting an heiress — glossy marble floors, rich gilded molding, and scarlet museum-quality drapes. If you added our ages together, we'd still be the youngest people in the hotel by a ridiculous margin.

"Checking in," I said in Italian. "Anastasia Phoenix."

The man behind the mahogany desk tapped his keyboard, eyes peering suspiciously as if expecting me to shoplift a vase from the lobby. After a few clicks, he held out the plastic key cards, almost begrudgingly, as if we didn't deserve to touch them. And it wasn't until we slogged over to the mirrored elevators that I understood his reluctance — we looked like extras in a late-night zombie flick. Our hair was matted from the motorbike ride down the side of a mountain, our eyes were bloodshot from a heaping dose of wind and fear, my arm was bloody and bandaged, my neck was bruised, and my shirt had a giant brown coffee stain from the two-hour train trip.

"We look hot," I joked as we entered the elevator, and Marcus snorted a laugh. We rode to our floor in silence, then thumped across the floral carpet to our adjacent rooms, pausing at our doors.

"So tomorrow morning, Allen Cross?" Marcus confirmed.

I nodded, not meeting his eyes, as an awkward pause fell between us. We'd kissed a lot at the train station, like *a lot,* then we spent the entire ride to Rome acting like it never happened. Instead, we focused on Keira, travel plans, and our date with the professor. Only every time our arms touched on the armrest, one of us jolted like we were hit with an electrical current.

That same buzz was building between us now as we stood in front of our hotel room doors, and it felt not only awkward but inappropriate. I had no right to feel good about anything, ever, until I found my sister. I had to focus.

"See you in the morning," I said abruptly.

"*Sí. Hasta leugo,*" he replied, but I'd already entered my room and was closing the door.

I needed time alone. I needed to think.

I fell asleep in my clothes.

I awoke the next morning to a text from Charlotte detailing her itinerary. She'd be arriving in Rome tomorrow, and she wanted me to delay my visit with Allen Cross until after she landed. But I couldn't do that. According to his online

schedule, Cross taught at the University at nine o'clock
this morning then wouldn't be back on campus until next
week. This was my chance to confront him and, if it were
a trap, I'd rather have the bad guys spring it at a very
crowded collegiate institution during regular business
hours. Let Cross tell me what he knew about my parents,
my sister, and a potential DNA test while there were lots of
presumably well-educated witnesses lurking about.

Marcus and I took the subway to the Sapienza
Universita di Roma, a campus that reminded me so much of
BU—with red and white flags lining the bustling city streets
and boxy, modern architecture—I almost expected to see a T
train rumble past.

"Cross is teaching International Business Law," I told
Marcus as we walked toward the marble library at the end
of a grassy quad. The street bordering the school was called
Via Aldo Moro. Honestly. Our jaws dropped when we saw
it, as if the universe had put my family madness in motion
when it laid out the Roman street grid.

We entered a flurry of chatty students, and I couldn't
help but notice how we blended with the crowd. We were
the right age, wearing the right clothes, doing what kids
our age should be doing—going to class. I suddenly hated
them; I so wanted to be them. I wanted their problems. I
wanted to go to Poli-Sci too hungover to take a pop quiz.

"Reminds you of Boston, right?" said Marcus, echoing
my thoughts.

All I could do was nod as we stepped toward the archi-
tecturally uninteresting Business School, slicing through
bored, pouty Italians crowded by the entrance texting
through a cloud of cigarette smoke. He was in Room 102,
and as we neared, I heard a deep voice bellow from inside
the classroom. The voice was familiar, and suddenly a

memory sprung to my brain. Only it wasn't of Allen Cross, but of a man named Aleksandr.

I was crawling under a Christmas tree, a party underway in our living room. My parents were home for the celebration and had invited all of their friends from the Los Angeles area to spend Christmas Eve in our home. We rarely celebrated holidays on their actual date, so in an effort to make this the most perfect Christmas ever, I insisted we display the nativity scene my parents kept tucked on the top shelf of a hall closet. They agreed, and I was lying on my stomach under the tree, pine needles pricking my black velvet dress, smelling of sap as I tried to arrange the display—Mary, Joseph, baby Jesus, three wise men, an angel, and an array of farm animals. One sheep was missing a leg, and as I attempted to prop it against the manger, a man walked in.

I recognized his socks—bright red, sticking out from under his gray wool trousers. I knew without looking that they'd match his bow tie. Uncle Aleksandr always had matching socks and bow ties. He'd been a part of our family for as long as I could remember. We didn't see him much, on account of our constant relocations, but he usually visited twice a year, bringing armfuls of presents that spanned the globe—a shadow puppet from Bali, nesting dolls from Russia, soap from Paris, chocolate from Switzerland, and corn husk figures from Prague. Only, before I could slide out and ask what he'd brought me for Christmas, he and my parents began to argue.

He was begging for help, and my parents refused. They sounded cold, hardly uttering a word as he pleaded, and finally he started to threaten. His voice grew deep, and he switched to another language—Russian, maybe Czech—as if he were so heated he couldn't be bothered to translate his thoughts from his mother tongue anymore. I tried to crawl off, but my mother spied my black patent leather Mary Janes jutting out from under the branches, and everyone immediately stopped talking.

I never saw Uncle Aleksandr again. I hadn't really thought about him much, either. Maybe that was why I didn't recognize his image in the crime scene photo. Because if I was right, and it was him, he was probably in his twenties when the picture was taken. I doubted I would have recognized anyone but my parents with that many decades of change on their faces.

I peeked in his classroom, and his figure confirmed what his voice already told me—there stood Uncle Aleksandr with black plastic glasses and a liver-spotted bald scalp above a ring of wiry hair (a bit grayer than I remembered). He wore a royal blue bow tie, which I already knew would match the royal blue socks protruding from his slightly too-short pant cuffs.

"I know him," a voice whispered in my ear.

For a second, I thought I was talking to myself, but I felt Marcus squeeze my shoulder. "In London. I've met him before," Marcus continued.

"What?" I hissed, glaring at him with a twisted expression.

"When we lived in the UK, a couple of years ago, my dad got me a part-time job as a cycle courier. I used to deliver packages to *that* man. I didn't recognize him in the photo; he had hair when he was younger, looks different now. He was a professor at the London School of Economics, and he got *a lot* of Dresden mail. Only I thought his name was different…"

"Aleksandr," I confirmed. Marcus eyes snapped to me, wide with the revelation.

"*Sí.*"

"I knew him, too." Nerves twined in my gut. "He was

close to my family for years."

"I guess Charlotte was right," Marcus noted. "If Keira was in touch with somebody in Rome, someone who could help with information on your parents—"

"This would be the guy," I finished for him. "Luis said he'd be more receptive to *me*. I think I should go in alone." I looked at Marcus. "The two of us showing up at the same time, it might seem suspicious. And we still don't know if it's a trap. I need you out here."

He nodded. "I'll be your lookout, but I'm here if you need me."

"I know." Our eyes held for a moment, and I realized Marcus *was* here, really here, with me. I wasn't alone in this. He had my back. I trusted him.

It was an unfamiliar feeling.

Only, before I could express it, students began pushing past us, shuffling into the classroom. They dropped book bags onto the floor and gave their phones one last check. The lecture was about to begin, and without another distracting thought, I slid inside with the masses. Cross was at the board, erasing the previous class's notes, his short arm reaching up, tufts of white hair dotting his splotchy pale hand. I sank into a desk in the back, dropping low behind the horizon of students, but he immediately paused— his arm halted as if locked in an outstretched position.

Maybe it was a sixth sense, or maybe I was paranoid, but I swore he already knew I was there. The class settled down, growing quiet as they waited for the lecture to begin, and slowly Professor Cross turned his head. He didn't scan the room. His gold-hazel eyes seemed programmed on me like a missile. He drew a quick breath, recognition clear on his face.

"*Studenti, tranquillo*," he began in Italian, silencing any lingering chitchat, his eyes set on me and the eraser clutched in his hand like a weapon. "I assume you read the chapter on contract law; today we'll be discussing termination rights…"

He flowed into his lecture in Italian as if I weren't there. Students feverishly typed on their laptops as Uncle Aleksandr conducted the ninety-minute session with utter professionalism. No one acknowledged my intrusion.

It wasn't until class had ended and the room had emptied that his eyes finally turned my way once more.

"You're not in this class," he said in English with barely an accent.

"Nope," I confirmed, rising up from my metal desk. "But I think you know who I am." I was trying to sound confident, but really my hands were shaking.

"Anastasia." He greeted me with a gentlemanly nod.

"Do you know why I'm here?"

"I have a good guess, but I'm not discussing anything right now." He rearranged some papers, stuffing items into a scratched leather satchel as if this were an ordinary conversation about an upcoming chapter reading.

A fly buzzed past my ear, and I swatted, more aggressively than the insect deserved. If this man fed my sister information, then he was partly responsible for what happened to her. He pulled her into this mess, likely knowing the danger that my parents' pasts possessed. Though I wondered if he shared his knowledge of that danger with her.

"I'm not leaving without answers. My sister, Keira, has been kidnapped. So I'm gonna get right to the point—there are people who think she was being fed information about my parents from someone in Rome. Was it you? Because these men went through a lot of trouble to get me here, and I need to find my sister fast. So if you know anything, start talking." I was done with cryptic conversations.

He shifted his weight, eyes scanning the room as if a band

of assassins might descend from the ceiling. "Who have you spoken to exactly?" He cautiously looked out the windows.

"Salvatore and Luis Basso. It was Luis who admitted Keira was alive; that was before he nearly choked me to death. He said his partner, Craig—"

"Stop. Talking," Cross said forcefully, rushing to my side and gripping my elbow. "I'll tell you what I know, but not here." He glanced at his watch. "Meet me at five-thirty at Santa Maria's Basilica in Trastevere. It's across the river."

"They wanted me to find you. Why? How are you involved in this?"

"I'm not your enemy," he said curtly.

"And I'm just supposed to trust you? I'm supposed to go somewhere alone with you?"

"If I were you, I wouldn't trust anyone. But Santa Maria's is about as crowded as you can get. Five-thirty. Now go."

He pushed me to the door, and before I exited, I stopped, looking back.

"Fine. I'll meet you there. Don't be late, *Uncle Aleksandr*." I couldn't be sure, but his eyes seemed to lighten when I said the nickname, as if he liked it.

CHAPTER TWENTY-THREE

Seven hours. That was how long I had to wait. Really, Cross might as well have told me he'd be happy to set up an appointment to discuss my kidnapped sister two months from next Tuesday, because that was how long the wait felt.

So Marcus and I ate pizza—when in Rome, right?—then left to meet Sophia Urban, hoping she could offer insights into the lying criminal adults in our lives. The *gelateria* was set near the Trevi Fountain, which was a bit like meeting someone for a hot dog in Times Square; it wasn't exactly an intimate setting, but Sophia and I weren't intimate friends.

"Aren't you prompt?" she greeted as she approached us outside of the store's ancient mustard facade. The rustic exterior clashed loudly with her designer outfit—a tight white dress and black stiletto heels so high she deserved a Fashion Medal of Valor for making it across the cobblestones.

"It's been too long," I said with a fake grin before gesturing to Marcus. "This is my friend Marcus."

"Dipping into the Spanish well. Not bad." She smirked,

eyeing him like a prize show horse. She swished her strawberry blond hair behind her shoulder—it looked professionally blow-dried.

"Good to see you, too." I grunted, and headed into the quaint shop, my Converse sneakers squeaking on the cracked tile floor. A large crowd hovered in front of the teal and cream marble bar, surveying the colorful bins of Italian ice cream.

"When did you get to Rome?" she asked, clutching her Italian leather bag as she scanned the gelato selections.

"Yesterday." Though I was pretty sure she knew that. "Didn't your grandfather tell you why I'm here? Keira's missing—"

"Oh, yeah. I heard. *The tub*," she moaned, pumping her plucked eyebrows. "That must've sucked."

I gritted my teeth, my hand clenching into a fist so tight, Marcus had to grab it before I could act. He massaged my palm open with his thumb. "*Tranquilo*," he whispered in my ear. Only he wouldn't be telling me to calm down if he knew exactly how overdue this girl was for a good smack to the teeth, starting with the day my parents were buried.

The post-funeral brunch was about as over-the-top as one could imagine. Randolph Urban insisted on "celebrating my parents' lives" by inviting the entire Dresden Corporation, all three-hundred-plus employees, to share memories while sipping mimosas and dining on seafood. There were enough Maine lobsters for every guest to have two. There were crab cakes brought in from Maryland, sea bass from Chile, salmon from Alaska, enough caviar to fill a dump truck, and even a sushi station.

My parents preferred steak, but I kept this to myself.

I leaned against the polished doorjamb to Urban's mahogany-paneled dining room. His mansion had eight bedrooms, a servants' wing, an eight-car garage, and a pool that would make Michael Phelps drool. The brunch was being held in the West Wing, (yes, it had a "West Wing") and, despite the massive crowd promising that, "their prayers were with me," I'd never felt more alone.

Keira was so much better at this. She circulated the room in her black tea-length dress with her hair in a low bun accepting condolences like she was the second coming of Jackie Kennedy. A tear never fell, not even when they lowered their bodies into the earth. She just hugged me repeatedly and said, "Everything will be all right." Sometimes I believed her.

I glanced at my watch, willing the day to end. I'd buried my parents. I'd thrown a white calla lily on each of their caskets. And I wanted the day to be over, finally over.

"Bet you can't wait to get out of here," droned a voice from behind me.

I turned to find Sophia Urban, sipping a bottle of imported spring water between her pearly front teeth.

"I'm surprised you came for this."

"Didn't have a choice. Grandfather made me."

At least she was honest.

"When do you go back to London?"

"Hopefully tomorrow. Though a lot of people want to use the jet." She gestured with a tiny porcelain hand to the crowds of Dresden staffers chatting about corporate projects. Many had traveled from Singapore, Germany, Japan, and Prague to be here.

"Well, at least you got out of school."

"I like school."

Of course she did.

I shook my head and skimmed the collage of photos that timelined Urban's thirty year friendship with my parents. At ten years their senior, it was weird to imagine him ever having dated my mother, especially when she was just nineteen years old. But it was true, and if you looked carefully, you could see that there were more photos of my mother exhibited than of my father.

"You going to stay in Boston now?" Sophia asked, sucking another gulp.

"I guess. I think we were gonna move to Canada. You know...*before*..."

"Yeah, I guess that's over now," she said flippantly. "I still can't believe they died in a car crash. Nuts."

I set my jaw. *Yes, Sophia, my parents dying in a mess of fiery wreckage was* nuts.

I hadn't seen her since that day. Actually, I hadn't seen most of the Dresden family until Keira's memorial. I guess Sophia didn't think my sister's "death" warranted a trip. Not that I would have wanted her there. She would have just continued with the insults. Like when I won the school science fair in fifth grade and she accused the teacher of awarding "mediocre talent," or the Dresden company party I went to a year before my parents' deaths when she said my dress made me look like "a little choir girl."

Sophia Urban didn't like me, and I didn't like her in return.

"Yes, Sophia, holding a memorial service for my presumed-dead sister did sort of suck," I spit before ordering the largest cup of *lampone*—raspberry—gelato they had. If I was going to be forced to talk to this girl, I was going to do it with a lot of ice cream.

"So what, now you're here looking for her? Since when did you join law enforcement?" she asked flippantly before ordering a dish of pistachio fit for a toddler.

"She's my sister. I'd do anything for her, which you wouldn't understand, because the only family you've got is a grandfather who lives in a different country." I cocked my head, eyeing her pointedly. If she could be rude, so could I. And really, this was a girl who lost her mother almost at birth and had a father who never stepped up to the plate to claim her. You would think that would make her a bit more sympathetic to my situation.

She clucked her tongue. "Yup. All I've got is the man who's paying for your trip."

I shut my mouth, and Marcus carefully guided us to a table, sitting between us like we were professional wrestlers about to reach for the folding chairs.

"So, I came with a purpose," Sophia said more calmly as she pulled a small cream-and-white-checkered sack from her bag and placed it on the table before us. She nodded at Marcus. "You sure you want him here?"

"He's a Dresden Kid," I noted.

"Oh, I hadn't realized. Welcome to the party." Her tone was glib.

"Thanks." He shot her a look.

Good for him.

She returned her gaze to me. "So, you were right. Grandfather told me about your little situation with Keira." Just hearing her refer to my sister's violent kidnapping as a "little situation" made me want to *accidentally* throw my fuchsia ice cream all over her white dress. "He said you know about the 'enemy of the state' thing that happened after your parents' funeral."

"*You* know about that?" My brow raised.

"He is *my* grandfather. Why do you think I'm here? He said you think the person who killed Keira—"

"*Kidnapped* Keira," I briskly corrected.

"Oh, right. Sorry." She didn't look sorry, and I dug a giant scoop of hot-pink gelato onto my plastic spoon and aimed it at her dress like a catapult. Marcus grabbed my hand. "He said you think whoever did it might be involved in your parents' *secret spy missions*?"

She fluttered her long lashes like the words were ludicrous, which they were. At least, that was what I thought a few days ago. Now, everything in my life seemed cloaked in espionage.

"Well, if that's the case, I think I might know someone who has a grudge." She opened the small cotton bag with her manicured hands and slid out a black and white composition book.

Instantly, I knew where this was headed. I recognized the handwriting. The front page read, "Operation Manual." It was my father's script.

I snatched the book, flipping it open. "What's this?"

Sophia smacked her lips, casually picking up her pistachio cup and taking a tiny bite like we were chatting over Sunday brunch. "A few years ago, when I was at LSE, I dated this guy, Julian. We're still good friends. His family's super rich, owns all these media outlets…"

As she spoke, I thumbed through the notebook, viewing page after page of my father's cursive handwriting. It looked like a blueprint—maps, diagrams, and text, all written in English, almost like the outline for a military operation.

"Julian spent a summer working at one of his father's newspapers, the *London Gazette*. Don't ask me why, he doesn't need the money." Of course Sophia would think this. "But he had this whole complex about wanting to prove he could write something other than an exposé on William's and Kate's latest fashion trends. So when this 'source,'"—she put air quotes around the word—"approached him and said there was going to be a terrorist attack on the London Tube, Julian was a bit too eager to believe him."

I scanned the book. The words "C4 Explosives" jumped from the page. My stomach turned. Suddenly, I didn't like where this was headed.

"Anyway, Julian wrote a whole story about the supposed terror plot. It ran on the front page, claiming that a group of Islamic *women* were plotting to blow up thousands of subway commuters. He had a ton of evidence to back it up, but the biggest piece was an operation manual that he had translated from Arabic into English."

She nodded at the book I was holding, and I dropped it like the pages were on fire.

"Obviously, it was bullshit. The 'source' who fed Julian the story was lying. The man who translated the manual was in on it. The whole thing was a setup. Only Julian didn't figure that out until *after* the police raided the women's apartment with riot gear and attack dogs." She cocked her head, her eyes almost smiling. "Can you guess who translated the manual?"

She looked back and forth between me and my father's handwriting with a teasing grin. She was enjoying this, and I wanted to punch her in the face.

"Anyway, it was a total mess," she continued when I didn't say anything. "Julian practically started race riots in the United Kingdom. Muslims from around the world accused Scotland Yard of roughing up innocent women. You didn't read about this in the papers?"

If it wasn't in *Us Weekly*, it was safe to say I was un-informed. I squeezed the muscles on the sides of my neck, staring at the book as if it might melt like a surrealist painting; none of it seemed possible.

"I remember this story," Marcus said, aggressively biting into his thumbnail, his eyes edgy as he glared at the book. He seemed to grow paler. "I was living in London at the time…"

"So you know what a laughingstock Julian became. I mean, the Stones are one of the most powerful families in Europe. At least, they *were*."

My hands fell to the table. Julian *Stone*. That was who she was talking about? The Stones were the Rockefellers of England, only their money came from media conglomerates — newspapers, publishing, TV stations, entire cable companies.

My brain flashed to the tabloid I'd purchased at the airport, the one I'd read on the train to Cortona, the British "media heir" with the word "Wanker!" scrolled above his head.

That was Julian Stone.

"You think my dad was involved in this?"

"What do you think?" Sophia nodded to my father's handwriting, then licked her plastic spoon clean and dropped it in her empty cup. "I didn't realize it until a few weeks ago, though." She shoved the composition book back into its sack. "Grandfather told me about Keira, and I went on *Boston.com* to read some of the articles. I was with Julian at the time, and he saw what I was reading. One of the stories had a picture of Keira right next to a photo of your parents and the crash. He totally freaked, recognized your dad right away."

I remembered that article. It was one of the first features the *Boston Herald* ran on Keira. "*Bathtub of Horror,*" read the headline. It included a sidebar called, "*A Family Tragedy,*" with photos of my parents and their flaming car wreck. Now, I was picturing Julian Stone thousands of miles away gawking at it, making the connection.

Sophia stowed the manual in her purse, and I reached for her hand.

"Can I keep that?" I asked, my voice pathetic. It was the only solid evidence I had of my parents' double lives, and I'd barely had a chance to glance at it.

"Sorry. I snagged it from Julian when he wasn't looking. He's probably freaking out by now."

I rubbed my fingers against my tightening jaw. If what Sophia was saying were true, then my parents really were linked to an alleged terror plot against the U.S.'s greatest ally, just as the FBI had accused. Luis's assertions that he and my parents didn't work for the CIA rang in my head. What type of spies were they?

"So let me get this straight," I replied. "You came here to tell me that you think your ex-boyfriend is responsible for what's happening to Keira? Like, he took her from our bathroom out of revenge for something my dad did years ago?" It sort of shattered the DNA test theory.

"Oh God, no. Julian's way too obsessed with clearing his name—kidnapping Keira and committing an *actual* crime wouldn't accomplish that. But his father, that's a different story. The man lost a fortune." Sophia rose to her feet, pulling her elegant bag onto her shoulder.

"You think *Phillip Stone's* behind this?" Marcus asked, his face growing paler.

"It's a hell of a grudge." She looked at her diamond-studded watch. "I gotta get back to work."

Sophia swished her glossy strawberry blond hair behind her back, straightened her stark white dress, and patted the corners of her perfectly painted lips. Even in a massive, noisy crowd of tourists, she stood out—beautiful, porcelain, and fake. This girl never did anything that didn't benefit herself.

"Why are you telling me this?" I asked.

"Because Grandfather said I had to." She shrugged. "He wants to help you. Obviously. He's bankrolling this little vacation of yours." My left eye twitched. I wouldn't exactly call a death match on top of a mountain in Cortona a vacation excursion.

"You work for Dresden, right?" I asked, trying to sound nonchalant, but I saw a shift in Sophia's face.

"Uh, yeah," she snipped. "It *is* a family business. You used to know that."

Yes, before I lost my family. Thanks for the reminder.

I cut the politeness. "Your grandfather is one of the richest men in the world, and probably one of the most intelligent. You really think he didn't know what my parents were involved in?"

She paused, her gaze hardening. "*You* didn't, and you're their kid."

I swallowed the truth like a ball of fire, and Sophia stepped toward me, her stiletto clicking on the marble tiles. "I don't know what you're implying, but as soon as I told Grandfather about Julian and the manual, he insisted we meet. He doesn't want to withhold any information from you, but I guess this is how you repay his generosity." She hiked her purse onto her bony shoulder and turned for the door, her strawberry hair swishing.

"He was their best friend," I called after her. "How could he not know?"

She spun back toward me. "Because your parents were liars." Then her gaze turned devilish. "Also, you should know, Julian may no longer be my boyfriend, but he's still my friend. He got royally screwed by your dad, and I value *my* friendships."

"Your point being?"

"Julian's in Rome, and I gave him your hotel info. I'm sure you two will have a lovely chat." She smiled smugly, then strutted out the door.

Great, like I needed another enemy in my life.

CHAPTER TWENTY-FOUR

We walked to Trevi Fountain without saying a word, as if all the thoughts in our brains were too tangled together to separate a single sentence to utter. We stared at the tourists chatting simultaneously as they tossed coins over their backs, reenacting an old movie, and we watched as their wishes landed in an enormous ocean-themed Bernini fountain, water roaring from the masterpiece as it rose up in front of a giant palace.

All I could see was my father's handwriting.

"Phillip Stone..." I finally muttered, not even realizing I'd said it aloud until Marcus's head whipped my way.

"I was thinking the same thing."

"Someone with that much money could hide Keira anywhere. She could be in a hut in Zimbabwe by now. She could be dea—"

"Then why would he take her?" Marcus interrupted my dark thought. "Whoever did this could have done worse right in your apartment, but they didn't. They took her alive. There must be a reason."

"Assuming Luis was telling the truth. We don't know

that for sure." I stretched my legs as I sat on a marble step across from the water-spouting statues.

"Allen Cross—Aleksandr, or whoever he is—was not surprised to see you," Marcus pointed out from beside me. "I think these people *want* something from you and your sister."

"But what? It's not like we have any money. I can't pay Phillip Stone back whatever riches he lost." I propped my elbows onto the step behind me.

"This isn't about money. It's been months. You would have gotten a ransom demand by now. But if you listen to Luis, this is all about potentially exposing your parents' former cases. Maybe the Stones want to prove what your father did, that he set up Julian?"

"But wouldn't DNA *help* their case?" I asked, thinking aloud. "If my father caused the international incident that damaged their family, there could be DNA connected to that crime that might prove his guilt. So why would they want to *stop* the test?"

"Maybe they didn't. Luis *claims* he was hired to stop the test, maybe *that's* the lie. Maybe he was really hired to retrieve the results," Marcus guessed.

"But it's just a DNA test! It's not that hard to run, or stop, some lab work." My eyes tensed with concentration as I glared at the puffy clouds. "I don't get it. If they want something from us, then why don't they ask? I'd give them anything to get Keira back. So why am I here? I just...I think there's something *else* going on, something we're missing."

I looked at Marcus, whose expression was as blank as my own. I felt like a pawn, like there was some massive chessboard I wasn't being shown, and a king or queen behind it playing ten moves ahead. For me, the endgame was finding my sister, but I was growing increasingly convinced that for them (whoever *they* were), checkmate was something else entirely.

Just then, a man not ten feet away dropped to one knee, ring box in hand. He held up a diamond and the crowd cheered as the bride-to-be nodded yes, tears in her eyes.

"Marcus, maybe it's time you go find your brother in Milan?" I said, changing topics.

"What?" He flung a shocked expression at me.

"This whole thing with Keira, my parents—we had a *gun* pointed at our heads."

"Do you really think I'd leave you here by yourself?"

"Charlotte will be here tomorrow." I'd left her a message about Julian Stone, hoping she could verify what Sophia had said. But even if she did, it wouldn't change much. From the Bassos to the Stones, my parents obviously had an impressive list of enemies. I couldn't exactly track them all and accuse them of kidnapping my sister.

Marcus grabbed my hand. "I'm not leaving. Not until you do. Dresden Kids stick together."

Only the look on his face suggested he had his own motives now. His parents and brother worked for Dresden, and if my parents were espionage superstars, it wasn't a far leap to question whether Dresden was involved as well, whether Randolph Urban was involved—despite everything Sophia said to the contrary. Because if he was, it meant Marcus's entire family could be as embroiled as mine.

Only we left this unsaid. Instead, I glanced at my watch. It was time to go.

I sat in a center pew. Incense filled the air. A priest stood at the altar reciting the rituals I recognized from far too many funerals, and I wondered how many Catholic services my parents had attended without me knowing. I already knew they sponsored a baptism.

I was raised by strangers, I thought as I scanned the aisles for Uncle Aleksandr, or Allen Cross. I had intended on waiting outside, feeling safer in the open, but then I realized how right Cross was, the throngs of tourists flooding the church were so huge it would be hard to kill me here. So I entered a quiet pew and left Marcus as lookout in the plaza.

When the parishioners stood, I stood, when they sat, I sat, all the while trying not to have flashbacks of mahogany caskets, memorial posters, and white calla lilies. I squeezed my eyes. *God, if you exist, bring my sister home. Please. Don't punish her for things our parents did,* I prayed futilely. Then a hand shoved my shoulder.

I spun to see Allen Cross in the row behind me. He dropped a postcard on my pew—Michelangelo's *La Pieta*, Jesus's crucified body sprawled across Mary's lap. Then he quietly walked out of the church.

I picked up the postcard and read the note. *Meet in the first pew when mass is over.*

I did as I was told, waiting for the last organ note before moving to the front pew and sinking down amidst a thinning cloud of incense. A grand mosaic covered the altar—each shiny, gilded scene representing the life of Mary.

"Beautiful, isn't it?" Cross said as he sat beside me, his royal blue bow tie slightly cockeyed. "Sorry I disappeared, but I had to make sure you weren't followed."

"Was I?" I should have thought of that. Luis and his father clearly wanted me to meet with Cross. They probably had people tailing me to make sure I went through with everything.

"No, not if you discount my old cycle courier, Marcus Rey." He clasped his wrinkled hands, gray hair covering his knuckles.

"Yeah, I hear you and Marcus go way back." I tried to mask my surprise that he was able to spot Marcus like a living *Where's Waldo?* amongst the crowd.

"The Reys have quite a history with Dresden."

"So do you, if I remember correctly. Though your name wasn't Allen Cross then, *Uncle Aleksandr*." I cut him a look.

"Ah, yes. You knew me as Aleksandr Chromy." There was a hint of Czech in his voice. "I changed it when I became a professor. Allen Cross is more accessible to the masses."

"Is that the only reason? Because I recently learned my parents were crazy super spies."

His golden hazel eyes narrowed with a condescending smirk. "What exactly do you think you know?"

I could practically hear the words "little girl" being tagged to the end of his question. "It seems I was raised by liars deemed terrorists by the U.S. government, and it's possible Keira running a simple DNA test got her snatched from a tub full of blood. For some reason the Bassos, the Stones, and hell, maybe Santa Claus, are behind her kidnapping. And they want me in Rome. They think that *you* were feeding Keira information, and that you'll be more 'receptive' to talking to me."

Cross snorted. "Well, they definitely wanted us to meet, I'll give you that, but I haven't spoken to your sister since you were kids."

My chest sank. More confusion. More wrong turns. "So, why am I here? How are you connected to this? Is it Dresden? You worked there, right? Please tell me Randolph

Urban's not behind this. Please tell me I'm not wrong about everything." I thought of the hug he gave me in his office, that smell—warm, woodsy, and familiar. It was the first time I'd felt safe and cared for in a long time. I didn't want that to be a lie. I didn't want every fuzzy family memory I had to decay into cow manure.

"Before I answer, you need to realize how much danger you're putting yourself in." He eyed me pointedly. "People get killed in this line of work. Do you understand that?"

My fingers lightly brushed my bruised neck, the cut on my biceps pulsing. Obviously, I knew how lethal this was; that was why I was here. I wasn't going to let my sister fill more hazmat jars of blood while I safely returned to Boston for the Homecoming dance.

"I understand."

"Okay." He nodded once. "I never spoke to your sister, though I was close friends with your parents, so I can see why people would think I was her source."

"Who are these 'people'? Who's behind this?"

"I can't say with certainty." His tone was emotionless. "Your parents had a lot of enemies."

"So you're a spy?" I asked. "Because Luis claims my parents did so much covert work that a DNA test on them might blow up the planet." I shook my head, all of it sounding ridiculous.

"Yes. Your parents and I handled a lot of jobs for Department D that could come back to hurt some very important people."

"Wait, *what*? What's Department D?" Pure shock filled my voice. These were answers, *real* answers.

"We weren't the type of spies you're picturing." He turned to me, his voice even, like he was giving a well-paced lecture on contract negotiations. "We worked for an organization called Department D. Your parents ran it."

They ran *it? Wonderful.* "Please tell me that's a branch of the CIA, right?" I asked, doubtful hope in my words.

"No. It's a private organization. Unaffiliated with any government entity."

"What does that mean?"

Cross slid off his tweed blazer and folded it in his lap. There were sweat stains under his arms reaching half his torso. At least I wasn't the only one so amped up I could use a sponge. My knee bopped anxiously, rocking the ancient pew.

"Department D does jobs that governments can't do for themselves, jobs that would compromise a country's public image. We're masters of manipulating the masses..." There must have been such confusion on my face that he immediately took a breath and started over. "The organization excels at misleading the public and the media. We specialize in disinformation."

My eyes scrunched. *Disinformation? Is that even a word?* My mind clicked to the photograph in Cortona—the assassination, the news coverage, my parents' images being removed. "You mean the Aldo Moro thing? The dead prime minister? Did my parents kill him?'

His head jerked back. "No, of course not. How did you see the photo?"

"Salvatore Basso."

Cross nodded thoughtfully, like he was absorbing a revelation that was still obscured to me. "Well, that confirms it." He popped his lips. "Aldo Moro was our first op. We were hired to make sure the prime minister wasn't found. We needed to buy the kidnappers time, so we planted false leads, misdirected the press, led the authorities down the wrong path..."

For some reason, hearing this aloud was like an ice pick

splintering the last frozen remnants of what I thought was a happy childhood. My parents were criminals—conniving, calculating bad guys who helped political assassins. They didn't stumble upon any crime scene. They made these enemies, and they probably killed Luis Basso's uncle and set up Julian Stone. *They did this.* "So my parents weren't witnesses? They were involved in the assassination from the beginning?" I could hear my voice shake—from anger or disappointment, I wasn't sure.

"Yes." He nodded.

"But, why? How did my parents get involved in this? I mean, a dead prime minister?" My mouth hung, stale incense coating my tongue.

"You have to realize, we had no involvement in the kidnapping plan whatsoever, and we never expected Moro to be killed. We were hired after the fact and thought he'd be returned alive…"

"Oh, that makes me feel so much better." I pressed the bridge of my nose. It felt like I was one giant headache lately—eat, sleep, breath, Tylenol. "Well, Luis is holding a serious grudge against my parents—something about what they did to his uncle. He wants Keira dead. How do I know she's not dead already? How do I know he's not *disinforming* me now?"

Cross wiped a sheen of sweat from under his thick plastic glasses. "The Bassos were bonded to your parents for decades, and what happened to Salvatore's brother, well, I'm not going to get into that. It was unfortunate, to say the least, and the Bassos probably would now sell themselves to the highest bidder if it meant getting back at your family. It's why they would take part in this whole mess to begin with. But they're not the ones pulling the strings. Neither am I. As for your sister, I know why they sent you to me. They want me to show you something, force my hand." He looked me head on, the gaze of a man full of stories, each wrinkle revealing a piece of history like the lines read by a fortune teller. "I have a picture of your sister in captivity, a proof of life."

I blinked, unsure of what I'd heard, like a parent who's been told their missing child has returned yet is too fearful to believe it. *A picture...of my sister...in captivity.*

"Wait, you didn't mention this until now!" I suddenly shouted, my voice reverberating off the marble surfaces.

He shot a warning glare, then reached into the breast pocket of his blazer and pulled out a slim black cell phone. He swiped at the screen. "This was uploaded onto a website our organization uses to communicate. I still frequent it occasionally, but when the picture went live, everyone in the espionage community was talking."

I grabbed the phone and stared at a black-and-white photograph of my sister's body contorted in the back of a European car in what appeared to be the same alley in Rome where Aldo Moro was found. She was posed the exact way.

"Is she..." I couldn't bring myself to finish the sentence.

"No," he interjected quickly. "We're fairly certain your sister's alive. She was last seen in Venice *after* this photo was taken."

"How do you know?" My grip on the phone tightened as I glared at my sister's twisted body, her closed eyes. Her cheekbones were protruding a bit too sharply, and her chin was pointier. She'd lost weight. Her collarbone was exposed under a wrinkled white T-shirt, and her hair was longer. There were dark roots near her scalp, contrasting with her platinum blond ends. She must hate that.

"The photo was posted exactly fifty-five days after she

went missing. That's exactly how long Moro was held before his body turned up. Obviously, when I saw this, I feared the worst, but then she was spotted in Venice, at a flat used by our organization long ago." His voice maintained his matter-of-fact demeanor that I was starting to hate.

"Did you talk to the cops? Did you go after her?" Accusations were thick in my voice.

"We don't deal with the cops, but yes, we did go to the flat. By the time we arrived, your sister had been moved. I have no idea where she is now, but we're working on it. This was about two weeks ago."

"You knew where Keira was two weeks ago?" I breathed in a dumbfounded whisper. That was when I snapped out of my pseudo-coma. That was when the cops found the surveillance footage. Someone had given an anonymous tip. "Two weeks ago, someone called the Boston PD and informed them of a surveillance tape showing Keira with her attacker, Craig. It was what ultimately led me to a photo, which led me to Tuscany, which led me here."

"They probably called in the tip. They're dragging you into this to force a reaction from us."

"From *who?* What are you talking about? Because if they want me, they can have me!"

"You don't know these people."

"Do you?" I yelped, my eyes flaring. "You already said you don't know who's behind it. Was that a lie? Is it the Stones?"

"Phillip Stone? Who told you about that?"

"Who do you think? Randolph Urban, you know, the guy I thought you and my parents worked for, has a granddaughter who lives in Rome. I met with Sophia, and she showed me some manual my father used to set up her ex-boyfriend, Julian Stone. She and her grandfather seem to think his father,

Phillip Stone, might have a financial motive for snatching Keira."

"How long have you been in contact with Randolph Urban?"

"My whole life! You know that," I spat. "He's paying for my trip."

Cross tapped his finger on his lips, his eyes deep in thought. "Phillip Stone's a bastard. Stay away from him, as a point of fact. But I doubt he's behind this…" His voice trailed off, his gaze distant like he was solving calculus equations in his mind. Then he shrugged off the thought. "Be careful who you trust, Anastasia, who you talk to about this."

"You mean, like you?"

He *tsked* in response. "The only reason I'm telling you any of this is because I want your sister found. As much as you do. You may not realize that, but I do." He ripped his cell phone from my hand and tucked it back into his jacket pocket. "There are a lot of people who are trying to help you."

"Where? Who?" I tossed my hands around the empty cathedral. "Because right now it seems to be me, you, and some kid from my high school."

"There are agents from Department D who are still loyal to your parents. We're trying to end this without dragging you further into it." He slid his arms into his blazer, hiding his massive sweat stains. "Your parents wouldn't want you following in their footsteps, you or your sister."

"Are you seriously worried I'll join the espionage team at my high school?" I snapped, shifting loudly in our pew. "Because I can assure you kidnapping prime ministers won't be the 'Future Goal' listed in my yearbook."

"I'm more concerned you won't *have* any future goals. You're currently following the steps of our first mission—Cortona, Rome, and I'm guessing, soon Venice. Your sister was *posed* like Aldo Moro. You must see the symbolism?"

"No, actually, I don't. All I see is my sister's blood filling our tub." My knee bounced harder, the creaking boards of our pew echoing through the thousand-year-old space. "I spent months thinking she was dead. It practically sent me into a coma. I thought it was my fault. I left some guy in her room…" Just then, the face of a wannabe Kurt Cobain flashed behind my eyelids. He was the one I really wanted to find; he was the one who deserved to pay. "Do you know Craig? Twenty-something with a scar on his lip? Raspy voice? Tall with dirty blond hair. *He* took Keira."

I pictured his head on a stick, his greasy hair dripping with blood. I used to be horrified by films set in medieval times where people would cheer for executions held in the town square. Now, I completely understood. I would stand in the front row to watch Craig the Psycho get the rack.

"We think it was Craig Bernard. I've never met him myself, but the description sounds right."

Craig Bernard. My pulse spiked. He was a real person with a first and last name. "Where can I find him? Who does he work for?"

"Anyone. Everyone. He's a hired gun. A cockroach. He probably lives in a gutter someplace." He rose from his seat, checking his watch like he had somewhere to be. "His involvement is a dead lead. He has no loyalties."

"You can't go." I shot up, grabbing his arm and wincing from the cut on my biceps.

"What happened there?" he asked, nodding to my two bloody Band-Aids.

"Luis Basso. Apparently, he's capable of strangling me with one hand and stabbing me with the other. Marcus saved me."

"It doesn't look deep."

"It's not. I got lucky."

Cross paused, thinking. "It's gonna get a lot worse than that if you keep after this."

"It's already worse for Keira," I pointed out. "Where's the apartment in Venice? Where were they keeping her?"

"She's not there. The flat's empty." He buttoned his jacket, stepping into the marble aisle.

"Please, you have to help me, help *her*! God knows what they're doing to her. Luis said those men…" My voice cracked, unable to finish the thought.

He turned toward me, a sudden softness touching his face for the first time. "They haven't harmed *you* yet, not really, but they easily could have." He flicked a casual glance at my arm like it was a skinned knee. "I'm sure the same is true for your sister. Believe me, I want her found as quickly as possible. Meet me tomorrow at eight a.m. at Sant'Eustachio. There's a café there; you'll know it when you see it. I should have more information then."

He didn't wait for a response. He simply walked out, leaving me in the empty gilded cathedral with more questions than I had when I'd walked in. A few days ago I believed my parents were engineers, and a few months ago I believed my sister was happy, if not a little boy crazy. I was wrong. About them, about my own life. I felt like I was drowning in lies with no life raft in sight, instead only more weights pulling me down. What scared me most was that I knew, deep inside, that I hadn't even gotten close to the bottom of this dark abyss. How far would I have to sink to find my sister?

I felt the funk circling overhead. The weight of our grave situations left a heaviness on my chest, the air constricting my lungs. Thankfully Marcus came to find me before my mind could darken further.

CHAPTER TWENTY-FIVE

Bits and pieces of the conversation trickled back like the details of a nightmare I was determined to recall—a look in Cross's eye, a gesture he made. Everything had meaning.

My parents were spies, and not the good kind you root for in movies. They were the villains in a Bond flick.

I wrapped my arms tighter around my knees as I sat on the edge of my hotel room bed, the mattress plusher than anything I'd ever experienced. Marcus was seated in the crimson silk wingback chair across from me, hardly blinking as I relayed the story.

"So you're meeting him again tomorrow?" Marcus confirmed.

I nodded.

"Do you have a copy of the photo? The one with your sister?" He was trying hard to politely refer to the photo without mentioning her body crammed into a hatchback trunk, but his omission didn't help me forget. I was already suffering from chills that had nothing to do with the air conditioner.

"There was so much going on that I didn't even think

to get a copy," I snapped, irritated with myself. "Charlotte's looking for it now."

I'd called her as soon as we left the church. A photograph existed of my sister in Italy *after* her supposed death. With that sort of evidence, somebody in some sort of official law enforcement capacity would have to listen to us, and if they didn't, then I was pretty sure CNN would. Of course, Charlotte agreed to help only after screaming at me for meeting Allen Cross without her. Her flight to Rome didn't leave until tomorrow, and I had a feeling it was going to be a long twenty-four hours for her.

It wasn't feeling any shorter for me.

Marcus rose from his chair and dropped down beside me, the mattress slumping under his weight. My body rolled toward his, a fresh bandage covering the wound on my arm. I let myself lean in to him and slowly felt better, warmer.

"There's something I haven't told you." His voice took on a cautious tone, and I squeezed my eyes. I didn't want him to ruin this one peaceful moment. I wanted him to hug me and tell me everything would be all right. I wanted to forget what was going on outside of this hotel room and just feel *him*. But Marcus continued. "Remember how I said I delivered packages in London?"

I nodded, an anxious pit opening inside me.

"That was my first real job, so I wanted to take it seriously, show my parents I had a *strong work ethic*." He seemed to be repeating their words. "I was the fastest courier on my team, and I loved how proud my dad looked, like I was the responsible one. Unlike my brother, who was drinking and fighting every guy who bumped into him."

"The brother who now works for Dresden?"

"He's changed a lot." Though Marcus sounded like he didn't see this as a good thing, and I was starting to realize he missed his brother in more ways than one. "To be fast, you need to make sure you don't waste too much time talking to customers," Marcus went on, biting his lip as he now stared at the floor like he didn't want to look at me. "I'm not typically chatty with old men in suits. I hardly even looked at my clients. That's why I didn't realize it before..." His voice trailed off, and my head slumped toward my chest.

Don't say it. Only I saw Marcus's reaction when we were at the *gelateria* listening to Sophia Urban and, if the way he was biting his thumbnail with a panicked expression was any indication, he was about to say something very bad.

"I delivered that manual to Julian Stone," he blurted. "I've seen it before, the composition book and checkered sack. I remember it."

I nodded, peeling my body away from him, away from the quiet moment I so desperately wanted. *Of course he did.* Marcus was a Dresden Kid, my father "worked" for Dresden. My dad probably used their cycle courier, their copy machines, and their staples for his criminal activities.

"Who gave you the manual?" I asked, though I already knew.

He bit his thumb. "I swear, I didn't realize it before. I got paid by the amount of items I was able to deliver in a day, so I hardly spent more than a second with clients, but the package was memorable. Who uses composition books anymore? And the checkered sack... It was your father who gave it to me."

I continued nodding robotically, wanting this day to end, wanting all the duplicities my parents fed me to stop. My biggest question now was whether Dresden and Department D were the same company. Because no matter how many times I asked Cross today, he refused to answer. And I was not leaving that coffee shop tomorrow without a yes or no.

"I'm gonna force Cross to tell me about Randolph Urban and Dresden and *all of this*." I threw up my hands like we were surrounded by madness, which we were.

"There is no way they're connected. That would mean that my parents and my brother are spies too," he spat.

"I'm sorry." I shook my head, having nothing more to add.

Marcus stood up, moving away from me, like he might catch the disease of deceit that was infecting my family. "I get that my brother's a little nontraditional for a corporate sales guy, but my parents are biomedical engineers. I've seen them at work, I've been to their labs. My father grew human tissue out of nothing. Their projects are in the news. Are you saying the entire world is in on it?"

"It would be a very elaborate front…" I conceded.

"And Randolph Urban? You've known him your whole life."

"I thought I knew my parents, too." I flopped back onto the bed, the crisp white cotton duvet enveloping me as I closed my eyes, information swirling like a kaleidoscope, every word warped and twisted. It took all my strength right now not to let the funk in, not to drift away and just feel numb.

"I should go." Marcus turned toward the door, and I swiftly reached for his hand.

"Don't." I peered at him, my lids hooded with exhaustion. If I spent the night alone tossing and turning in five hundred thread count sheets reliving every word that was said to me today, recalling every suspicious moment I spent with my parents, every excuse they gave for moving us across the globe, I didn't know whether I'd be able to get out of bed in the morning. The funk would take me, and I'd let it.

"Will you stay?" I whispered.

Marcus squeezed my hand, his thumb gently caressing my palm, then lowered himself onto the bed. He spread his long body beside mine and draped a heavy arm across my waist. I closed my eyes, my mind finally quieting from his touch. I needed him.

A hand nudged my shoulder, gently rocking my sore arm until my eyelids crept up. Marcus was perched on his elbow, staring at me from across a goose down pillow.

"It's time to go," he whispered, nodding toward the digital clock as I peered tentatively through my lashes. "It's seven fifteen."

Oh my God! We were supposed to meet Cross at eight. I shot up, the white sheet falling to my waist. I'd slept in my clothes. I glanced at Marcus; he was naked from the waist up. My eyes turned back toward the sheet, a flush spreading across my face.

"I need to get ready," I muttered quickly, my mouth tacky. I could taste my teeth.

"I tried to let you sleep as long as I could. You needed it." He cracked his neck, his bull tattoo stretching my way.

I didn't know when he'd removed his shirt, but it was hard to look at him with all those muscles showing. I'd never spent the night with a guy, in any sense of the term. I'd fooled around with a competitor after a karate tournament once, but it never got to nakedness—just some awkward kissing, nothing like kissing Marcus in Cortona. Having him in my bed right now felt intimate.

"Um, okay. We should call down to the concierge, get a cab." I flung back the crisp sheets in a jerky motion and jumped out of bed, not looking at him.

He'd saved me from myself last night. Just his presence

calmed the chaos in my brain. I could breathe. I could relax. I could sleep. It was good that he stayed, only I wasn't expecting him to undress.

"Is everything all right?" he asked as he watched my eyes flick about the room for fresh clothes, shoes, a brush, anything to offer a distraction.

Calm down. You look like a freak. Nothing happened.

I took a long breath and forced my eyes to meet his. "I'm going to hop in the shower. I'll be ready in ten minutes," I stated as composed as possible.

"Okay. I'll get ready next door." He stepped out of bed, then peered down at his bare chest and back at me as if finally catching on. "I get hot when I sleep," he muttered, having the good sense to finally sound embarrassed.

"Yeah, sure, no problem." I spun toward the bathroom, my face ready to combust. At least he was still wearing shorts. I rushed inside and flicked on the recessed lights, exhaling audibly. You'd think I'd never been to a beach, never seen a guy's shirt off. Only this felt different. This was the type of naked that sent a buzz of excitement through my belly followed by a rush of guilt. How could I get so distracted? If I was being held captive somewhere and learned that my sister was busy flirting and cuddling with some random guy, how would I feel? I couldn't do that to Keira. I had no right, especially after all the years of judgmental snipes I threw at her.

I turned on the shower and listened as Marcus exited the room.

We took a cab to Piazza Sant'Eustachio, and Allen Cross was right—there was no guess as to where he wanted to meet—everyone was funneling into one overwhelmingly crowded café. We entered the caffeinated chaos, snaking our way to the counter, the steamy scent of espresso permeating my skin. Patrons all around stood shoulder to shoulder sucking down coffee as the impatient mob continued to grow. And people think Americans are pushy. Most of our coffee shops were full of hipsters lounging with screenplays and stay-at-home moms feeding toddlers five-dollar cookies.

I scanned the crowd for Cross as Marcus waved euros at the baristas. A pretty brunette with unnaturally long lashes fluffed her hair as she moved toward Marcus. It took moments for drinks to land in our hands. We leaned against the rounded edge of the bar, holding our scalding cups.

"Do you see him?" Marcus asked, eying me over his tiny espresso.

"Not yet." I licked my foam.

"What if he doesn't show?"

"He will."

Charlotte had left a voicemail overnight saying she was able to confirm Sophia's story, which unlike me, she had recognized from the news. Julian Stone's reputation was destroyed by that London terror scandal—every media outlet from Fox News to *El País* carried the story—but she couldn't verify that my father was involved, nor that he was even in London at the time, but I guess that went with the spy territory. She *could* confirm that Julian was currently in Rome; he'd boarded a first-class flight yesterday. I wasn't sure what that meant. Was he following me because his family was behind Keira's kidnapping? Or because my dad set him up and he was hoping to destroy everyone in my dad's bloodline?

Surprisingly, Charlotte couldn't locate the photo of Keira in the trunk of the car, and without proof, Boston PD seemed unwilling to seriously consider the lead, which made me feel like Luis was right—maybe there were agents working to ensure no one looked into my sister's case.

I lifted my ceramic cup, the scent of cinnamon filling my nose as an elbow bumped my back. Cappuccino splashed onto my hand, and I cursed, wiping my fingers on my jeans. I turned to see Allen Cross standing behind me, wearing a canary yellow bow tie and holding a small cup.

"I see you had no trouble finding us," I greeted, as I dried my sticky fingers on the only clean pair of pants I had left.

"Americans are pretty easy to spot. Spaniards, too." He turned to Marcus. "Good to see you again." Then he nodded toward the door with his balding head. "You seem to have drawn a crowd. Julian Stone is in the café across the piazza."

We swung our heads toward the glass doors, morning light shining through in defined rays as I scanned the faces in the crowd outside. No one looked familiar.

"Sophia told him I was here," I noted, surveying the masses.

"I wouldn't talk to Sophia Urban anymore, *or* take any more of her grandfather's money," Cross instructed.

"Are you admitting it then? Urban is involved in this?" I braced myself for the awful truth. As much as I didn't want to believe Urban could be connected to a plot to harm my sister, I couldn't ignore that all the roads seemed to lead back to Dresden.

"Of course he is. You went to his office and asked for his money." Cross eyed me over the rim of his tiny cup.

"That's not what I meant, and you know it. If I'm not supposed to take his money anymore, then tell me why. Are Dresden and Department D the same thing?" I looked at Marcus, watching the fear slip into his eyes.

"Dresden is a real company," Cross defended carefully.

"But yes, it *is* connected to Department D."

Marcus's chest caved like a balloon had been popped within him.

"So it's Urban who took Keira?"

"I can't say that for sure. Believe me, he loved your parents, especially your mother. I would think him the last person who'd want to hurt their kids."

"The Bassos loved my parents, too!" I huffed, slamming my drink on the bar with a thud. "So did *you*. But that didn't stop you from screaming at them on Christmas Eve like you hated them."

"That was a long time ago."

"Why were you so angry with them?" My eyes narrowed.

"Because I wanted out of the organization, and it's not exactly an easy business to leave."

"So what happened?"

"I'm a law professor now, aren't I?"

"A professor with criminal ties, a professor who still peruses espionage chat rooms and receives Dresden mail. You were like family to us, showering us with gifts, then we never saw you again. How am I supposed to trust you now?"

He swallowed a gulp, his throat tight. Then he exhaled a loud, coffee-drenched gust and looked at me with a softer expression. "When your parents died, your sister dropped out of college, right? She was pre-med?"

I nodded, not knowing where he was going with this. I peered at Marcus, but his face had drained to the color of day-old oatmeal. If Dresden was in on it, so were his parents, so was his brother. He needed a minute.

"She reenrolled unexpectedly," Cross continued, "because she won a grant to go back as a nursing student, tuition free, correct?" He stared at me, unmoving, letting his words hang in the air.

I took a step back, clarity sinking in.

"It was you?" I could hardly form the question.

He glanced away, almost embarrassed. "Randolph Urban wasn't the only one helping you all these years. Your parents were dear friends. And they had a lot of cash that was *rightfully yours* tied up in the organization." He hissed the last words through his teeth.

"You think I want their blood money?"

Old men don't typically roll their eyes, but it looked like Cross wanted to. "Your sister graduated, didn't she?"

"Because she worked her butt off."

"And because she had the money. You also stopped eating potato chips for dinner."

"You want me to thank you?"

"I want you to realize I'm on your side."

If you added me to the list of people on my side, we wouldn't even be able to play doubles tennis. I had two allies—Charlotte and Marcus. That was it. Maybe Cross was responsible for upgrading Keira and I from ramen noodles to frozen lasagna, but I had no proof of that. Only his word. And so far his words weren't telling me everything I needed to know.

"You want me to believe you? Then prove it. Who's behind this? Urban? The Bassos? The Stones? Who?"

"Julian Stone is harmless." Cross waved me off. "I'm not even sure he's aware of his father's criminal activities."

"So *his* dad's a spy, too?" I asked, sounding more defeated than bewildered. How could I have been so oblivious to the world around me? To the world my parents built?

"Phillip Stone's not a spy, but think about what we do." Cross cut me a look, head tilted. "Department D uses the press to mislead the world about major international incidents, and Phillip Stone *owns* the press. He's a media giant."

"Is that why my parents went after his son?" I pictured my father's handwriting on that manual, him deliberately writing false information, smirking sinisterly as he crafted an elaborate scheme I could barely understand or could have ever dreamed him capable.

"They didn't *go after* Julian. Phillip was making business difficult, and he needed to be put in his place."

"But you didn't put *him* in his place. My parents went after his kid, so maybe now *he's* going after *theirs*."

"It was a long time ago, and his business has rebounded. Besides, that photo of Keira, the Aldo Moro connection, the Stones had nothing to do with that." Cross rested his empty cup on the bar, and immediately a crowd flocked toward us, shooing us away.

I thought of the black-and-white photo of my parents at that awful crime scene. Randolph Urban and Phillip Stone weren't there, but there was someone else who was. "There were four people Photoshopped out of that Moro photo. My parents, you, and the future Deputy Director of the CIA."

"Martin Bittman?" Cross chuckled, then glanced around to ensure no one was listening. The name was probably recognizable. He cleared his throat. "He's as straight and narrow as they come. He really was a random witness to that crime, a college student backpacking while on break from Stanford. Only he remembered every detail he saw, every face, including ours, and he was majoring in world languages with a perfect score on the SATs. The CIA recruited him the next day."

"So, if he works for the CIA and my parents *didn't*, that puts them at opposite ends, right?" I shivered, hating that my parents were the Lex Luthors of this scenario. "Maybe he has a grudge? You said whoever's behind this had to be there at the beginning."

"It's not him." Cross shook his head definitively. "Besides, your sister was running a DNA test; that's what started this mess. Do you really think the CIA would kidnap an innocent woman just to stop a lab test?"

"I don't think anyone would kidnap someone to stop lab work!" I yelped a bit too loudly, but I didn't care. There was more going on in this situation, and I was certain that Cross knew but wasn't sharing. "Luis said that there were double agents in every branch of law enforcement, including the CIA."

Cross pursed his lips. "He wishes his reach were that deep. Now, I wouldn't trust the *Italian* authorities—the story about his Uncle Angelo is true. But the CIA is definitely *not* involved in this. In fact, I might be able to enlist their help. I'll make some calls." His eyes flicked toward the glass doors, as if hearing a sound I missed. He paused, straining to listen, then turned back. "You should know, we think your sister's still in Venice."

A puff of air escaped from my chest, like I had been holding it and didn't realize it, just waiting for my sister to be found. She was in Venice, only hours away, and she was alive. I wanted to bust through the café doors and run there, full speed, right now. I bounced on my toes, ready to sprint.

"She's at the apartment? You said yesterday that it was empty."

"It is, but there are certain procedures for transporting a kidnapping victim, and none have been taken."

"So you think she's still there?" I grabbed Marcus's arm, my heart leaping, and he seemed to finally jolt back from his daze. I could see the question marks swirling behind his dark eyes, what this meant for his family, who they really were. We were Dresden Kids, and that was no longer a good thing. Given how much he'd helped me, I knew I should comfort him, come up with the perfect thing to say, but there were no words. Hallmark doesn't make an "I'm sorry your parents are criminals" card. Maybe we should add it to Happy Legal Guardian Day.

"I can't say for sure, but every other move they've made has mimicked our first mission. We flew into Florence, completed the job in Rome, pit stopped in Cortona with the Bassos and, when things got hot, we hid out in Venice. You and your sister are hitting each of those spots. It's like they *want* to be easy to follow. They *want* you on her tail. They showed you the Aldo Moro photo, posted a picture of her crammed into a trunk, and practically gave you my address. At this point, they might as well send you a postcard of Keira riding a gondola."

Gondola. My mind sprung to the small photo mounted on the wall of Randolph Urban's office—he was steering a gondola, with my parents, looking about the same age, with the same hair, decades ago, *in Venice.* "*He was there*," I whispered, the revelation thick in my voice. "Urban may not have been in the Aldo Moro photo, but he was part of that first mission, wasn't he? He was with my parents in Venice. There's a photo in his office."

Cross's jaw twitched, a slight pulse by his ear, then a loud shuffle broke out near the doorway. "Anastasia! Anastasia!" yelled a voice with a British accent. "Run!"

I spun to see Julian Stone barreling toward us.

CHAPTER TWENTY-SIX

Julian's bright blue-green eyes were frenzied as he zigzagged through the crowd. Marcus stepped in front of me, his hand across my torso in protection. It seemed he was finally refocused on our conversation, and his first instinct was to jump in front of danger. I liked that about him.

"Anastasia! You must leave! Now! *They're here!*" Julian yelled.

"Who are you?" I spat, though I knew the answer.

Julian stopped inches away, panting, sweat on his brow. "Pardon. I'm Julian Stone." He smoothed his freshly ironed white button-down, which fell over his crisp dark jeans. His blond hair looked flatironed. "I'm a friend of Sophia Urban's. I was across the piazza."

"Yeah, I know. Why are you stalking me?" I looked at Cross as if to ask *what the hell is going on?* but Cross was looking at Julian.

"Mr. Stone, how many of them are there?" he asked.

"At least three, two men and one woman," Julian replied, his eyes frantically darting toward the entrance. "I've never seen them before."

I peered toward the glass doors not knowing who I was looking for, and in an almost comforting way, Marcus seemed just as lost. He kept his hand held out, and I grabbed it in solidarity.

"You sure they don't work for your father?" Cross asked, like he wanted to see his reaction.

Julian jerked back. "What? No. Of course not. Bloody hell." He peered at me, azure eyes wide. "I realize you don't know me. But I know you. Or at least, I knew your father…"

"Yeah, I heard. You guys were best buds. You know, my sister is missing." I cut to the point.

"I had nothing—"

"Not now," Cross insisted, surveying the entrance. Then, something must have caught his eye, because he began shoving me toward the back of the café. "The bathrooms. Go."

"What? Why?" I twisted toward the windows again, and that's when I saw him. Luis Basso. He was standing across the piazza, a scowl on his face. "Oh, no."

"Yeah, I see him." Marcus grabbed my hand and began yanking me toward the dimly lit hallway that led to the bathroom. The cut on my arm throbbed as if recognizing the man who delivered the wound. We barreled into the men's room, Julian locking the door behind us, and Marcus squeezing my palm like he was never letting go.

"What are you doing here?" I yelled at Julian.

"Presently, warning you about the men with guns," he replied.

Cross shoved a set of car keys at me, interrupting the argument, and I let go of Marcus's hand. Marcus immediately stepped closer to my side, as if our physical contact kept us safe. It didn't. But it did keep me sane. He pressed his chest against my back as if ready to dive on top of me to shield me from danger, and I liked the way that felt. I wasn't alone.

"There's a silver Fiat parked in front of a restaurant nearby." Cross's tone was stern.

"What?" I stared at the foreign keys. "You want me to take your car?"

"It's a safe car. Plates are untraceable." His eyes skimmed all of us. "Do not use credit cards. Do not use the internet. Get as far out of town as you can before stopping. Use cash. Conceal your faces when you go through tolls. Do not use an ATM. The car is parked two blocks from *Hostaria Pantheon*; walk there like tourists, gaze at the architecture, blend in with the crowd. Do not run. Do you understand?"

I nodded stiffly. "But why is Luis here? What does he want? He let me go in Cortona."

Cross looked jittery, as if warring with the words in his head, with the information he clearly knew but didn't want to share. "They want something from *me*," he admitted reluctantly. "You're right, they do want you and your sister in Italy for a reason, and *I'm* a part of that. They're hoping I'll tell you what I know about past *events*." His golden eyes looked cagey, even more elusive than usual, like he was not just withholding something, but something vital. "It took me decades to get out of this business, and I'm not going to draw you and your sister in now. I'll do whatever I can to get her back, but that's as far as I'm taking this."

"They want information from *you*," I realized, finally catching on. "And they thought you would tell *me*?"

"Yes. But I won't. All I'm going to say is that your sister is in Venice, and we *will* find her."

"You mean the flat?" Julian interjected, stepping between us. "Because I have the address where she was held."

I gawked at him, openmouthed.

"I'm sure Sophia told you I saw the articles," he blurted.

"My family's media holdings afford me many useful contacts throughout the world, and there was chatter about an American girl being held at a flat in Venice."

What in the world? My eyebrows wrinkled together. "You know, your dad's on the short list of people who might have taken her."

"Impossible. It wasn't my family. I assure you." Julian shook his head, his blond hair swaying with overly styled perfection. "I *can* help you, though. I know the address. Campo dei Frari, Building 3070."

I sucked a quick breath and looked at Cross, who seemed equally impressed. "You've got good intel, Mr. Stone. Your father should be proud." He gripped my shoulder. "Now, out the window. All of you."

"You want me to take him with us?" I spat.

"I doubt he's in on it," Cross said as he cut a sideways glance toward Julian. "But his father's a bastard who you should avoid at all costs."

"No argument here," Julian grumbled.

"Besides, I'm sure Mr. Stone can solve a few cash flow problems now that Randolph Urban's funds are out of the mix."

"Yes. I have money! Lots." Julian's face lit up. "I just need you to—"

"Quit while you're ahead, kid," Cross snapped.

"How is his money any safer than Urban's? His father's a criminal, too," I shrieked, and Julian recoiled as if he'd been slapped. "And why should I take your car? You're just as bad. Every adult in my life is a lying psycho!" I knew I sounded like a melodramatic soap star, but my life was starting to feel unreal. I was just waiting for the evil twin to pop out.

"Anastasia, it was a job," Cross sounded exasperated.

"I know you want a loftier explanation than that, but it's really that simple. We were good at what we did, and we made lots of money. Money I tried to give to you and your sister." His hazel eyes softened, that hint of kindness gleaming through. "Your parents loved you. Everything they did was for you. But people don't become powerful without having secrets."

Just then a crash erupted inside the café as if a large tray of cups clattered to the floor. Everyone looked to the bathroom door. "That's them. Go!" Cross shoved me toward the window. This time no one hesitated.

Marcus jumped onto the closed toilet seat and cranked the grimy window open. "I'll catch you on the other side," he said, looking only at me.

He squirmed face-first through the small rectangular opening, and Julian guided his feet, though I doubted Marcus wanted the help. Then Julian scurried out behind him, and I stepped onto the toilet, turning back toward Cross. His eyes looked sad.

"If you go to Venice, they'll be waiting for you," he warned.

"She's my sister," I replied, summing up every choice I'd made since I saw that tub. Keira was out there, right now, praying for someone to find her. And I was the only one looking. I had to go.

"Do not talk to the Italian police. They encountered your parents often over the years, and they are loyal to the Bassos. They won't do you any favors, but I'll send help when I can."

I reached down and hugged him from my perch on the toilet, feeling a sudden burst of emotion for the Uncle Aleksandr of my youth. "Are you sure about Julian?" I asked in his ear.

"Keep him close. He could be an asset. Think—if it *is* his father who has your sister, then it'll be beneficial to have *his* son. But do not let him plaster you on the front page of some newspaper." His words were hushed, though there was no way Julian could hear from outside. Then he shoved me toward the window. "Now go. Stay safe."

"I will."

I reached onto the gritty ledge and shimmied my way through, Julian and Marcus guiding me down to the cobblestones. Then we all left together, for better or worse.

CHAPTER TWENTY-SEVEN

We cut through the massive crowds surrounding the circular Pantheon, walking as calmly as our panicked bodies would permit until we located Cross's silver car. Marcus took the wheel while I sat shotgun, and Julian spouted directions from the back like a local on his daily commute. He even took us past the Coliseum, the only time in my life I'd ever seen the iconic structure, not that I got the chance to appreciate it. Though I did imagine all the gladiators who'd been here before us; at least they had spears.

Once we were on the *autostrada*, with no gun-toting crazies in sight, I finally was able to absorb the fact that I was stuck in a compact car with a guy whose family may have potentially arranged for my sister's kidnapping. Not that I was afraid of Julian, at least not physically. He was only a few inches taller than me, probably about ten pounds thinner, and his jeans looked too skinny for the Olsen twins. I doubted he could fight in those things. But still, for the sake of our getaway, I waited until we were safely on the highway, cruising past lush green mountains and soaring over sky-high bridges, before I allowed myself to address the size zero elephant.

"Sophia told me she sent you," I said, turning toward his perch on the hump of the backseat. "But I don't really get why you're here."

Julian smiled like a teeth-whitening ad, looking relieved for the opportunity to finally speak. He spouted his saga. Supposedly, he and my father met while Julian was seeking a linguistic expert to translate the Arabic manual. He said that my dad was using the alias "John Frazier" (*Joe* Frazier was his favorite boxer), and that his knowledge of world languages was extensive, which I knew. My father became somewhat of an advisor, sharing pints at the pub as he praised Julian's efforts to bring down the terrorist cell. Then he ultimately destroyed the Stone family name and crippled their media holdings. Julian never saw it coming, nor did he ever meet my mother.

Additionally, while he was aware of his own father's questionable ethics, he denied that his family was guilty of any criminal activity that didn't involve a corporate boardroom. He swore the Stones had nothing to do with Keira's kidnapping. I didn't know how much I trusted my instincts anymore, but it didn't seem like he was lying.

He leaned between the front seats. "After I was publicly flogged, our fortune diminished, my family completely cut ties with me. While I still have my trust fund, no one speaks to me. Not my parents, not my siblings." He shook his head in a mixture of disgust and humiliation. "All I want is to fix the damage I caused, to set things right for everyone and to clear our family name."

"That's why you're here? You think *I* can help *you*? Because if you haven't noticed yet, I'm a little busy." I scanned the drivers whizzing by, fearful of spotting Luis Basso or another assassin. I knew that there was a trap waiting for me in Venice, but I had to go. I had to find a way to give them what they wanted, if it meant bringing Keira home.

"I'm sorry about your sister. That's why I looked into your situation, that's how I discovered the address where she was held."

"For all I know, your father *gave* you that address." I pumped my shoulders like I didn't believe him. "That man back there, Allen Cross, says that your dad's a criminal, that everything my father did to you was because *your* dad wanted too much power."

"Well, he does love to be in control." Julian scratched his forehead with a shiny buffed fingernail. "But he's a successful, well-documented entrepreneur. His corporate holdings are extremely public. There's no way he's a criminal, unless you count corporate espionage or illegal stock trades."

"Julian, my parents were very successful and well-documented engineers. So are his." I pointed to Marcus, who flinched at my words as if still unready to accept what our situation meant for his parents, his brother. "Dresden employees have had their pictures taken with government leaders from around the globe. Their contracts make headlines. Yet apparently, the company is also a front for a ring of criminal spies. So you can understand why I'd think your father is capable of anything, including kidnapping."

He sucked his lips between his veneered teeth, then shook his head defiantly. "If my father is what you say he is, it would mean that everything that happened to me, the last few years I've spent being slandered *by his own papers*, was because of him." Julian knotted his hands in his lap, his gleaming leather shoe tapping furiously on the floor mat. "It's not possible. I don't believe it…"

Though it sounded like he already did. Unfortunately,

I knew the pain of that betrayal all too well—from every adult in my life.

Two scenarios started to formulate in my brain. The first, that Randolph Urban never loved me, that he took my sister for some unknown reason and that he sent me here to find her for an even more obscure reason. The second, that Randolph Urban was a criminal just like my parents, who knew exactly which enemy not only held the greatest grudge against them, but also would be willing to use a child for revenge, because my parents had used his child against him—Phillip Stone.

"Think about it." I looked at Marcus, who glanced at me from behind the wheel. "What if Randolph Urban *knows* that Phillip Stone has Keira, and that's why he sent us to Europe. Look at what he's done since we've been here—he sent his granddaughter to talk to us, gave us that manual, then told *Julian* to find us. Maybe he's trying to help."

"But if Urban knows who has your sister, why wouldn't he get her back himself? He has the resources," Marcus pointed out.

"Maybe he tried," I continued. "Cross said a team of Department D agents raided the apartment in Venice. It was empty. Maybe Urban was working with them. Cross was very reluctant to say that Urban was behind this. Maybe Cross is trying to protect him."

"But then why send *you*, or me?" Marcus snapped, his forehead tense with wrinkles. "I thought Urban cared about you. If these lunatics are going after kids, why would he send us here?"

I thought he cared about me, too. Of course, I also thought that my parents were good people, and that my sister believed our espionage theories were crazy jokes. Clearly, I'd been wrong about a lot of things.

"I don't know." My voice swelled with emotion as I acknowledged the lies around me. "But he hasn't returned my calls since we got here, and have you heard from your family once?"

"How is *your* family involved?" Julian snapped, his blue-green eyes glaring at the back of Marcus's head. "I'm supposed to sit here while you attack *my* family, but have you told her that you brought me that manual? Your tattoo's rather memorable."

Marcus rubbed his neck, where the angry bull was inked, his eyes locked on the road. "I had no idea what I was delivering. It was just a job."

"Been hearing that a lot lately," Julian huffed.

I watched Marcus's jaw flex, out of guilt or irritation, I didn't know. Probably both.

I stared at the road in front of us, my mind racing faster than the car. If all this really were true, then somehow the children of three very high-ranking criminal families were now seated in the same car, heading toward a foreign city, where *someone* somewhere wanted us. We were purposely brought together, and it was clear there was much more waiting for us in Venice than my sister.

CHAPTER TWENTY-EIGHT

We crossed a long bridge into Venice, the afternoon sun bouncing off the glassy water of the bay so brightly I had to shield my eyes. Ahead, I spied a smattering of drab, smoggy industrial buildings and a generic concrete parking garage, but no submerged homes, no flowing canals, and no gondolas. It wasn't the Venice I'd imagined.

We parked the car near the swarming bus station, a cloud of diesel exhaust enveloping us as we crossed the four-lane street. Julian had booked a hotel, swearing he had enough cash in his wallet for us to stay as long as we'd like, which now conveniently left us at the mercy of someone whose family was leading the race for most-likely-to-have-kidnapped-my-sister. But I didn't have many alternatives. If his father did have Keira, keeping Julian in my sights was a good idea—as Cross suggested. And given that I had about ten euros in my pocket, it was either let him pay for dinner and a warm hotel or sleep in a two-door Fiat and pray for stale crackers between the bucket seats. I chose the former.

"Follow me," Julian said as he led us to a wide concrete staircase.

We began descending the steps, and a broad canal of thick turquoise water came into view.

Now, *this* was the postcard.

Ancient, colorful residential buildings sat with their foundations fully immersed in the rising tides of the canal. Arched pedestrian bridges crossed the muggy current at random intervals. Shutters framed every window, and the remains of centuries-old front doors peeked from far below the water line.

"Wow," I gaped in wonderment. It was like seeing the ruins of Atlantis.

Marcus grabbed my hand, as if on autopilot, as if the scene was too romantic not to hold someone's hand. "How does this even exist?" he asked, echoing my sentiment.

"The Venetians were a powerful empire," Julian replied. "They built things to last, somewhat." He led us to a private water taxi and we climbed aboard, not a piece of luggage between us; everything was abandoned at our hotels when we darted from the café. I was even without my laptop, which gave me that feeling you have when you forget your watch and keep looking at the lonely freckle on your wrist. I sank onto a faux leather bench in the back of a wood-trimmed speedboat and wondered how long I'd be wearing this beige peasant blouse, which most likely reeked of panicked sweat given the events of the day.

Marcus sat beside me, grabbing my hand as our boat skimmed the water, passing under one pedestrian bridge after another, the setting sun casting a tangerine glow on the buildings painted in bright hues of cobalt, rose, mint, and every color in between. The fact that my sister was potentially being held someplace so beautiful almost made the ordeal even more twisted.

A cloud of white mist sprayed my face as we sped into

the mouth of an expansive bay and pulled into a bustling dock. Crowds of tourists meandered on the walkway before us, shopping at tiny vending stands selling elaborate feathered carnival masks and cheap plastic key chains.

"Piazza San Marco's." The driver pointed. Julian handed over a wad of cash, his grin so smug it was clear he loved the power his money gave him.

"Thank you," I said, a little tight-lipped.

"My pleasure." He offered his hand to help me out of the boat, then lowered his voice. "I plan on buying a burner phone as soon as possible. I'll have people look into whether my father is behind this, and if he is, I'll do everything I can to help."

I nodded, unconvinced, but trying to look grateful. It took a lot of internal pep talks to remind myself that someone was working hard to blame me and my sister for actions that our parents committed, so even if Phillip Stone was behind this, it didn't mean Julian was, until proven otherwise.

Julian booked three rooms at a pleasant, understated hotel near Piazza San Marco. Given his pompous demeanor, I had expected him to demand designer water and a minimum number of fresh-cut flowers, but an all-cash budget seemed to limit his provisions—especially since he was now purchasing three new wardrobes, which included a black-tie affair.

Within minutes of procuring his new mobile device, Julian contacted an old news informant who he swore, "knew everything going on in Venice." The man was working to track down an address for where Keira may have been moved, and he expected to have more information within hours. However, the man also had tickets to the symphony that evening and would meet only during intermission. According to Julian, this necessitated that we all dress for the occasion.

"Do you really think this guy knows something?" I asked as we walked toward the city's version of Rodeo Drive.

"He's been right in the past," Julian offered.

"Says the guy who published a fake news story," Marcus grumbled. If I was annoyed at Julian holding the monetary power in this little trio, then Marcus was straight-up hostile. Though I had to assume that Marcus's anger had more to do with his family being full of potential underground criminals than Julian being rich and entitled.

Julian halted in front of a posh boutique so sparsely stocked, each clothing item was displayed like a work of art. Even the hardwood floors gleamed as if they'd never been stepped on. "Let's get dressed for the symphony, shall we?" He offered me a bended arm.

"I already told you, I'm wearing jeans," Marcus rebuffed.

"Brilliant. Then you'll stand out in the crowd like a sodding tourist, and everyone will notice you." Julian peered at me for assistance.

There was a trap waiting for us somewhere in Venice; whether it was being set by Phillip Stone, Randolph Urban, or an evil overlord I had yet to meet, I didn't know, but drawing undue attention to ourselves did not seem like the brightest plan. Besides, I literally could not afford to offend Julian. I had to eat and sleep. And Charlotte wasn't arriving in Italy until sometime later tonight—in Rome. I'd used Julian's new phone to leave a message telling her of our change in location, but who knew when she'd make it to Venice.

"Marcus, I can't ignore this lead," I insisted. "Cross said Keira was still in Venice, and this guy might know where.

Do you have another suggestion as to how to find her?"

Marcus gritted his teeth then finally hissed an irritated, "fine," before adding something in Spanish about throwing the spoiled *pendejo* off the nearest canal bridge.

We entered the store, bells ringing overhead.

"Mr. Stone, wonderful to see you again," greeted a forty-something sales associate in perfect English the moment we crossed the threshold. She flicked her shiny black hair behind her shoulder. "What are we shopping for today?"

"Casual wardrobes for my friends and me, plus outfits to wear to the symphony this evening." His tone was authoritative.

"Excellent." She smiled, brown eyes twinkling with dollar signs. She glanced at me. "My name is Isabella, and I understand you'll be needing a dress for this evening." She quickly guided me toward a rack, her graceful hand on my back, and plucked a sunny yellow cocktail number. "You have the perfect figure, and this canary tone will make your smoky eyes pop. Doesn't she have beautiful eyes?" she cooed, gazing at Julian.

"Yes, she does," he replied politely.

Marcus aggressively slammed down a thick chrome hanger. "Does it really matter what we look like?" he spat.

The associate gasped like he'd offended her reason for being. "Let me find you a fitting room." Then she scurried me away before Marcus could ruin her commission.

Moments later, I stepped out in the silk cocktail dress, the color of a dandelion, with a pair of gold heels on my feet. The climate-controlled store felt frigid against my bare legs, and the straps of my uncomfortably high dress shoes dug into my pinkie toes. I couldn't be expected to wear this in public. One good breeze aimed at this short flowy skirt, and all of Venice would see my undergarments—also being provided by Julian. I tugged at my hemline, ready to rip off the dress, only I heard a quick intake of breath. I glanced up to see Marcus and Julian smiling at me the way you expect a prom date to beam when you walk down the stairs.

"It's too short, right?" I pressed the thin fabric against my wildly exposed legs.

"Nonsense! It was made for you," countered the sales associate, glowing with such pride, I almost thought she'd sewn it herself.

"*Que hermosa.*" Marcus stepped toward me, gazing as if he were seeing me for the first time, like I'd changed somehow. It was only a dress.

I fidgeted with the spaghetti straps. "It's too much." I peered at Julian, referencing the price, the fabric, the style, everything. It was too much for what we were really doing in Venice.

"It's quite stunning, actually. Perfect." He nodded politely at Isabella. "Well done."

She shined at the recognition, then swiftly whisked Julian away to find his own fancy attire. An hour later, many shopping bags were filled and promised to be delivered to our hotel. Marcus and Julian were both dressed in black pants and pale button-downs, though Julian added a sport coat and Marcus insisted on keeping his motorcycle boots, which I loved. Apparently, Marcus could even make formal attire look edgy—with his boots and his chain-link wallet—and I couldn't help but notice his chest filled out his slim shirt in a way Julian's couldn't. It wasn't that Marcus was big or bulky, or thin and scrawny; Marcus was solid and defined like someone who used his muscles outside of a gym, like an athlete or a soldier. And the light blue fabric illuminated his maple eyes and hair. It was nice seeing him in something other than black.

"You clean up well," I said as I strolled beside him, trying to stifle the swooning smile that wanted to stretch across my face. I was in Italy to find my sister, not stare at Marcus in a new shirt. But it was so hard not to notice.

"You do, too." He slowly looked me up and down, not even pretending to hide his lingering gaze. "You should wear that dress all the time, like to sleep, eat breakfast…"

I blushed and stared at my feet. "Might be a little impractical."

"Maybe, but I still think *all* our outfits are unnecessary."

"Oh, really?" Julian countered, then pointed ahead.

We had reached La Fenice Theater, and the plaza was filled with symphony-goers dressed like attendees of a black-tie wedding in uptown Manhattan. In fact, we might have been underdressed.

"Whoa," I muttered, surveying the glamorous scene.

"Exactly." Julian nodded to me before stopping in front of the white marble staircase to the structure's columned entrance. "Now, my contact is going to meet me in the men's bathroom. He left only one ticket at will-call, so you'll have to wait here."

"What?" I snapped, skidding to a halt. "Since when?"

"It's a new development. He just sent me a text."

"You got us dressed up for nothing?" Marcus barked, reaching for his collar like he was prepared to yank off the shirt right here.

"This is *my* sister, Julian. You can't expect me to sit outside." My eyes insisted he couldn't be serious.

"But he's *my* contact, and he doesn't know you." Julian shrugged. "I can't help it if he doesn't trust you."

"Well, what if *we* don't trust *you*?" Marcus practically ripped the words from my lips.

Julian sighed, running his hand through his boy-band

hair. "I realize you're under the impression that my father is behind this, but I don't yet share your view. Even still, I have my own reasons for wanting your sister back." He looked me squarely in the eyes. "You and Keira may be the only two people on Earth who can clear my name; you know your father set me up."

"And you think I'm going to go public with that? Look what's happened to my sister for just quietly researching my parents' pasts."

Marcus grunted in agreement.

"That's exactly it." Julian smiled like someone who'd been struck by an epiphany. "Everyone thinks your sister is dead, but if she comes out of this alive—which I'm sure she will—and you go forward with your story, everyone will believe you. *And* no one will be able to touch you. You'll be public figures. *Girl back from the dead.* I can plaster your faces on every news outlet from here to New Zealand, making it way too dangerous for any harm to ever come to you again. Think about it."

Marcus rolled his eyes, stepping back as if the offer were ridiculous.

I didn't scoff.

If we did come out of this alive and returned to being anonymous nobodies in Boston, whoever did this could keep coming at us again and again and again. We'd always be looking over our shoulders for one of my parents' countless enemies. But raising our profile would make it riskier to take us out, though I doubted it was safer than going into hiding altogether, which might be our only other option. Not to mention, Cross sternly advised us not to let Julian plaster us on some newspaper. Still, it would be a decision Keira and I would have to make together, once she was safe. In the meantime, it did give me a new perspective on Julian. If he needed us, then he might genuinely be trying to help us—assuming he wasn't working for his father.

"Fine. Go talk to your contact. We'll wait," I replied grudgingly.

"What?" Marcus snapped.

I looked at him, my eyes trying to stress how limited our options were. I needed to know what his informant had to say. "If you're screwing me…" My voice trailed off as I shot Julian a heated look.

"I'm not. I assure you." Then he darted into the theater, passing through a towering gray metal detector before striding toward the will-call booth.

Meanwhile, Marcus and I lingered in a café across from the theater, passing time with a bottle of Pellegrino as we imagined every worst-case scenario—from Julian being attacked in the bathroom, to Keira being relocated to the Amazon jungle, to Phillip Stone popping out of the bushes with a bazooka aimed at our heads.

Finally, Julian emerged.

"We're in business. Let's go," he said as he approached our table.

We popped from our seats, and I threw my last remaining euros on the table. I couldn't ask Julian to pay for everything. I had some pride.

"What did he say?" I asked, hope ringing in my voice.

"Let's not talk here." His voice was low as he led us toward a nearby walkway. There were no cars in Venice, at all, just water taxis, ferries, gondolas, and pedestrians—a city utterly blocked from the clutches of big auto, a true time capsule.

"He knew about your sister," Julian whispered as we hurried on foot through a dimly lit alley. No one was around. "Not her name, but he heard about an American girl being held at the same flat that I mentioned. It's a well-known safe house. He agreed it's empty now. But for weeks, two men were spotted routinely entering and exiting the building."

Two men. I didn't want to think about what they were doing, what Keira was going through, especially after what Luis said on that mountaintop about his colleagues feeling lonely. My stomach rolled as I swallowed the bile that rose in my throat.

"Where is she now?"

"He has *some* leads. He thinks she's in a hotel."

"Where exactly?" My voice was desperate. There had to be at least a hundred hotels in this tourist town.

"He's still working on it. He expects to hear more tomorrow."

I couldn't wait another twenty-four hours. I'd spontaneously combust from anxiety alone. We were so close.

"We should go to the apartment, the one where she *was* held, see if there's evidence." I was ready to run there in high heels. It was like I was starting to feel her, in this city, in my gut. I wanted to reach out and grab her.

"The flat's a trap, don't you think? And my contact is reliable. We should wait," Julian insisted, as we moved through shadowed walkways.

"How do we know your contact isn't in on it?" Marcus accused, his eyes small as slits. "He could be telling us what *they* want us to hear, purposely keeping us away from the apartment, or making up anything to keep your *dinero* flowing."

"He's got a point, Julian. Are you paying him?" I asked, and Julian looked away guiltily. He should know people say anything for money; his family owns tabloids. "I'll text Charlotte your contact's name and have her look into him. She's probably in Rome by now."

"I can't give you his name," Julian shot back, shoulders pressed to his ears. "He's a source, and I have a terrible reputation as a journalist as it is. Why don't we give him a day and see if he comes up with anything?"

He clearly didn't know me very well. We had an address. I was going. At least it was something we could do.

Julian stopped walking, grabbing my elbow as we halted in a near-black piazza. The square looked abandoned, full of dilapidated buildings with drawn shutters and closed chipped doors. An empty flagpole stood dead center as a reminder of the life that used to occur here. I imagined it was hard to attract permanent residents to a city with no cars and sinking real estate. "How about we agree on dinner tonight? We haven't eaten in a while. We'll talk after we've had a good meal? Regroup?"

Marcus audibly sighed in time with his growling stomach. It was the first thing Julian had said right to him all day.

My own stomach was bubbling with hunger, but my heart was telling me to run in the potential direction of my sister, and my brain was telling me I needed to stop and think before I got myself killed. I was at war with myself. "Okay." I nodded reluctantly, finally siding with my brain.

We continued winding through the dim alleys, the straps of my gold shoes digging into my toes. I squirmed in my heels, Marcus's motorcycle boots beginning to look ingenious.

"So what have you been doing since you got fired, Julian?" Marcus suddenly asked, grinning as if this were a cheery topic of discussion.

"Oh, just trying to clear my name. You'd be surprised how time consuming it is," he replied sardonically.

"Yeah, I'd imagine you'd do just about anything."

"Well, I wouldn't work as an errand boy for international criminals."

"No, you'd just accept daddy's money, who *is* an international criminal."

"Quit it," I interrupted, shooting Marcus a look. I didn't care how much he disliked Julian; I'd join forces with the devil himself, if it meant finding my sister.

"*Lo siento*," Marcus replied, sounding slightly embarrassed, as we stepped into St. Mark's Square.

It was exactly like the postcards. An elaborate basilica stood on one end with a soaring brick bell tower anchoring the other. Couples were actually dancing under a bright full moon to the classical music of string quintets, gliding past the intricate rosy exterior of Doge's Palace with the serenity's only interruption coming from fluttering flocks of pigeons. It was so dreamy, it felt like a backhand to the face. This was where you should fall in love, not fight for your life.

"*Hermoso*," Marcus said, resting his hands on my shoulders, only I didn't feel butterflies in his touch. Instead, a thick mix of guilt and dread wound within me, as if this majestic scene showed just how far away I still was from my sister, as if I were on the brink of failing her yet again, standing on the other side of that bedroom door so close, but still unable to open it, still too late.

"She's here somewhere. She has to be," I whispered, almost to myself, and Marcus dropped his hands, acknowledging the ache in my voice.

We continued toward the restaurants lining the canal, water lapping over the edge as gondoliers waited for lovers to take a ride. My eyes stared longingly at the tourists, slipping from wine glass to wine glass, fish entrée to entrée, wanting to be them, until my gaze stopped short. Every muscle in my body suddenly clenched reflexively.

"Oh my God," I murmured, horror in my voice.

"What? What is it?" Marcus looked about, head jerking frantically, searching for the danger.

I nodded toward the restaurant, my throat constricting in a visceral reaction. "That's him," I choked, my hands involuntarily balled into fists. "The guy who took Keira. That's Craig Bernard."

CHAPTER TWENTY-NINE

Every night, for months, the face of Craig the Psycho haunted my nightmares—the man who came to our party, who drank our booze, who rocked the headboard of my sister's bed, and who left me with a bathtub full of her steaming hot blood. Now, he was standing before me, the personification of everything that was blazingly putrid in this world, and he was wearing a skinny suit.

A bolt of rage seared inside me, my nails burrowing into the flesh of my palms. His dark blond hair was pulled into a slick, low ponytail, contrasting sharply with the shaggy grunge look he sported on Mother's Day Eve. His scar was still visible in the light of the restaurant, and his smile looked crooked as he glanced about the tables seemingly searching for someone.

I could hardly breathe. It felt like my chest was being crushed by a boulder. I continued staring, unmoving, until suddenly my hatred swept in and tapped him on the shoulder. Craig Bernard looked my way. As soon as his eyes locked on me, he smiled like I'd made his day.

"Son of a bitch," I muttered, faintly hearing Marcus and

Julian arguing behind me, but their voices churned into white noise, a distraction I could easily ignore.

I stayed locked on Craig as he moved slowly through the open-air restaurant, never breaking eye contact, weaving past tables, seemingly amused. I longed for a grenade to launch at his cocky face, to erase the dare in his eyes begging me to confront him. He was going to get his wish. I exhaled and straightened my posture as the pianist inside broke into Beethoven's Fifth Piano Concerto, like he knew the drama about to unfold.

"Screw. Him," I hissed as I yanked off my golden heels and tossed them at Marcus. Craig seemed to appreciate the gesture, because he smiled. Then he blew me a kiss, just like he had the night of our party, when my sister wasn't looking. Only this time, I didn't feel nauseated, I felt fire.

He started running, and I took off after him like a championship sprinter, my bare feet flying over stone pavers, slipping in the rising tide as my yellow dress whipped in the wind. If this was a trap, if this was what Cross had been warning me about, I was running into it. Literally.

"I'm right beside you," Marcus confirmed as he and Julian kept pace.

I tore down the promenade bordering the Grand Canal. Vendors lined the strip as tourists strolled casually eyeing the colorful feathered masks. Craig slammed into anyone in his way, his stride awkward in his skinny suit pants. Even in bare feet, I was gaining on him fast.

He tossed a middle-aged man to the dirt, sending the crowd into a burst of panic as a cell phone flew into the air. I hurdled the victim lying face down on the pavement, not caring how much glass, rock, or twisted metal my bare feet caught. I didn't look back.

"Stop him!" I shouted in Italian. "Thief! Thief!" (Yelling

"Crazy psycho!" didn't seem like it would help.)

I splashed through a puddle at least an inch deep, water speckling my dress. I had no idea what I would do when I caught him. Craig was at least fifty pounds heavier and trained to kill; if my confrontation with Luis taught me anything, it was that this was not a sparring match. I could lose. Permanently. Plus, even if I did get in a few hits, I still needed him to tell me where Keira was, and I had no idea how to accomplish that.

But I couldn't get ahead of myself.

I couldn't think beyond: *Stop. Him. Now.*

Craig flew onto a nearby boat.

"Julian, you know that money you got?" Marcus gasped between breaths as Craig revved the engine. "Now would be a good time to use it." He pointed to the water taxis.

I dove into the first one I saw.

"*Via!*" I screamed at the driver to go, my pulse racing faster than the motor. "*Via! Via! Via!*"

Marcus and Julian jumped in beside me.

"Follow that boat!" Julian threw the driver a wad of cash, tucking a cell phone into his pocket.

Our boat took off into the inky night. The only things illuminated were fellow cruisers with their red and white taillights dotting the water like starbursts. I knew exactly which taillights were Craig's; it was as if I could smell his scent.

"Go! Now!" I hollered, pointing toward Craig's boat. Adrenaline gushed through me as we zipped across the black water, cool spray smacking my face, the water cooling the blazing heat in my cheeks.

Marcus stepped beside me. "What's the plan? Follow him? Hope he leads us back to Keira?"

"Bloody hell, he's a spy! This is crazy! He's not going to

lead us anywhere!" Julian countered.

"Maybe that's because you don't want him to," Marcus accused. "Maybe you're in on this. Did you tip him off? Is this your family's doing?"

"Enough!" My eyes stayed superglued to the boat. "We're going to stop him."

"How?" they both asked in unison.

"I don't know, but we will. This is the man who took my sister." That was all that needed to be said.

Julian grabbed my wrist. "Anastasia, he likely has a gun. This is a trap. You knew it was coming."

"So you think Craig Bernard was just sitting in San Marco's hoping we'd wander by?" I barked, disbelieving. "You saw him at that restaurant; he was looking for someone else, a dinner guest, a boss, someone. Not us. Yes, we don't have a plan, but neither does he."

"*His* plan is to kill us," Julian pointed out.

"If they wanted me dead, I'd be dead! Luis Basso had all the time in the world on that mountain!"

"Yeah, and according to Marcus, he choked and stabbed you." Julian nodded to the now-healed wound on my arm.

"I didn't even need stitches," I retorted, as if that mattered. Wind crashed against my face, tears forming, streaking my cheeks—hopefully from the breeze. "Luis had a gun, Julian, and he didn't use it. Regardless, what do you expect me to do? Let him get away? You want my sister to stay in shackles somewhere? For all I know, you and your father are the ones who've locked her up." I pointed my finger inches from his face. "You said you want me to trust you? Fine, then help me, otherwise get off the boat."

We were probably traveling at more than forty miles per hour. Julian couldn't exactly jump off the boat. I knew that, but at this point, I was ready to throw him off if he attempted to stop this chase. I was going to catch those taillights, and I didn't need his money to do it.

"I've got your back." Marcus pressed closer to my side as we rocked with speed. Whatever fears I may have developed for motorized vehicles after my parents' accident oddly seemed to evaporate in the face of my sister's attacker. Maybe immersion therapy works.

Craig's taillights continued flying down the canal, racing toward a crowd of gondolas full of couples cuddled side by side with young Italian men gliding their boats through the water using sky-high poles. It reminded me of the picture from Randolph Urban's office. I couldn't believe that I took his money, that I blindly trusted him.

What if it isn't Phillip Stone who has Keira? What if I just want it to be the Stones? This could all be Urban's doing. Has he been laughing at me this whole time?

Gondoliers hollered as our impending speedboats approached, Craig never veering off course. He sliced into the Venetian traffic jam, splashing waves of white water and nearly capsizing the defenseless tourists. Couples screeched as gondoliers shook their fists, screaming obscenities, and our driver began to slow.

I jumped in his face. "Keep going!" I shouted in Italian.

He continued carefully, ignoring my request.

My eyes shot toward Julian. "Make him go! Now!"

Julian approached the driver, whispering something I couldn't overhear, and immediately our speed increased. But it wasn't enough. Our distance from Craig was expanding.

"Julian, if this son of bitch doesn't drive faster…" I hissed.

Just then Craig made a sharp turn down a dark side canal, and I bounced on my toes, hands waving furiously. "Over there! Go! *Hurry!*"

Julian instructed the driver, who subtly increased his speed but failed to steer into the same canal.

"What is your problem?" I shrieked in Italian, shoving the man's shoulders. "Follow him! Now!"

The driver yelled something about taxis being prohibited from traveling in certain waterways, about needing to stick to the Grand Canal, and no matter how much I hollered, nostrils flared, he refused to follow my orders. Julian joined in, also screaming, until Marcus shoved the driver aside and took the wheel.

"*Siéntate!*" Marcus shouted in Spanish, and I could see he was about a second away from punching the man in the face (which I would have appreciated).

He spun the boat toward the side canal, throttling the engine as he raced perpendicular to oncoming traffic. Craig's taillights trailed off as he skimmed down the narrow waterway, and before Marcus could veer down the same path, we were jolted by the blare of a deafening foghorn. We swung our heads and spied a large passenger ferry headed our way. Marcus swerved, avoiding a near collision as the massive ferry cut in front, its nearly one hundred passengers snapping pictures of the just-missed crash. I bounced in my bare feet, waiting impatiently for the ferry to pass, only as it did, I peered down the black canal and saw no lights.

"We lost him," I whispered, a pain piercing my abdomen. I hunched over.

"We don't know that," Marcus insisted, speeding into the canal, but I knew it was useless. We were too late.

Craig Bernard was gone.

CHAPTER THIRTY

I collapsed onto my hotel room bed. My yellow silk dress splayed out, stains blotching the hem. All the determination that had kept me going was left on the floor of that boat.

After we lost Craig Bernard in the canals, we went to the only logical place—the flat where Keira was held. Only there wasn't a single light in a window, nor a swish of a curtain. It was empty.

I dropped my head against my lumpy down pillow and sprawled wide, staring at the mustard yellow watermarks seeping through the hotel's popcorn ceiling. I'd stood within yards of the man who took my sister, and I let him get away. Cross had sworn they were purposely leading me here, but tonight I'd walked right up to the apartment building where Keira was held hostage and nothing happened—no trap, no evil super spies, and no Keira.

Maybe she's already dead? A hole ripped inside my chest. *Don't think like this... Don't think like this...* She had to be out there. Somebody wanted something from us, right? We were useful to them. We had to be. Otherwise, they could have killed her in Boston; they could have killed me in Cortona. But they didn't. Still, that didn't mean she was okay. I already knew they shoved her into the trunk of a car, I knew two men were holding her. What was she going through right now because I failed her? Yet again.

My lungs tightened. This was my fault. I let him get away. I shut my eyes, a burning sensation building behind my eyelids. I didn't want to cry. I was tired of crying. I was tired of all of this. I wanted to go back to the way things were. I wanted Keira back. I wanted my parents back. I wanted to be the daughter of two happy engineers. I wanted a normal life. We didn't do anything wrong. We didn't deserve this.

I dug my teeth into my lips, chewing—hard—hoping the pain would divert my tears.

Don't cry, I commanded myself, biting harder. Only images flashed behind my eyelids—the bloody tub, Keira's memorial, her body twisted in a foreign car, my parents' caskets, the cocky smirk of Craig Bernard. The tears gushed like levees giving way, and I sobbed, curling tight, grabbing my knees, my breath hyperventilating. I had nothing. I had no one. The funk enveloped me, and I let it, curling tighter.

A knock sounded on my door.

I tried to ignore it. It was either Marcus or Julian, and I didn't know which one I wanted to see less. I had unabashedly lost it on the boat when Craig disappeared. I screamed at them, called them pathetic, useless, cowards. It wasn't exactly my shining moment, and it wasn't until Marcus reminded me of the apartment that my head stopped spinning in circles.

Then we sat in the plaza for hours, waiting for something to happen, waiting for someone to show, and all the while I didn't say a word. I wouldn't speak to either of them, not even when they asked direct questions. Finally, when it hit two a.m., I left. I didn't say good-bye or where I was going. I just walked away and left them behind. They didn't follow.

Until now.

"Anastasia?" It was Marcus. "Let me in."

I scrunched my eyes tighter, trying to will him away. I didn't feel like apologizing. I wasn't ready to be sorry.

"I know you're in there. Just let me in. We don't have to talk."

My eyes pulled open and stared at the door. If I stayed alone, I knew I'd sink back into the coma, back into the funk. I wiped at my cheeks.

"I, um, I just want to see…" he stammered. "I don't know. Let me in. *Por favor.*"

I hardly had the energy to stand, but I did, robotically. I dropped my bare feet onto the floor and staggered over, left foot, right foot, left foot, right foot. I turned the knob.

Marcus's eyes bugged in their sockets. I must not have looked good.

"It's not over." He reached for me.

But it was, and I cried harder. Marcus pulled me to his chest, shutting the door behind him. The louder I sobbed, the tighter he squeezed, my tears soaking his fancy new button-down. I nestled my face against the tattoo on his neck, sniffling, trying to compose myself, but it was too hard. I wanted to dissolve into him, to disappear. The loss was overwhelming—my sister, my parents, now Craig Bernard.

"It's not over," he said again, stroking my hair. I knew it wasn't true, but I needed to hear it. I needed to believe it.

I needed him.

I drew a slow, stammering breath and peeled my head from his sweaty chest. I looked up, remembering that train station in Cortona, wanting to erase the pain inside me, wanting to lose myself, wanting to forget what was happening. He seemed to register the new expression in my eyes as I slowly moved toward him. He didn't pull away.

I kissed him. Hard.

I crashed my body against his and he responded, knotting his fingers in my hair. He pressed me against the wall of the entry, his lips moving against mine. The hot energy oozing from him eased the ache inside me. He moved his leg between mine, clutching me tighter, biting my lip. My breath was ragged as I held on to him, clinging to the passion, clinging for dear life.

Then he suddenly jerked away. And I gazed up, confused and breathless.

"Are you sure this is what you want?" he panted. "I don't want to take advantage…"

"You're not. I—I just don't want to feel sad anymore. Make me not feel sad anymore."

He hesitantly moved his lips toward mine, then paused, barely a whisper between us. I could smell his sweat, feel his breath. I knew he didn't want to stop.

"Are you sure?" he asked again, leaning his arm against the wall above my head, dark eyes heatedly locked on mine.

I didn't want to answer. I didn't want to talk. I just wanted *him*. I thrust myself at him once more, and he didn't resist. He grabbed me tight, the blood whooshing from my brain. My heart accelerated, but not out of fear or desperation or frustration. I felt something new. I felt excited.

He pressed my head against the wall, my face firmly in his hands. Then he abruptly pulled me toward him and guided me to the bed, kissing me as I stumbled backward. I knew where this was headed, and it was what I wanted.

I needed to feel this. His lips moved to my neck, and his hands slid toward the zipper of my dress. Hot tingles flushed my skin.

This is it, I thought. He moaned my name, and I suddenly felt a surge of power. I gripped his hair, kissing him harder.

Then a knock pounded on my hotel room door.

I groaned, pulling away.

"Ignore him," Marcus whispered, still kissing my neck.

The knock got louder. "Anastasia?" Julian yelled.

"*Ignore him,*" Marcus said again, lightly sucking my skin, hoping to retain my attention, but I turned toward the door.

"I have a surprise for you!" Julian yelled enthusiastically, still pounding. "You'll never believe what I found!"

"Go away!" Marcus yelled, his voice winded as he forced himself from me and glared at the entry.

"Anastasia?" asked an awkward female voice.

Charlotte.

A smile sprung to my face that I didn't know I still had in me. I shoved Marcus's hands away and darted toward the door, adjusting my dress. I turned the knob and heaved it open.

"You're *here*!" I squealed.

Charlotte smiled with the purity of a toddler, her hair messy from hours of travel but her eyes delighted. She looked exactly the same. I knew it had been only about a week since I'd seen her last, but I felt like I'd aged a decade. "Well, you didn't think I'd let you find Keira without me, did you?"

I flung my body at her, wrapping my arms around her chest until they crossed on the other side. "You got my text?"

"Obviously. Sorry for the late hour, but getting a last-minute flight out of Rome was insane." She pulled away. "And I gotta admit, I was a little surprised to get to the hotel lobby and find Julian Stone." Her eyes cut toward him.

"She approached me at the hotel bar," Julian explained. "At first I thought she was hitting on me, which was rather exciting—"

"Then I asked if he stalked you here," Charlotte interrupted, and I could see from her expression that the verdict was still out.

"We actually gave him a ride. Sorry I didn't mention it. It's been a long day, longer night…" My voice trailed off as I grabbed Charlotte's arm. It felt so good to have her here.

"I want to hear *everything*," she said, then looked at Marcus, the flush of his cheeks and the sheen on his skin. Her brain flipped topics. "So good to see you again. You know, you missed a button." She pointed to his shirt, and he immediately glanced down, eyes alarmed, but saw everything buttoned just right. His cheeks flamed even more as he ran a hand through his disheveled hair.

"*Slut*," she taunted, her eyes glancing at my partially unzipped dress.

"You're here!" I shrieked, hugging her once more.

CHAPTER THIRTY-ONE

I didn't sleep much that night. It was already close to three a.m. when Charlotte arrived, and she grilled me like a prime-time news anchor as I relayed everything that happened with Craig Bernard, the boat chase, and the empty flat. Then, she updated me on her progress. She was still unable to locate the photo of Keira in the trunk. Even worse, the Boston PD removed Detective Dawkins from the case, leaving McCoy in charge—a cop I'd hated since he accused my sister of attempting suicide and magically evaporating.

Add to that, Tyson and Regina were asking if I'd be available for Back to School festivities, which only reminded me of how far I'd fallen from a normal teenage life. I didn't know what I wanted after I found Keira. Part of me yearned for simplicity—dating, college applications, and pep rallies—while part of me already knew I surpassed the ability to meld back into that life. I was like a soldier returning stateside; my adrenaline was in such perpetual flow, could I ever be content with daily commutes and homework? Could I pretend this entire world of espionage wasn't lurking in the shadows? And did I want to?

Charlotte eventually drifted off with jet lag, while I lay in bed, staring at the clouds of rust-colored water stains blotting the ceiling. I may have dozed for a few minutes before the sun crept through the hotel curtains in a gray morning haze. I had to get out of here, start moving, clear my head. It was five thirty when I exited the hotel, and even the front desk clerk seemed surprised to see me. Outside, the canals were motionless. Only a lone, rank-smelling trash boat passed as I veered through the walkways that led back to the building where Keira was held, like a beacon was calling. The storefronts selling colorful Venetian glass and bottles of wine were closed. The city was sleeping.

I crossed a small pedestrian bridge and spied a large church ahead—Campo dei Frari. I stepped into the familiar square. Irish-green shutters flanked every window, with sienna bricks peeking through the beige stucco façades, perfectly matching the exterior of the Basilica di Santa Maria Gloriosa dei Frari, which anchored one side.

I stared at building 3070. Supposedly, Keira had been held in apartment 302. It was time for me to go in. See it for myself.

I strode into the center of the empty square, the newsstands closed, the cafés covered with metal security protection. The only movement came from a fluttering leaf. I looked up at the smoky gray sky, reminiscent of my eyes, and a wave of defiance surged through me. I held my arms wide, turning in a loop of circles, faster and faster. If anyone were waiting for me to show, if some evil spies were tailing my every move—here I was. I'd done what they'd wanted. I walked into their trap. They could have me. Now. Just take me to my sister.

A few moments passed, my dark hair whipping my

cheeks as I spun, but no one appeared. I dropped my arms with a sigh and scanned every window along the square, willing a curtain to shift, a light to flicker, a shadow to move.

But I was alone. I could feel it.

I trudged to the door of the building. It was crafted from solid wood, painted hunter green to match the shutters, though the thick layers of paint had long ago begun to chip. I placed my fist on a carved wooden panel and knocked. (Hey, you never know.) It barely rattled, and no one answered.

My eyes moved to the long, thin, rectangular windows lining the vestibule door, their glass ribbed and frosted. They looked modern, almost new, and a lot less solid than the door. If I was ever going to break the law, now was the time.

I glanced back at the nearby newsstand; sienna bricks coated with white chalky dust held a plastic tarp over its cashier window. Before I could overthink it, I darted over and grabbed a brick, its clay leaving a film on my palm as I moved back to the door. I closed my eyes, made a silent wish that buildings this old did not have alarm systems, then crashed the brick against the glass windowpane. Millions of shards clattered at my feet, and I wasted no time. I shoved my hand into the hole, trying to avoid the jagged edges as I felt for the doorknob.

It opened easily.

I slipped into the building, rushing up the stairs as quietly as possible, then stopped on the third floor. The door to flat 302 was slightly ajar, and I couldn't help but think of the door to my apartment that fateful morning, before I found the tub, before everything changed.

I exhaled deeply and went inside. The door creaked like a horror film as the stench of garbage smacked my face. I turned and saw a stack of grease-stained pizza boxes and overflowing trash bags filling the entry. Someone had been here recently.

"Keira!" I screeched, charging into the living room. There was a lone sofa, its striped brown fabric ripped to show the dirty yellow foam beneath. Two newspapers rested on the coffee table. I picked one up. It was dated only a week ago.

"Keira!" I hollered again, my voice cracking in desperation. "Are you here?"

I looked in the small galley kitchen. There were dirty dishes leaning like the Tower of Pisa in the porcelain sink; stale-smelling bottles of Peroni beer with floating cigarettes sat on the white-tiled counter, and a couple of flies buzzed near the scraps of rotting food. I rushed toward a short hallway. There were four doors. I flung open the first to see a closet with a few bare wire hangers. I ran to the next—a bathroom, the shower curtain pulled open, no one inside. The last two doors had to be bedrooms.

"Keira," I squeaked, my voice shaky. Whoever was here had left in a hurry.

I placed my hand on the scratched brass knob of the first door and turned. No one was inside, only two metal cots about as luxurious as those you'd expect to find in your local prison. There was a rumpled sheet on each. I tore off the bedclothes, looking for a clue, any sign that my sister had been here. But all I saw was a thin, stained mattress. I searched under the bed—clotted dust bunnies rustled about, nothing more. I opened the closet door, more metal hangers and the musty smell of dirt. I pulled the drawers on the tall dresser in the room—only a safety pin and a broken plastic button.

I headed back into the dimly lit hall and moved to the final door, my last hope. Beads of sweat dripped down my forehead as I placed my quivering hand on the knob, almost too scared to turn it. But I did.

The second the door swung open, I could instantly sense Keira. The room smelled of her.

I dashed to the bed, queen-sized with an old wooden frame covered in pink sheets and a rosy quilt that looked brand new. It was nothing like the room next door. I yanked back the covers, desperately searching for something, maybe another piece of jewelry, a lipstick, a note. I lifted a long platinum blond hair from the wrinkled white pillowcase and stretched it in my hands. If my years of experience with our shower drains were any indication, I'd bet my future life savings that this hair belonged to my sister. I held the pillow to my face. She was here. I could breathe her. I dropped the pillow back onto the mattress, and my eyes caught a small etching in the wooden bedframe, right where the pillow had rested. I ran my finger along it.

KAP.

Keira Alexandra Phoenix.

My mind skipped back to our days in Singapore, the night I wandered into the wrong hotel room and everyone thought I'd been kidnapped. They were panicked. When I finally turned up, Keira joked that if I were going to hop from bed to bed I might want to leave a trail of breadcrumbs.

"Aren't there starving people in Africa who need that bread?" I teased.

"Okay, so carve your initials in the beds. Or leave a message in blood. *Whaahhaahaa.*" She faked an evil laugh.

"I think the hotel people might complain about that."

"But think of the trail you'd leave around the world. When you're old and have kids, you could take a scavenger hunt to find all your old initial carvings, like a real-life Gretel."

She was only kidding when she'd said it, but as my fingers ran along the carving hidden behind the bed pillow, I knew she wasn't kidding now.

KAP.

She was here. Maybe as recently as a week ago.

And I was too late.

No. I shook my head, pushing out the thought. *There has to be something else. She has to have left a clue.* It was what I would do. I would hold on to hope that someone would find it, that someone would find me.

I tore through the room, yanking open every drawer, ripping through the sheets, searching under every dresser. Finally, I crouched low and peered under the bed. That was when I found them, suspended between the bedframe and the wall, directly behind the wooden post where she'd carved her initials.

There were two photos.

I slid my hand behind the splintery column, my fingers cutting through a mess of cobwebs as I yanked the photos free. As soon as my eyes caught the first image, a gasp escaped my lips. It was of me. Actually, it was Marcus and me kissing in Cortona, on the train platform. We looked like happy young lovers. Chills rushed across my skin, raising the hairs on my neck, my arms, as I realized we had been followed. Someone was watching us as we kissed, and we were completely oblivious. Maybe it was Luis, maybe that was why he hadn't chased us out of town—he was too busy lurking in the bushes snapping pervy pictures. And they'd shown this to Keira. She probably thought that I'd forgotten about her, that I was having a blast on vacation, that I didn't care. They'd used me to hurt her. I was making things worse.

A sense of hollowness consumed my chest. Was there

anything else I could do to fail her?

I reluctantly turned to the next photo and saw Keira. Her platinum blond hair was grown too long, her dark roots were at least two inches from her scalp, and her face was gaunt and greasy with dark purple circles under her eyes. She was holding a piece of paper, scowling for the camera. I peered closely and recognized that she was clutching what looked like a church bulletin for the basilica across the plaza. It was dated two weeks ago.

Who did they send this to? I wondered, examining the image.

It looked like proof of life, like they wanted to assure someone that Keira was alive. But *I* never received it. Did they send it to Allen Cross? To agents at Department D? Maybe that was why Cross said that men had raided the apartment. Surely the church bulletin would have tipped off their location. The kidnappers literally drew them a map; they wanted to be found. But why? And why didn't Cross tell me if he received a second photo?

It didn't make sense. A photo was taken of Keira and not sent to me—the sister who's been searching for her, the sister who these men supposedly wanted to trap.

Unless they didn't.

My mind considered the alternatives. *Maybe this trap isn't for me.*

These guys could be luring someone else. Randolph Urban? He was the one who sent me. Maybe Urban was trying to track down the daughter of his old friends, and he fell into their clutches. Maybe something happened to him, and that was why I hadn't heard from him. Because I couldn't think of anyone else on the planet who would care about the lives of Keira and me.

...

I darted out of the apartment building, my sneakers crunching on the window's broken glass as I sped across the empty plaza. I bounded up the steps of the basilica. Keira was holding a bulletin from this church—she had to have gotten it somehow. I yanked open the heavy wooden doors to the shiny marble foyer. The church, with its soaring vaulted ceiling and exposed beams, was surprisingly cool for August. I crept up the rose-and-ivory-checkered tiles of the center aisle, passing towering marble columns as I searched for a priest, a nun, or an altar boy to question. No one.

I scanned the ornate gilded alcoves and confessional booths for any signs of movement, listening for whispers, until a door slammed shut behind me. I jumped, my Converse squeaking as I spun toward a side entrance to see a young priest descend a red-carpeted ramp.

"*Mi scusi, padre.*" I walked toward him. "*Hai un minuto?*"

"You shouldn't wear that in here," he replied in English, eyeing my black tank top and bare shoulders.

"*Mi dispiace.*" I tugged at my fitted shirt. I might as well have had "American" stamped on my forehead. "I wasn't expecting to come in this morning. I just have a few questions," I continued in English.

"About what?" He nodded to the first pew, and we sat together. He was younger than most priests I saw back home—his shoulders were broad, and his neck was thick, and there was a little paranoid piece of me that worried he wasn't a real clergy member. Still, I continued, summoning whatever nerve I had as I stared at the fresco before us, cherubs packed on dense clouds ascending toward heaven as worshippers reached desperately from below.

"I'm looking for someone," I admitted, inhaling the sour stench of religious incense. "My sister, Keira. She's been kidnapped." I held out the photo of my tortured sister clutching a crumpled church bulletin.

His thick black eyebrows squished together, a deep wrinkle forming above his nose. "Is she all right? Have they found her?"

I shook my head. "No. That's why I'm here. Somebody took this photograph of her. On *this* day." I pointed to the date. "Which means the kidnapper had to have been in this church."

"I conducted this mass." His brown eyes widened.

"Do you remember anything? Did you see my sister? Anyone suspicious?" My heart leaped.

He eyed me cautiously. "Where are the *polizia*?"

I twisted my hands in my lap, the conversation reminding me of McFadden's Bar. It felt so long ago. At the time, Charlotte and I were evading the police to keep ourselves in the loop. Now, I was paranoid that all government agencies were corrupt and out to get us, which didn't seem like a rational response to elicit assistance from him.

"The evidence just came into my possession," I admitted truthfully. "And my sister's American. There's a lot of red tape over whose jurisdiction this is."

There. That sounded legitimate.

Besides, now that we had a time-stamped picture of my sister alive, the FBI, the Boston PD, the CIA, and every other agency in the world, couldn't ignore us. Maybe we finally could get some help.

The priest nodded, seemingly satisfied. "Your sister was kidnapped in Venice?"

"No. She was taken from our home in Boston, then brought to Italy. I found that photo in an apartment across the piazza." I pointed to the doors. "It looks like they moved her recently. Do you remember anything?" I asked hopefully, shifting toward him in our creaky pew. He stared at the photo. "There were two men holding her in building 3070. One of the men I saw in San Marcos Piazza last night. His name's Craig Bernard. He's in his late twenties. About six-foot-two. Dark blond wavy hair to his shoulders, raspy voice, a thick scar on his upper lip."

The priest cleared his throat, a strange flex in his eyes, then glanced about the empty church. "I'll look into it. I'm so sorry about your sister, but I need to get ready for mass." He glanced at his watch as he handed back the photo.

"Should I wait? Will you ask around?"

He stood, moving toward the aisle as he offered me an all-too-familiar pity smile. "You can always stay for mass; it can only help. I promise I'll pray for you and your sister."

My jaw clenched. I didn't need his prayers, I needed his help.

But I said nothing. Yelling at a man of the cloth would probably do me no favors. So I silently stewed as he walked down the massive center aisle toward the back of the church, his shoes echoing off the five-hundred-year-old marble. I *would* stay for mass, and I'd question every person who walked through those doors. I'd do it every day if I had to. Keira was being held across the plaza. Someone had to have seen something.

I pushed myself upright and charged toward the entrance, prepared to camp out on the front steps with the photo of my sister. I should blow it up to poster size, march back and forth like a picketer. I spied the priest in the vestibule, frantically scribbling in a bulletin, absorbed in his work. I shot him a thanks-for-nothing look and he stopped writing, hurrying toward me.

"Please, take a bulletin. Stay for mass." He handed me the folded sheet of paper.

I held up my hand to refuse, but he shoved the bulletin into my palm, manually closing my finger on the pages. "I hope you find her," he whispered, and there was something in his tone that made me pause.

I exited the church, prepared to wage a sit-in on the steps, when I finally looked down at the paper. There was a message written in elegant cursive script.

I saw a man fitting the description you gave. I remember the scar on his lip, and I remember him talking loudly on his mobile after mass. I asked him to keep it down, and he did, but I still overheard his conversation. He said that he had "her," but that he needed to move her soon. He arranged a meeting at La Fenice Theater during tomorrow night's symphony. I have tickets for that show, so the date stood out in my mind. If I had known your sister was in danger, I would have called the authorities. I hope you do so now. May God bless you and your sister.

I sprinted back into the basilica, heart pounding like the bass in a techno rave. My eyes darted around, but the priest was gone. The church was empty. I ran to the side entrance where he'd originally entered and heaved at the solid wooden door. It was locked.

Why didn't he say this to me directly? Was he scared for his life? Was he worried about breaking his vows of secrecy? I had only a sketchy knowledge of religion, but even I didn't think eavesdropping on a cell phone conversation was the same as listening to a confession.

My mind flicked to the boat chase through Venice. I could have altered Craig's plans with our run-in; maybe the symphony meeting would be canceled now, but if not, then it meant I knew where my sister's kidnapper would be tomorrow night. It was the same theater where Julian had met his contact. That couldn't be a coincidence. That informant had to be in on the kidnapping, maybe Julian was in on it, too. I didn't know who to trust, who was behind this, but it was the closest I'd gotten to Keira so far.

La Fenice, I thought, almost smirking to myself. It meant "the Phoenix."

CHAPTER THIRTY-TWO

I walked toward the sloping pedestrian bridge, the two photos I found in the flat tucked into the back pocket of my dark, low-slung jeans, one thought ringing in my head—what if Keira is with Craig at the symphony? What if this is it? I could finally have the chance to save her and simultaneously bash Craig's head on the concrete. It was my recurring fantasy sequence. I imagined the blood on his face, the pain in his eyes.

Then I heard a stampede of running feet.

"Oh my God! You're alive!" Charlotte screeched as she sprinted from the opposite side of the bridge, Marcus and Julian behind her. She threw her arms around me, crushing me into her, then pulled away and punched my shoulder. "What is wrong with you?"

"How late is it?" I looked at my watch. "I'm sorry, I thought I'd be back before you woke up."

"You don't just run off on people! You don't come to a place like *this* by yourself! You could've been killed." She punched my shoulder again. It barely hurt. Actually, it probably hurt her wrist more by the way her fist was flopping.

"I'm sorry. I didn't mean to go off alone, but we were up so late, and you were sleeping. I didn't want to wake you. I thought I could come here and look around one more time," I said apologetically. I probably should have left a note.

"Why didn't you wake me? I would have come with you," Marcus offered.

"Did you see anything?" Julian asked.

I stared at my sneakers as we continued trudging across the sloping bridge, the canal of turquoise water lapping below. If Julian's father was behind this, then revealing Craig's symphony plans would be akin to handing the enemy my playbook. Until I knew which side Julian was on, I couldn't share any leads in his presence.

"I went into the apartment, but the place was empty," I stated.

"You got in?" Julian sounded impressed. Or was he alarmed? Protecting his interests? My gut twitched.

"Yeah, it was wiped clean. No sign of Keira."

"You could have been killed," Charlotte muttered. "But I'm sorry you didn't find anything."

The time stamp on the proof-of-life meant we could finally communicate seriously with government agencies, something Charlotte desperately wanted, but I had to consider everything. Like why was a photo taken of Marcus and me? To upset Keira, make her think I no longer cared? Or was it sent to someone else? Who would care about my romantic involvements? And who wanted proof of Keira's life other than me? I needed time to process this information before I shared it with anyone else.

"Hey, it's not a total loss," Charlotte offered, digging into her gray denim purse. There was a patch of a pirate skull on the flap. "While you were breaking into apartments, Julian and I were hacking into this." She yanked out a thin black smartphone.

"Whose is that?" My forehead wrinkled.

"Craig Bernard's," Julian answered, sounding smug.

My sneakers skidded to a halt. "What?"

"He dropped it last night while you were chasing him. I picked it up," he said with a self-satisfied shrug.

"Why didn't you say anything?" I snatched the phone, sliding my finger along the bottom. A password screen popped up.

"Because I couldn't crack the code, and you already called me an idiot." His blond eyebrows arched high. Sure, I had flung a few insults after the ill-fated boat chase, but that didn't mean he should omit something this important. "I wasn't sure what the best course of action was. I was thinking of sending it to a mate of mine who's good with computers, but then Charlotte showed up." He nodded to her, as if already impressed by her skills.

"I'm making progress. I should be able to hack in by tonight." Her eyes were excited, thrilled to have a way of assisting.

"I told you I would help you find your sister," Julian added.

"Yeah, if I just give you an exclusive interview on CNN," I huffed.

"CNN's American. I'd want more of a European market."

"Good to know." I rolled my eyes, my faith in him eroding further. Marcus grunted beside me, muttering something about him being a "*gilipollas*," or dumbass, and I tried not to smile.

At this point, Julian was either on his father's payroll and helping to stash my sister in a hole somewhere, or he was capable of ruining the symphony meeting tomorrow just to ambush my sister's kidnapper with a mob of TV cameras and redeem his journalistic reputation. I couldn't risk either scenario. And while I could tell Charlotte and Marcus the truth, I worried one of them would inadvertently slip to Julian. Additionally, Charlotte would never support a face-to-face confrontation with Craig Bernard, and while Marcus might under normal circumstances, given the revelations about his family and his current angry mood, he was probably too conflicted to think clearly.

I ran my fingers against the hard edge of the photos tucked in my pocket, and stayed quiet for now.

"Want another Coke?" Marcus asked as he crumpled his empty can and tossed it into the trash can next to the bed.

"I'm good," I replied robotically, mindlessly staring at the flickering colors on the hotel TV.

It had taken all day, but I'd mentally constructed a plan for *La Fenice Theater* tomorrow night. It was detailed, layered, and a result of my battle with Luis—I was never throwing a wild punch at an assassin again, not if I didn't want to end up on the ground with a knife in my arm and a hand at my throat. This time I would be prepared. First, I'd lie in wait for Craig in the café I'd sat at with Marcus—it was discreet and had a good view of the symphony house. Then, I'd watch as Craig entered the theater through the metal detectors, and I'd instantly know if he was armed. Without a gun, we could have a fair fight (relatively). I'd take him by surprise and land every punch I'd fantasized about since I first heard Keira's bed squeak.

I decided I couldn't tell Charlotte. She'd insist on calling the police, and while I realized that was probably a good idea and that I needed the authorities, the core of my being craved one shot to face him, alone, before there was a legal barrier between him and me, before he was locked in an interrogation room with cops potentially working for Department D. Still, I didn't have a death wish. So I'd leave the photos I'd found behind Keira's bed in Charlotte's suitcase. She'd find them eventually and call for help. But I'd have a solid head start.

"I thought this was supposed to be a comedy. It's not funny," Marcus said, cracking open another soda as he stared at the movie. It was intended to "take our mind off things," per Charlotte's orders. It wasn't working, though that wasn't the movie's fault.

"Yeah, it's boring," I agreed, not sure what Marcus was even referring to on-screen.

He took a long sip and turned my way, his breath coating the air with the scent of cola. "I've been thinking about my family." His tone was serious as he muted the film. "I know given everything we've learned, their closeness with Urban, it seems like they must be in on it. I just don't see how that's possible. My dad grew a jawbone out of nothing. How could they fake that?"

"I don't know," I commiserated, remembering my parents' specialty in thermochemical process design. That seemed real to me too. But it wasn't.

"We don't know for sure if Urban is involved in this. Maybe he really is trying to help you? Maybe he isn't evil?" he rebuffed, his voice almost squeaking.

"Cross admitted that Urban was a part of the first mission." I thought of the gondola photo. I'd seen the proof, hanging in a five-by-seven frame in Urban's office. But I could understand Marcus's doubts. If he wanted to go home and confront his family when this was over, that was probably a good idea. But guessing now about their involvement, or non-involvement, would only worsen his mental state. His eyes were already rung in dark circles, and he seemed far too eager to take the night off. If I told him about my plans, while he was in this mood, he might tell Charlotte; they might team up to stop me. And even if he did agree to join me, I wasn't sure he was ready to hear the truth about his family. He was in such denial, he could make a mistake. While I had given up any hope of learning my parents were anything but evil pathological liars. Nothing said about them could shock me now or distract me from my mission, which was finding my sister. Alive.

A knock sounded on my hotel room door, someone pounding with all their might. "Anastasia, open up! It's me!" Charlotte shouted.

I looked quizzically at Marcus, then crawled out of the queen-size bed.

"Anastasia! Hurry up!" She continued pounding.

I flung open the door. "What?"

"I cracked the password! I'm *in*!" She rushed into the room, Craig Bernard's phone in her hand. "There are emails, text messages… I know where to find Keira!"

My jaw fell. Whoa. "What does it say?"

"Craig Bernard is going to be at the Venezia soccer match in three days! The text says he's bringing 'the package.' You know it has to be Keira. It *has* to be!" She was bouncing on her flip-flopped feet, waving the thin black phone in the air.

Julian squeezed in behind her, his own burner phone pressed to his ear as he looked at Charlotte. "I'm speaking with him now…"

"What's going on?" My eyes darted between the two of them, sensing an uncomfortable closeness that left me out of the loop. I thought Craig was going to the symphony tomorrow night. Had his plans changed because of our boat chase? Was he now going to a soccer game?

Julian moved his phone to his chest, muting it. "I'm speaking with a mate who works in British intelligence. He's going to send a team to the soccer match. Turns out Interpol knows Craig Bernard bloody well. They've been looking into him for years. He's wanted in connection with countless crimes." Julian shook his head, his turquoise eyes glowing. "It's going to be a huge story!"

I was ready to smack him across his pearly white teeth. Of course he would care more about what this could do for *him*.

"Julian, stay focused," Charlotte snipped, shooting him a look of warning. Then she grabbed my hands. "Anastasia, in three days, this will all be over. We're getting Keira back! We did it!" She flung her arms around me, hugging me so tight she cracked my back. I tried to smile, to will myself to believe her, but it just didn't feel right.

Craig, a highly trained spy, accidentally dropped his cell phone where we could retrieve it? My amateur hacker friend was able to crack his password in less than *one* day? His covert orders were just sitting there in a text message?

Everything they'd done so far had been purposefully easy to follow. Cross warned me that I'd be walking into a trap in Venice, but I hadn't yet. Maybe *this* was it. Maybe the phone was a piece of expertly placed disinformation meant to lead us where they wanted us—the soccer match.

Was the symphony house a bogus lead, too? It seemed so unlikely anyone would know I'd talk to that priest. *Keira* hid those photos for me, not them. And even with Charlotte's new lead, there still wasn't any harm in staking out the theater. If Craig didn't show, fine—I'd wait for Interpol to do its thing in two days. But if he did...

Charlotte leaned forward and whispered in my ear,

"You should know, Julian's been calling every member of his family nonstop. They don't know anything. They think he's mad. I really don't think they're involved in this." Then a smile burst from ear to ear. "Can you believe it? We found Keira! Do you realize that? You did it!"

There were tears in her eyes, and I wanted more than anything to share that feeling, but we were dealing with an organization that specialized in misleading the world. No matter what Charlotte thought, I couldn't trust anything that came from a phone Julian Stone happened to pick up. And I couldn't discount everything I'd learned from the priest.

My plan was still on.

CHAPTER THIRTY-THREE

I t was a quarter after five in the morning when I awoke, my brain still exhausted as if having reviewed my strategy all night while I slept. I lifted Marcus's heavy arm from my torso. He'd slept at my side, groaning in his sleep, the suspicions regarding his family seemingly twisting his thoughts. I considered every Dresden Kid I'd ever met. We were all raised by criminals. How many knew the truth? Sophia Urban surely did. She could have warned me days ago, maybe years, but she didn't. Of course.

I slid out of the hotel into the rainy morning, hopping a passenger ferry traveling the length of the Grand Canal. I watched as one hotel after another passed and wondered which one held my sister, or if that lead was false, too. A soft drizzle tumbled outside my window, casting a gray haze on the otherwise colorful buildings, sucking the life out of Venice.

My goal was to get as far away from Piazza San Marco as possible before my friends awoke and searched for me in every walkway, bar, and restaurant in the area. I knew I was leaving them in panic, Charlotte especially, but I couldn't sit around all day acting like everything was normal. I had to confront Craig tonight; this was my family, my call. If anything bad happened, Charlotte would eventually find the photos in the front zippered pocket of her carry-on luggage, and she'd know what to do.

I stared out the window as the ferry glided over the turquoise water, passing under a stone pedestrian bridge full of tourists lining the arched metal railing with umbrellas in one hand, snapping pictures with the other. It was just another morning in Venice, everyone blissfully ignorant to the lives in the balance.

The ferry pulled into the train station, and I exited with the crowd, trying to look casual as I glanced up at the massive departures board: Verona, Milan, Amsterdam, and Munich. I imagined my sister and I boarding a train, leaving together. It was the one place no one would look for me. With my sister so close and a plan set for the soccer match, it was inconceivable that I'd leave town. So I'd have time here alone to prepare, and money thanks to Julian's unattended wallet. I needed a black T-shirt and pants, and a pare of army boots if I was going to fight—not a sunny yellow dress. I spent the morning shopping, then the rest of the day preparing for the confrontation, surveying the symphony house, planning my routes.

I was ready. It wouldn't be another impulsive attack like my disastrous fight with Luis.

My dark hair was pulled back, and my mind was focused.

It was time for Phase Two.

I dodged droplets of rain as I hurried to a ferry. A crowd of passengers waited to board on the outdoor platform, their voices forming a collective hum in my ears. *Do you know how to get to the Bridge of Sighs? Aren't the gondolas expensive! I can't believe it's raining!* I wanted to be them.

I wanted to sit in a water taxi with Keira and worry that the driver was hiking up our fare. I wanted to go home and lie on the couch and complain that there was nothing to watch on TV, I wanted to yell at my sister for leaving her shoes piled in front of the doorway, and I wanted to hear her whine that I used up all the hot water. I wanted my life back.

I plopped down on a ferry seat and stared out the window.

But I guess that never really was our lives. Our parents were spies. They lied, broke the law, conducted secret missions, and moved us around the world to fit their criminal needs. I had no idea who we really were, what our last names even were, but I had to hope that whatever super-spy skills they had were somehow passed down in my DNA, because I was going to need every killer instinct my family had to get my sister back. Tonight.

"Miss, would you like another glass of water?" asked a young male waiter as he stepped into my line of sight. I was seated in the shadow of the café's cloth awning, nursing a large glass bottle of Pellegrino like I had the other night with Marcus. Only this time, I was waiting for my sister's kidnapper to emerge in the crowd of elegantly dressed Italians arriving at the symphony.

"I could bring you some wine? Maybe some pasta?" the waiter continued.

"*No, gratzi.*" I flicked my hand, shooing him away like a rude American as I scanned every face, analyzed every walk. Couples strolled arm in arm up the marble stairs with gowns brushing their soaring heels and designer suits tailored to perfection.

I squirmed in my seat, peering at the walkways, scanning every shadow, until I finally saw his face emerge from the crowd. It was like I could feel him in every cell of my body, a tingle rushing through me.

His stride was quick as Craig Bernard moved up the steps of the theater, a hand running aimlessly over his greasy low ponytail. He was wearing a dark suit and shiny black dress shoes.

He was alone.

CHAPTER THIRTY-FOUR

He stepped through the towering gray metal detectors—not a beep, not a flash. He had no gun. My knee started bopping, rattling my water glass as I watched him walk through the lobby. My sister wasn't with him. Not that I actually expected her to be, but I had hoped.

I bit my thumbnail. The show was sold out, so I couldn't get inside. I'd have to wait for him to exit, which thankfully would be the same way he'd entered. There was only one set of doors. I'd checked the perimeter twice.

Twenty minutes later, Craig reappeared, pacing the theater's stark white lobby, a cell phone pressed to his ear. (So much for the one he'd "lost.") Frown lines deepened as he argued on the phone, then he charged out of the building and headed toward a walkway. I knew exactly where he was going; the path led to the Grand Canal. It was the same route we'd taken with Julian the other night.

Craig turned the corner, and I rose from my chair, tossing euros on the table as I raced quietly behind, his hard shoes clicking the way. I'd practiced every possible course to the Grand Canal, so I knew this walkway led past three piazzas. Two were packed with restaurants and shops while one was nearly abandoned—the same one Marcus, Julian, and I had briefly stopped in days ago. I'd confront him there.

My lack of covert skills limited my ability to follow Craig undetected in the hope he'd lead me back to Keira. He'd either catch me tailing him, or he'd hop on a speedboat, leaving me at the mercy of another lazy water taxi driver. This left me with only a face-to-face confrontation before he reached the canal. And it would be on my terms.

I listened to his footsteps echo farther away, and as soon as it was safe, I sprinted down an adjacent alley—my combat boots thudding in time with my heart as I dashed through the shortcut I'd carefully rehearsed. If I ran at full speed, I could beat him to the abandoned plaza by at least a minute. I inhaled the musty scent of algae on the swishing canals as the empty piazza came into view.

I entered the eerily black square, the flap of a pigeon taking flight rattling me as I ducked into the first darkened doorway, my hands quivering as I pressed my back against the peeling paint of the door's wood panels.

It may have taken months, but I'd found the man who'd pretended to be my sister's boyfriend, who held her hand, dried her tears, rocked her bed, then ripped her from a bloody bathtub.

This was happening.

I took a slow inhale through my nose, trying to control my breathing as I pictured the fight in my head. The objective was to strike first and focus on my legs. I could kick harder than I could punch, and I had to make sure he didn't punch me, didn't get my throat. I'd learned that lesson in Cortona. Instead, I'd wear him out. The more he swung and missed, the more tired he'd be, and the more likely he might be to mess up.

Blackness spread in front of me like the curtain to the symphony as I heard a heavy set of footsteps drawing closer. I recognized the click of his fancy Italian shoes. He was headed straight toward me, and there was no Department D, or CIA, or local cops, or group of friends, waiting in the wings to interfere.

Just him and me.

I closed my eyes and breathed down to my belly. The sound of his steps scraping the gravel reverberated off the walls.

I pictured his mouth bleeding and his eyes blackened.

Step......Step......

I imagined him wincing in pain.

Step...Step...Step...

I remembered him touching my sister.

Step. Step. Step.

I recalled every feeling of guilt, every comment I regretted, every tear I shed.

He turned the corner of the narrow alley, and I flung my fist into the base of his throat.

Kill him now, I thought as he bent forward, grabbing his neck. Before he could breathe, I kneed his nose. A loud crack followed, and blood splattered like abstract art onto the slate pavers below. He gripped his face, standing upright, purple liquid dripping down the scar on his lip. It reminded me of my sister's tub.

I shifted my weight, then kicked his face with a straight leg, my boot connecting loudly with his jaw. Craig stumbled, spitting blood, and glared at me as if just realizing what was happening. He tossed up his fists and abruptly moved toward me, snarling with a homicidal look that sent a spasm of fear to my belly.

"You fucking little bitch," he hissed.

He swung his right arm toward my face, and I ducked. He threw three quick punches, which I batted away with my forearms. My final block spun him backward. I precisely struck his kidney, and he yelped, pausing, before he thrust his leg back in a donkey kick—connecting with the side of my gut. I winced, then quickly jumped into my fighting stance. There was no way I was going down easily, not this time.

Craig rushed toward me, and I swung a roundhouse to his face, but he batted my leg, spinning me around and grabbing my arm behind my back, twisting my shoulder. I elbowed his side, and he released me, growling. Then I whipped around and jabbed his Adam's apple with a row of straight knuckles. Craig gagged and stumbled, gasping for air.

It all happened in seconds, and unlike Cortona, I felt more exhilaration than panic. I wanted this. I moved forward, attempting a jump-kick to his knee, but he saw me coming. He swung at my leg, his hand knocking me off-balance, then he thrust his fist at my face. I bobbed perfectly, but his other fist connected with the side of my gut. I yelped involuntarily.

"Not so fun, is it?" He sneered.

All the rage inside me wiped away the pain. My eyes flamed as I sprung upright, right arm protecting my face. I glared over my fist.

"Where is my sister?"

"Heard she bled to death." He rubbed his bloody nose.

"Bullshit! I know Luis Basso brought her to Italy. I know you took her picture in the trunk of a car in Rome. I found her initials carved on her bed at Campo dei Frari."

His eyes narrowed. He didn't know that one.

"I'm smarter than you think," I snipped.

"*You* might be. But your sister's the one who invited *me* into her bed." He winked before blowing me a bloody kiss. "She's got one hot little ass."

A fresh wave of fury washed through me, and I charged at Craig, faking a right jab before swinging with my left. My fist crunched his ear, and he instinctively grabbed his head. So I jump-kicked his groin, slamming my boot between his legs in a massive uppercut. *Let's see what you can do in bed now, douchebag...*

He yelped like a dog, doubling over, and I prepared for a kick to his head, but he barreled at me. I twisted to the side, letting him brush past like a bull to a matador. He hit the ground face-first.

"Where is Keira?" I shouted.

"Where do you think? She'll be at the soccer match on Friday. Or didn't you get my text?" He smirked, and considering he was bleeding from the mouth, nose, and ear, he shouldn't be so smug.

Still, it was all the confirmation I needed. The soccer game was a setup. He'd dropped his phone on purpose. He wanted us to find it.

"Why are you doing this? What do you want from us?"

"We don't want anything *from* you." He wobbled on tired legs. "In fact, you already served your purpose."

"What are you talking about?" My face crumpled in confusion. "You know what, I don't care. Glad to have helped. Now, let us go home!"

"Oh, sure. Why not? Let me buy you a ticket." He spat blood. "After all, we practically drew you a map here to begin with."

"No shit. You went through a whole lot of trouble to get me here. For what? Who's behind this? Phillip Stone? Does he want some sort of revenge because of what my parents did to Julian? Because if he hasn't noticed, my parents are dead! Revenge achieved."

"Wow, you really are clueless," he scoffed.

"Then fill me in! Where's my sister?"

"If you had stuck to the plan, you would have found out in two days at the soccer match. Now, who the hell knows what's gonna happen. On to Plan C, I guess."

With that, he took off across the piazza.

I bolted after him and, given his multiple injuries, I was significantly faster. There was no way he was getting to the Grand Canal and hopping on some stupid getaway boat. Not this time. I spied the water ahead, the lights of the taxis moving across the current. Our narrow alley opened onto another plaza that ended in a small wooden bridge curving over the canal.

I increased my pace, my eyes determined as I dove onto Craig's back, wrapping my arms around his throat. I fish hooked his mouth with two fingers, digging my nails into the flesh inside his cheek. He angrily twisted, flinging me off, which sent me soaring into the square. I crashed onto the stone pavers, landing on my side, my forehead butting the earth as my body skidded a few feet. I screeched as my skin scraped the uneven gravel. Stumbling, I got to my feet, wiping the abrasions on my face. My cheek and eyebrow were cut, and I could feel the warm sticky blood begin to flow.

I ignored the pain as Craig attempted to brush past, heading for the pedestrian bridge. I flew at him with a diving kick to his knee, and this time I connected with a thundering pop. He dropped instantly, screaming. His knee was either broken or dislocated. Either way, he wasn't getting far.

"Luis said you were going to kill Keira, but you changed your mind. Why? Why did you take her? What's going on?" My voice cracked with naked desperation. But I needed him to talk. This was the only chance I had. I couldn't fail her again.

Craig looked up, the pain from his knee obvious, but

more than that he seemed almost irritated that I'd managed to hurt him. He struggled to his feet, using the bridge's railing for support. "You know, we should all thank your sister for that asinine DNA test, because if it weren't for her, we may never have learned the truth."

"The truth about what? Why did some stupid lab work get Keira in all this trouble?" I was trying to sound strong, but my voice was shaking.

"Ask your *father*."

"My dad's dead."

Craig smirked, a fresh glint in his eye as he watched me, pausing as if enjoying the moment. Then he took a long breath. "Which one?" he asked, his lips curling to the side.

That was when the world stopped. Literally. I think for a second I was in an *X-Men* movie, because I swear even the flies over the water halted in midair.

What was he talking about? My dad was dead. Both of my parents were dead.

"Haven't you wondered why no one's shot you? Why Luis Basso cut your arm?" He nodded to the now-healed wound on my biceps. I'd gotten lucky; Luis was about to stab me before Marcus intervened.

"What, what are you saying?" I stuttered, shaking my head in denial.

"I'm saying there was more than one DNA test being run, sweetheart, and you might owe someone else a belated Father's Day gift."

I glared at his cocky grin, his thick scar covered in blood, his eyes smug despite his numerous wounds. Then he raised an eyebrow, as if proud of himself, and that was when something inside me erupted. It felt like ants were crawling on my skin. My mouth turned dry. The lights gleaming on the water blurred, and all I could see was

Craig Bernard in a fiery red film.

He was lying. He was trying to make me doubt my father, my *dead* father. Hadn't this psycho already done enough to me? To Keira?

I ran at him, leaping what felt like a mile as my foot swung into his jaw. The crack was loud. He crashed onto his back, and I kicked his gut, then his groin. He rolled over, crawling up the bridge, and I thrust my boot into his tailbone. He fell flat.

Then I heard the screaming, the sirens. I whipped toward the sounds, hair flying, dazed with rage, and saw people sprinting along the other bank of the canal. They were racing for the bridge. They were holding guns.

It was the police.

I snapped my eyes toward Craig and caught him crawling pitifully toward the center of the bridge. He grabbed a handrail and pulled himself upright on his broken knee.

What is he doing? My brain was still foggy. *The cops are here.*

The officers on the other bank pointed their firearms, yelling for us to freeze, screaming for Craig to stay where he was.

That's when I saw the ferry. It was a few hundred feet away and preparing to move under the bridge. *He's gonna jump.*

I ran forward. "You can't make it! You'll die from the fall. Give up! Just tell me where my sister is!"

"You *still* don't get it?" he mumbled with a swollen jaw, his eyes drawn to the ferry. "You're doing all this for a girl you're only half related to, and you're missing the family you really have. Are you telling me you never wondered, you never suspected? You never saw the way your parents acted around *him*?"

Every follicle on my being rose up as if hit with an icy

wind. *No…no…no. It's not true. He's lying…he has to be.*

But Craig saw my doubt. "Ahhh… You're starting to see it. Why we're in Venice? Why we went to *that* apartment? Your father stole your mother, right there in that flat. Banged her in the kitchen from what I hear." He looked me up and down, loving this. "But it didn't end there."

Randolph Urban.

My mother was dating Randolph Urban before she met my father. But it ended, right? It had to have ended. She couldn't have cheated on my dad…

Craig watched my doubt gleefully. "In case you're wondering, the blood from Luis's knife confirmed it. Congratulations, Anastasia, you're officially an Urban! You're rich! And I guess that makes Sophia, like, your niece or something…" He snorted, blood splattering from his mouth.

"You're saying *Randolph Urban* is behind this? *He* did this? Not Phillip Stone. Not some random enemy. Why?" The motive didn't make sense. Why would he want to hurt me? Or my sister? Especially if he thought I was his kid.

"It's not because you're his offspring. Don't take it personally. That's just a knife twisting old wounds. Pun intended." He winked, then looked around at the chaotic scene of whipping helicopter propellers, blazing sirens, and pointed guns. He seemed amused by it all. "Honestly, none of this was even about you, *or* Keira, or the lab work. It's about what happened when we went to intercept the DNA test."

I stared blankly.

"Luis went to the lab that night in Boston, only before he could make a simple change to the records, a *couple* broke in. Shots were fired, Luis's shoulder was grazed, and the couple got away. But not before Luis got a good look at them, an eerily familiar husband-and-wife duo who looked a lot like people we worked for not long ago, people we thought were *dead*." He eyed me carefully, savoring my devastated reaction and seemingly oblivious to the vortex of police activity swirling around us. "You see, we weren't trying to draw *you* to Venice; we're after dear ol' mom and dad. So consider yourselves bait to lure those betraying bastards out of the hole they've been hiding in."

No, it's impossible. I pressed my fists to my ears, shaking my head. It was too much. He was a psychopath. He'd say anything to hurt me. My parents were dead. I'd buried their bodies. He was just trying to distract me from finding my sister. I had to stay focused.

"Where's Keira?" My head snapped up.

"You mean your half sister?" He cocked his head. "You'll have to ask your bio dad."

"Tell me where she is!" I shouted as my eyes caught a gondola in the distance. It was moving slowly behind the ferry that was heading toward the bridge, and suddenly my mind flicked back to that infamous photo: my parents in a gondola in Venice, Randolph Urban pushing the boat, his hand on my mother's shoulder. Maybe they were still dating then. The photo obviously meant something to him. He kept it on his wall. I focused on the image: them, the gondola, the canal...the hotel.

There was a hotel in the background. A large, grand white hotel in the heart of the bay, steps from St. Mark's Square. I'd run right past it the night I'd chased Craig Bernard, and if I'd learned one thing during this entire miserable journey, it was that nothing was a coincidence.

"The hotel," I sputtered in a barely audible voice, but Craig heard me. I could see the shift of his eyes. "The Londra Palace." I pictured the hotel's sign in my mind, the photograph crystal clear. "That's where Keira is. She's at the Londra Palace. There's a picture on Urban's wall. That's where they stayed during that first mission. Everything else you've done has mimicked that mission…"

"What better way to draw two dead spies out of hiding than to kidnap one daughter and convince them that the other is about to follow in their footsteps."

Draw two dead spies out of hiding? Was this really happening? I couldn't speak. I could hardly see. *No, no, no. They can't be alive. They burned in a car wreck. They wouldn't let us bury them, mourn them. They wouldn't leave us on our own.*

Craig glared at me, his face swelling badly, blood slowly dripping like the spigot in our horrific tub—but in that moment, he could see that I was the one who was really in pain. "Room 204. Tell Keira I say hi."

He blew another disgusting kiss, then jumped off the side of the bridge.

A passenger ferry moved underneath as he soared through the air. I rushed to the edge, searching the darkness as his body crashed onto the boat's upper deck. Passengers shouted, tourists scattered, and cameras flashed. Then Craig rolled to his side, staggered to his feet, and dove into the canal.

The water was black, motionless. I searched for air bubbles, signs of movement. But I saw nothing. No shift in the current, no paddle of hands, but somehow I doubted people like him died that easily.

Die… My parents. They're alive!

Randolph Urban is my father…

No. Not now. I couldn't let my mind go there; it might never come back. I had to get to Keira. I had to find her before anybody tried to move her again, before they had time to use us in any more schemes.

I pushed off the railing and ran across the bridge, sprinting in the direction I'd come, back toward San Marco's, back toward the Londra Palace, away from the police.

Voices barreled behind me like angry gusts of wind.

"Anastasia! Stop! Are you okay? *Stop! Please!*" It was Charlotte.

I could hear Marcus and Julian yelling beside her. I could hear the stampede of footsteps. I could hear the blaring sirens, the bullhorns, the rescue dogs. I could see the helicopter beam illuminating me from overhead. I could feel the swirl of its blades.

But I didn't stop.

"It's Keira! I know where she is!" I shouted.

I kept running.

CHAPTER THIRTY-FIVE

I beat the authorities to the hotel. Not by much. But I beat them—sirens chasing me all the way and a helicopter spotlight tracking me like I was Harrison Ford in *The Fugitive*.

It seems illogical. I could have hopped on a police boat and taken a nice, leisurely ride to save my sister. But I didn't trust the police. And as selfish and immature as it sounded, *I* wanted to be the one to burst into her room, I wanted to save her, I wanted to be the first safe face she saw. And I wanted to see if it was all really true.

I tumbled into the lobby of the hotel; if I thought my accommodations in Rome were luxurious, they almost seemed middling when compared to the spectacle that was the Londra Palace. The floor was an interesting mosaic set to a damask pattern, and the front desk was lit up with blue electric lights that made it seem like the water from the Venetian lagoon outside was pouring down the front of it. Not that I had much time to appreciate the décor. I ran straight to the first desk clerk I saw, screamed that I needed to get into Room 204, and hollered that it was life or death.

I shook the lapels of his navy wool blazer and pounded on the desk with my other hand.

Considering I was bleeding from the head at the time, I created a stir.

Only, before the clerk had a chance to respond or to register the sound of police alarms blaring from every direction, I charged up a nearby marble stairwell. I had to run up only one flight, which was probably all I could handle given that my adrenaline was wearing off. I was beginning to feel the pain in my side from where Craig had kicked me, and the pound of my head from where it had hit the pavement.

I dizzily stumbled onto the second floor, staggering across the damask patterned carpet as I searched for 204. The room practically called to me, light oozing from the crack underneath the door. Someone was in there.

"Keira! It's me! Anastasia! Can you hear me? Are you in there? Are you okay?" I battered the wood with my fists, but it was so solid, it barely made a sound. Tears streaked my face mixing with blood as I continued to shriek, knocking harder and harder.

Out of nowhere, a clerk appeared with a plastic keycard. He looked afraid to get too close. "*Scusa,*" he said timidly as he stepped to the door, smoothing his suit. I moved away, and he slipped the plastic into the reader. The light turned green.

He opened the door.

I charged in, my eyes wildly racing about. The bedroom was empty. The elegant nineteenth century décor was completely undisturbed, the embroidered bedsheets were pulled tight, the silk curtains were drawn.

Then I heard the kicking.

I charged into the spacious marble bathroom to find

my sister curled on the shiny cream floor, her hands tied to the gleaming metal support legs of the modern vanity sink and her mouth gagged with a rag.

She was alive.

"*Keira*," I cried, tears spilling from my eyes. I rushed over, pulled the rag from her mouth, letting the knotted ring of damp cotton drop to her chest, then I collapsed onto the floor beside her. Sobbing.

"*Keira*." I pressed my face to her chest. "*K… Keira*." My breathing was staggered. I wrapped my arms so tightly around her, I heard the wind rush from her lungs.

"It's okay. It's over," she said, nuzzling her chin against my bloody hair. "You're all right. Everything's all right."

Here she was, a girl who had been held hostage for months, and *she* was comforting *me*.

"I…I'm so sorry," I sputtered, my tears soaking her white tank top.

She yanked her head back. "What?"

I lifted my face to look at her. She'd definitely lost weight, her eyes were a little sunken, but I saw no major bumps or bruises.

"What are *you* sorry for?" she asked, her pale forehead wrinkled, faded platinum hair falling into her eyes, her roots a light chestnut.

"For not coming back from the supermarket sooner, for holding a funeral, for not finding you months ago, for not opening that bedroom door, for being a complete asshole the past three years. I'm so sorry. *What did they do to you?*" I broke down in sobs again, pressing myself into her, never wanting to let go.

"You have nothing to be sorry for; you have no idea. *I'm* the one who's sorry. Anastasia, I think…" But before she could finish her sentence, the police barged in.

The room quickly filled with men in uniforms prying me from my sister's body, untying her hands, dabbing my forehead. I was dragged from place to place, alcoholic cotton swabs stinging my skin, cold compresses pressed to my skull. It was hard to even see my sister in the crowded hotel room, and it would be hours before I'd get to speak with her alone again.

They took us via speedboat to the local police station. Just like everything else in Venice, the building was ancient, marble, and located on a canal. I sat in a small room at a wooden table that looked better suited for an underfunded elementary school. I briefly caught a glimpse of Charlotte, Julian, and Marcus as the police dragged me from the hotel. Charlotte looked like she'd been crying hard.

"You okay?" she mouthed as they hurried me past.

I nodded.

"She's alive," Charlotte mouthed with a smile, tears spilling.

Marcus simply gazed at me, his twinkling eyes practically shouting, "We did it!" He'd helped me save my sister, just like he promised. He was there to the end. Whatever role his family played at Dresden, or Department D, or with Randolph Urban, didn't matter. Not right now.

A door opened to my little interrogation room, and I dug my nails into my thighs, preparing myself. I wasn't well versed on Italian law. Given that in the past twenty-four hours, I had used a brick to break into an apartment building, I'd critically beaten a wanted criminal, and I'd left a trail of blood through half the city's tourist attractions, I was betting there were some legal snafus in there somewhere.

"Miss Phoenix?" asked a man in perfect English. He was American.

Well, at least they contacted my embassy.

He sat across from me. His head was bald with just a few white wisps, and his face was round and full, the skin sagging at the cheeks much like his drooping eyes. There was white stubble on his chin and tight veins in his neck, but what stopped me was his expression. He had the look of someone who had seen a lot, who knew a lot. He was important.

He rested his wrinkled hands on the wooden table. "My name is Martin Bittman."

My head jutted back.

The Aldo Moro photo. The Deputy Director of the CIA.

"You know who I am," he confirmed, obviously noticing my reaction.

I nodded, swallowing hard. *The CIA is here? Now?*

"Allen Cross called me a few days ago," he said, matter-of-factly. I imagined if he were relaying that aliens had landed on Mount Rushmore, he'd say it in much the same manner. "Cross briefed me on your situation, told me you were read in on your parents' history. I came here as a favor to him, to help you find your sister. I owe Cross from a run-in a while back."

"Well, you're a little late," I snipped.

The corner of his lip twitched up. "I see that I am."

"Is it true? Are my parents alive? Were they criminal masterminds? *Are* they criminal masterminds?" I sat back, shaking my head in denial. I refused to believe it.

His face didn't budge. "We have not been able to independently confirm anything Craig Bernard said to you on the bridge, but I can tell you that you saved your sister's life tonight. We found explosives in the hotel room. The plan at the soccer match, we believe it would have included a bomb. It could have been devastating."

The air puffed from my chest. A bomb. Were they going to strap Keira to a bomb? I blinked rapidly.

"Did you find Craig Bernard?" I pictured his dive into the black water.

"The police are still searching for him and his accomplice. His partner cleared out of the hotel room only moments before you arrived. We're looking for them both. Tomorrow, we'll send divers into the canal to try to locate Bernard's body. I hear you had quite a fight." He looked at my forehead, which was now stitched and bandaged.

"Am I in trouble?"

"Of course not."

I exhaled in relief, then glanced around the room I was *locked* in. "Then why am I stuck here? Why aren't I with my sister?"

"Right now, it's for your own protection. What do you know about who's behind this?"

"Who do you think? It's Randolph Urban. I already told the detectives who questioned me." I slumped back in my chair. It was like Boston all over again. "Craig Bernard told me that Randolph Urban, *of Boston, Massachusetts*, took my sister," I said slowly. "He cut my arm, ran some DNA, and now he thinks I'm his daughter. *And* he thinks my parents are alive. All of this,"—I tossed my hands around—"was supposedly some crazy scheme to draw them out of hiding— put my sister in danger, convince them I was about to become the next Jane Bond, and hopefully make them break their cover. It's ridiculous. It's not true, is it?"

Bittman pressed his lips tight, his eye twitching. It was the first shift in his demeanor, the first break in his I-volunteer-nothing persona, and it felt like a dagger to the chest. "Oh my God," I breathed. It was one thing to hear wild accusations coming from a sociopath like Craig Bernard, it was quite another to get confirmation from the Director of the CIA.

"The DNA test was real. We believe you're Randolph Urban's daughter. I'm sorry." He sounded like a doctor giving a terminal diagnosis.

"And my parents?" I croaked.

"We honestly don't know. Unfortunately, there's no hard evidence to link Randolph Urban to any of this. Your sister never saw him, her captors never mentioned him, and the only people who claim to have seen your parents alive are wanted international criminals," he stated plainly. "But I knew your parents. If they're alive, we'll find them."

If the CIA didn't know for sure, that meant it still might not be true.

"When can I see Keira? How is she?" I didn't care what some DNA test said. She was my sister. My *full* sister, and they had kept us separated for hours, probably to get our stories straight. But I'd already told my story, again and again and again. It was time to end this.

"Soon. She was checked out by the local hospital. Aside from some dehydration and malnutrition, she seems fine."

"Then take me to her. I want to go home." I rose to my feet, and he stood, blocking my path.

"You know you can't go home." He held up his palms. "This isn't over. We've been watching Randolph Urban for years, and he's never once broken his humanitarian, entrepreneur, *Fortune 500* persona. Until now. He believes that your parents are alive, that they betrayed him, and that you're his daughter. He's acting emotionally, recklessly, and that makes you the biggest chess piece in the criminal espionage community."

"Did you just call me a pawn? This isn't a game. And no one's using me, including you."

"You may not have a choice." He reached into his jacket and pulled out a passport.

It was royal blue with the United States emblem on the front. I opened it to find my passport picture, the one I'd taken two years ago in a crappy camera store on Comm. Ave. Only the name read, "Faith Sparks."

That is so Keira. I rolled my eyes.

"Your sister chose it," he confirmed.

I felt tired, defeated. "So where are we going? And for how long?"

"I can't say for sure. But you leave in two hours."

CHAPTER THIRTY-SIX

We sat in a private car on a high-speed train bound for Amsterdam. My sister was beside me. It was exactly what I swore I'd do when I found her. This wasn't a dream, or worse, a nightmare featuring assassins. I'd done it. Keira was back. Only we couldn't go home.

"So Faith," Keira teased. "Hope you like your new name."

"It's better than *Penelope Storms*." I shot her a look. "Seriously? The 'weather girl' fantasy?"

"It could happen." She shrugged, arching her brow in a mocking sisterly way.

"Why did you pick different last names? Just because we're on the run, doesn't mean we can't be sisters." I rested my head against the back of the train's cushy seat. I was long overdue for some sleep, like I planned to find our hotel, hit the bed, and wake up sometime next month. Hopefully, by then my wounds would be healed and I could convince my mind I'd spent these last few weeks at a pleasant summer camp.

Keira squirmed beside me, and I turned my sluggish eyes her way.

She looked nervous as she fidgeted in her seat. I forced

myself to sit up. "Do you want to talk about it?" I didn't want to rush her, or more accurately, I didn't want to ruin things. I was so relieved to be reunited with her that I didn't care if we ever spoke of these events again.

She looked at me, her hazel eyes full of worry. "There's stuff you need to know." Her fingers twirled in her hair with a look of worry, fear of what I might think. "I caused this mess. All of it. It's my fault."

I instantly started to object, but she cut me off with a flick of her hand. She'd earned the right to speak.

Keira exhaled, straightening her posture like she was mentally steadying herself for what came next. "Back in March, on the anniversary of Mom and Dad's deaths, I got depressed. I don't know why. I don't know what made this year different. I was just feeling sorry for myself. I kept wondering what my life would be like if they hadn't died." She gave me a sideways glance, guilt in her eyes as if she was breaking our long-standing policy—I won't talk about my resentment if you don't talk about yours. Only that policy didn't work, and it took a desperate and dangerous search through Italy for me to realize I didn't blame her for missing all the freedom that caring for me took away. I was wrong for judging her, for screaming that she wasn't my mother, for making fun of every boyfriend she had. I felt so horrible now for how easily I overlooked her sacrifices, her struggle, but when I tried to reach for her hand and slather her in overdue apologies, she waved me off.

Keira continued. "I couldn't get past how random it was, the car crash. How our whole lives could be ruined in a trip to the airport. They seemed like such pointless, unnecessary deaths—a drunk driver? So I started to *really* think about them. Our lives, all the moves, the languages, the bruises. I built it up in my head and I thought, what if it wasn't an accident? If they really worked for the CIA, that would make them important, that would somehow make their deaths matter. It's ridiculous and *clearly* misguided, I know." She shook her head, appearing embarrassed, and I grabbed her hand.

"It's not," I interjected, squeezing her palm in commiseration. It's what any person would hope for, a noble death, and what any loved one would find comforting. I got why she wanted that, I just didn't get why she didn't tell me.

"It snapped me out of my funk," she went on, and I almost smiled at her choice of words. The fact that we both saw our grief as a "funk" goes to show what a sisterly bond really is. We shared a language. I didn't care what anyone said about our father, or *fathers.* She was my person. "I became obsessed, completely convinced that my suspicions were right. I just needed proof. So I connected online with this guy from BU who now works for the CIA. We had drinks, and I gave him samples of Mom's and Dad's DNA, from their old hairbrushes. He swore that if they worked for the agency, they'd be in some government database. I guess that's when everything went wrong. As soon as he entered their names into the CIA's system, red flags went up in evil lairs around the world." She snorted, trying to make light of the situation, but in her eyes, I could see the pain she was in, the guilt that consumed her. I knew that look well. I saw it every morning in the mirror. I squeezed her hand tighter.

"Then I met Craig." She cringed. "He just showed up at the bar, buying me drinks and acting like I was the most interesting person in the world. He used to ask me about Mom and Dad all the time." She scoffed, yanking her hands away to dig them into her overly long hair, pulling way too hard. "I thought that meant he was different, that he was trying to really get to know me. What guy asks questions about your family? So I told him everything I was thinking about Mom and Dad, and he never made fun of me for thinking they were spies. He kept telling me how smart I was, how brave. I am seriously the stupidest person alive!"

"You are not!" My eyes widened. I leaned toward her, wanting to take away her pain, take away all of our pain. We were choking on a shared sense of guilt—who failed who more, who should have known better, done better. We both screwed up so much, and we were so ready to forgive each other, I just wondered if we'd ever forgive ourselves. "I'm so sorry you didn't think you could tell me about Craig, about Mom and Dad. I could have helped you, especially if you were depressed. Why would you hide something like that?"

"Because I'm supposed to be taking care of you!" she said, as if it were obvious. "And I was doing a shitty job. Of course you resented me for barking orders, because you knew I didn't want to give them. I didn't want to be a mom. I didn't want to be in charge." Tears clung to her eyes. "I'm so sorry. If I ever made you feel like it was your fault, like you were the reason I wasn't a doctor, that I was stuck in Boston. I know that's not true. I *know* it."

"Stop. It's okay. You don't have to apologize." I hugged her from my seat beside her, holding her to me, so glad that I could, so glad she was with me. "I'd resent me, too."

"But I don't resent you! The whole time I was being held, all I wanted to do was apologize. I wanted to make sure you wouldn't hate me forever," she sniffled, struggling to hold back her emotion. Even now, after everything she'd been through, she was trying to be the strong one, the one who wouldn't shed a tear at the funeral, the one who was determined to make things easier for me.

"I could never hate you. You know that, right?" My eyes pleaded for her to listen. "I came after you, because it's what you would do for me, what you *have* been doing for me. I owe you...so much," I choked out, sniffling back my own tears.

Keira shook her head, not accepting my words. "You owe me nothing. Not after what I've done. Look at this mess we're in!" She tossed up her hands in disgust. "And for what? As I waited for those test results, talking to Craig who was constantly pumping me for every memory I had that implied Mom and Dad were spies, it all started to feel real. Then I realized—if that were true, and they were spies, then that meant our whole lives were a lie. Why would I want that? Why would I want to hurt either of us like that? I started to regret ever running the test. Then Luis popped up."

She pulled away, meeting my eyes. "The day I was supposed to get the test results, about a week before the party, Luis just showed up in the hospital with a bullet wound to his arm. He refused to let me enter him into the medical records, and eventually I learned he was a spy. I thought that confirmed my suspicions. Because if he was a spy, and Mom and Dad brought us to his house, then there was no way that could be a coincidence."

She was right. About everything. Though I doubted that was much consolation right now.

"So I invited him out to drinks with me and Craig. I kept hitting him up for information. I thought I could get *him* to tell *me* what he knew. I was soo stupid..." She rolled her eyes, the hindsight on the situation clearly making her hate herself. "Then the two of them started to gang up on me, tell me I was going overboard. And I was. I was constantly checking my phone, waiting for the test results. I threatened to walk into the CIA and ask the girl at the front desk if she knew my parents. I was shooting my mouth off, completely consumed. And Craig kept insisting

I stop, let it go. I was scared that I was turning into 'the crazy chick,' that I was pushing him away. I can't believe I even cared. So, I decided to throw a party. I thought it would take my mind off things, get us back on track."

"How did you and Craig even communicate?" I asked, glaring at her with such confusion for all the secrets she'd managed to hide from me. "Charlotte and I couldn't find him in your phone, your email."

"He bought me a cell phone, said it was our private line, for just him and me. I thought it was *romantic*." She spat the word like she was disgusted for ever thinking this. "So I invited him to the party, and I thought this would be my chance to introduce you guys, but you seemed to hate him at first sight. Why couldn't *I* see that? It took you two seconds!" She threw her head back against the train seat, groaning in aggravation.

"Because he was being nice. He was listening to you when no one else was, when *I* wasn't."

"Don't you dare act like any of this is your fault." There was heat in her voice.

"You didn't think you could come to me, about our own parents! I was so horrible to you!"

"I deserved it!"

"You did not!"

Keira took a huge breath, eyes closed. "Let's not go there right now." She straightened her frame. "Because there's more."

I wasn't sure I wanted to hear it. I was so tired, my brain so drained, my body so wounded. But I placed my hands firmly on my thighs and braced myself for the question that had been plaguing me since I realized my sister was being held captive.

"When they were holding you," —I dug my nails into my

legs—"did they…hurt you?"

"*No*. No," she said definitively, gripping my shoulder. "They never touched me. They didn't feed me much, just water, coffee, bread, and pasta. They wanted me to lose weight for those photos. But that's it. I swear."

"Who were the photos for? The proof of lifes, the shot of me and Marcus? They never sent them to me."

She gave me a look that said, "I'm not sure if you really want to hear this." But I nodded. We might as well get it all out at once.

"I was sedated whenever they moved me. That's how they got me out of the country, drugs and a private plane. Well, that and threatening your life." She pumped her brow as if those were memories she'd rather not recall. I completely understood. If I could, I'd have the image of our tub surgically removed from my brain. "I remember them making that anonymous tip to the Boston PD about the surveillance footage of me and Craig. They were purposely trying to involve you, and I was so angry, which they loved. They found me absolutely hysterical. Then they made me shoot that awful photo in Rome—and by the way, I don't recommend hanging out in a trunk too long in summer, it's bumpy and a little warm."

"They made you ride in the trunk?" I screeched.

"I don't want to talk about it." She shook me off. "After that, I took *another* photo in Venice. I obviously thought they were both for you. Only everyone suddenly started acting all edgy, like something big was about to happen. That night, they drugged me and started dragging me to a boat. I could hear tons of people shouting, feet running, guns firing. It was pitch black, and my mind was spinning from the drugs, but I heard voices." She turned toward me with a look as grave as the one she held at the funeral.

"Anastasia," she swallowed hard, "I swear I heard Mom and Dad. They were yelling for me."

I scrunched my eyes, my forehead clenched. "No. It's impossible. That can't be true." I shook my head, like I could stop the words from landing on me.

"I know, but...I think it was *them*."

I dropped my chin to my chest, pressing my fists to my ears. I wanted to believe with every cell in my being that it was the drugs in her system, that the voices were warped in her head, but after what Craig said, it was hard to bury this reality and ignore its existence. *If they're alive, then what they put us through, what they put Keira through, is sadistic. They couldn't seriously let their children plan their funerals? Grow up orphans?* But then another thought defiantly slithered into my brain. *They could be* alive. *I could have my parents back, I could have my family back...*

"Look, I was drugged. I could be wrong," Keira continued, interrupting my dangerous train of thought. "But the whole time those guys had me, it felt like they were laying a trap, only as time went on, it felt like the trap wasn't for you. The way they were talking, it was like they wanted revenge, like they couldn't wait to see someone's twisted face. Only why would anyone have a grudge against *you*? And if you didn't get the photos, who did? Who else would care about pictures of me?"

Mom and Dad.

My jaw tensed so much, my teeth ground audibly. I couldn't take anymore—the lies, the fear, the anger. Keira swung her arm around me, hugging me to her, feeling my pain, *our* pain. I remembered the car crash, the wreckage, the dental records. It was too much.

"I'm sorry," she whispered.

"You did nothing wrong."

"I left you."

"I found you," I retorted, trying to sound cheerier. "Well, with Charlotte and Marcus's help, of course."

"You know I want to hear all about Marcus. That photo of the two of you sucking face was the best part of my captivity. I might get it framed."

"Shut up." I pushed her away, teasing as I realized I might never see him again. The CIA shuffled me and Keira out of the country so fast, with new passports and new names, we weren't allowed to speak to anyone. No one knew where we were going, not even Charlotte's parents, my pseudo legal guardians. What would the world think? That we were dead? That we disappeared? Would Tyson and Regina have to attend a funeral for me? Would I be making them grieve my fake death the same way that I had grieved my parents? Then there were Marcus, Julian, and Charlotte—they knew what really happened in Italy. Were they expected to keep quiet? Were they being sent into hiding, too?

I couldn't imagine never seeing Charlotte again, after everything she did for me. She deserved to be here now, hugging Keira. I couldn't have gotten to this moment without her help.

And Marcus. I would have slipped back into the funk a dozen times over if it weren't for him. My stomach flipped at the thought of him, then sank when I realized that was all he'd be now—a thought, a memory. I'd lost him, and I never got to tell him how I felt. I wasn't even sure how I felt. I just knew that I needed him, that I wanted him.

I closed my eyes and rested my head against the seat. Keira didn't say anything else for the rest of the ride, not until we got to Amsterdam.

CHAPTER THIRTY-SEVEN

I awoke in a sunny hotel room. It had been days and, so far, Keira and I had kept our promise. For one week, we swore we wouldn't think or talk about what happened. Instead, we'd visit Anne Frank's attic, ride bikes, cruise the red-light district, and hit the "cafés." We were going to live the touristy fantasy I'd imagined having with my sister every night since she'd disappeared.

We even continued the family tradition of testing the local cuisine, and this morning we set out to find the best *spakdik* place in Amsterdam.

"So you really had a funeral for me?" Keira asked as she ate her fat pancakes stuffed with bacon and syrup.

"Yeah, sorry," I grumbled between gooey bites. "It wasn't my idea. Charlotte's parents insisted. They printed programs and everything. A choir sang 'Danny Boy.'"

Keira snorted. "I can't believe people gave speeches. I wish I could have heard them."

"Dr. Baskin from pediatrics told that story about you spilling the bedpan." I cracked a smile.

"Don't tell me anyone talked about the Nurse's Ball

and the piña coladas!"

"Of course they did," I chided, then changed my expression. "But we're not supposed to talk about this."

"I know. It's just so surreal." She took a long sip of coffee, the bells above the shop's front doors ringing as they opened.

We both turned and saw what felt like a mirage. Marcus, Charlotte, and Julian stood in the entry with smiles wider than a bridal party.

Air expelled from my lungs as I rose in shock, in joy.

"Omigod! How did you find us?" I yelped, racing toward them, throwing my arms around Charlotte.

"How do you think?" Charlotte mocked. "I'm not a hacker god for nothing."

I pulled away and looked at the three of them. They were all here. Even Julian.

"She only figured out you were in Amsterdam," Marcus interrupted, stepping to my side. "I'm the one who figured out you would come here. You said your family always tried the local cuisine, so I figured it was only a matter of time before you looked for the best *spekdik*."

I flung myself at him, wrapping him in a tight hug. "You remembered."

"You okay?" he whispered into my hair.

I nodded, watching Keira and Charlotte in a tight embrace. Despite everything, I was okay. I had Keira. We were safe. And the guilt that had constantly consumed me since I saw that bathtub, that rushed over me every time Marcus flashed his dimples, was finally gone. I felt only butterflies, and gratitude, and comfort.

"You shouldn't be here," Keira warned as she simultaneously gestured for everyone to join us at the table. We all took seats, and my sister scanned the group. "This is too dangerous."

Marcus looked at her from across the table, his seat

close to mine. "You must be Keira. *Mucho gusto.*" He held out his hand. "I've heard a lot about you."

She snorted. "I'd imagine. Nice to meet the boy from the photo."

"Don't start," I shot her a sisterly glare before turning to Charlotte. "Seriously, how did you guys find us?"

"I lived with you for three years," Charlotte stated as if it were obvious. "*Penelope Storm?* Don't worry, unless the evil spy overlords know of your dream of being a weather girl, I don't think they'll hunt you down. We covered our tracks."

"I told you it was a stupid name," I hissed at my sister, then looked at Julian who was sitting quietly beside Charlotte. "I'm surprised *you're* here."

"You should thank him," Charlotte replied. "If it wasn't for Julian, we never would have found you in Venice. We were all running around absolutely panicked, and it was his contact from the first night who was able to track you down at the symphony. Hey, did you know *La Fenice* means 'the Phoenix'?"

"Yeah." I nodded, glancing at the Londoner squirming awkwardly in his wooden chair. "Thank you for bringing the cops. I know it wasn't your dad who took her. I'm sorry I accused you."

"Don't thank me just yet." He shot Charlotte a nervous glance, and she bit her lip.

Something was wrong. "What is it? What happened?" My heart seized.

Charlotte glanced at Marcus, nodding as if to say "the floor is yours." Marcus peered at me, his voice lowered. "It's my brother, Antonio. We can't find him. And not like before. He's completely off the grid, even from my parents. And Urban's disappeared. No one knows what's going on." He swallowed hard. "I'm worried something's happened to him..."

"Because you helped me," I finished for him. Another

family member in danger. Because of me.

"I've tried all of my contacts and nothing," Julian offered. "All I was able to turn up was his call list from the last day his cell was in service."

Marcus gave me a serious look. "My brother's last conversation was with Allen Cross."

Uncle Aleksandr.

"Did you talk to Cross? What did he say?" I asked, looking at Charlotte.

"He hasn't returned our calls," Charlotte admitted, her tone obviously concerned.

Marcus looked at me, a new fear in his eyes, so raw, so familiar. This was never going to end, was it?

"We'll find him," I promised, taking Marcus's hand. "Dresden Kids stick together, right?" Now it was my turn.

"Good, because that's where you girls come in." Julian looked at me and Keira. "Mr. Cross might ignore our calls, but we don't think he'll ignore *you*. We need you to call him, email him, send some Morse code. We need to find out what he knows, about everything."

"You have to help me find Antonio," Marcus squeezed my hand tighter, his eyes pleading with me like I held the fate of his family in my hands.

No pressure, I thought. My dreams of returning to Boston, of returning to Tyson and Regina and the life of a teenage girl flaking off her senior year, were unequivocally shattered. This was my life now, all of our lives. We weren't safe. and we never would be, as long as Department D was out there, as long as Urban was in the wind.

I looked at Keira.

We had to end this.

We had to bring down Department D.

THE TRUTH

Aldo Moro was the prime minister of Italy from 1963 to 1968 and from 1974 to 1976. He was kidnapped on March 16, 1978 by the Red Brigades, a Marxist-Leninist terrorist organization, and killed after fifty-five days of captivity. There are many conspiracy theories relating to his death, including ties to a meeting with Henry Kissinger, advisor to President Nixon, and links to the KGB. Moro's body was discovered in the trunk of a car on a street in Rome. The photo Anastasia and Charlotte uncover is based on the actual photograph of the crime scene, only with Anastasia's parents added to the background.

-*The Guardian and The Telegraph, 2008*

• • •

Disinformation and Department Ds really exist, and these forms of subterfuge are said to have had a considerable impact on world affairs. They were a major component of the KGB and Czech STB during the Cold War.

-*KGB and the Soviet Disinformation, Ladislav Bittman, 1985*

...

Lawrence Martin-Bittman, formerly Ladislav Bittman, was the former Deputy Commander of Disinformation for Czechoslovakia during the Cold War. He led many successful disinformation and propaganda campaigns, most notably Operation Neptune. After the invasion of Czechoslovakia by the Soviet Union in August 1968, he sought political asylum in the United States, and a communist military court in his home country sentenced him to death in absentia. He went on to become a professor at Boston University, where he taught budding journalists how to identify if they were being fed false information. As a graduate of BU, the author met with Bittman in preparation for this novel and lent his name to the CIA agent featured in the final scenes, Martin Bittman.

-New York Times, 1994

DON'T MISS
BOOK TWO IN THE
Anastasia Phoenix Series

LIES
THAT
BIND

LIES THAT BIND

CHAPTER ONE

Everything smelled of fire.

It was coming from the torches, obviously. They were all around me, the smoke pluming in thick streams. I coughed, choking, the taste of charcoal coating my tongue as my lungs burned from the black ash. I couldn't breathe. I could hardly see. There was no moon, and even with the aid of the blazing embers, my eyes filled with more tears than clarity.

And this was a holiday celebration?

Not that we were here to celebrate. We were searching for Antonio, the brother of my pseudo-boyfriend, Marcus. Though boyfriend might be the wrong term—adventure-junkie companion? Guy who saved my life? Fellow Dresden Kid whose family might be as twisted as mine? It was a complex relationship.

I wiped at my nose, which was running from a conflicting mix of frigid night air and burning smoke.

"How much f-farther?" I asked, coughing, my hand clutching to Marcus's leather jacket as we cut through a dense crowd.

"The place is supposed to be on the corner," he replied, pointing.

Spectators stood shoulder-to-shoulder, moving through the tiny village streets of Lewes, England, like Times Square tourists on New Year's Eve, each fighting to obtain the best position to view the upcoming spectacle.

It was November fifth, Guy Fawkes Day in the United Kingdom.

Being an American, I had no ties to the holiday. I imagined it would be like celebrating the Fourth of July in Germany, or Cinco de Mayo in Boston. Oh, wait, we *do* celebrate Cinco de Mayo in Boston. I had a picture of my sister, Keira, with Craig Bernard and Luis Basso at a pub to prove it—that was a week before those two criminal spies kidnapped her. Still, I had never heard the name Guy Fawkes until Charlotte explained the unusual festivities as I booked my train ticket.

Turns out, Guy tried to blow up Parliament more than four hundred years ago, but he sucked at his job. He got caught, in the bowels of the historic seat of government, holding a match about to light enough barrelfuls of gunpowder it would have been seen from the New World. He was branded a terrorist and mutilated in the town square. (It was a standard pastime back then, though Guy somehow managed to hang himself before they got to the really gory bits.) Afterward, the country began to annually mark the day of his screwup with open flames that screamed, "Yay! We saved Parliament! Long live the king!"

Only hindsight has a way of shedding new bonfire light on the situation.

To many people, Guy had a point. He wasn't just some crazed lunatic bent on mass murder; he was protesting the British government's treatment of Catholics at the time. Priests were being killed, Catholics were being forced into hiding, and crazy laws were being passed. Fawkes's violent attempt at protest came to be seen in an anarchist light. *Fight the power!* And all that. His face is the symbol of the hacker group Anonymous, and today there are as many people who view Guy as a freedom fighter as there are those who view him as a terrorist.

"I think I see it," Marcus said, gesturing to a pub and its adjoining bed-and-breakfast, a gold logo displayed on a brick wall. The front of the building featured weathered white siding and large plate-glass store windows, showing a pub interior full of aging wooden booths and a rustic tin ceiling. A small inn rested above it, its windows lined with black shutters and its roof pitched. The entire structure looked like it had been transplanted from Beacon Hill in Boston. Except for the castle in the background. Because what self-respecting town doesn't have a castle on a hill? They are to Europe what McDonald's restaurants are to the United States—old, plentiful, and, lately, overlooked.

I squeezed past a young couple holding a toddler wearing protective plastic goggles, as they watched a parade move along the ancient cobblestone streets, torches in hand. Only this parade had no feathered costumes or giant balloons, no two-story colorful floats or celebrity performances. Instead, there were lines of marching people who appeared, to this American, to be dressed in train conductor uniforms bedazzled by Michael Jackson. The men's dark sport coats featured gaudy glittered rhinestone patterns worthy of a moonwalk, only instead of a single sequined glove, they wore sparkling train conductor hats, red neckerchiefs, and carried flames on sticks. All were filing toward a giant pile of wood and kindling that they planned to light ablaze at midnight—in a narrow street, lined with buildings built hundreds of years ago, mostly constructed of wood, surrounded by hordes of people, many of them drunk.

There was no way this holiday would ever exist in America.

"All right, we need to find this place before someone seriously singes my hair," I joked, still clutching Marcus's leather sleeve as we edged past a Tudor-style shop selling used books with a picture-perfect flower box anchoring its front window. More kindling. "I saw a five-year-old holding a torch back there."

"Americans are so uptight."

"Not playing with matches makes us uptight? Haven't you heard of Smokey Bear?"

"No," Marcus stated plainly. "And if you think this is bad, you should see *Las Falles de Valencia*. Puts this little *fiesta* to shame."

"Oh, so the Spanish light things on fire, too?" I raised an eyebrow.

"Bigger than this," he said proudly. Then he cocked his head in a teasing way. "Americans, *Puritanos*."

"You can't call me a Puritan in a crowd of Brits. They invented the term."

He stopped short and pulled me toward him, gripping my waist. "I didn't mean to offend." He gazed into my eyes from inches away.

There was smoke and literal fire encircling us. Only the heat I was feeling right now seemed to be coming from within me rather than the torches around me. I stared at his lips. We hadn't had much time to be romantic. After rescuing my sister from super spies in Venice (following her captivity of four months, one week, and two days), I finally had my family back—my sole wish since I walked in on a claw-foot tub full of her steaming-hot blood. But Keira and I barely had time to enjoy our reunion before we learned of the sudden disappearance of Marcus's brother.

Marcus needed our help, and we owed him. So we aborted

our reunion celebration and spent the last two weeks trying to locate Antonio, who was supposedly still working for Dresden but missing in action ever since Keira was rescued. This led to two theories—one, that Department D dangerously targeted Antonio because Marcus helped me find my sister or two, that he was safe and purposely laying low on the advice of Allen Cross. Julian, the billionaire son of a former Department D colleague, and Charlotte, our best friend and tech genius, confirmed that the last call made to Antonio's phone was from Allen Cross, who had the honor of being the only person who knew my parents who was actually trying to help us. Except Cross insisted that he only left Antonio a voicemail informing him of our situation in Venice, just in case Marcus's association with my family's mess put Antonio in danger. If Department D went after my sibling, why not Marcus's? We didn't know if Antonio got the warning in time.

But Charlotte was hacking around the clock to try to locate him. Despite many pleas from Keira and me, Charlotte refused to return to her regularly scheduled life in Boston, insisting she'd "seen too much to go back now." (She'd been watching a lot of Netflix in the wee hours of the morning while scouring databases.) Instead, she moved to London and had been working alongside Julian. During that time, Antonio's passport, credit cards, and bank accounts were completely inactive. Then, this morning, his name suddenly popped up on the registry for a B&B at the Guy Fawkes festival in Lewes, England—only an hour and a half from where we were staying in London. This from a man who hadn't so much as touched an ATM for weeks and who hadn't called his parents or brother to let them know he was okay. I thought it suspicious, Marcus thought it lucky, and Julian thought it a potential setup.

But like me, Marcus was willing to walk into that setup willingly if it meant finding his brother at some quaint bed-and-breakfast. And like him, I wasn't going to let him go alone.

Keira wasn't too thrilled about our plan, but there was no way I was letting her accompany us on a potential Department D setup operation. I'd already lost her once. And given I was the one who found her, I knew I could handle myself. I'd proven that, and I was not going to argue this point with her or anyone else. Marcus needed me, and I was going.

He squeezed my waist. "Thank you for coming here, for helping me," Marcus said for the millionth time.

"Dresden Kids stick together." I repeated his infamous line.

"I don't know if I could have done this by myself."

"I know the feeling." I thought back to my sister, to Marcus saving me in Cortona while Luis cut me with a knife. I was plagued by nightmares—sometimes of Keira's dead body in our tub, sometimes of Craig Bernard fighting me in Venice, and sometimes of Luis Basso pointing a gun at my head. I didn't tell anyone about what woke me up at night (I didn't want Keira to feel worse), but the puffy purple circles under my eyes were becoming more noticeable.

"Once we find Antonio, we'll be okay. It'll be over," Marcus said, lightly brushing my dark circles with a fingertip, his voice so monotone it was obvious even he didn't believe his words. We weren't safe. Keira and I were living under assumed names. Marcus dropped out of high school. Charlotte was hacking databases against a criminal empire. And Julian was funding the entire anarchist operation.

We were so far from okay, I didn't even remember what it felt like.

"I'm sure Antonio's here," I lied, not really knowing what we'd find but really hoping it wasn't a B&B full of assassins. Or worse, another bloody tub.

Marcus nodded too quickly, eyes distant, like he was forcing himself to agree with my words. Then he pressed his forehead to mine and sighed, his whole weight leaning into me. I closed my eyes, feeling his hair brush against my cheekbones.

"I have to find him," he whispered, his mouth incredibly close.

"I know."

He breathed against me, the heat of his face adding to the heat in the burning air.

Then his face shifted slightly, his lips moving toward mine, almost blindly, like he was searching for me by scent in a pitch-black room. When we touched, it was barely a flutter—a kiss so sad, it felt desperate. And the sensation was oddly familiar—only I had never been on this end. I could sense him trying to forget the world, forget his fears, forget where he was. I knew what he needed. I had been there myself not too long ago.

So I grabbed his hair in my fists. I pressed my mouth hard, moving my tongue against his until I felt a sudden shift within Marcus, like a light turning on. He pushed me against the brick wall of the building behind us, the stones sticking to the wool of my peacoat as his mouth moved with a new excitement. I moaned slightly, and he slid his hand behind my head, gripping my hair, protecting my scalp from the hard brick and pulling me closer.

Around us crowds cheered; the bonfires must have been starting. I could feel torches glowing brighter, hotter, closer.

Much closer.

I cracked open my eyes and was instantly startled by

a man standing inches away, a fiery torch in his hand. He was watching us with a creepy grin on his face. I pushed back Marcus—visions of Department D, Craig Bernard, Luis Basso, and endless threats of setups flashing in my head. Marcus jerked, panic spreading across his flushed face as he noticed my reaction.

Then he turned toward the stranger.

Only then, did the man move the torch closer, illuminating his skin.

That was when I recognized his familiar features—the dark hair, the double dimples, and the near-black eyes that clearly ran in their bloodline.

"Hola, hermano."

ACKNOWLEDGMENTS

Before I even got to Boston University, I met a student who talked about a professor in the College of Communication who used to be a communist spy during the Cold War. This man specialized in disinformation, before emigrating to the U.S. and teaching budding journalists how to tell when they were being fed false information. I never had the pleasure of taking a class with this professor; he retired before I got there, but something about his story stuck with me. So when I decided to write a YA spy thriller and needed to create a specialty for Anastasia's parents, I instantly thought of this spy from BU and the concept of disinformation. Thus, I would be remiss if I didn't start my acknowledgements by thanking Lawrence Martin-Bittman, a real-life 007 from the Czech Republic and now a painter in Massachusetts. You were my first spark of inspiration for this book. Thank you for meeting me in your home all those years ago, and thank you for corresponding with me on email since. Without you, Department D wouldn't exist.

• • •

There is someone else who has supported this book since the very first draft in 2008—my agent, Taylor Martindale Kean. You were an intern when I first dreamed up Anastasia, and you were one of my first readers. I'm so glad that you remembered this book years later when I decided to dive into the manuscript yet again, and I'm beyond delighted that we've accomplished this together. I believe this is how it was always meant to be. Thank you!

•••

To my editor, Alycia Tornetta, I will forever be indebted to you for seeking an "international YA thriller" right when we decided to go on submission. I've loved working with you, and I know you are the perfect editor to help me craft this trilogy. Thank you to everyone else at Entangled, especially Stacy Cantor Abrams and Melissa Montovani, who has supported this book, through countless book covers and millions of promotional questions. You truly go above and beyond.

•••

Thank you to the friends, family, and colleagues who read Anastasia in one of its many drafts. Your notes made this book what it is today, and the generosity of your time and effort is greatly appreciated. Specifically, major thank-yous go out to: Jenoyne Adams; Melissa Jeglinski; Megan Kelley Hall; Aisha O'Connor; Ellen Larson; Candice Smith; my BFF since seventh grade, Melanie Raby; and my wonderful copy editing in-laws, Paula and Larry Wallach.

•••

Special thanks to Chris Klock for taking every author photo I've ever had. You're an awesome photographer (and your wife, Sheri, is pretty awesome, too). Thank you to those who have helped with marketing this series, from social media advice to interning to media attention, specifically: Riley Londres, Jenee Chizick, Kari Oriolo, and my teenage book-blogging niece, Marissa Nicole Rodriguez. Thank you my BU family for help with marketing and networking, specifically Steven Schaefer, Evan Schapiro, and Tom Fiedler. Thanks to my awesome Street Team members, I love and appreciate all your enthusiasm!

· · ·

Thank you to the generous friends and family who let me use their homes as a writing retreat—Jen and Ed Hanna, and Matt and Cristina Wallach. It's amazing what peace and quiet can accomplish.

· · ·

To all of my friends—my Ridley Girls, my college friends, and my new mommy friends and neighbors—thank you for encouraging me and acting interested as we shared a few drinks. Thank you to all the family members who resisted asking me "how the writing was going" even though I know they wanted to. I hit the jackpot when I joined the Wallach family, and I thank you all for your support.

· · ·

Thanks to my Rodriguez family! My brother, Lou Rodriguez, is probably the most generous entrepreneur in the world, and he's always been willing to introduce me to anyone who might help promote my books. My sister, Natalie Jansorn, has been a copy editor for me and has never questioned why I keep writing. Thank you to Nicole and Prao for always being fun. And of course, a special thank you to my parents, who read the first draft of this book and insisted every day since that it would be on the shelf one day. Your belief in me, and this novel, kept me from giving up.

· · ·

If there's one person who deserves a lifetime achievement award for supporting my writing, it would be my husband, Jordan. You've read and edited this book more times than anyone else. You never told me I was crazy when I said I was going to try to rewrite it *one more time*. You supported me emotionally and financially to make sure I had room to give this writing thing a shot. And you've always dreamed bigger for me, and this book, than I ever could. Thank you for loving me.

•••

To my kids, Juliet and Lincoln, I hope one day you read this and realize you were toddling around when I first sat down with a blank page. I know the stories ahead of you will be epic, and I can't wait to watch them unfold.

Grab the Entangled Teen releases readers are talking about!

CHASING TRUTH
By Julie Cross

When former con artist Eleanor Ames's homecoming date commits suicide, she's positive there's something more going on. The more questions she asks, though, the more she crosses paths with Miles Beckett. He's sexy, mysterious, *arrogant*...and he's asking all the same questions.

Eleanor might not trust him - she doesn't even *like* him - but they can't keep their hands off of each other. Fighting the infuriating attraction is almost as hard as ignoring the fact that Miles isn't telling her the truth...and that there's a good chance *he* could be the killer.

LOST GIRLS
by Merrie Destefano

Yesterday, Rachel went to sleep curled up in her grammy's quilt, worrying about geometry. Today, she woke up in a ditch, bloodied, bruised, and missing a year of her life. She's not the only girl to go missing within the last year...but she's the only girl to come back. And as much as her dark, dangerous new life scares her, it calls to her. Seductively. But wherever she's been—whomever she's been with—isn't done with her yet...

FORGET ME ALWAYS
BY SARA WOLF

It's been three years, twenty-five weeks, and five days since Isis Blake fell in love, and if she has it her way, it'll stretch into infinity. Since then, she's punched Jack Hunter—her nemesis-turned-maybe-something-more—in the face, survived a brutal attack by her mom's abusive ex thanks to Jack's heroics, and then promptly forgotten all about him.

The one bright spot for Isis is Sophia, the ephemeral girl who shares Isis's hospital stay as well as a murky past with Jack. But as Isis's memories return, she finds it harder and harder to resist what she felt for Jack, and Jack finds it impossible to stay away from the only girl who's ever melted the ice around his heart.

As the dark secrets surrounding Sophia emerge, Isis realizes Jack isn't who she thought he was. He's dangerous. But when Isis starts recciving terrifying emails from an anonymous source, that danger might be the only thing protecting her from something far more threatening.

Her past.

OLIVIA DECODED
By Vivi Barnes

This isn't my Jack, who once looked at me like I was his world. The guy who's occupied the better part of my mind for eight months.

This is Z, criminal hacker with a twisted agenda and an arsenal full of anger.

I've spent the past year trying to get my life on track. New school. New friends. New attitude. But old flames die hard, and one look at Jack—the hacker who enlisted me into his life and his hacking ring, stole my heart, and then left me— and every memory, every moment, every feeling comes rushing back. But Jack's not the only one who's resurfaced in my life. And if I can't break through Z's defenses and reach the old Jack, someone will get hurt...or worse.